DEVLIN. CAROLINE. MAGGIE.
THEY KNEW SO MUCH ABOUT LIFE
AND SO LITTLE. . . .

One created CITY GIRL, the fabulous spa for wealthy women . . . but only after she learned what innocent girls don't know: that men lie, families keep secrets, and only friends stay around when a woman is pregnant with her lover's child.

CITY GIRL

One changed from ugly duckling to irresistible gamine, but that didn't stop her from marrying the first man who asked. Then the beatings began, the pills, the alcohol, until all that stood between her and death were Devlin and Maggie.

CITY GIRL

One fooled herself—and the world—into thinking she had a perfect life, not the reality of passionless sex and a dreary marriage. Now she planned a shocking change, the kind no one would understand except a woman's two best friends.

CITY GIRL

"GREAT . . . A THOROUGHLY ENJOYABLE READ . . . CRACKS ALONG AT A GREAT PACE!"
— *"U"* Magazine

City Girl

PATRICIA SCANLAN

Island
BOOKS

ISLAND BOOKS
Published by
Dell Publishing
a division of
Bantam Doubleday Dell Publishing Group, Inc.
666 Fifth Avenue
New York, New York 10103

ISBN: 0-440-21275-8

Reprinted by arrangement with Poolbeg Press Ltd

Printed in the United States of America

Published simultaneously in Canada

August 1992

10 9 8 7 6 5 4 3 2 1

OPM

This book is very lovingly dedicated to my mother, father, sister and brothers, and to Gemma O'Connor, playwright and author, whose warm praise and constructive criticism set me on the right track. Thank you, Gemma.

One man in a thousand, Solomon says,
Will stick more close than a brother...
But the thousandth man will stand by your
    side
To the gallows-foot—and after!

Rudyard Kipling

Contents

City Girl

prologue

Devlin Delaney gave a big wide yawn, stretched catlike for a moment and then jumped out of bed. Naked, she walked to her en suite bathroom and stepped under the shower, enjoying the feel of the warm water as it cascaded down her body. Briskly she soaped herself, humming cheerfully.

She felt good. It was a beautiful day and the world was hers for the taking. Wrapping herself in a soft terry-towelling robe, Devlin padded out on to her balcony and surveyed the view that she never tired of. It was still early, just after seven, and the air was fresh and tangy, the salt-laden breeze of the sea caressing her wet tangled hair, blowing it across her face. She loved this time of day. Everything was fresh and young: even the city and the docks on the other side of the river seemed calmer, less frenetic and jaded at this hour of the morning. Only the milk man below shared the sight of Dublin across the Liffey, soft and serene in the dappled pink hues of early morning.

Devlin liked living in Clontarf. It was so near the city and yet so picturesque, the vast panorama of Dublin bay always a pleasure to view.

To her left, Howth glowed like an enormous emerald, mysterious, reserved, the sun-sparkled water surrounding it, giving the impression of thousands of glittering diamonds in a bed of velvet blue. She breathed the air deeply, enjoying the salty tang, pulling it down into her lungs like a smoker does the first cigarette of the day. After a while she walked back into the bedroom to prepare herself to challenge the day and be ready for all it held.

Devlin particularly enjoyed Fridays, starting off with her work-out class at eight. Although she exercised three mornings a week, she always preferred the Friday class. There was something different about the Friday group, an added air of energy and excitement as people prepared for the excesses of the weekend ahead. She always left the Friday class buzzing with energy, much to the dismay of her secretary.

Well, no doubt Liz would be relieved to know that today she would be leaving the office early. For the first time since CITY GIRL opened, its part-owner and boss was taking some time off.

God, she was looking forward so much to the weekend in Rosslare Harbour with the girls. It had been years since the three of them had been away together. Devlin's aquamarine eyes sparkled with anticipation at the thoughts of what was to come when Maggie, Caroline and she got together. But she was going to have a hectic few hours before she got away though and she'd better get cracking. After dressing in a light pale pink tracksuit she packed some clean lingerie, her shoes and a clutch bag into an elegant holdall and took a cellophane-covered black and white Dior suit out of the mirrored wardrobe that stretched the width of her spacious apple green and white bedroom. She had better look the part of the upwardly-mobile successful young business-woman, she mused wryly, as today she was taking part in a programme on national TV about successful entrepreneurs.

She'd come a long way, that was for sure. Little did she think, as she grew up in the affluence of her Foxrock home, that she would live for a time in a high-rise flat in Ballymun. And little did she think, when she was in Ballymun, that she would end up living in a penthouse apartment in Clontarf, a wealthy and successful young woman! Sadness darkened her eyes. All she had been through. Had it been for nothing? Maybe today she would ring her mother. She had been putting it off for so long and Luke was right: it was time to forgive and forget.

Devlin smiled as she thought of Luke Reilly. Once she had thought she would never trust a man again. How gently he had pierced her armour. Luke had told her to make a new beginning and that was exactly what she had done. It had been difficult, very difficult; there were always reminders. Only last week at a glittering social function, a smiling, elegant woman had tapped her on the shoulder and said pleasantly, "You're Devlin Delaney aren't you? You used to work for my husband.".

Devlin had nearly died. Not Colin Cantrell-King's wife! It couldn't be. But it was, and then to her horror she had seen Colin heading in her direction, smiling suavely at her, hand outstretched. "Devlin my dear! What a pleasure. It's been so long. We must get together for old time's sake," he gushed. Devlin thought she was going to be sick. The bastard! How could he just stand there as though nothing had happened, smiling insincerely at her. Fortunately a photographer from one of the society pages of a popular magazine had spotted her and whisked her away to take her photo, saving her the necessity of answering her former employer. The encounter had upset her. She supposed it was inevitable they should meet again in Dublin's tight-knit social scene, but even so, the memories of the past were so painful that it was worse than she had thought it would be.

Luke, eagle-eyed where she was concerned, had noticed that she was upset, although she thought she had disguised it well.

"What's wrong?"

"Nothing."

"Devlin! I know you too well to be palmed off with 'nothing,' " he smiled. "It was that tall man over there, wasn't it?. Did he say something to upset you? Wait a minute…" He stared hard at Devlin. "That's that bastard Cantrell-King isn't it? I've been waiting to meet him for a long time!"

"Luke!" Devlin exclaimed, alarmed at the expression in his eyes and the set of his firm jaw.

"It's alright, Devlin. I'll be back in a minute," he said reassuringly.

Devlin watched anxiously as he strode over to Colin and took him aside. She saw a deep flush suffuse her former boss's face as he stared in startled horror at Luke. Then Luke was walking back to her and she felt limp with relief. She'd been afraid of her life that Luke might have punched Colin.

"What did you say to him?" she asked heavily.

"Take it easy, Devlin," Luke said, putting an arm around her and drawing her close. "I told him if he ever came within ten feet of you again he'd be singing soprano for the rest of his life."

Now, standing in her bedroom, Devlin smiled at the memory. Luke was so protective of her and she had to admit that it was a nice feeling after all the years of being on her own. Still, she had managed, she had stood on her own two feet, made and paid for her mistakes and there was no looking back. Memories were strange things; they could spur you on or bring you down. Today was a day for spurring, that was for definite, she decided briskly. Today was going to be a happy day. In a few hours she and the girls would head off for Rosslare and a weekend of unmitigated pleasure. She had even decided to take the Monday off, so they had three whole days to themselves. The last time they had been away together had been the Shannon cruise just before

Maggie's wedding and it seemed like a lifetime ago. It *was* a lifetime ago. She glanced at her watch. Seven forty-five. Time to leave. As Devlin stepped into the lift she wondered if Caroline was waiting for her at the car.

***

Caroline Yates had been awake since before six, letting thoughts wander at will. Today would be a special day for her. A new beginning. It was going to be a lovely day, she could feel it in her bones. It was time to get up and get dressed for the first item on her agenda for her special day; her work-out session at CITY GIRL, the most exclusive health studio in Dublin.

When it had opened in a blaze of publicity nine months ago, Richard had made sure they were at the opening and had paid the substantial sum for her yearly subscription without a thought. Devlin had not wanted to charge her, but Richard had insisted on paying. He was able to boast to his colleagues' wives that his wife was a member of CITY GIRL. They were then as impressed as hell, while his colleagues, who couldn't afford the yearly subscription, could only fume.

In Richard's eyes it was money well spent. Poor Richard; such petty things gave him immense satisfaction. If their photograph appeared in the society pages of the newspapers and the up-market social magazines read by the trendy Dublin set they socialised with, he was delighted.

The last one had put him in a good humour for a week with its heading of "Mrs Caroline Yates, wife of well-known young legal eagle Richard Yates, wearing a beautiful Ib Jorgensen gown at the Red Cross Ball." Or had it been the Law Society's Gala, or so and so's bash? She went to so many of them, she couldn't remember.

God! How she hated the superficiality of it all. One day! She promised herself. One day she was going to tell them all with their "Hello Dahling absolutely smashing to see you," kiss, kiss, exactly what she thought of them. Caroline smiled wryly knowing she'd never have the guts!

Turning her head she observed her husband sleeping in the next bed. He slept tidily. He didn't snore or rumple the covers, just lay neatly in bed breathing precisely and calmly. No noisy slurping from Richard! He was so..."prissy" was the word she was looking for. Even in bed he never had a hair out of place. Years ago, it seemed like another lifetime ago, she had been so impressed by these exact qualities. His neat immaculately-groomed person, so different from your usual untidy Irishman. Always dressed in a well-cut, pressed suit. Tawny hair always neatly styled, nails pared and white. She had thought him so sophisticated. But then she had been so desperate to get married, so terribly afraid of being alone and left on the shelf. Well she had made her bed and she was lying in it, and lying in it alone too.

No! She wasn't alone. Caroline had discovered that much and more in the last year. She had the girls, Devlin and Maggie, two of the best friends anyone could wish for. She had her family. She had Charles. And despite all that had happened between them she was still living with her husband and was closer to him than she ever had been. If she had told him this time last year that she was going to spend a long weekend with Devlin he would have beaten the daylights out of her. Of that there was no question!

Sighing at the memories she wondered what the reaction of The Set would have been if she had sent in a photograph detailing in glorious technicolour her profusion of bruises to one of the gossipy mags that were so avidly devoured by their crowd: "Mrs Caroline Yates, wife of prominent solicitor Richard Yates displays the newest fashions of mauve, purple and yellow occasioned by a savage beating given to her by her loving husband. Joining her in this particular fashion show are some other well known ladies!"

Caroline grimaced at the memory. She wasn't the only wife in the so-called "professional" classes to be beaten. That was for certain. Battering was not the privilege of the working class as many falsely presumed. But at least she had found out why! Had found out the tortured guilt-ridden reason her husband used to wallop the daylights out of her. Since that awful night she had never received another battering.

Her life had changed so much and she had come a hell of a long way from the valium-ridden lush she had turned into. She'd got her old job back. Richard hadn't wanted her to go back to work and in the old days that would have been that. But these weren't the old days. These were *her* days, as her husband was slowly learning. It was strange to have him in the same room as her: usually he slept in the other bedroom of their luxurious penthouse apartment. A friend of his from London had stayed the night so he had moved back into the room she had made her own, decorating it to her taste, transforming the awful stark, sterile decor that the interior decorator had favoured. Richard had been so impressed he had actually asked her to do something with the lounge! Caroline smiled to herself; she enjoyed decorating very much, she seemed to have a flair for it. Devlin had even used some of her ideas in CITY GIRL. She was seriously thinking of taking a course in interior design and decorating. That would really give her an interest and who knows she might be able to start up a little consultancy, set up in business for herself.

How nice it was to have these thoughts. A year ago she would have been terrified of standing on her own two feet. Now here she was, thinking of starting up her own business! Caroline laughed as she stood under the bracing spray of the shower. She really was a new woman. She'd been through the mill of drink and valium and come out of it a stronger more determined person. Richard was finding it a little hard to get used to the new Caroline, but he was coping. She didn't know whether she would leave him or not, that was something she would have to decide in the future, but for now she was happy enough to be finding her feet again and starting on the path to independence. It suited Richard and it suited her right now, and she had never felt so good about herself.

Wrapping a robe around her she padded into the kitchen and switched on the kettle. Across the landscaped lawns of the apartment complex, she could see Devlin's French doors open. Devlin was up too, preparing for her workout class. Caroline smiled. Devlin was her closest friend. They had been through so much together and at last things seemed to be going right for them both.

This weekend was going to be just like old times. No husbands to annoy them, just the three of them having fun. The crack would be mighty, the irrepressible Maggie would make sure of that...

***

Maggie Ryan felt her heart sink as her husband sleepily pressed himself against her, indicating his good morning intentions. Whoever invented the morning erection was certainly not a woman, she thought glumly, trying to decide which would be better—to have sex and not have him moan about her weekend away and the cost of her membership of CITY GIRL, or to suit herself and not have sex and have to listen to an earbashing. She knew it was sexual blackmail, a subtle form, but blackmail all the same that her husband exerted on her. He'd end up moaning either way, especially about CITY GIRL and how much it was costing him and what did she want to be hobnobbing with those snobs for? Couldn't she just go to Unislim like anybody else! It was so annoying: Devlin hadn't wanted to charge her for membership, but when Terry heard that Richard had paid the fees, he had insisted on paying too. Maggie told him he was crazy, but he retorted: "I'm not having Yates going around thinking I'm a pauper!"

The foolish pride of men! his wife had thought with disgust. Oh God Almighty! Were all marriages like this or just hers, she wondered wearily, hearing two of her three children in the next bedroom shrieking their little heads off as they announced to the neighbourhood that they were awake.

"Shit! The kids are awake. Come on, Maggs, before they come in on top of us," her husband said groggily, as he nuzzled her earlobe with a stubbly jaw. Closing her eyes reluctantly, she tried to pretend that it was Sean Connery and they were lying on a fur-covered water bed.

"Atta girl!" murmured Terry triumphantly. Maggie's eyes flew open.

"Atta girl!" For crying out loud! Who the hell did he think she was? Bloody Arkle!

Arkle's a male, you fool, she thought idly noticing a sneaky little cobweb behind her Norman Rockwell print. Must dust that! Sean Connery wasn't working so well. Think of Harrison Ford, she instructed herself gently. In spite of herself she giggled as she pictured Terry with a bullwhip on the back of an elephant. Her husband gave a breathless grunt.

"Ya like that, love. I always know how to turn you on!"

Maggie sighed, amused at the incongruity of it all. Her husband's ego was as big as her belly when she was in her ninth month. Terry thought Warren Beatty had nothing on him.

"Mammy, what's Daddy doing to you?" An inquisitive voice spoke from the distance as two eyes observed them with interest from the door of their bedroom.

Giving a satisfied gasp, Terry rolled off his wife and Maggie said mildly and truthfully, "Daddy's doing absolutely nothing to me. He was trying to get out of my side of the bed. Now go and get your pyjamas off. I'm coming to wash you in a minute. And don't wake Fiona."

The sarcasm had sailed over her husband's head, as she knew it would, as he relaxed in the afterglow of his husbandly performance. "You're some woman, Maggie!" he said, smiling at her and swatting her rump as she got out of bed.

"I know," she responded dryly, but she leaned

over and gave him a kiss. Sometimes she reflected, she didn't have three children, she had four. And often Terry was the biggest child of all.

"Tell you what," he said magnanimously. "You go and get ready for that old exercise class of yours. I'll get the kids ready for playschool and feed the baby. How about that?"

"Thanks Ter," she said, knowing Josie, the woman who came on Fridays, would be along at eight and that it would be she who would oversee breakfast for the twins and nappy changes for the baby.

"Blessed art thou among women to have a hubby like me," Terry informed her modestly as he leapt athletically out of bed, pausing to admire himself in the mirror.

"No flab there," he observed in satisfaction, patting his lean flat belly. "Not bad for a forty-year-old! I don't need fancy exercise classes. I'm telling you, Maggs, a couple of games of squash a week and that's all you'd need to keep trim. And it would be much cheaper!"

"Ah don't take all the good out of it," Maggie snapped back.

"Well, it's alright for Richard Yates. You should see the money *he's* earning." Terry was Richard's financial consultant.

"And what's more," came the voice from the bathroom, "he doesn't have three little mouths to feed and clothe. He's too bloody cute!"

There was a silence as toothbrush assaulted teeth; then, "and you know something else? He's driving around in a brand new BMW with the plastic still on the seats because he's too mean to tax the bloody thing until the start of the month. He wouldn't give you the steam off his piss the cute hoor..."

Maggie threw her eyes up to heaven as she brushed her gleaming locks. Was it any wonder she was sorely tempted to have an affair with Adam? She missed him badly while he was away in London, but he'd be back next week, and her generous mouth curved in a smile as she thought of what she had to tell him. It was the most exciting thing! And it was because of his advice that it had all happened. Wait until she told the girls!

She was so looking forward to their weekend away. What bliss! A bed to herself, a full night's sleep. No babies to be fed or snoring husbands to keep her awake. Time to talk, and confide and laugh. Thank God for Devlin and Caroline, real honest-to-God friends. Not like Marian Gilhooley. Forget her, she's not worth it, Maggie told herself firmly. She was going to have a carefree weekend and she couldn't wait!

Twenty minutes later Maggie sailed out the door. Friday was hers and had been since she had found out about her husband's affair with Ria Kirby, the hard-faced bitch! She felt no guilt as she heard the twins squabbling and Terry bellowing at them. It was a beautiful morning. She heard the baby start to wail. For a moment Maggie was tempted to turn and go back in. Her maternal heartstrings tugged. It had taken her a long time to get to the stage where she could leave for the day and think nothing of it.

"No, dammit!" she muttered aloud. It wouldn't kill Terry. It was twenty to eight, he'd only have to put up with it for twenty minutes. She'd been the perfect wife and mother for long enough. All the years of giving to her family, in Wicklow, to Marian Gilhooley, her so-called friend, to Terry and her children. Well it was time now for taking. Time for her. Time to begin her life again. Briskly Maggie strode to her car, meeting the postman en route.

"Hello Mrs Ryan, letter for yourself."

"Thanks," she said calmly, but as she took the long slim envelope he handed to her, she wanted to throw her arms in the air and do a dance.

At last, it had actually arrived! She knew it was coming, but for it to arrive today made everything perfect. She couldn't wait to tell Adam and the girls; they had been so encouraging. It would mean nothing to Terry, she'd tell him later. In a daze of excitement Maggie drove to her morning rendezvous with Devlin and Caroline at CITY GIRL.

Devlin's Story I

one

She knew she was pregnant. No doctor had
confirmed it yet but she knew, just as thousands
before her had known and thousands after her
would instinctively know that their bodies were
no longer theirs alone, their wombs no longer
just parts of their anatomies but vibrant living
things that for nine months would dictate to and
rule over the host body.

Devlin felt an awful fear deep in the pit of her
stomach. Her period was five days overdue. But
she was on the pill, it was impossible to get
pregnant on the pill.

"No it's not. Maggie Ryan got pregnant on the
pill," a little voice in her mind whispered maliciously. Devlin sat up in bed.

"Oh Jesus God please don't let me be pregnant. Holy-Mary-Mother-of-God-pray-to-Jesus-
for-me," she babbled, deriving some comfort
from the prayer of her childhood to which she
now turned only in moments of deep distress.
She waited a moment, as if expecting her period
to appear miraculously; maybe it had come in the
night. Devlin inspected her knickers; they were
as pure and virginal as the driven snow and

frustration rose in her. Getting out of bed she paced the floor of her bedroom.

"It's not fair, I don't want to be pregnant. Why should it happen to me? God Almighty I only did it once and I didn't mean to. Colette and Brian have been doing it for over a year every night of the week. How come you didn't pick on them? Oh God please let my period come!" she prayed silently, hopefully.

She had to get out of the flat; being on her own was driving her crazy. Caroline had gone away with Richard for a long weekend. She supposed she could go home but the thought of facing her parents in her present state chilled her; she knew guilt would be written all over her face. Lydia, her mother, would probably start picking on her and she just couldn't face it right now. Panic assailed her and she sat down on the bed. There must be something she could do.

"I mean for heaven's sake it's my body, my body, my body." She whispered the words like a mantra, rocking backwards and forwards on the bed and hugging herself. A thought struck her. She flew downstairs, almost breaking her neck in her haste to get to the sitting room.

Yes! Oh thank God! Grabbing the half-empty bottle of gin Devlin didn't even bother with a glass. She flew back upstairs almost crying. Rushing into the bathroom she turned on the taps of the bath. Why didn't I think of this before? she chided herself.

"That's abortion," a mean little voice was

saying in her brain.

"Don't listen. Don't think about it," she muttered feverishly as she waited for the hot water to explode through the pipes. The water remained stubbornly cold. She checked the immersion heater which was switched off, and cursed angrily. Viciously she snapped it on, frustration and misery written all over her face, knowing that the water wouldn't heat for at least fifteen minutes.

I suppose I could start on the gin, she mused doubtfully. Devlin wasn't too sure exactly what gin was supposed to do. She knew a scalding hot bath was supposed to bring on an overdue period and maybe you were supposed to put some gin in the bath as well. Well, there was no harm in trying it both ways. Taking a big slug of gin she spluttered and gasped as tears came to her eyes.

Devlin caught sight of herself in the mirror, naked except for the treacherously white briefs, her slim body tanned golden after a holiday on the Algarve. Blonde hair bleached by the sun lay tousled around her face and aquamarine eyes, big and frightened, glittered with tears as she stared at the gin bottle clutched in her hand.

"This has to be the pits," she groaned and depression enveloped her in a cloud of torment. She took another slug of gin. It didn't feel so bad this time so she took another.

An hour later Devlin sat in her very hot bath to which she had added a measure of the gin just in case. The bathroom was steamed up and the sweet cloying smell of the gin seemed to be everywhere. She was very very drunk and starting to feel extremely sick.

Just as well Caroline's gone away for the weekend; she'd be horrified, Devlin thought woozily. Caro, her flat mate, was easily shocked and very innocent. She'd probably faint if Richard put his thing near her, that was, she thought nastily, if Richard had a thing.

Oh God! She was going to be sick. Drunkenly she stood up in the bath swaying in the steamy heat and barely making it to the toilet. She noisily retched feeling that everything inside her was coming up. The violence of the attack left her dizzy and weak and grabbing a towel she wrapped it around herself and crawled into the bedroom on her hands and knees. Somehow she managed to haul herself into bed, where she passed out. It was three hours before she came to from her drunken stupor and she felt as though there was a fireworks display going off in her head. For a while Devlin just lay there not daring to move, not even sure if she was dead or alive. Then the telephone rang. Harsh, piercing, the sound penetrated her throbbing head with a savage intensity. Sticking her head under the covers she tried to ignore the sound and eventually it went away. Silence descended once more and she dozed off to sleep. When she woke again she felt much improved, although her mouth tasted vile and her head was muzzy and heavy. Dragging herself out of bed she made a cup of very strong coffee and decided to go down to the seafront. She had to think and the sea had always calmed her. Catching sight of the calendar in the small kitchen of their flat, Devlin stopped in front of it, grimacing ruefully. This day three weeks ago she had been on a beach in Portugal with not a care in the world and here she was feeling decades older, having just experienced the most awful shock in her entire life. She looked at her watch. Three fifteen. It was on this day two weeks ago at around this time that Colin had impregnated her. Colin Cantrell-King M B, M D, F R C O G, gynaecologist to Dublin's gentry. Employer and impregnator of Devlin Delaney.

Heavy-hearted, Devlin tidied away her coffee cup in the untidy but friendly little kitchen that she shared with her best friend Caroline Stacey. They had been lucky to get such a nice flat after the awful grotty hole they had first moved into in Rathmines. What a rip off that had been. The shower hadn't worked properly; you were either scalded or frozen to death. The beds were lumpy, the walls damp and the landlord was a right gurrier. They had stuck it a month before they were off again scouring the evening papers where they found this jewel of a flat in a big old house on the Sandymount seafront overlooking Dublin Bay. It was clean and airy and they had a bedroom each as well as a sitting room and kitchen. It suited them both perfectly and was fairly close to their working locations.

Looking out the kitchen window, Devlin could see that it was a beautiful late summer's day. In the distance the distinctive ESB towers at Ringsend were bathed in sunlight and children danced up and down in the warm puddles of water left by the outgoing tide, screaming with pleasure as they wriggled their toes deep in the wet squelchy sand. The Shelly banks! That's where she'd go: down to the "Shelliers" to watch the tugs tow in the huge cargo ship that had just appeared as a dot on the horizon of the bay.

Leaving the flat she began to walk towards Ringsend, turning right before she got to the village so that she was heading down past the attractive new homes built on land triumphantly reclaimed from Dublin Bay, down towards the Glass Bottle Co and then on to the river, that long blue winding vein that flowed right through the belly of the city and on out to sea. Devlin sniffed the air that was laden with the smell of Dublin and the sea and began the long walk down the Pidgeon House Road towards her destination. On her right, small terraced houses faced the panorama of dockland. Cranes, containers, small boats ploughing up and down the river and gulls circling and screeching. Soon the tugs would be heading out down the river to meet the big ship coming to its journey's end. Her pace quickened; she wanted to be there to see it all.

Deliberately she emptied her mind of all worrisome thoughts. Only this was important now. Don't think about anything else. Not that you've taken the day off work because you couldn't face the thought of going in when Colin wasn't there. Don't think that you'll be in the house alone until Caroline gets back. Don't think...don't think!

Down past the ruined dwellings of the coast-guards, past the coalyards. Her tense face relaxed briefly into a smile. Once she'd been to a party on a ship in the days when Ireland had possessed a National Shipping Company. She'd been dating one of the second officers from Irish Shipping and one day his ship had sailed proudly into its mother port having traversed the wide powerful Atlantic. She had seen the pride on his face as he stood uniformed and smart on the gangway to meet her for the party the crew were throwing. It had been a wonderful party and she had seen the pink gold sun rise over the city of her birth from the impressive bridge of the vessel. They had been good times, before unemployment had become rampant and an air of hopelessness had enveloped the towns and cities of the country as jobs got fewer and the dole queues swelled like big malignant growths.

Almost before he knew it, her good looking sailor had been made redundant, as the government had liquidated the shipping company, leaving some of its crews under arrest in foreign ports, its workforce destined for the dole and the liquidator earning thousands a week. The arrested crews had eventually been repatriated and Devlin had marched down

O'Connell Street one Saturday with them and their wives and mothers. The men were proud and dignified in their braided uniforms and white-topped caps. All they wanted was justice and their dues but sure who had listened to them? The ordinary man and woman in the street wished them well but they were only one protest group among many on the streets of Dublin.

Devlin felt a bitterness rise within her. Frank had emigrated to America and how could she blame him? She too had seen the long queues waiting at the dole office once a week. Not that she had ever really wanted for money—her parents were well off— but how people without any other means existed on social welfare was beyond her.

Glumly she walked on down past the power station, around the dump where birds scavenged like something out of a Hitchcock movie, then down the road where the sea lapped up against the rocks and she could see Sandymount, where she had come from. On she walked, the wind rippling her thick blonde hair, the sun caressing her still tanned face, oblivious of the children with their mothers, the lovers sitting in their cars, the old men smoking their pipes chatting and reminiscing with their lined weatherbeaten faces, keeping a close eye on the fast-approaching cargo boat. She passed the fishermen and boys hooking their mackerel and bass with excited grunts of satisfaction and sat down halfway along the narrow finger of the South Wall that penetrated the bay for two miles. She concentrated on the nautical activity in front of her as the two small tugs pushed and pulled the enormous ship up the river. The powerful throb of the engines, the white-capped wash breaking against the wall over which her legs dangled and drenching her with spray made her forget the huge black shroud of worry that enveloped her. Fascinated she watched as the ship glided majestically past her, so near that she could see the men on deck. All too soon it was gone, up into the heart of the decaying dockland and out of her sight. If only she could get on a ship and sail out of Dublin, leaving all her worries behind her.

She'd have to tell Colin. He would know what to do; he was always so firm and decisive, exuding an aura of calm authority. It was one of the things she found so attractive about him. Then she remembered. He wouldn't be back for a few days. He had gone to Paris with his wife.

Misery attacked her again, so physical that she could feel it stabbing her like a knife in the heart. Colin had told her that his was a marriage of convenience when Devlin had said that she didn't go with married men. He had laughed and told her that he loved her innocence. Why hadn't she listened and believed the nuns when they had warned about "married men" and "rampant lusts." Had she listened she wouldn't be in her present predicament. She remembered how Sister Dominica had been so pleased for her when she had heard that Devlin had secured a job as private secretary to Mr Cantrell-King.

"A wonderful man, my dear. You know several of the sisters have had little jobs done by him."

Theirs was one of the better off religious orders. Southsiders, of course.

"And my dear, you know he gives very generous donations to the Order every so often. You're a very lucky girl indeed, Devlin. Come now, let us go and give thanks to the Lord. It's not easy getting jobs these days."

Devlin had given thanks not only to God but to her Dad, who happened to be Colin Cantrell-King's bank manager. When Colin mentioned that his secretary was leaving to get married, Gerry Delaney told him that Devlin had recently been made redundant from her secretarial post in a small arty publishing firm but that she was well qualified.

"Excellent! Send her along for an interview," Colin had instructed.

Devlin, desperate for a job that would get her out of her mother's hair, had prepared very carefully for the interview, making sure that she looked well groomed and elegant but not overdressed for the occasion. Usually she took interviews in her stride but she was nervous as she faced the tall good-looking man in front of her. Her mother was driving her crazy with her constant nagging and drink-induced rages. She need not have worried. She did an impressive interview and her references were excellent. She was given the job along with a generous salary. C C K, as she had privately christened him, was an extremely busy gynaecologist, whipping out wombs that needed whipping out and some that didn't! Delivering babies, some that were wanted and some that were not. Comforting menopausal and premenstrual tensioned females and charging hefty amounts to the many affluent fur-coated private patients who came from all over the country, day in day out, to his rooms in Fitzwilliam Square.

Devlin got to know them all. Some would pour out all their woes to her. Others looked down their haughty noses at her and demanded to be seen instantly. The coldness would melt instantly when Colin appeared at the door of the waiting room with a warm smile and reassuring handshake.

"Ah Mrs Cochrane! Good to see you. Come in now and tell me what's bothering you."

Invariably eyelashes would flutter and tremulous voices would waft down the hall as he led them to his surgery, sometimes winking at Devlin behind their backs. He was an immensely charming man, only forty but at the height of his career. He had, of course inherited a large practice from his father and was a prominent member of Dublin's high society, seen at many social gatherings around the city. He knew her father well. An ex-rugby player, he hadn't an ounce of flab on his tall muscular body and the faint traces of grey at his temple lent him a distinguished mature air that Devlin found exceedingly attractive. All his patients were madly in love with him.

Devlin, who was twenty, had always dated men of her own age or men in their middle twenties. Her only experience with older men was trying to avoid their sweaty roving hands in the dimly lit, faintly seedy night clubs they always ended up in on their Saturday nights on the town.She was an outgoing girl with a broad circle of friends and aquaintances who lived a relatively untroubled and carefree existence. Her only experience of the hardship of life occurred when she had been made redundant for a brief period, and rather than give up the freedom of flat-dwelling and return home to the uncomfortable atmosphere her mothers's behaviour caused, she had survived, well cushioned by a generous allowance given to her by her father. But it was not the same as having a salary.

At present, it was nothing for Devlin to go into town on a Saturday and spend a small fortune on clothes. She loved her little week-end sprees. After a lie-in, Saturday would be spent shopping in Grafton Street with friends. She might treat herself to a little something from Benetton or Pamela Scott or if she was really in the money she'd hit Brown Thomas. Strolling past the colourful street artists, past the cheerful flower sellers she and her friends would meander along to Captain America's to grab a quick lunch before she had her hair done in one of the many exclusive, expensive hair saloons. Then it would be time to drop into the Powerscourt Townhouse Centre with its bright airy plant-filled ambience, to browse through the shops for a while before relaxing over a cup of coffee. Her biggest decision might be whether to buy the snazzy little suit from Private Collection or a Lainey Original. Devlin loved shopping in Grafton Street with its winding elegance, its stores filled with up-to-the-minute fashions. There was a buzz about Grafton Street that couldn't be found anywhere else in the city.

Then hurrying back to her little Fiesta parked on the Green, she would drop her friends home and drive like the clappers to get home herself to prepare for the night's activities. By half past eight a crowd of them would be found drinking in the Shelbourne. Later they would stroll down to the Bailey or Davy Byrne's for last orders, then head off to a disco where they would bop the night away before ending up in one of the city's many night clubs. Dawn would frequently be upon them before Devlin's tired head hit the pillows and Sunday would be spent recuperating after the excesses of the night before. But by mid-afternoon, revived and refreshed, she would meet the gang to go stock-car racing in Mondello, or to watch a rugby match in Wanderers. Sunday night she would go to the pictures or for a meal with whatever boyfriend happened to be in tow.

Looking back she would realise what a charmed and sheltered life she had led and how she had so matter of factly taken it as her due. When she started to work for Colin she had no steady relationship, unusually for her. But Frank, her most recent boyfriend, had emigrated and so she was ripe to fall prey to the overpowering charms of C C K.

At first he had been businesslike but friendly, asking her if she was settling into her job, urging her to ask him or Nurse McGrath if there was anything she wished to know. Gradually Devlin had settled down and taken control of all the secretarial aspects of the practice. Being quick and efficient she took pride in seeing that everything ran smoothly. One day Colin told her he would like to take her and Nurse McGrath to lunch and brought them in his luxurious metallic grey Merc to a quiet little Italian restaurant off Stephen's Green, where they gorged themselves on pasta cooked as only the Italians know how. He had been all charm and after several glasses of wine Devlin had lost her slight awe of him.

From then on she was much more relaxed in his company. At work he would come out to her office between appointments and sit against the edge of her desk chatting casually. He might tell her about a difficult operation he had to perform, and confide that the Moore woman was an awful pain in the neck or that such and such was having an affair with so and so and what was her attitude to broken marriage and divorce? Devlin found him easy to talk to and she never took exception to his probing questions about her boyfriends and lifestyle, because she sensed his underlying interest. Because she was young, beautiful and very immature the challenge of exciting the interest of a very suave, older man was more than a little thrilling.

Her friends, who had called on the pretext of seeing her but really to assess whether he was in fact the dish Devlin made him out to be, ended up agreeing wholeheartedly with her. He was much nicer than some of the geeks they encountered in the fleshpots of Leeson St. Their obvious envy added immensely to Devlin's pleasure.

One day Colin strode into the office and found her pale and cranky.

"What's wrong with you, for heaven's sake?"

The query was laced with concern. Devlin blushed with embarrassment...and pleasure.

"Nothing...I just don't feel well," she said offhandedly, unwilling to tell him that she was suffering from severe and crippling period pains. She had often wondered what attracted so many men to gynaecology. After her own experiences in that area she would decide it was because of their immense envy that they could never reproduce and give birth as women did every day, every living minute of time the world over. The only way they could exercise their power was by controlling women's pregnancies from the moment of conception and being there for the births. "Now push when I tell you...," or by removing the life giving organ: "I'm sorry, it's got to be taken out." If they couldn't themselves reproduce, being in control was the next best thing. It was a well known fact that there were far more male gynaes than female.

Later, much later on Devlin would realise just how much Colin had manipulated her but then, in her naïveté she had been pathetically grateful when he had just nodded wisely, gone into his office, written a note and given it to her.

"Devlin pet, in this day and age there's no need to suffer from period pains. Haven't you ever heard of the pill? Now take this to the Well Woman Centre when you've finished your period and they'll look after you. Hmm?"

She nodded in a frenzy of embarrassment. Laughing, Colin chucked her under the chin.

"Devlin, you fool, I'm a gynaecologist for heaven's sake! Don't be embarrassed with me. Now take the afternoon off, go home and lie down for a while and take these." He handed her some tablets. "And go and get yourself seen to."

He was smiling down at her, his eyes so warm and exciting and crinkling up at the sides in the most attractive way. Her heart melted at his kindness and swam around inside her on a tide of ecstasy as she drove home.

"He cares! He cares...ooohh he cares," she hummed to herself, letting herself into the flat.

From then on the nature of their relationship changed. Subtly it became more intimate and there were more lunch dates, only this time Nurse McGrath did not accompany them. Colin confided to her that his marriage was on the rocks, that he and his wife only kept up appearances for the children's sakes. The picture he painted was a bleak and lonely one and Devlin felt a mixture of pity and admiration for him, plus a strong sense of desire.

After all she reasoned with herself, the poor man needed the comfort of loving arms. If his wife was so cold and frigid, always out socialising, never home to cook his meals after a hard day in the operating theatres of Dublin's hospitals and private clinics, it was only to be expected that he would seek companionship elsewhere.

I mean it's not as if you were setting out to cause trouble deliberately in his marriage, the trouble is already there, she comforted herself. She was in fact a little scared. Devlin had never really had a fully-fledged relationship with any man, sexual or otherwise. True, she had dated many boyfriends but it was really only social dating, being part of the crowd. She had indulged in a certain amount of fumblings and fondlings in the back seats of cars but she had never slept with anyone, fear of her mother and fear of pregnancy being the major deterrents when it came to losing her virginity. Unlike many of her peers she had led a sheltered life. The only daughter of an affluent banker and his wife, she had lacked for nothing materially. Having been educated in an exclusive Dublin school, she mixed with the young upper class set commonly known as "Yuppies" or the "Yaws." "Why do you

call them the 'Yaws'?" she had asked Maggie,
who was living in the same house as herself and
Caroline.

Maggie had grinned cheerfully at her and said
in her down-to-earth no bullshit manner:
"Because they say 'Yaw' instead of 'yes' and if I
catch you at it...!" She had shaken her finger
warningly at the amused Devlin. Trust Maggie
who wasn't the slightest bit affected to bring her
down to earth every so often. Devlin would have
denied that she was a snob, but unknown to
herself she contributed to a subtle social snobbery that was rampant within their social class.
Had Colin been an Indian doctor or a working-
class man she would never have considered an
affair with him. Unconscious though she was of
them the prejudices of her upbringing were too
strong.

Having an affair with a married man was not
something to go public about either. Ireland
might have entered the Nineties but by European standards Dublin was a small intimate city
where it was almost impossible to go anywhere
and not meet people you knew. Although
sometimes it seemed to Devlin that everybody in
Dublin was having an affair and everyone else
knew about it but didn't let on. It had often
amazed her how husbands and wives who were
both conducting liaisons would appear together
at Mass on Sundays, the very picture of unity, or
at some social bash, while that very night they
would fornicate happily.

The hypocrisy of it sickened her and yet here she was contemplating doing the same. How confusing life was. Sometimes she felt she was a split personality. Her desire to love and be loved by Colin was intense, yet at the back of her mind lurked the shadow of her strict Catholic upbringing. The little voice of her conscience reproached her frequently and although a nun had once warned the class that the worst thing that could happen to Catholics was for them to lose their conscience she wished heartily that it would disappear for the duration of her relationship with Colin.

And then there was her mother! Lydia would go crazy if she ever suspected that her daughter was even contemplating something so sordid as an affair. There had been a huge row when Devlin had said she was going to move into a flat.

"What are you moving into a flat for?" she had stormed, her tone of voice suggesting that Devlin was deliberately going to live with the lowest of the low. It had been bad enough when she had started going to discos and pubs. There would be the interrogations the next morning, lectures about the hour she had come in at and dire warnings about burning the candle at both ends. It amazed Devlin that her mother would concern herself so. Usually she was so busy with her charitable works and hectic social life and running her immaculate home that she never really bothered about what Devlin was doing. It was only since Devlin had started working that

she had begun to take such notice of her
daughter's activities. Gerry, her father, would
try and mediate between them but Lydia would
turn on him in fury and another row would start.

"You'll end up just like..." her mother had
shouted at her once, stopping suddenly at the
expression on her husband's face.

"That's enough, Lydia!"

Devlin had never heard her father sound so
stern. "Just like who?" she had asked, puzzled
and angry.

"Just don't come into this house with any bad
news, Madam, that's all I'm saying."

"Mum!"

Devlin was shocked at her mother's implicat-
ion. Didn't her mother realise that she was
practically the only girl in her class who still
hadn't had sexual relations with anyone? Most of
the girls she had gone to school with and still
kept in touch with were sleeping with their
boyfriends. Two of her classmates had become
unmarried mothers with one of them handing
her baby up for adoption, forced to do so by her
parents, and the other kicked out of home completely. Devlin was under no illusion about what
Lydia would say were she ever so unlucky as to
be in that predicament. Sick of the rows, she
moved out.

All this she tried to explain to Colin but he
always seemed to come up with the most logical
arguments in favour of an affair, arguments that
made her reasoning seem flawed and foolishly

childish.

Once they'd had a shouting match and Colin's patience had really worn thin. "For Christ's sake, Devlin, will you grow up!" he yelled at her. "You can't stay a damned virgin all your life. What a criminal waste, for crying out loud." He took her in a savage grip and marched her over to the mirror in the foyer. "Look at yourself!" She turned away. "Go on. Look! Why are you wasting your beauty? Your youth? Just because of what some frigid old nuns told you. You can't hang on to mammy's apron strings for the rest of your bloody life. You've got your own life to lead. My God, Devlin you were made for loving, you're twenty years old."

His eyes were hard, angry and frustrated. She bit her lip to stop it from trembling and he said in disgust, "Don't start bawling for God's sake. Do you know something, Devlin, you're the typical Irish female. The body of a woman, the mind of a child, not able to make a decision on your own about whether to love someone or not. If that's your religion and your attitude to life you're welcome to it. Wrap yourself in your little cocoon, you stupid little girl and let me give you a word of advice," he glowered at her. "You shouldn't flirt and tease if you're not prepared to carry it through."

"It's easy for you to talk," Devlin retorted. "You'll never have to worry about your next period. You'll never have to worry about getting pregnant." Her voice was bitter, hurt. Devlin had never seen him angry before and she wasn't sure she liked it.

"You're on the pill, aren't you?" he retorted coldly. You won't have to worry either so don't give me that hard-done-by female crap. If you feel like taking control of your own life let me know. Otherwise, Devlin, let's keep our relationship purely business."

He slammed out the door and into his office, not even giving her the satisfaction of making a response, and she felt a strong desire to imitate Scarlett O' Hara and throw something at his treasured le Brocquy. Her fingers curled around a heavy glass ashtray but her courage deserted her. The painting was worth a small fortune and seeing as she was going to the Algarve the following week she could not afford to replace it. Reluctantly she let go of the ashtray but compensated by pounding hard on her typewriter for the rest of the afternoon.

The following day Colin arrived in, cool and business-like as if their confrontation had never taken place. He did not look at her, dictated briskly and she was glad Nurse McGrath was away on holiday. At least she didn't have to endure her poking and prying. It was with relief that she welcomed the temp who was taking over from her for the two weeks she would be away, because when Friday finally came she felt drained and mentally exhausted.

Colin had called her into his office at five o' clock when the last patient had gone and handed her an envelope. "Enjoy your holiday," he said drily. "Who knows, you might be overcome by passion and come back a fully-fledged member of the human race. I believe Portuguese men are very charming and virile. Maybe one of them might succeed where I've failed." Devlin tried to swallow the deep sense of hurt that engulfed her. Deliberately moving around his desk, she looked him straight in the face, held the envelope that she knew contained her holiday bonus between finger and thumb and disdainfully dropped it into the waste basket. Head held high, she turned on her heel and walked out. To hell with you! she thought unhappily.

Devlin drove home in the heavy rush-hour traffic of a Friday evening, the roads clogged with the big buses taking people back home to the country, clogged with weary city-dwellers escaping the fumes and dirt of the city as they drove bumper to bumper to spend the weekend in the wide open comforting spaces of the countryside. Heavy-hearted, depressed, she negotiated her way through the barely controlled chaos that surrounded her as cyclists, bikers, motorists and pedestrians jockeyed for position. To her left meandered the Grand Canal, the evening sun glittering on the calm surface that was untroubled by the lanes of fume-belching traffic. Already people sat in seats shaded by bright multi-coloured umbrellas, outside some of the canal-side pubs, drinking cool frothy glasses of dark rich

Guinness, and Devlin swallowed, hot and thirsty and envious of their happy weekend joie de vivre.

"Blast Colin," she muttered grumpily as she glared at two lovers entwined, oblivious, on Patrick Kavanagh's memorial seat by the Baggot Street lock gates. The lights were out at Baggot Street Bridge and she wanted to scream with frustration as she jammed on her brakes for the umpteenth time to avoid a cheeky cyclist.

When she got home, in a rare bad humour, she found Caroline in a tizzy of excitement. It was Caro's first foreign holiday. Devlin had previously been to Greece and the South of France but Caroline was new to it all and was engaged in a packing marathon. "Well, if we're going out every night I'll need fourteen different outfits and then there's day wear and beach wear!" Caroline explained reasonably.

"Oh Caroline, you goose! Haven't you ever heard of mix 'n match? Go and put the kettle on and I'll sort out this lot for you."

Although Caroline was two years older than Devlin it didn't seem like it. If Colin thinks I'm a child, he should see Caro. She's a baby compared to me, Devlin mused as she started to sort out the chaos that confronted her.

There were four of them going on holidays— Caroline, herself and two of Devlin's friends— but right now all she wanted to do was to go to bed. She had a thumping tension headache and the thoughts of packing only irritated her.

As the evening progressed her headache

lightened. Cases were packed and plans were made and the kettle was constantly on the boil as vast quantities of tea were consumed. Devlin had just had a bath and was sitting with her hair wrapped turbanwise in a towel with yet another mug of tea in her hand when the doorbell rang. Half-expecting it to be Caroline's boyfriend, Devlin stayed where she was. Richard had seen her often enough in her dressing gown, although she faintly suspected that he was taken aback by her lack of inhibition. Caroline would certainly never parade around in her dressing gown in his presence. Richard was so straight-laced and prissy he irritated Devlin, but Caroline seemed happy enough with him and that was what mattered. Her friend's voice interrupted her thoughts.

"Dev, Mr Cantrell-King is here to see you for a minute."

Behind her she could see Colin's broad outline and her heart gave a crazy lurch. Maybe he was going to tell her not to bother coming back. Defiantly she stood up.

"Sorry to disturb you, Devlin," he was saying smoothly. "Could I speak to you for a moment?"

"I have some packing to finish. Excuse me." Caroline, always courteous, disappeared. Colin shut the door and stood before her. "I'm sorry, Devlin" he gave a smile. "I guess I'm behaving like a love-sick teenager. Forgive me?"

A burden was lifted; Devlin's heart danced.

"I'm sorry too." She touched his face lightly

with her fingertips. "A lot of what you say is true." For a brief moment she thought she saw a flicker of triumph in his eyes but she dismissed it as he bent his head and kissed her long and lingeringly and sensually. She returned his embrace ardently, utterly happy.

"I'll be mad with jealousy while you're gone," he murmured against her earlobe. "Promise you won't lose your heart to any romantic Alfredo."

"I promise," she whispered, burrowing her face against his chest and wishing she could hold the moment forever, loving the male musky scent of him.

He drew an envelope out of his pocket and smiled down at her. "I think you forgot this!"

Devlin laughed. "I was so mad..."

"I know you were, my hot tempered little witch," he murmured, as he drew her close to slide the envelope into her dressing gown pocket, his hand lingering against the softness of her body through her robe. She trembled.

"I'd better go before I forget myself. This is not how I plan to seduce you," he smiled warmly at her. "Be good! I'll see you in two weeks Devlin."

Her face, innocent of make up, freshly scrubbed and pink after her bath, lit up like a Christmas tree. Impulsively she threw her arms around his neck and whispered, "I'll miss you, Colin."

"I'll miss you too, you little baggage. I wish I could chuck up everything and come with you." He grinned at her. "I'll tell you one thing: if I was with you, you'd never get a tan; I'd have you in bed all day." The doorbell rang, saving Devlin's blushes and, laughing, Colin walked out into the hall just as Richard was walking in. Hastily Devlin made the introductions.

She couldn't put a finger on it but she just couldn't take to Caroline's boyfriend and she felt the feeling was mutual. Not that he was ever anything but suavely charming and polite to her. The two men talked casually for a minute or two as it seemed they were already acquainted and then Colin was gone. Richard and Caroline were in the lounge so Devlin was alone, hugging her happiness to herself.

He had actually come and apologised...and at such a late hour! And what's more, the cheque in the envelope was for a hundred pounds! He had to care as much as she did. In one way she wished the holiday was over. Still, now that her mind was at ease she decided that she was going to have the best holiday of her life.

Devlin raised her face to the warm evening sun, blind to the people strolling along the sea-wall and only vaguely conscious of the seagulls circling, screeching and bawling raucously above her. It had been a great holiday, she thought sadly, and now all the good was gone from it. Now that she was almost sure she was pregnant. Never again would she be so carefree and happy as she had been for two weeks in the Moorish heaven where time stood still and no-thing was more pressing than deciding whether to drink by the pool or by the sea, or selecting which outfit to wear and who to date. Oh it had been a fantastic holiday all right! In spite of herself she grinned.

two

Oohhh...OOHHH! Melinda groaned in ecstasy as her body flamed with violent passion. Ramon's hands were caressing her intimately where she had never been touched before and again she cried aloud in pleasure as her insides turned to liquid fire...

"It gets better, girls. Listen!" The four of them lay shrieking with laughter beneath a scorching sun, on a golden beach lapped by soothing white-crested waves, as Ailish read aloud from a stack of bodice-rippers she had brought on holidays. Noeleen, the fourth member of the party, turned over on her stomach and gave a muffled exclamation.

"My Gawd girls! Look at that...what a bunch of grapes!"

Noeleen had an exquisitely vulgar turn of mind and kept them highly amused by her running commentaries on the daily parade of male sun-worshippers up and down the beach. The rest of them snorted and giggled as two young Portuguese men, wearing only the briefest of G-strings, strutted past, parading their wares.

"Oh crikey! Here comes Big Wobbliers! I'm going for a swim. Anyone else coming?"

"Big Wobbliers," so named by the irrepressible Noeleen because of his more than obvious attributes, had taken a fancy to Devlin from the first moment she had arrived on Oura beach and because the feeling was not mutual, she spent her time trying to avoid him. Shrieking and giggling the girls dived into the foaming surf, leaving the lovesick Wobbliers testing the water with his toes. Love would go far but diving into the Atlantic waters was too much to ask. Huffily he turned on his heel and walked further along the beach to try his luck elsewhere.

And so the days had passed in a haze of sun and fun, the nights bringing new adventures and experiences as they stuffed themselves at the beachside cafes under the stars, drinking bottles of cool delicious Mateus Rose, discoing in the KISS, the biggest disco on the Algarve and tumbling into bed exhausted with the dawn...

It had been a great holiday, the best Devlin had ever had, and in spite of her woe she smiled at the memories. Restlessly she got up from where she had been sitting and began to walk back along the sea-wall, her hands in her pockets, her head down, turning over and over in her mind the events of the past few weeks, her thoughts spinning crazily like a ferris wheel until she wanted to scream. Never had a girl been so happy to come home from holidays as she had been on that Saturday, as she sat in the huge Aer Lingus Jumbo gliding through the skies with the towns and cities of Spain passing beneath them. Her reunion with Colin was foremost in her mind. What would she wear to show off her deep golden tan? The sun had bleached her hair even blonder and she knew without vanity that she was glowing and healthy-looking in spite of a dose of Spanish tummy. In her mind she discarded one outfit after another before deciding on a simple white broderie anglaise top and matching skirt. Thank God she didn't suffer any inhibitions about going topless, there was nothing worse than strap marks she thought, eying her partly revealed golden globes with satisfaction.

Her parents had met her at the airport, Lydia offering her a cool reserved cheek for a kiss, Gerry enveloping her in a bear hug. She had practically danced into the office on Monday, only to have her bubble of anticipation burst ever so slightly by a note from Colin saying he would be delayed. An emergency operation had come up and he wouldn't be in the office until after lunch. Nurse McGrath had a migraine and apart from a few polite comments about Devlin's tan was in no mood to chat.

Restlessly Devlin organised her desk, noting that the temp had done a good job in her absence. At around eleven thirty Nurse McGrath announced that she was going home and with one hand clutching the bottle of wine Devlin had

presented her with and the other rather dramatically clutching her aching temple she gave a
martyred sniff and made her exit. Devlin had
been so absorbed in the latest Jackie Collins
novel that she didn't noticed Colin's arrival and
it was only his low whistle of appreciation that
alerted her to his presence.

Leaning over her desk he kissed her full on the
mouth, long and lingeringly. Jackie Collins, eat
your heart out, she thought happily, wrapping
her arms around his neck, hungry for him.

"Oh Devlin, I missed you like hell!" Colin
nuzzled her earlobe.

"Aren't you afraid Nurse might come in?"
Devlin murmured dreamily, forgetting that the
martyred one had left.

"The doorman told me she's gone home. For
God's sake Devlin, come out from behind that
desk before I go crazy!" Roughly he pulled her
into his arms and kissed her passionately, his
hands busy with the fastenings of her blouse.

Devlin felt a twinge of panic. "Colin, wait!
What if someone comes in? No!...wait." His
hands were inside the flimsy blouse caressing
her breasts and the sensations he was causing to
ripple through her were delightful and new. She
had never felt so melty and soft, her insides felt
like warm marshmallow. Part of her wanted
more, part of her was scared.

"Devlin, Devlin!" He raised his head. "I've
thought about nothing else but wanting you
since you started working for me." He grimaced.

"Don't ask me how I've kept my hands off you until now..."

Swiftly he locked her office door and taking her hand led her in past his own surgery into the tastefully furnished cubicle where he examined his patients. His eyes were warm and full of desire as he turned to her and said huskily, "You know you arouse me, don't you? Make love to me darling, here, now, I need you."

Later, when she reflected on the moment she lost her virginity she would wonder how she had ever let his ridiculous corny words impress her. But at the time his words, uttered in husky passionate tones, had thrilled her and she wanted him to love her. She had felt a sense of power that she, Devlin Delaney, a twenty-year-old virgin, could inflame this suave experienced man so much that he wanted her passionately, urgently.

She could feel the physical evidence of her power as he pressed her against the couch and, feeling a quick flash of relief that she had shaved her legs and under her arms the night before and that she was wearing her sexy lace panties, she lay back and waited for the earth to move. By now Colin was frantically removing her skirt, his breathing harsh and heavy, his body writhing urgently against her. A moment later she gasped in surprise and pain as he undid his fly and penetrated her.

"Christ! So you are a virgin!" he groaned in surprise, pausing for a moment to stare at her lying beneath him. He felt her body stiffen as an expression of pain crossed her face.

"Relax, relax," he said soothingly and started to move against her. The movements became faster, stronger and then with a final thrust he collapsed groaning on top of her, leaving her sore, wet and utterly dismayed.

Was this what it was all about, this painful unpleasant heaving? Where were the waves of pleasure lifting her to heights of passionate fulfilment that she had read about so often in novels? Or seen in films, as the heroine, her face contorted with pleasure, lay beneath her hero saying dreamily, "That was beautiful, lover." Was it all a big hoax? Nobody had ever told her about the soreness, the messiness. She was sure her broderie anglaise skirt was ruined. Devlin knew the first few moments were supposed to be painful the first time it happened, but pain was supposed to give way to pleasure. Maybe she was one of these frigid women she had heard about. Devlin felt strangely sad. She was afraid she was going to cry and disgrace herself completely. It must have been a disaster for Colin...how could she face him? Colin, his breathing almost back to normal, was drawing away from her to give her room to move. To her surprise he was smiling.

"That was fantastic, sweetheart. God, you were so tight I thought I was going to explode. The next time will be better for you, I promise." He pulled her up beside him. "Listen darling, run into the toilet and fix yourself up. I have someone coming in at four and we don't want them to see you in a state of undress, now do we?"

Mortified, Devlin realised that she was half naked. Laughing at her blush he kissed her tenderly on the mouth. "Oh Devlin, my little virgin, that was an added bonus. I'll teach you all about love, my pet, I have a share in a penthouse out in Dalkey. He gave her a wink. "Some of my colleagues and I maintain it to entertain visiting specialists." He winked again conspiratorially and Devlin knew with a sinking sensation that specialists were not the only ones he entertained. She wondered had there been many before her.

Hastily pushing the thought to the back of her mind she drew her clothes around her with as much dignity as she could muster and walked out to the toilet. As she wiped the blood from between her legs she could hear him whistling cheerfully in his own office. Would it be better for her the second time? He seemed to think so and he thought it had been fantastic. Maybe she wasn't frigid after all.

There hadn't been a second time. Devlin had put her foot down when he tried to make love to her again in the office and he promised to take her to the place in Dalkey. They had been kissing and cuddling once when Nurse McGrath had almost walked in on top of them, scaring the daylights out of Devlin. She was so nervous as a result that she would tense up if Colin came within a foot of her. Then Colin's mother-in-law died suddenly and after the funeral he told Devlin that he felt obliged to take his wife away for a few days.

It was while he was away that she sensed that she was pregnant. A slight dizziness that was gone in seconds was her first indication that life would never be the same. It brought with it a strange heightened intensity of emotions that she had never before experienced. Walking along the South Wall, Devlin reflected wryly that this certainly didn't happen in romantic novels or in *Dynasty* or *Dallas* either. She couldn't imagine Alexis Carrington-Colby-Dexter missing her period.

Why did it have to happen to her? What in the name of God was she going to do? Lydia would freak altogether, she had no time for unmarried mothers.

"There's no excuse!" she had said coldly, upon hearing of the unfortunate girl in Devlin's class. "Haven't these people ever heard of self control? And anyway in this day and age people can prevent pregnancy occurring. She probably wanted to trap him into marrying her!"

"Oh Mum! Who'd want to do a thing like that?" Devlin had responded heatedly.

"It's been done before, my girl," Lydia had snapped, her eyes bright and angry, her voice strangely bitter. Devlin, unwilling to risk an argument, had said no more, but she often thought about her mother's words and the sense of bitterness behind them. Maybe she knew someone that it had happened to. The thought horrified her. She couldn't conceive of doing that to someone. Marriages were supposed to be based on trust. How awful to be trapped into a lifetime of living with someone who had deliberately got pregnant.

How on earth was she going to face Lydia and tell her she was going to have a baby? If only she had a sister to confide in. Caroline would undoubtedly be shocked speechless; she was never any help in a crisis. Maggie, yes, she could tell Maggie alright, but she was in Saudi, five months pregnant herself and she too had got pregnant on the pill.

Oh God, if only Colin was back. She sobbed aloud, not caring who saw her. How she longed to feel his arms cradling her against his shoulder, soothing her, calming her fears, taking charge of the situation. If only there was divorce in Ireland he could leave his dreadful wife and marry her and she could have the baby and everything would be fine. Damn the referendum on divorce. Why couldn't people get a divorce if they were living in an unhappy marriage? Maybe Colin's wife had trapped him with an unwanted pregnancy, maybe that's why their marriage had failed and now because of the mean dog in the manger attitude, the rigid narrow dogmatic views of people who imposed their beliefs on every section of society, people like Colin were trapped for life in unhappy loveless marriages. It just wasn't fair!

Her eyes were so blurred with tears, her mind so clouded with anxiety that she collided with a man coming in the opposite direction.

"Oh, excuse me!" She fought to regain her composure as he steadied her with a firm hand.

"Not at all. Is something the matter?" The voice was deep and attractive and Devlin noticed that the brown eyes staring down at her were kind and concerned.

Shaking her head hastily she lied, "Some sand blew into my eyes. Please excuse me, I should have been looking where I was going." Wiping the tell-tale tears from her eyes she noticed that the man who spoke was accompanied by another, older man. She gave them an embarrassed smile and walked on leaving them both staring after her, a thoughtful frown on the younger man's face.

"There's one miserable young woman, Dad. I wonder what's wrong with her?"

His father shook his head slowly. "There's plenty in this world to make young girls cry, son, don't you forget that."

The man smiled down at his father. "Come on Da, let's go and murder a pint and you can give me your lecture about settling down," he grinned. "I know you've wanted to all day and it wouldn't be the same if you didn't." They walked on slowly, the son curbing his stride to suit his father's.

Devlin walked in the opposite direction towards the bus stop, savagely telling herself to get a grip on herself. She had got herself into this mess and she and Colin would have to discuss what was to be done. But how in the name of God could she have got pregnant when she was on the pill? She just couldn't figure it out.

***

"Did you forget to take it?"

She couldn't believe the coldness in Colin's voice or the horror on his face as she told him of her predicament when he arrived back two days later. She shook her head emphatically. "I took it every night, the pack makes it easy."

"Did you have vomiting or diarrhoea while you were on holidays?" The cold professional voice chilled her to the bone, making her cringe inwardly. Remembering her bad attack of Spanish tummy at the end of her holidays Devlin nodded miserably. It had lasted even through the week-end she had come home and of course, that was it. It even said in the instruction on the packet to take added precautions in the event of having vomiting or diarrhoea. It hadn't even crossed her mind at the time of her deflowering that the pill would not adequately protect her.

"When?" Colin's question was curt.

She told him and this time her own voice took on a cool edge. To hell with him! she thought. It was as much his problem as it was hers but of course there was no such things as "unmarried fathers." It was always the girl who got the blame.

"Why didn't you tell me?" His irritated accusing voice growled at her, a bad-tempered frown marring his handsome features. Was this the same loving man? Funny, she had never noticed the slightly pockmarked texture of his skin, which was beginning to hint at jowls around his jaw. Another couple of years and his good looks would certainly fade if he didn't look after himself. She thought this in a strangely detached way as if seeing him for the first time.

"For heaven's sake, Devlin," he rasped, his brows drawn down in anger. Thrusting a small specimen jar at her, he sharply ordered her to fill it and bring it back to him.

So much for loving arms and words of comfort, Devlin thought, as she tried to perform with accuracy for the required sample. She knew with certainty that this was only the beginning. Somehow, deep down inside her she realised that things were very definitely going to get worse. Looking at the little jar of urine that would shortly confirm what she already knew, she longed with all her might to have the guts to fling it in his face and walk out of the office and never see him again. What a fool she had been! How naïve! Thinking that Colin might perhaps divorce his wife! She felt as though she hated him and bitterness surged through her. The emotion shocked Devlin and she stared at herself in the mirror. This was the man she had thought she loved only hours earlier. It now seemed like decades ago.

She had given him what she had once been told was a woman's greatest gift. Her precious virginity. Impotent rage gripped her. It wasn't fair! Why was it such a big deal? Why did men not have the same pressure about their first time doing it? Did they ever feel dirty and used? And she had always thought she was so sure of herself, so sophisticated. What a laugh...how could she have ever imagined that she loved Colin or that he had loved her.

"Be honest." Devlin made herself stare at the image reflected in the mirror. "You wanted to find out what it was all about, you used him as much as he used you." The truth of it made her squirm but she acknowledged it. It horrified her to think that she could be so shallow but although she did not realise it, this was her first real step on the ladder of maturity. She would know many soul-searching moments in her life but none of them would ever be as difficult as this.

Several hours later, when his last appointment was finished Colin came and stood in front of her desk. "It's very early but it's positive all right." Still the cool professional voice. "I presume you want an abortion?"

Devlin sat very still as his words sank in.

"Well, Devlin?" he queried, coldly, impatiently.

"I...I...um I hadn't really thought about it," she said quietly.

"Well, darling," he drawled somewhat sarcastically, "isn't it time you started. Do you want to carry the pregnancy to term? Do you want to keep the child or have it adopted or do you want to get rid of it?

Devlin looked at him squarely. "You're the father, Colin. What would you suggest?" His eyes hardened and he turned his back to her and walked over to the window.

"I have three legitimate children, Devlin. I don't want another one and you'll have to prove I'm the father; I'm not accepting responsibility for it. I suggest," he turned and looked at her coldly, "that I make arrangements for you to go to London to be seen by one of my colleagues over there and I suggest you go soon. This week in fact if I can arrange it: it will be less traumatic."

"Jesus, Colin, you don't mean that!!" Devlin thought she was going to be sick. Her mind tried to accept his words. He wanted her to abort his own child and he hadn't even discussed any alternatives. Colin pulled her out of her chair and gave her a little shake.

"Listen, you stupid little girl! Don't think for one moment that I'm going to let you ruin my life as well as your own. Hell! If this ever got out I'd be the laughing stock of the medical profession." He saw the disgust and repulsion in her face and let her go. "Look, Devlin," he said heavily. "Do you really want to have a child outside wedlock? A little bastard? What's the point of going through nine months of misery only to hand it over for adoption? Are you going to keep it and suffer the finger pointing and gossiping and ostracism that goes on no matter who you are once you're an unmarried mother? And you'll never have another moment of freedom." He stared intently at her. "You have to think of your own future too and I'm telling you here and now, London is the best option for you. I'll take care of you financially—don't worry about that—but..." his voice was steely, "if you decide on anything else you're on your own and I won't keep you on in the job. Don't give me any crap about unfair dismissal either, I've good friends in the legal profession so I'll be well advised."

He pointed a long manicured forefinger at her. "And you would be well advised to go to London. Think of yourself," he urged and this time his voice was less authoritative, kinder, more like the old Colin. "Look," he said quietly, "we've both had a shock. Go home and think about it and I'll see you tomorrow." Silently Devlin gathered up her things. Her heart was pounding with a mixture of fear and anger. If she had the baby she would get no help from him and she would lose her job. If she had an abortion, which was murder, according to her religion and the laws of the land, she would have to live with it for the rest of her life. *Only you would know*. The thought flashed through her mind and she had to admit that abortion would be so simple. It would erase the problem like a duster on a blackboard. A clean slate. She could start again.

Pausing at the door she looked at Colin. "Thanks for all your help." He coloured faintly but said nothing as she closed the door, hating him as once she thought she had loved him. How could he do this to her? She wanted to kill him, to hurt him in some way for what he had done to her. Bitterness so strong that she could almost taste it flooded through her. She could go to a Garda station and say that he had counselled her about abortion and was prepared to refer her to an abortion clinic. Would he be arrested? She wasn't sure; she knew that the law prohibited abortion referral. How would he like his handsome face plastered over every newspaper in the country? That might knock the smug superior attitude out of him.

She knew she wouldn't. She wouldn't have the guts to do it and expose herself as well. "Oh Devlin, you fool," she cursed herself quietly as she got into her Fiesta. Her heart sank even lower as she realised she had to go home to her parents for dinner this evening. Usually she went home for a meal once a week but lately she had really begun to dread going home. There was such an air of strain between her parents and she guessed it was because of her mother's worsening drink problem. She hated when Lydia had too much to drink. She would become strident and then later start weeping, saying that Devlin had deserted them by moving into a flat. Her father would intervene and then her mother would turn on him, hurling abuse as though she hated him.

It was a side of Lydia only the two of them saw. To her friends and neighbours Lydia Delaney was a gracious cultured woman involved in many church and social activities. She had a distinguished-looking husband in a prestigious job who worshipped her, a beautiful home, an affluent lifestyle and was the envy of many of her neighbours. Yet Lydia Delaney was not a happy woman. It was as if she carried inside her some secret sadness that had embittered her and warped her life and prevented her from ever being truly satisfied with her lot. Because theirs was not a very close relationship, Devlin couldn't talk to Lydia about her drinking and her unhappiness. Her mother was a cool and very reserved person as regards giving and receiving physical affection. Not for Devlin warm loving hugs when she was a child. Not for her to be loved as other mothers loved their daughters.

"Mind my dress, dear," or, "I've just put on my make up," Lydia would say to the young Devlin when in her spontaneous way she would throw her little arms around her mother. So the child got out of the habit. Not that she had ever really seen an awful lot of her mother. Lydia was on many committees and involved in fund-raising for various charities. She played a round of golf almost daily unless she was on one of her drinking binges, and so Devlin had more or less been raised by a succession of dailies and babysitters. Her father did not especially enjoy the hectic social life Lydia forced upon him, but because he loved his wife and it seemed to keep her happy he went to openings and first nights, charity galas and church socials and it always seemed to Devlin that no matter what he did it was never enough. It was as if Lydia had set some invisible goal that he could never reach.

How, Devlin thought, could she go home and tell her elegant reserved status-conscious mother that she was going to bear an illegitimate child? Devlin hoped to the depths of her soul that Lydia would not be drunk tonight. She couldn't cope with a scene; she was near enough to a nervous breakdown as it was. How could Colin be so unfeeling and cold? How could she have been such a fool? Why wouldn't her thoughts stop racing around her head, which felt as if it was going to explode? Why did her heart keep palpitating, causing her to feel dizzy? Was this what it was like to have a nervous breakdown or was it because she was pregnant? Tears came to her eyes again and she cursed herself for being so weak.

three

Eventually she turned off the dual carriage way up the exclusive road they lived on and into the long shaded avenue of their tastefully planned garden. The elegant Edwardian house lay in a curve of silver maple trees, their lovely glossy leaves catching the rays of the evening. She loved the way the ivy grew around the large bay windows that now reflected sparkling prisms of sunlight.

Two magnificent red hawthorns dominated the lush green lawn and Devlin smiled at the sight of them. They had been Gerry's pride and joy and when she was a child and the soft red fragrant flowers would begin to fall he would throw handfuls over her hair and tell her she was a flower fairy. Gerry loved his garden and spent many hours of solitude hoeing and weeding and planting. Lydia shared his love of gardening and when they worked in it together they never fought. Devlin had always been happy to see them both in the garden on the rare evening that they weren't going out. At least there would be no rows.

As she parked her car she saw that her father

was not yet home although Lydia's car was there. Slowly she got out as if putting off the fateful moment of entering her home in her pregnant state. She carefully picked up the bouquet of flowers she had bought for her mother on the way home—a weekly tradition. She could no longer put off going in so, taking a deep breath, she inserted her key and entered the elegant grey and pink hall.

A veneered Georgian side-table bearing an urn filled with roses was the only piece of furniture there—simple, understated and utterly right. Whatever her faults, Lydia had an eye for colour and decor that would have made her a natural for a career in interior decorating had she been so inclined. Her home was stylish and tasteful and the envy of her less talented friends. Poking her head into the superbly equipped pine kitchen Devlin saw that her mother was not there, although the preparations for dinner were well under way. Sighing, she walked into the lounge and found Lydia relaxing with coffee and a cigarette.

"Hello Mum, hope I'm not too late," she forced a cheerful note into her voice as she handed her mother the flowers. Lydia smiled. Thank God she's not drunk, Devlin thought, greatly relieved at her mother's seemingly affable humour, although she knew from experience that what started out as a pleasant family dinner could often end in disaster.

"Thank you, dear, these are lovely," her

mother's cultured tones intruded on her musings. "You're not late at all. Dinner won't be for a while. Your father is entertaining a client and he's invited him back for a meal. You don't mind, do you?"

Devlin's heart sank. Just what she didn't need, making social chit-chat. But for her mother's benefit she said brightly, "Of course not, Mum, I'll just go and freshen up."

"Good idea," Lydia said, a trifle drily. Devlin let it pass. She knew she looked a sight. Trust Lydia to rub it in. Her mother was always impeccably groomed except during a very bad binge, and she expected nothing less of her daughter. Tiredly Devlin made her way upstairs to her bedroom with its cheerful Laura Ashley floral paper, matching curtains and bedspread. Usually the sight of her immaculately tidy bedroom bathed in sunlight lifted her spirits, but not today. She was feeling a little strange. She'd just lie down for a while, she decided, flopping onto her bed.

It was funny, she reflected; she felt as if she was getting her period. Her PERIOD!! Galvanised, she flew into the bathroom and inspected her briefs. Frustration welled in her at the sight of their unblemished purity. She did not realise that many women in the very early stages of pregnancy often feel as if a period is imminent. Flinging herself on the bed she lay staring at the ceiling, knowing she would have to start making a decision soon.

Reluctantly her hand moved down over her stomach. It felt no different. She couldn't feel the presence of a life. Maybe it was true what some argued that life didn't begin until much later. After all she was only a little while gone. It couldn't be bigger than the top of a pin.

"Devlin! Devlin! I was wonder..." Her mother stood at the door staring at her. "Good gracious, Devlin, what's the matter with you?"

Scarlet with guilt, Devlin shot off the bed, the colour draining from her face as dizziness overcame her. Hastily she sat down on the bed, trying to keep from fainting.

"Heavens above, Devlin, what's wrong with you?" Her mother's voice, sharp with concern, pierced the woolliness of her mind.

Devlin wanted desperately to blurt out the truth and get it over with, but caution restrained her and she murmured slowly, "Honestly it's nothing Mum, I skipped lunch and I felt a bit faint."

"It's living in that...flat. You're not feeding yourself," Lydia said sharply.

Don't let her start, Devlin prayed.

"I hope you're not on one of those faddy diets?"

Diet! Devlin thought she was going to laugh hysterically. Not the best diet in the world was going to be able to save her figure unless she had an abortion. In a few months everybody who met her would know exactly what she had been up to. There was no need to write the word "Adultery" on her forehead in bright red paint...it would be there for all the world to see in the bulge of her belly, which was now so flat and slender.

"I'm not on a diet, Mum. I just skipped lunch. I was shopping, that's all!"

"Well, tidy up. Gerry and Mr...er...Reilly I think his name is, should be here soon."

"Is there a Mrs Reilly?" Devlin inquired as she cautiously stood up, not wishing to have a repeat of the previous dizziness.

"Gerry just said Mr Reilly had a very sharp business brain and was self made. He lives in London most of the time, I believe, as most of his business is over there, but he does have some property in Dublin. I think his father lives here." She eyed her daughter thoughtfully. "I wonder what age he is?"

It was one of her mother's aims in life to make a good match for Devlin and all the more so as the obnoxious Carol Jones down the road had just landed a most eligible bachelor and was sporting a dazzling hunk of diamond on her left finger. The said bachelor, son of a prominent politician who had made millions in land speculation deals, had been very keen on Devlin who disliked him intensely, hating his arrogant assumption that because his father was a rich powerful man he could do what he liked and have what he wanted. He had wanted Devlin badly but neither his manners nor his wealth impressed her and it had been a relief to her when he had started seeing Carol.

Her mother gave one of her cultured sniffs.

"You could have had that Gaynor fellow if you had wanted to, I must remind Cecilia of the fact the next time she starts on about Carol's marvellous match." Then the sound of a car coming up the drive sent Lydia to the bedroom window from where she could see the drive.

"They're here! Do brush your hair, Devlin, and don't be long," she admonished before drifting downstairs, leaving the faint scent of *Je Reviens* wafting on the air behind her. Automatically running a comb through her blond sunstreaked hair, Devlin washed her face and added a trace of lipstick to her mouth to please her mother, before dabbing some *Magie Noir* behind her ears.

Glumly she descended the stairs and walked into the lounge. As she entered, she saw a dark haired man of tall muscular build talking to her father.

"Hello, love," her father greeted her warmly as she raised her face for his kiss.

Good God! thought Luke Reilly, his dark eyes narrowing, That's the girl who was crying her eyes out on the South Wall. He felt a flicker of interest. Several times since she had bumped into him he had wondered why a girl like her would be weeping in broad daylight in such a public place. He had never dreamt he would meet her again.

Devlin turned to find a pair of amber eyes regarding her thoughtfully. Her father said swiftly. "Luke, I'd like you to meet my daughter

Devlin. Devlin, Luke Reilly."

Her hand was taken in a warm firm handshake and his deep voice was saying "it's a pleasure." Then Lydia was coming in, laughing and talking animatedly, and Devlin was content to melt into the background to sip her soda water. She had turned down the offer of a drink. Now that she knew she was pregnant she might as well abstain.

"But you're going to have an abortion, so it doesn't matter," her little voice interfered again. "And anyway you've probably turned the poor child into an alcoholic already with all that gin you drank."

How she hated that taunting prying voice that was always there to torment her. It must be the voice of her conscience, she thought, unaware that Luke was studying her unobtrusively as he stood, one hand in his pants pocket, the other holding his whiskey sour, his head bent attentively as he pretended to pay attention to Lydia over the pre-dinner drinks.

The daughter fascinated him. Those darkly lashed eyes of such an unusual shade of blue were staring unseeingly out of the window as if she was deep in some private argument with herself. Obviously she hadn't recognised him. She was dressed simply in a peach tee-shirt mini dress that hugged her shapely figure and showed off her tan to perfection and he decided she was stunning. And the thing was, she was completely unaware of him too, he mused wryly, not used to being ignored.

The combination of dark, almost foreign looks, thanks to a Spanish mother, powerful personality and considerable wealth ensured that beautiful women invariably fell for Luke Reilly and Devlin's behaviour was a decidedly new experience for him. Usually he wasn't attracted to young girls, preferring women to be a bit nearer his own age of thirty-three but there was something different about this cool, distant girl that intrigued him.

Over dinner, Devlin forced herself to join in the conversation. She didn't wish to appear rude but she was certainly not her usual exuberant self, a fact her mother noticed.

"Darling, I thought you were ravenous?" Lydia remarked lightly, noticing Devlin picking half heartedly at the smoked salmon that lay appetisingly on her best fine bone Royal Doulton.

"Oh!..I...am," Devlin murmured, forcing herself to swallow a mouthful. Her eyes met the stranger's and as she came under the scrutiny of those heavy lidded amber eyes she felt that the word PREGNANT was written all over her face. Defiantly she lifted her chin and stared back at him. He wasn't good looking in the conventional sense, his face was too lean and long. Rawboned would be a good word to describe it, she decided. He had the dark swarthy looks of the European, a broad forehead, straight nose and a firm sensual mouth, which now had an amused grin which displayed strong white even teeth. There was an intense magnetic air about him and she felt she didn't like him or his strange amber eyes that seemed too penetrating. He laughed aloud at the joke Gerry was telling him, a rich deep laugh, and she felt irrationally irritated that he should be laughing while she was in the depths of panic and despair.

Moodily she toyed with the rest of the delicious meal her mother had prepared: the mouthwatering rack of lamb, the sinful baked alaska. She was beginning to feel somewhat nauseous and it was with relief that she heard her mother ask Luke to go and relax with her father in the lounge. Devlin helped Lydia to clear the dishes and stack them in the dishwasher before joining the men for coffee in the gracious pale apricot and cream lounge with its luxurious sofas and chairs and enormous French panelled bevelled mirror. Through it, she caught once again the interested gaze of Luke Reilly upon her.

"Your father tells me that you are not long back from Portugal. Did you enjoy your holiday?" he inquired politely.

"Oh, it was very nice." Her tone was polite but offhand. She wished he would leave so she could make her own excuses and go back to the flat.

"I sailed into Lisbon several times when I was at sea some years back. It's a lovely city."

Lydia's eyes opened a little wider. "Oh Luke! Do you have a yacht?"

He laughed. "Not at all, Mrs Delaney, I was a

seaman for a while."

"Oh!" The disappointment was audible and Devlin nearly laughed. Poor Mother. A sailor! she thought, aware of her mother's rampant snobbery. Embarrassed, she caught a twinkle in Luke's eyes as he observed her private smile and she could have sworn that he knew exactly what was in her mind. Then, unfolding his well-built body from the depths of an easy chair, he stood up and she noticed how muscular he was across the chest and shoulders. Although his suit was well cut and looked expensive, it hardly seemed to contain him and she felt instinctively that he would prefer casual clothes.

He was thanking her mother for a lovely meal, shaking hands with Gerry and telling him he would be in touch and then he was standing in front of her, his hand held out. For the second time that evening Devlin felt the strong firmness of his handclasp. "I hope we meet again," he said suavely.

I hope we don't, she thought nastily, unable to explain her sudden dislike of this man, for it was not like her to be so irritable and irrational. But he seemed to have sensed that something was wrong with her and it made her feel strangely vulnerable the way his eyes had been watching her all evening. She murmured some non-committal reply even though Lydia, who had been drinking quite steadily, was glaring at her. And then he was gone and the room seemed bigger as if he had somehow dwarfed it with his presence when he had been there.

"Really, Devlin!" Her mother's irritated voice brought Devlin sharply out of her reverie. "You might have been a little more pleasant during dinner. That man could become an important client of your father's." She eyed her daughter crossly. "Since you've gone to live in that flat," the word was uttered with utter distaste, "you've become a different person."

Oh no, don't let her get started, Devlin thought wearily, feeling that she couldn't take much more as Lydia launched into a tirade. Sometimes Devlin felt that her mother begrudged her every moment of her independence. Was it because she had never had any herself? Lydia belonged to an era where women went straight from school to matrimony to motherhood.

"And what's more, Devlin, I think..." What Lydia thought Devlin never discovered because a wave of nausea overcame her and she had to flee to the bathroom. She retched miserably, cursing the day she was born.

When she came out of the bathroom her mother was waiting for her and there was a granite-like grimness about her features that caused Devlin's heart to sink.

"I want the truth from you, Devlin." She stared at her daughter with eyes as cold and forbidding as a fjord in winter. "This dizziness and sickness. Is there any reason for it and the peaky way you've had about you lately?"

Shocked into silence Devlin could only stare back mutely.

"Were you misbehaving in Portugal?"

Misbehaving! Devlin felt a wry amusement at the term. It always brought to mind children playing in puddles or pulling hair and spitting. It was a word of childhood, not a description of the act she had performed with Colin.

"Are...you...pregnant?"

Each word was enunciated with a savage intensity that stunned Devlin. The words hung in the air between them like a guillotine ready to descend on her admission of guilt. Speechless, she could only stare at her mother.

"Jesus! Will you answer me!"

Devlin had never heard her mother use the Holy Name and it gave her a funny little shock. Coming from her mother's lips it seemed like blasphemy. Swallowing hard, knowing there was no point in denying it, she met her mother's eyes. "Yes Mum, I'm pregnant...I'm sorry," she said inadequately.

Pain, anger, horror, were etched on Lydia's fine features as she stared at her daughter.

"Oh Sacred Heart of Jesus!" she muttered almost to herself, in a voice of such anguish that Devlin felt a lump rise to her throat.

"I didn't mean to," she whispered, frightened at the expression on her mother's face.

"You didn't mean to..." Lydia raged at her. "Do you know what you've done...don't you know how people will talk? My God Almighty, is this the way you repay Gerry and me for all we've done for you? Oh my God, the shame of it...the shame of it!" She was sobbing harshly now, her mascara running down her cheeks in black smudgy streaks. Her hands, heavy with jewellery, were grasping each other so tight that the veins in them bulged bluely.

Her father, who had heard the commotion and raised voice of his wife, came hastily up the stairs, puffing a little as he got to the top. "Lydia! What's wrong?"

"What's wrong? Ha...ask *her* what's wrong!" his wife cried noisily, almost hysterically, her natural restraint gone because of the brandy and wine she had consumed during the course of the evening.

Shaking with reaction, dry-mouthed, her heart thudding so loudly that she was sure it was audible, Devlin told her father and watched and hated herself as his face crumpled in pain and disappointment.

"Ah Devlin, Devlin," was all he could say, shaking his head in disbelief. Gerry had never been able to chastise her; that had always been left to his wife. The pain of her father's reaction was a memory of guilt she would always carry, the way he had seemed to age visibly before her, his shoulders sagging as he saw his daughter fall from the pedestal that he had so proudly erected for her.

"I knew something like this was bound to happen when she went to that flat," Lydia was sobbing and hiccupping into his shoulder.

"She's just like her mother!"

"Shush! Shush, Lydia, you're distraught. Go and lie down for a while," her husband urged.

Devlin felt icy tentacles of fear curl around her insides, gripping and squeezing. "Wait a minute, Mum! What do you mean?" Her voice became high-pitched as various little memories of past years flashed through her mind, like the time Lydia and Gerry had been arguing and Lydia had been shouting, "We should have told her at the beginning," and Devlin had run upstairs, her seven-year-old heart beating so quickly and loudly that the noise of it deafened her when she had buried her sobbing little face in the pillow. Tell her what? Instinctively she knew it was something to do with her, something nasty and threatening.

"It's all right, Devlin! Your mother doesn't know what she's saying. She's had a shock. Go down and make us some strong coffee like a good girl." Gerry Delaney felt as if his world was crumbling around his ears.

"No Dad! Wait! Why did she say that?"

There was an unconscious pleading in her voice and then Lydia was saying wearily, "Oh for God's sake Gerry tell her, I wanted to tell her long ago, it might have prevented this."

Through a mist of anguish Devlin heard Lydia's bitter upset voice tell her she was adopted.

"No!...NO!" Screaming, Devlin raced down

the stairs, grabbed her bag and ran out to the car. "Oh Jesus, Jesus, don't do this to me...please God, let it be a nightmare." It must be a punishment for committing adultery with Colin. Why else would this be happening to her?

As if in a dream she started up the car and saw Gerry, distraught, calling her back. Ramming her foot down on the accelerator she raised dust as she sped down the drive onto the road. She half-hoped a car coming in the opposite direction would collide with her and send her crashing to oblivion so that she could forget the fear and aching misery that engulfed her.

Adopted! Adopted! Adopted! The sound of the word filled her mind like loud clashing cymbals as automatically her hands and feet operated gears and clutch and brakes and she emerged onto the dual carriageway. Lydia wasn't her mother...Gerry wasn't her father. Who were her parents? Why had they abandoned her? Were they still alive?

"I hate you, I hate you," she sobbed aloud, great gasping shuddering sobs that blurred her eyes and made her body shake. The car behind her beeped loudly at her erratic driving and becoming conscious of the stream of lights and the busy flow of traffic she pulled herself together and concentrated grimly on just driving.

four

How long she drove she did not know. She vaguely remembered the turn-off at Bray and then the traffic eased until it seemed she was the only car on the road for long lonely miles. It was with numbed surprise that she realised she was driving into Arklow, a town about fifty miles from Dublin on the main Wexford road. Tired and disorientated she pulled in and rested her head on the steering wheel. How had she got this far? What was she going to do for the night? Devlin checked her watch: it was almost twelve. She knew at the back of her mind why she had instinctively come this way. She needed someone and Katie was the only one who could help her.

Her Aunt Katie had always been close to her and given her the warmth Lydia had never been able to provide. Now she needed Katie more than ever. Although she was pregnant she knew that Katie would never reject her as Lydia had. She'd have to ring home...Gerry would be frantic. Even if she wasn't his daughter he did love her, Devlin thought, torn between bitterness and sadness. She drove until she got to a phone box, praying that it wouldn't be vandalised. She was in luck and she asked the operator to reverse the charges.

"Are you all right, Devlin? What in the name of God are you doing in Arklow? Please pet, come home and let's talk about all this." Her father sounded so upset that Devlin felt tears springing to her eyes and her throat constricted painfully.

"Oh Dad, Dad I'm so sorry. I didn't mean to hurt you." In spite of herself she burst into tears.

"Devlin, please check into a hotel and I'll come and collect you. I'll get Cecilia to come and stay with Lydia."

Somehow she managed to compose herself. "Honestly, Dad, I'd like to go to Katie for a day or two, I think I'll carry on down to Wexford."

Her father sighed. "Well if that's what you want, pet." He knew how close she and Katie were and he didn't try to stop her. "Will you phone as soon as you get there?"

"It'll be late," she protested.

"Devlin, we won't rest easy otherwise. Oh and Devlin..." He paused as if unsure how to continue. "Pet, try not to think too badly of your mother. She's not herself these days...I think she's going through the change."

The lump rose in Devlin's throat again but she swallowed hard and said quietly, "Bye Dad, I'm sorry and I do love you." She could sense him smiling at the other end of the line.

"I love you too, don't forget that. Drive carefully now."

"I will," she promised and replaced the receiver.

For the next hour she banished all other thoughts from her head and concentrated on her driving and it was with a physical sense of relief that she saw the lights of Wexford in the distance, the twin steeples of the churches seeming to pierce the black star-studded sky. Driving slowly over the bridge, Devlin, despite her trauma, felt her spirits lift as they always did when she crossed the bridge into the town. She loved Wexford: the warmth of the people and the beauty of the place always soothed her. Slowly she drove along the quay, looking at the myriad glittering lights reflected in the water that softly lapped the quayside. Katie lived in Rosslare Harbour, about twelve miles further on, but the road was excellent and she made good time and turned up the winding lane that led to the farmhouse less than fifteen minutes later.

Checking her watch, Devlin saw it was almost one thirty. She reflected that Katie would be long gone to bed. One of the dogs started barking and a minute later Devlin saw the bedroom curtain being drawn back and her aunt stuck her head out the window.

"Who in the name of…? Merciful hour, is that you, Devlin?"

Minutes later the door was thrown open and Katie stood there, a dainty elf, her soft grey hair tumbling about her shoulders.

"There's something wrong, isn't there?" she

exclaimed, enveloping her niece in a warm embrace. "Is it Lydia or Gerry? Is it the drinking?"

Devlin shook her head sadly. "It's me, Katie. I had to come and see you. You're the only one who can help me."

"Well come in, alanna, out of the night. Sure it can't be that bad. Nothing is ever as bad as it seems."

Tears smarted in Devlin's eyes. How typical of Katie to be so loving and reassuring. Katie gave her niece a soft shove into the house and Devlin could feel its peace and serenity envelope her like a comforting eiderdown. Before long she was sitting before a crackling fire, hot chocolate and a plate of fresh homemade scones dripping with jam and cream on her lap. Between mouthfuls she poured out the whole sorry tale.

The relief of unburdening herself was enormous and Katie let her talk, merely interjecting a softly-spoken comment here and there. When Devlin told her about Lydia's revelation her face turned hard and cold and she said grimly, "Typical of Lydia. She was always the most self-centred and selfish person I ever knew and believe me it hurts to say that about my own sister."

"Katie?" Devlin's voice was raw with pain. "Do you know who my mother was?" Her aunt wrapped a comforting arm around her and rocked the now sobbing girl softly, soothingly.

"Cry all you want, alanna, and get it out of

your system. There's no point in bottling it all up inside because it will only affect you later." She held her for a long time and when Devlin had stopped weeping those long haunting racking sobs, Katie said quietly, "Your mother was our youngest sister, Tara. She died at your birth. Robbie and I wanted to adopt you but Lydia wouldn't have it." She looked down at her niece. "I wish I'd fought harder to get you but Lydia had just married Gerry and he had money and good prospects whereas Robbie and I only had the few acres. Lydia said we would never be able to give you the opportunities they could." She sighed deeply. "It's something I've always regretted, especially as Rob and I did well for ourselves."

"But why did she adopt me? The way she spoke to me tonight made me feel as though she hated me."

The question was anguished and bitter and for a moment Katie felt a deep resentment of her sister. But she continued reassuringly: "Ah Devlin, she doesn't hate you. She wanted to adopt you to try and make up for the way she had treated your mother. When Tara died they were estranged. You have to understand, Lydia's normally a very restrained person and when she loses control she's angry with the person who causes it. The drinking isn't helping either."

Devlin shook her head. "No Katie, it was more than that. I know!" she said emphatically.

Katie sighed. "All right, Devlin, I'll tell you what's wrong with Lydia. Maybe then you can understand her attitude to your having a baby and find it in your heart to be sorry for her."

"I'll never forgive her," Devlin vowed savagely.

"Hush pet, don't say that. If you let yourself you can come out of this experience more mature and self-reliant than you've been. Don't be so negative...that's one thing I've learned from life." Katie smiled lovingly at her niece. "Negative thoughts and bitterness get you nowhere. I learned that when Robbie died."

Devlin gave a sniff, wiped her eyes, blew her nose and said brusquely. "Well tell me why I should have sympathy for her." Katie threw another log on the fire and settled back comfortably.

"It was like this, you see. Lydia was beautiful when she was young and she knew it." She laughed. "I was the plain one and Tara, your mother, was fat and spotty until she was seventeen and then...well she went away to her penpal in France for a whole summer and when she came back people didn't recognise her, she was so slender and tanned. All her puppy fat had just melted off her." Katie nodded at Devlin. "She was very much like you are now. Anyway, Lydia had been dating a young doctor and she was crazy about him. He was the only one of her boyfriends who didn't hop at her command and who wasn't always at her beck and call," she smiled wryly. "You know Lydia! He was the only man she couldn't dominate. To make a long story short,

Tara came back from France looking like a million dollars and Brian, that was his name, fell for her hook line and sinker. Tara was a lovely soft generous person, you couldn't but love her. They didn't plan it that way. They tried to fight the attraction. But it was one of those things. Tara fell in love with him and he started dating her. Lydia never forgave either of them and in a way, Devlin, I always feel she married Gerry very much on the rebound.

"Then Tara became pregnant with you. Brian was in the middle of his internship in a Northern hospital—that was where he lived—and there was no way he could afford to marry Tara immediately although he wanted to. Mother, God bless her, took the whole thing very calmly; she was always a brick in a crisis. She told Brian to save enough to get decent lodgings. She wanted to be sure that Tara would have somewhere proper to live with her new baby. She never once reproached Tara and always told her to hold her head high."

Katie smiled "It's a pity you never knew your grandmother, Devlin. She was a lady with a lot of class. Anyway, Brian and Tara had made plans to marry two months before you were due but two days before the wedding Tara went into labour and died shortly after the birth. Everyone was devastated. You weren't expected to survive," she gave her niece an affectionate smile, "but you were a little fighter, Devlin, and you made it." She sighed. "After much discussion

Lydia and Gerry decided, with Brian's blessing, that they would adopt you. Your father was in no position to take care of you, darling. He felt that Lydia and Gerry could provide a stable home. So that's why Lydia reacted as she did. Don't blame her too much, Devlin. She's had hardships too."

"What happened to my father?" Devlin asked, unable to keep the bitterness from her voice.

Katie's eyes were full of compassion as she saw her niece's obvious torment. Gently she said "Your ah...that is, Brian continued living in the North. I believe he married and had two children. They emigrated because of the troubles, Australia I heard. He died of a heart attack last year."

Devlin shook her head in disbelief, unable to grasp all she had been told. She actually had a half-brother and sister or maybe two brothers or two sisters. It was all too much to take in. Her blonde head drooped exhaustedly and, briskly, Kate urged her up the small stairs into the tiny guest bedroom. Devlin undressed automatically and climbed naked into the welcoming double bed piled high with downy white pillows. Pulling the patchwork quilt up around her, she stretched her limbs against the softness of freshly laundered sheets and giving an exhausted yawn fell into a deep and dreamless sleep, as the horrors of the past few hours were temporarily erased from her mind.

five

A week later, a harder, more determined Devlin stood in front of the check-in desk at Dublin Airport. She was alone. As she thought of the events of the past week, she felt a strange sense of relief that she had made her decision. She had stayed with Katie for two days. Her aunt had discussed all the options with her, offering her the haven of her home for the duration of her pregnancy...and afterwards. Devlin knew that Katie was deeply opposed to her decision to have the abortion. She tried gently but firmly to dissuade her from the idea.

"Tara could have had you aborted, Devlin, but she didn't, so think hard about what you are going to do. I know the stigma of being an unmarried mother is a hard cross to bear, especially in this uncharitable country. I've seen the way girls have been treated, thrown out of their homes, left to have their babies alone and dumped in lonely flats in Ballymun and the likes. I know what you're afraid of facing, alanna, but you're strong, you can cope and I'll always be here for you, so think hard..."

In a state of indecision Devlin had returned to

her flat in Dublin, ringing Gerry at work to tell him she was home. An hour later Lydia arrived on her doorstep. They stared at each other awkwardly and then Lydia said abruptly, "I apologise for my behaviour the other day. It was the shock!"

Swallowing hard, Devlin said, "That's all right, I'm sorry for what's happened."

Lydia drew a packet of cigarettes out of her bag and lit one. Sitting gracefully on the edge of the sofa in her superbly cut Michael Gall suit, her hair beautifully styled, it was hard to believe that this was the same ravaged sobbing woman who had ranted and cursed so stridently a few days earlier. Pulling deeply on the cigarette she said firmly, "I've told Gerry I'll handle this my way." Exhaling the smoke in a long thin stream, she said matter-of-factly, "I think an abortion is the best thing for you." Two bright spots had appeared on her cheeks despite her meticulous make-up. The hand holding the cigarette was not quite steady.

Devlin walked over to the window and stood staring out. In spite of herself she was shocked and surprised. She had felt that Lydia would have been totally against her having an abortion on religious grounds and she had dreaded telling her. But here she was, the same Lydia who went regularly to Sunday Mass and who chastised Devlin for not going, Lydia, who was on first name terms with some of the bishops as a result of her charity work, Lydia who had been so shocked when it was rumoured that Jennifer Quinn had gone to England and had an abortion. This Lydia was now advocating that her daughter—sorry, "adopted daughter"—do the same.

Devlin smiled bitterly. How easy it was to judge other people until one of your own got into trouble. How easy to accuse other people of committing murder, as Lydia had, when she heard about Jennifer. I wonder how she'll justify the change of attitude, she thought. She didn't have to wait long.

"It's a bit late for morals and scruples now," Lydia's voice was crisp. "After all Devlin, you're only twenty. There is no point in ruining your life with an unwanted pregnancy. I mean I presume you are not going back to Portugal to confront the gigolo who fathered the child?" The cultivated voice paused, and then, "What kind of life could you give a baby? It would be unfair to both of you."

She stopped to take another pull of her cigarette while Devlin struggled to keep her temper. Had she not known the facts of her adoption, had she thought she was Lydia's own child, she would have argued heatedly with her mother and pointed out her hypocrisy. How she longed to scream that the bastard who had impregnated her was none other than the supremely socially acceptable scion of Irish medical circles and Dublin's high society, Colin Cantrell-King and not, as Lydia so disdainfully put it, "a Portuguese gigolo." With great difficulty Devlin restrained herself. She knew Colin was a valued client of her father's and if he knew the truth he would feel obliged to speak to Colin about the matter. As a result Colin might withdraw his business. It's your problem, not theirs, she told herself, the empty cold feeling inside her making her feel utterly alone and frightened. Lydia's voice impinged on her consciousness like a malevolent laser piercing and probing deep inside her brain. She wanted to put her hands over her ears and scream at her to go away...leave her alone...Again Devlin struggled for control. She was just not going to get into an argument with her mother. Breathing deeply, she heard Lydia say coolly,

"You do realise of course Devlin that with your father's position in the bank, an...um...episode like this could be rather embarrassing. I mean after all we do keep a rather high profile...so if you insist on keeping the baby, I think it might be better if we could be a little discreet about it. We'll give you an allowance of course and do our duty by you financially."

The silence that hung between them was broken only by the erratic tick of an old carriage clock on the mantelpiece.

We'll do our duty by you financially. How kind, thought Devlin bitterly. But on no account let the neighbours see that I'm an unmarried mother just like the poor unfortunates you hold coffee mornings for, the ones that are put on the streets with no where to go. Well, I might as well be one of them.

Lydia, seeing the expression on her daughter's face, stubbed out her cigarette rather crossly, stood up and said in her best "I know what's best for you" tone, "I think my first suggestion will be best all round, I'll provide the money. I'm sure you could make discreet inquiries from Colin. Say you have a friend in trouble. I know it's supposed to be illegal but I'm sure you'll get the information from him. I just hope he won't put two and two together when you take the few days off." Giving one of her sniffs she said agitatedly, "You can say we are going on a shopping trip."

Lydia picked up her expensive Italian clutch bag and walked towards the front door, hips swaying gracefully. "Ring me tomorrow, dear, and let me know what you decide but, as I say, I think you should consider my suggestion."

Devlin bit her tongue. Say nothing. It's your decision to make and no one else's, she thought in despair. Whatever else she had been expecting from her mother, she had never dreamt that Lydia would condone, let alone suggest, her having an abortion. Watching her get into her Ford Capri, Devlin wondered what was Gerry's opinion on the matter. Did he agree with Lydia about the abortion or was he letting her handle it just to keep her happy? Lydia dominated him totally and always had done, yet it took a kind of strength to love and stay with a woman like Lydia as Gerry did. She wondered sadly would there ever be a man who would love her totally and unreservedly. How would such a man cope with the knowledge of the abortion she was about to have? How would he cope with her illegitimacy?

Not once in their conversation had Lydia referred to Devlin's adoption, nor would she ever again do so unless Devlin brought up the subject. Had it not been for Katie she would probably never have known the full truth. Never in all her life had she felt so isolated, so utterly rootless. From being somebody with an identity and family history she had become totally anchorless. She felt she was floating around like a leaf in a storm. But, she decided firmly, it was time to take stock and face reality. From now on the only person she would depend on would be herself.

The following morning she informed Colin that she had decided to go ahead with the abortion. She watched as a brief smile of satisfaction crossed his features and she hated him.

Briskly he made the arrangements with a colleague in London and twenty minutes later was handing her a page from his note-pad upon which, scrawled in his flamboyant handwriting, were the name and address of the doctor she was to go and see and the time of her appointment.

"That's all settled then!" he said heartily in his best doctor to patient voice. "Now go and book a flight and don't worry about a thing. It will be over and finished in no time."

Devlin observed that at no time had he looked her straight in the eye and as she watched him stride into his office she thought what a gutless bastard he was.

She was lucky and got a flight for the same day as her appointment. Ringing Lydia that evening she told her the date.

"Oh dear!" Lydia exclaimed in dismay. "That's the date of the Central Remedial Clinic's big do and I've promised I'll be there. I wonder would Katie go with you?"

Devlin grimaced at the vague tone of regret in her mother's voice. Truth to tell she was almost relieved that Lydia wouldn't be coming with her as the strain would have been unbearable.

"Don't worry, I'll be fine. Enjoy the do and I'll ring when I get home." Her voice was a little dry.

"Devlin dear, I hope you realise I'll be sick with worry." Lydia's voice now came sharply across the line. "Ring me from London and let me know the time your flight arrives. I'll collect you at the airport. Now give me your account number so I can lodge some money for you."

"It's all right, Mum, there's no need to," Devlin said heatedly.

"I insist, Devlin," her mother replied sternly "I told you your father and I would look after you financially."

But he's not my father and you're not my mother, she wanted to say...and I don't want to be looked after financially. I just don't want to be rejected.

"Do you hear me, Devlin?" Lydia insisted. Devlin gave her mother the required information. If Lydia thought that was the best way to help it didn't say much for her sensitivity. Despite herself Devlin felt sorry for the other woman. Lydia, so cool and reserved and worried about what other people thought of her, unable to give or to receive affection. That was probably why she had turned to drink. Maybe if she had had a child of her own it might have been different.

"Thanks Mum," she said quietly. There was a pause and then the sound of a throat being cleared.

"Just take care of yourself," Lydia said awkwardly, "and ring me when you are on your way home."

"OK," Devlin murmured wearily as she hung up and examined her side view in the mirror to see if there was any visible evidence of her pregnancy. There was nothing that she could see and sometimes she wondered if she was really pregnant at all. Maybe she was imagining the nausea and slightly swollen breasts. Maybe she was having one of those hysterical pregnancies she had read about and her period was ready to flood through her if only she could stop worrying about its arrival.

"Idiot!" she cursed her reflection. "Colin did the test. You're well and truly pregnant, so go and get packing." Now she was going loony as well as everything else, talking to herself. She viewed her wardrobe with distaste.

What kind of clothes do you wear to a murder? The thought came unbidden to her mind. Oh God stop it! Stop it! she screamed silently and flung herself sobbing onto the bed.

She did not hear Caroline coming in and wasn't aware of her until her flatmate sat on the bed beside her and said hesitantly, "Devlin what's the matter with you? Why won't you tell me? I'll try and help if I can." She put a timid hand on her friend's shoulder.

"Oh Christ, Caroline, if I tell you you'll be disgusted," Devlin muttered, her head buried deep in her pillow.

"I won't be!" Caroline declared stoutly, wondering what could be so awful. Maybe Devlin had crashed the car. Her eyebrows drew down in a puzzled little frown. She could recall nothing very odd about the car on the way in.

"Tell me, Dev...I mean we are supposed to be friends and I always come to you when I'm in trouble." Caroline's big brown eyes were earnestly staring into her own. Devlin dreaded the distaste that would soon be evident in their depths. She had always enjoyed the way Caroline looked up to her in spite of her being two years older. Well, it was true...they were friends and it was only fair to be honest and tell her.

Heavily she said "I'm pregnant..." and watched Caroline's eyes grow bigger and slightly rounder.

"Oh!" was her friend's inadequate response.

"And I'm going to have an abortion at the end of the week," Devlin informed her brusquely, deciding, in for a penny, in for a pound.

"Oh Devlin!" Caroline managed to murmur, completely stuck for words.

"There! You see! You are disgusted!" Devlin accused, half-angry, half-dismayed.

Caroline shook her head vehemently. "No! Oh no, Devlin, it's just such a ...a surprise... Ah Dev," she put her arms around her friend's shoulders. "How long have you been keeping this to yourself? Why didn't you tell me sooner?"

At the sympathy in Caroline's voice Devlin started to cry again. "I was so ashamed," she gulped. "Oh Lord I'm turning into a right waterworks lately."

"Well and no wonder," remarked the other girl soothingly, "with that burden to bear. Honestly, I'm mad you didn't tell me sooner."

"I thought you'd be shocked," Devlin admitted faintly, much surprised by Caroline's attitude.

"Oh for heaven's sake Dev, if Richard hadn't so much respect for me I might be in the same position." She laughed. "Sometimes I'm so frustrated with him I could almost rape him. He's so...restrained."

"Caroline!" Devlin expostulated in amazement at her friend's candour. Never in all the time she had known Caroline had she ever volunteered any information on her sex life or her sexual feelings for that matter.

Caroline blushed a delicate pink. "Well I have

hormones too, you know," she retorted, a little embarrassed by her outburst.

"Oh God, Caroline, I'm sorry! I know you do. It's just..." Devlin sat up and ran a hand through her soft blonde hair, "well, we don't usually have conversations like this do we?"

Caroline got up off the bed and laughed. "Maybe it's time we started. Come on, I'll make us a pot of tea and maybe we can talk about your dilemma."

They had talked for hours and Devlin felt a great warmth rise within her when Caroline offered to accompany her to London. But she wouldn't let her. Caroline worked as a saleswoman in a large auctioneer's firm and she could lose a lot of commission by being away as she was involved in selling an exclusive apartment complex just at that moment.

"Really, Devlin! I insist," Caroline said in an unusually firm tone.

"You don't know how much that means to me," Devlin had replied quietly. "But honestly Caro, I don't mind going by myself, it won't be for long."

"Well if you're sure..." Caroline murmured doubtfully, "but if you get lonely when you're over there ring me and I'll fly over."

"Thanks Caro, I will," Devlin assured her gratefully.

Caroline insisted on going with her friend in the taxi to the airport and, hugging her hard at the entrance to the departure area, had whispered supportively "Do whatever you think is right for yourself, Dev, I'll be here when you get back."

As Devlin sat in the departure lounge waiting to board she acknowledged to herself that she had never until now given Caroline the chance to prove herself as a friend. In spite of her shyness and timidity there was a solid core of integrity to Caroline. The words of Rudyard Kipling's "The Thousandth Man" flashed through her mind:

> *One man in a thousand, Solomon says,*
> *Will stick more close than a brother...*
> *But the Thousandth Man will stand by your side*
> *To the gallows-foot— and after!*

Caroline was her Thousandth Man alright and her support and friendship had certainly eased the pain and bitterness Devlin felt.

As the Aer Lingus 737 roared down the runway she felt a great knot of apprehension grip her. Now she was one of those yearly statistics she had read about, one of the thousands who had boarded planes and ships on the abortion trip to England. How had all those other thousands of women felt as they began their journey to one of the most traumatic experiences of their lives? Did the tiny little being in her have any idea of what was about to befall it? Would it feel anything? Would she feel anything?

She felt nausea rise in her throat and wondered what the suave executive type seated next to her would think if she puked all over him and his Gucci briefcase. He had been giving her the eye since they entered the departure lounge almost simultaneously.

Determinedly ignoring her discomfort—and him—she stuck her head in her magazine and read all about the "new celibacy" which was becoming the "in" thing and how to say "no" without hurting your partner or hurting yourself.

Pity I hadn't read this a month ago she thought. Flicking to her horoscope and finding the Scorpio piece she read "Follow your own intuition and you won't go far wrong. Finances will cause worry for a while but Scorpios are resourceful and it's only a passing phase. Romance..." Ha, thought Devlin there's no point in reading the rest but her eye slid surreptitiously along the column: "Someone is on the periphery of your life who will cause great changes in you. Be patient."

To her surprise the jet had begun its descent and she realised that they were making their approach to Heathrow. Idly she watched the glamorous hostesses in their elegant uniforms gliding up and down the aisle. Did any of them suspect what she was going to do?

Don't think about it she ordered herself. At least she could afford to fly. What about the poor unfortunates who had to come by boat and train? Although it wasn't all unmarried women who came on this particular journey. She had read a report in a magazine that said some married women came because they didn't want or couldn't afford more children. What a sorry mess women get landed in, she reflected glumly. Men just haven't a clue...

An hour later Devlin was getting out of a taxi at the address Colin had given her. While paying the cabbie she cast a longing eye at the spacious back seat. Oh God, if only she could drive around London all day long in that soft comfortable seat.

"Ta luv," the man said cheerfully, waiting for her to close the door. Reluctantly she did so. Did he know where he was bringing her? Had he brought many like her to this address? She turned to the impressive row of Georgian houses that faced her. Squaring her shoulders she took a deep breath and stabbed at the doorbell with her forefinger. A disembodied voice came floating over her head and hastily she gave her name over the intercom.

The door slowly glided open and as she stepped into a luxuriously carpeted foyer, it slid gently closed behind her with an ominous click. Feeling utterly trapped she had a wild desire to grab her case and run but she fought down the impulse and forced herself in the direction of the room marked "Reception." A brisk, efficient lady in her mid-forties greeted her and urged her to take a seat. "Doctor will be ready for you shortly," she informed Devlin in a high pitched sing-song voice. She swallowed, her mouth dry, her heart palpitating. She wished the piped music would go away. She found it irritating, reminiscent of funeral music almost.

Jesus, Devlin, will you stop it! she thought savagely, her nails digging into her palms. Her heart was beating so loud she was sure Sing-song could hear it but the woman gave no sign of being aware of her distress, just carried on typing briskly, back ramrod straight, wrists at the right angle over her keyboard. Is that what I'm like at work? Devlin thought in dismay, wondering how many palpitating women had sat in the same room as her of whose distress she had been completely unaware, too caught up in her own little world.

"Doctor will see you now, dear," Sing-song announced quite kindly and, catching her eye, Devlin saw a glimpse of compassion. She was led into a sparsely but tastefully furnished office where a man in his middle fifties stood behind an exquisite carved desk. He was small, dapper, and expensively dressed.

"Sit down please, Miss Delaney." He motioned her to take a seat.

"Now...my colleague Mr Cantrell-King has referred you to me for a termination, isn't that so?" He spoke calmly in his rather aristocratic English accent, his fingers joined together like a steeple, his eyes observing her through his bi-focals.

"Yes." Her voice was low.

"He tells me there will be severe mental trauma should this operation not go ahead.

Hmmm?"

"Yes." This time her voice was an octave lower.

"You are certain this is what you want?" he probed, bending his long slender fingers that held her eyes in an almost hypnotic gaze.

"Yes," she said quietly for the third time.

"I see." His eyes never left her face and she felt a prickly heat beginning to suffuse her skin.

"Well, I'm sure you've given the matter a great deal of thought—and you've received counselling of course?" She saw his eyebrows rise in interrogation.

"Yes," she almost hissed impatiently, although she felt an inane desire to laugh. Counselling. What a joke! To counsel somebody about abortion was illegal in Ireland and Colin had no more discussed any other options with her than the man in the moon. Her mother had urged her to go to London, anxious to have the matter finished with. The only counselling she had had was from Katie and Caro. Oh why couldn't this ordeal be soon over, why couldn't this irritating man do what he had to do and stop annoying her?

The doctor was getting up out of his chair. "I just want to do a quick examination before I refer you to my colleague. You need the signatures of two doctors. I'm sure Mr Cantrell-King told you all this." Devlin nodded; she wasn't going to say "yes" again. Colin had briefly explained the procedure and she knew that had she not said she had been counselled the abortion wouldn't be performed.

"Fine. I'll give you the address of the clinic. You can check in this evening. They are expecting you." He indicated his examining room where a uniformed nurse was waiting to assist her. Undressing, she lay on the hard white-sheeted couch and the nurse helped position her legs. As Devlin felt the doctor begin his examination her body tensed and she heard him murmur, "Gently now, relax."

Those long slender fingers were probing and examining between her parted legs and she wished mightily that it could have been a woman doctor. She couldn't help her feelings of distaste and violation as this small immaculate stranger pried and probed up her vagina. For an awful moment she thought she was going to fart and almost giggled nervously as she remembered Katie's stock phrase whenever someone was unfortunate enough to break wind in company. "'Tis a poor arse that never rejoiced!" she would declare good naturedly. If only Katie was here with her now. With superhuman effort she managed to contain herself and, red-cheeked, she allowed the nurse to help her down from the couch. Peeling off his rubber gloves the doctor instructed her to dress and come out to his office.

Again he sat steeple-fingered at his desk. "Good! Well now, I foresee no complications arising. We'll keep you in for twenty-four hours after the operation in case anything untoward should occur. I would also suggest that you receive some post-termination counselling if you feel you need it. I'm sure Mr Cantrell-King will arrange it." Standing up, he held out his hand. "The anaesthetist will most likely examine you tonight. Until tomorrow then." Devlin took the proffered hand, cool, slender, almost feminine, and felt a shudder of revulsion go through her. She couldn't take to him at all and found the idea of him fiddling with her insides quite nauseating.

"Er...what about your fee?" she asked almost rudely. He looked surprised.

"Ah...Colin....Mr Cantrell-King," he corrected himself, "told me to forward the bill to him. He's taking care of it from his end, I gather." The tone was even more aristocratic.

Humiliated, face scarlet, Devlin turned away and left the room.

She spent the next three hours walking disconsolately around the streets of London. She had taken the tube into Oxford Street but even the myriad displays of fashion could not distract her. Aimlessly she ambled around, her feet aching, her head throbbing. A big healthy-looking pregnant woman coming in the opposite direction and holding hands with her husband compounded her misery. The woman looked so glowing and vital and happy that Devlin couldn't bear to watch. Turning her head she stared unseeingly into a boutique until the couple had gone past. Wearily she headed for a small dimly lit café where she sank into a chair to relax her tired body. After tea and a salad roll Devlin felt somewhat refreshed and glancing at her watch she saw with some surprise that it was almost three-thirty. She couldn't face the tube again; the trains slamming in and out, and the crowds rushing up and down the escalators exhausted her. The sheer pace of London did not suit her mood of lethargy and ennui at this moment so giving in to herself, she hailed a passing taxi and gave the address of the clinic.

It was in the outer suburbs, a big rambling house set in its own grounds. Devlin could see several patients strolling around or sitting in the hot August sun. Lifting a damp lock of hair from her forehead she sighed deeply, feeling sticky and very tired. She paid the cabbie and entered the foyer with leaden steps. This was it! There was no going back.

Within minutes, details had been taken and entered into her chart. The second doctor had spoken briefly with her and it was almost a replica of her conversation with the consultant that morning. Then her bag was taken from her and she was led upstairs to a small but comfortably furnished room overlooking the grounds.

"I'm sure you'd like a shower, luv," the motherly Cockney nurse said, handing her a hospital gown. "Put that on. Mrs Harrison will want to examine you later." She directed her to the bathroom down the hall and hastily Devlin stripped out of her sweat-stained travel-crumpled clothes and stood under the warm refreshing cascade of water.

Later, sitting by the window in her room she eyed the crisply made up bed. The idea of getting into it didn't appeal to her one whit. She wasn't sick, after all...just unwantedly pregnant. But a sharp knock at the door sent her hopping into its hard embrace and she called out to the person to come in. A sullen-faced girl came into the room with a tea tray and said brusquely, "After this you'll be fasting, Nurse told me to remind you." She dumped the tray on Devlin's meal trolley and left the room as abruptly as she had entered it.

Devlin eyed the tray, deeply unmoved at the sight that greeted her. A poached egg wobbled watery and unappetizing on a piece of toast. A slice of paper-thin brown bread and a currant bun completed the meal. Her appetite vanished instantly. Pouring herself a cup of tea she sat forlorn in the strange hard bed wishing that the bright sun streaming in through her window would give way to the coolness of evening, yet dreading the night that lay before her. Her dark night of the soul, she reflected, wallowing in her melancholy humour. Somebody laughed outside her door and she found herself tensing. How dared people laugh! Didn't they realise the trauma she was going through? And whose fault is that? Trust her little voice to intervene. Nobody forced you to have sex. Nobody is forcing you to have an abortion.

"Oh shut up!" she snapped aloud and felt quite foolish. Honestly, there were days when she thought she was schizo. The sullen one arrived to collect the tray and gave an annoyed sniff as she saw the untouched food.

"You'll get nowt more till tomorrow evening," she declared in a "you'll be sorry" tone of voice as she self-righteously whipped the tray off the bed.

Marching out of the room, her broad hips swaying from side to side, her brown uniform stretched across their breadth like a wrinkled walnut shell, she managed, in spite of her load, to give the door a little slam and Devlin, annoyed out of her introspective moodiness, hissed, "Up yours too!" Only the back of the door heard her and Devlin decided she was definitely turning into a basket case. She pulled on her dressing gown, slipped her feet into her soft furry mules and left her little cell. Walking down to the TV room she was very much aware of the stillness of the place and her own solitude. The doors to the rooms on the corridor were all firmly closed and Devlin wondered if there were many like her behind them.

The nurse's station was at the end of the corridor near the stairs and a tall coloured nurse was busy filling in charts. She smiled as Devlin passed and asked if she was looking for anywhere in particular. She had beautiful liquid gold eyes and after the sullen one's bad humour Devlin felt warmed by her friendliness.

"I'm just going to the TV room, I think I'd like

to take my mind off tomorrow."

The nurse's eyes were sympathetic. "It's at the bottom of the stairs to the right. And Miss Delaney..." Her voice was soft and musical with the lovely lilt of the Caribbean.

"Yes," Devlin responded, half surprised that she knew her name.

"If you want to talk about anything I'm on duty till nine. If there's anything you need to know I'll be happy to tell you."

"Oh thanks! Thanks very much," stammered Devlin, embarrassed that this lovely girl with the serene air should know that she was going to abort her baby. The nurse nodded and smiled again. Shyly Devlin smiled back and descended the stairs. There were only two other women in the TV room, a young Indian girl and a haggard blonde woman. Neither of them acknowledged her.

She watched the antics of celebrities playing charades on the television but she couldn't concentrate as restlessness surged through her. She picked up a magazine and flicked through the pages but the print would not stay still and eventually she gave up and just sat and allowed her mind to wander.

What was Lydia doing now? Was she thinking of her at all? And Colin? Did he care that his own child was to die? Had he even spared her a thought? With a start she realised that a nurse was calling her name.

"Miss Delaney, the anaesthetist would like to

examine you now." Glancing at her watch, Devlin was surprised to see that it was almost eight-thirty. She followed the nurse back to her room and found a tall dark-haired lady waiting for her. Introducing herself as Doctor Harrison, she proceeded to examine Devlin's chest and lungs, asking her about childhood illnesses and previous operations as she went along. Devlin answered her automatically. She was beginning to feel unnerved by it all and just wanted to be left alone.

"Your pulse is racing a little, I think. I'll give you something to help you sleep and it will also relax you, Devlin. Have you any questions you would like to ask me?" the doctor inquired kindly.

Mutely Devlin shook her head. She wanted to ask if it would hurt the foetus but she couldn't bring herself to.

"Very well," the doctor said briskly, gathering her bag and Devlin's chart. "Nurse will give you something shortly. Goodnight."

"Goodnight doctor. Thank you," Devlin murmured politely. When they had gone she splashed cold water on her face, brushed her teeth and climbed wearily into bed. The hardness of the hospital bed provided little ease for her tired limbs and she tossed and turned, trying to find a comfortable position. Later she drank a cup of tea and obediently swallowed the medication handed to her by the nurse. She then lay back against the pillows awaiting instant oblivion.

But when the drug-induced sleep did eventually come, Devlin twisted and turned restlessly, tormented by nightmare images of distorted babies making eerie wailing sounds that terrified her. She woke and sat up in the darkened room, not knowing where she was, her heart pounding, rivers of sweat between her breasts and down her temples, her mind hazy from the sleeping tablet. Slowly her breathing returned to normal and she switched on the overhead light and lay back against the crumpled pillows.

A glance at her watch told her it was already five thirty and, slipping out of bed, she tiptoed slowly to the window and lifted the blind. Dawn was just breaking, a pale rose-tinted glow in the east, lightening the dark shadows of the night. Devlin watched as the glow slowly increased in strength, streaks of gold and pink exploding through the dark cloud until finally, the sun silently, majestically, rose over the horizon exploding into a brightness that encompassed the whole of the sky. Watching the magnificent orb pouring its rays like molten gold over the earth she knew she would have to make her decision. What right did she have to deprive the child within her of the chance of ever witnessing a sunrise as beautiful and miraculous such as she had just seen?

A sense of calm and peace descended on Devlin. In the distance she could hear bird-song. Her body relaxed as the tension that had been her companion for so long ebbed away and she stood looking out over the now tranquil grounds, the grass below her like a luxurious emerald carpet. The hibiscus and roses created a voluptuous profusion of colour as they drank in the sun's life-giving rays. As she stood quietly watching day's triumph over night Devlin knew that no matter what happened in the future, she would have her baby. No matter what Lydia, Colin, and the neighbours thought.

After a while Devlin got back into bed, leaving her blinds open and listened to the dawn chorus. Idly she picked up the health and beauty magazine she had taken from the TV room She flicked through the pages, reading whatever caught her interest until an item near the back of the periodical caught her eye. Sitting bolt upright, she read carefully and then neatly tore the section from the page.

Devlin smiled. Her mind was bright and clear, she felt strong and purposeful. Washing and dressing rapidly she packed away her overnight things. Already she could hear the noise of the tea trolleys as breakfasts were pushed along the corridors to the faceless ones behind closed doors. Quietly, she opened her door and walked towards the nurse's station. The nurse, relaxing after her night shift, looked up in surprise. Before she could speak, Devlin said with authority.

"I'm not having an abortion. Please give my apologies to the gynaecologist and Mrs Harrison

for any inconvenience I may have caused. The
bill for my stay has already been taken care of.
Good morning." She didn't wait for a response
but walked swiftly down the stairs and out the
front door into the sunlight.

Breathing deeply she stood on the steps for a
few moments before striding briskly down the
flower-edged drive, her long blonde hair lifting
behind her in the early morning breeze, Her
aches and pains were gone, her nausea had
disappeared, she was ravenously hungry and
ready for a hearty breakfast. Rashers, sausages,
eggs, pudding, fried bread. She could almost
taste it.

Without looking back she walked rapidly and
purposefully through the large gates hoping she
wouldn't have difficulty finding a taxi. Already
there was plenty of traffic on the road to the city
and it wasn't long until she was sitting in the
comfort of a roomy cab. "The London Tara
please," Devlin instructed crisply, giving the
driver the address of the Aer Lingus-owned hotel
where she always stayed when she was in
London. The Tara did the best breakfasts in
England and she would shortly be tucking into
one of them. Her stomach gurgled, reminding
her how hungry she was. Of course she was
eating for two now. Sitting back, she smiled and
stretched. Her decision was made; it was time to
think of the future and the first thing on her
agenda was breakfast.

Caroline's Story I

six

Caroline Stacey stepped gingerly on the weighing scales in the corner of her bedroom, took a deep breath and looked down. She did a double take. Nine stone five! She'd lost almost four pounds this week so far. She hugged herself with delight. Just wait until Martin O'Brien saw her in her jeans, the smart alec creep.

She hated Martin O'Brien with a deep and burning hatred. Were the gates of heaven to be closed in her face she could never forgive him for the pain, hurt and awful humiliation he had caused her.

Her face burned at the memory of the contemptuously cruel words he had spoken to his friend, almost a year ago, not knowing that Caroline could hear. "A big lump of lard," he had called her. And worse, he had stood her up on the night of her Debs Ball, leaving her sobbing in an enormous sack of a dress which the dressmaker, lying in her teeth, had told her "flattered her curves." Caroline, whose self esteem was almost non-existent, had pathetically believed her, trying not to see the ungainly bulky figure that filled the mirror. She had pretended she was losing weight; her waist had certainly gone in.

Nine o'clock arrived. Martin should have been there at eight and she knew in her heart that he was not going to come. She avoided the pitying yet ashamed looks her two brothers were giving her. Thank God her father was teaching a night class in the local comprehensive. At least she didn't have to listen to him. It had been bad enough having to get Declan, her brother, to ask one of his friends to go to her Debs with her.

"Aw feckin hell, Caroline! Do I have to? All me mates'll give me an awful slaggin," he had growled in irritation.

"Please Declan," she pleaded, in despair at the thought of being the only girl in her class not to have someone to go to her Debs with. Why couldn't she be like the other girls, so confident and self-assured, never tongue-tied with boys. Some of them had even slept with their boyfriends. Caroline had envied them so badly...she had never even been kissed. But the worst of the whole affair had been the week after the Debs she had not attended. She had been shopping in town, getting some of the weekly groceries. Hot, tired, she had lugged her parcels up the stairs of the bus, in the hopes of finding a seat on the upper deck. There was just one, near the front and she sank wearily into it, only to discover in horror that Martin O'Brien, stander up of fat debs, was in the seat in front. He was chatting to a friend and did not see her.

Even now, nearly a year later on, stones

lighter and no longer a schoolgirl but a third level student, Caroline felt a rush of blood to her cheeks as she remembered Martin's jeering comment to his friend who had accused him of chickening out of bringing her to the dance.

"Christ, would you be seen dead with that big lump of lard?"

Caroline would never ever forget the cringing sickening moment that she had heard herself being so cruelly described. Beetroot red, she had got off the bus a stop before the terminus, so she wouldn't have to face them, and taken the long way to her house. Heavy-hearted, lard-laden, she had trudged home, locked herself in the bedroom, stripped naked and looked at herself in the mirror.

Oh Divine Mother, what a sight she had been! Wads of fat bulging everywhere like great rolls of suet, white and yes, lardy looking. Pulling on her large passion-killer of a flannelette nightdress she had gotten into bed at five o' clock in the evening, much to the dismay of her father and two brothers who arrived home shortly after-wards for their evening meal.

Caroline smiled at the memory. Putting on her robe she slipped quietly out of the bedroom, noting with satisfaction that her friend Devlin was still asleep in the other bed. She would bring her up her breakfast in bed for a treat. If it wasn't for Devlin, she'd never have come this far.

Briskly, she placed strips of bacon, sausages, and tomatoes on the grill, enough for one. In times gone by, she too would have indulged in a large fry-up for breakfast. Now she settled for grapefruit and a slice of brown bread. Those cruel words and her friendship with Devlin had been a turning point of sorts, she mused, as she sat waiting for the breakfast to cook. Over the last year her life had certainly changed for the better. Her hands slid down over the outline of her figure. God, she had been so fat! Ever since her mother died four years before, she'd been fat.

Caroline's mother had died when she was fourteen and it was since then that she had slowly, steadily and unrelentingly eaten her way through her grief. The youngest child and only girl in the family, she was dominated by the three males in the house, her father Tony, a maths lecturer, and Declan and Damien, her two brothers. Until her mother died she had been happy enough. Shy and quiet, Caroline adored her vivacious good-natured mother who was always there for her, who always made a fuss of her little achievements and who made her feel important and cherished. When Caroline had got her first period, she had been so proud because her mother had said encouragingly, "Now you're a woman, honey, and we have even more in common." Caroline had felt ten foot tall. Her mother was treating her almost like an adult and they were starting to have such fun. The day she had gone to have her first bra fitted they had had such a laugh. Eva Stacey was a big woman and the fitting cubicle was a rather delicate hardboard affair. As Caroline struggled with unfamiliar hooks and straps, Eva had leaned against the cubicle, causing it to sway unsteadily. Horror-stricken, Eva and Caroline stared at each other before succumbing to a fit of the giggles that could be heard throughout the lingerie department. The saleswoman had not been amused. Eva loved town and shopping and each Saturday, mother and daughter would sally forth to hit the shops. On Sundays they'd go to the open-air markets.

Her mother was Caroline's best friend and when she died suddenly of a heart attack at the age of fifty-one, Caroline had been devastated. Her rock, her pillar of strength, was gone and she had never felt so alone in her life. Her father, grief-stricken, had just given up on life as his world collapsed around him. He was so caught up in his own grief that he hadn't seen what her mother's death had done to Caroline. He hadn't seen her increasing unhappiness, her total lack of self-confidence. All he knew was that he had a good daughter who took care of the house, fed himself and the boys and didn't go out dancing and boozing like some of the young rossies he taught. It never occurred to him that maybe his daughter might have liked to go out dancing now and again, that she might have liked some life of her own like her brothers. As long as his dinner was put in front of him and he could go for his pint at nine and then come back home and do his crossword, he was content.

Her brothers, unwittingly taking their cue from their father, treated Caroline as though she was a surrogate mother, expecting their meals when they were hungry and their clothes to be washed and ironed for them. They would give her the odd fiver and think they were great. It wasn't that they didn't love her; in their own way they were protective of her. It was simply that they just didn't think of her as a person. To them she was their sister Caroline who was shy and fat and could be a bit of an embarrassment when their mates were around. And so, quietly, uncomplainingly, Caroline took care of the three men in her family and kept their shabby but homely dormer bungalow in Marino as clean and tidy as possible, as well as attending school and trying to study for her exams.

To compensate for everything that was lacking in her life, Caroline ate. For the loss of her mother, for the demands made upon her, for her lack of self esteem, for the miserable time she had at school, for everything that was wrong with her life, the list was endless. The only joy in her life was food. She ate huge breakfasts, she made herself double-decker sandwiches for lunch, she would supplement this with crisps and chocolate during school breaks, and then when she got home she would have a big dinner. The more unhappy she became the more she ate and the stones piled on. Until Martin O'Brien's unforgettable insults she had been the fattest and unhappiest teenager in the world. Then

Devlin Delaney had come to her rescue and taken her in tow.

The smell of sizzling bacon brought Caroline out of her reverie and quickly and efficiently she dished up the grill, placed it on a tray already loaded with cereal and juice and set off for the bedroom. A sleepy tousled Devlin greeted her.

Caroline looked with supreme envy upon her friend, her blonde hair tumbling sensually around her tanned shoulders, small perfectly formed breasts holding up a pretty negligee. To be as slim and as self-assured as Devlin, who was after all two years younger than her, was her secret dream. It had never ceased to amaze her that Devlin, who was Declan's girlfriend, should have been the slightest bit interested in being friends with the fat dowdy person she had been. It was thanks to Devlin that she had got so far and lost so much weight.

Declan had met her at a rugby club dance. He came home raving about this beautiful blonde he had "got off with" and Caroline had listened to his delighted ravings with envy. Oh to be the object of someone's desire! This blonde bombshell obviously had everything that Caroline lacked: good looks, good figure, dazzling personality. She felt an uncharacteristic dislike for this unknown paragon. When Declan brought Devlin home Caroline's heart sank. She *was* beautiful! No doubt she was standoffish as well. After all wasn't her father a bank manager, and didn't they live in Foxrock?

Nothing could have been further from the truth. There wasn't an ounce of stand-offishness about Devlin. It was impossible for Caroline to be shy with the bubbling chatty younger girl.

Declan and Devlin had been going to a local dance themselves the night Caroline had overheard Martin's hurtful remarks. Devlin had been staying the night and had overheard Caroline sobbing into her pillow. Horrified at the other girl's misery, she had kindly but firmly got to the bottom of it and decided, as Caroline, pathetically red-eyed and embarrassed at her behaviour, tried to pretend that she didn't really care, that she was going to do something about Caroline Stacey and the way her family treated her.

The first thing she had done was to persuade Caroline to enrol in Unislim. "Let's do it, Caroline, I've heard some of the girls in my class talking about it, it's just what we need to keep us fit," she had said tactfully. It had been a turning point in Caroline's life. Never would she forget her first class when, dressed in a grey and pink tracksuit, selected by Devlin, and looking like a baby elephant, she had with the utmost reluctance climbed on the scales. Scarlet, she had heard Maureen, the attractive good-humoured woman who ran the class say kindly but firmly as the needle shot up to fourteen and a half stone: "Now Caroline, all this..." she took a wad of fat and gave it a little pinch, "is not good for you. You're an intelligent attractive girl with your whole life ahead of you. Starting now. Together we can do it."

Caroline was full of resolve as she accepted her "Quik-Loss" Diet Plan, her *Recipe for Successful Slimming* book and her attendance card which stated her disgusting present weight of fourteen and a half stones. Her target weight was eight and a half stone and Caroline decided grimly that if it was the only thing she ever did in her life she was going to reach it. After Maureen's humorous but commonsense talk— "bread is a time bomb, girls" and "let's put years of mindless eating behind us and re-educate ourselves," had come the exercise class that Caroline had been dreading. Puffing and panting and bending and twisting her ungainly body this way and that she was convinced that all eyes were upon her. Her heart sank lower and lower in mortification and she vowed she was not going to stay for the exercises any more. Lots of people just weighed in, left after the talk and did the exercises at home.

"You'll do no such thing, Caroline Stacey," exclaimed Devlin when Caroline informed her of her plan after their class.

"Believe me, Caro, no one is even thinking about you. Everybody is too concerned about doing the exercises themselves and anyway there are some girls there who are much heavier than you, so stop that nonsense!"

It was true of course, she saw herself, the next class she took. It had been marvellous—she had stuck firmly to her "Quik-Loss" plan for the week, as instructed, despite ravenous hunger pains, headaches and a constantly gurgling stomach. She went to bed early so she wouldn't be tempted in the kitchen and had the most satisfying dreams about cream cakes and chips and homemade scones dripping with butter, jam and cream. But she kept to her diet for the whole week and consequently floated along to her class a whole eight pounds lighter.

Maureen had been delighted for her. "An excellent start, Caroline; you're well on the way," she beamed at her as Caroline stood on the scales and proudly saw her weight-loss noted.

Devlin had come with her. "I might as well. I need the exercise," she said gaily when Caroline had asked diffidently whether she was going to go every week or not. She had been delighted at the younger girl's response; it was much easier to have company than to go alone. As she and Devlin sat waiting for the huge queue to be weighed in and listened to Maureen's witticisms, Caroline had viewed her fellow classmates— housewives, working girls, elderly women, teenagers, and yes, some of them heavier than her, she realised that Devlin had spoken the truth. Everyone was too concerned about their own weight loss or gain to be staring at her, but nevertheless there was a kind of comradeship about the class that warmed her and made her feel part of a group in a way she never had before. As the weeks flew by and she steadily lost weight by eating properly for the first time in years, she began to talk to people in the group, making conversation spontaneously and not sitting shyly until someone else spoke first. It had been great and she really came to enjoy her weekly class.

Devlin smiled with pleasure at the sight and smell of her breakfast. "You Pet! What a treat. Did you weigh yourself this morning?" her friend inquired sleepily, interrupting Caroline's musings.

"Four pounds gone!" Caroline said, doing a little twirl of delight. Usually she was quite restrained but she couldn't help looking in the mirror and seeing the new delightful curve of her waist, the firmness of a much-reduced bosom. Energetically she started her exercises, pushing herself to the limit. When she first started she had been breathless after two minutes. Now she could exercise for an hour and just be pleasantly puffed. Thoughts of the look on the Unmentionable One's face when she next met him, spurred her on, even though she hadn't seen him for ages.

For the next six months she slimmed and exercised, concealing her increasing slenderness under the old bulky clothes. Devlin and Declan stopped dating by mutual agreement, although they remained friends, but the younger girl kept in contact with Caroline, encouraging her on the path of self-improvement. In return Caroline coached Devlin, who was studying for her Leaving Certificate, in the intricacies of Sine,

Cosine and Tan, although it was a hard struggle, Devlin being deeply unimpressed by the delights of elementary trigonometry.

It was strange how they had become friends, so different in personality as they were and with such completely different lifestyles. Yet it seemed to Caroline that for all her out-going ways and many "friends," Devlin was a little lonely. She was an only child and at least Caroline had the boys. Although they weren't much use it was better than having no one in the house when she came home, as often happened with Devlin. Her mother and father always seemed to be out.

Caroline stayed over in Devlin's house occasionally and had met Mrs Delaney. Mrs Delaney was gracious, elegant and yet it struck Caroline that there wasn't an ounce of motherliness in her. Not like her own mother who had been so warm and loving and full of fun. What fun the teenage Caroline had enjoyed with her own mother on their weekly forays into town which usually ended with a trip to the pictures and then a meal in one of O'Connell Street's many restaurants, where they would have Caroline's then favourite meal, mixed grill and chips. Devlin and her mother never went anywhere together, a fact that amazed Caroline until she met Lydia Delaney. As the bond of friendship grew between the girls, Devlin confided in Caroline about Lydia's drinking and sometimes when things got really bad at home,

Devlin would stay over at Caroline's for a night or two until the worst was over.

Caroline loved the nights Devlin stayed. She would always make a special effort to have the house neat and tidy, shoving the boys' shirts into their wardrobes out of sight, hiding her father's multitude of textbooks under the sofa, hastily spraying air freshener around when she heard the door bell, to camouflage the heavy smell of her father's pipe smoke which seemed to invade every nook and cranny. Compared to her friend's luxurious abode, the Stacey house was functional and low key but Devlin never seemed to notice, and after a while it ceased to bother Caroline.

It was shortly after they became friends that Caroline began her Arts degree out in Belfield. Sitting on the number ten bus as it left O'Connell Street for the journey to the campus, she felt half-excited, half-afraid. Around her sat other young students chattering excitedly, looking forward to the new adventure ahead of them. Why couldn't she be like them, she thought in despair. Why was every new experience such a big trauma for her? Some of the girls on the bus had come from all over the country and were setting up home in strange flats and digs. How she envied their desire for freedom, their eager cutting of the ties that bound them to home. If she had to leave the security of her home and come up to a strange new city and find her way around she'd die of fright, she knew it.

The first few weeks on campus had been so

strange and unnerving. Compared to secondary school where every hour was mapped out, the loose unstructured style of University was a completely new experience. Along with hundreds of other young freshers Caroline wondered if she would ever find her way around the sprawling complex that made up University College Dublin, where she would remain in search of knowledge for the next three years. It was the proverbial melting pot, and from the big glass-walled restaurant Caroline viewed her peers each day with a faintly incredulous envy. Some of the way-out clothes worn so individualistically by many of the students amazed her. How wonderful it must be, she mused, as she saw one girl wearing purple ski pants and a vivid orange shirt, to have such confidence in yourself that you could carry off such an outrageous get-up. She would watch the eager clusters that gathered around the notice boards deciding which society to join. The Dramsoc and Literary and Historical societies were by far the most popular but she couldn't gather enough courage to join either of these.

The black tie debating contests fascinated her. Imagine to be able to stand up in front of a vast crowded theatre full of people and speak with fluent conviction on whatever topic was under debate! It was her dream, and often on the long traffic-jammed ride out to Belfield she would imagine herself in full flow making the winning speech, graciously accepting the loud applause of her audience. A few times she joined her classmates for a drink, after lectures, in the campus bar. The experience left her miserable as everyone else seemed to know someone. The music was loud and unintelligible, the smell of tobacco and pot permeated her hair and clothes and the battle to get to the bar through the jam of tightly packed bodies never seemed worth the effort. At the approach of closing time mention of parties in so and so's pad would filter down along the groups of laughing relaxed young people and a mass exodus would begin to the exciting, faintly seedy area of flatland in Rathmines. She had gone to a few, but the thought of getting drunk or stoned or laid terrified her and she was always on edge and never able to really enjoy herself and eventually she stopped going. And so she went to her lectures in the huge impersonal theatres and the social life and crack of the college passed her by. There were times when Devlin despaired of her.

"Honestly Caro! your life is one long drudge. Out to college in the morning, classes all day, home to cook for your dad and the boys, study all night. You're wasting your youth!" she would exclaim in exasperation. She would not let a little thing like studying for the Leaving Cert interrupt her own social life.

"You're different, Dev." Caroline would try and make excuses. "Anyway Dad would have a fit if I was out every night and besides, someone has to do the housework."

"Why does it have to be you?" Devlin had asked quietly. Caroline had no answer.

Near the end of her third and last year in college Caroline had let herself be persuaded to attend a class reunion. By now her figure had become so slim as to be almost boyish, her small heartshaped face dominated by wide dark-lashed brown eyes. Devlin dragged her to get her unruly black hair cut and styled and the hairdresser, one of the most expensive in Dublin, took a good long look at her and murmured something that sounded like "Audrey Hepburn eat your heart out," and then proceeded to scalp her.

Speechless, Caroline had eyed the complete stranger in the mirror. Was it really her? With the feather-cut hairstyle that now framed her face and made her eyes look enormous, she had a gamine yet sophisticated look and after the initial shock she was really more than pleased. Devlin had made the expedition a real day out for them. They had gone for lunch in the Westbury. It was the first time Caroline had been in the luxurious hotel and as discreet waiters took their orders Caroline sat back in her chair and sighed happily. "This is really living, Dev! Imagine being able to do this all the time? I'd love it."

"You should do it more often, Caro," her friend retorted, wishing that Caroline could develop more confidence in herself and, more important, a sense of her own worth as a person. It gave

Devlin great pleasure to watch her friend enjoy the delicious meal. Usually Caroline shopped in Henry Street on the other side of the city, never venturing south of the Liffey, but today Devlin was determined that her friend was going to splash out. That was why she had taken her to an expensive hair salon. Her hair had cost thirty pounds but it was worth every penny. Now she was going to take her to buy something expensively exclusive to wear at the reunion.

"What are you smiling at?" Caroline queried innocently.

"Oh nothing at all," murmured Devlin airily. "Come on, finish your coffee and we'll go and get your dress."

That night, dressed in a body-hugging soft black angora dress with a flamboyant royal blue cowl neckline to lesson the severity, Caroline stood in front of the mirror and gazed at herself in awe. Gone was the dumpy dowdy lump of lard of three years ago. In its place a small slender elegant sophisticate stared back at her from the mirror. Devlin was practically dancing around the room with delight.

"My God Caroline, you're stunning! You're so small-boned, look at your face. I'd love cheekbones like yours!" She scowled momentarily. "What a shame that Bollox O'Brien has emigrated."

"Devlin!" Caroline never failed to be shocked by her outspoken mentor.

"Tsk. Oh I know, Caro, but it describes the

cretin perfectly," Devlin said, unrepentant about her description of the boy who had stood Caroline up that fateful night so long ago. Arranging the cowl so that it fell perfectly around Caroline's shapely neck she said firmly, "My dear girl if I catch you in anything but tight-fitting clothes from now on, I'll murder you." She laughed. "In fact, Twiggs, I'm going to make sure you never get into those baggy jeans and sweatshirts again." Flinging open the wardrobe door, she dragged out an armful of the offending articles.

"Oh wait Dev! I mean you can't! I've nothing else to wear."

Devlin nodded crossly. "Well, it's about time you got some new clothes. My God, you slave around here for nothing!"

Caroline had to agree, although she hated when Devlin made comments about the way her family treated her. She knew that in his own way her father loved and depended on her: he just didn't think about buying new clothes. Since his wife died he just had no interest in anything and the boys were too busy with their own lives to worry about her. Besides, the thoughts of giving away her trusty baggy old jeans and sweatshirts caused a vague feeling of panic to flutter in her stomach. They concealed her new slenderness and she could hide in them. There was no way she was ready to flaunt her new body. Her figure might have changed considerably but her self-confidence was as non-existent as ever.

"Listen, Dev, I've only two months to go before

I get the degree. When I get a job I'll buy a whole new wardrobe. OK?"

Reluctantly Devlin surrendered her spoils. "And I'm coming with you," she warned as they made their way downstairs to say goodnight. Caroline's father just lifted his head over the top of his paper and his eyes widened slightly.

"Very nice. Don't be too late." he said mildly.

"I won't," she assured him. She really didn't want to go to this reunion: she had never been popular at school, being far too shy and introverted for anyone to have taken notice of her, and because of her weight she had never played games or gone to any of the school dances. The nuns had been kind to her after her mother died, often asking how she was coping and how was her father. Apart from that, school had been a nightmare and even now she could still cringe at some of the memories of her schooldays.

Valentine's day had been the worst. The trauma of going into class and being asked maliciously by one horrible girl how many Valentine cards she had got, had been soul destroying. One year in desperation she had sent herself one but even then at the last minute her nerve failed her and she left it lying in her school bag as she underwent her annual interrogation. So why was she going to this reunion? Why had she let Devlin persuade her to go?

"Listen to me," her friend had said. "You look like a million dollars. Take a deep breath and walk into that room. Tell them you are studying nuclear physics or something. Make them take notice of you. It's easy!" Devlin, of course, would take something like a reunion in her stride.

As she slowly approached the Gresham Hotel, where they were holding the function, Caroline could feel all her poise evaporating. Butterflies as large as elephants did tangos up and down her insides. It would be just like her to faint and cause a scene, she thought in self-disgust, as she stopped to view herself in a plate glass window. "You look fine," she reassured herself. Catching sight of a tough-looking young fellow staring at her, she clutched her bag against her and walked briskly along O'Connell Street. The sun was beginning to set, its dusky pink hues giving a softer edge to the harsh neon-lit facades of the capital's premier street. Queues were beginning to form outside the Savoy and, feeling lonely, Caroline watched the couples holding hands as they laughed and talked and were entertained by a wild-haired busker playing a jaunty tune. She walked on and taking a deep breath mounted the steps and found herself in the elegant foyer of the Gresham Hotel. The subdued air of genteel graciousness calmed her as she watched white-jacketed waiters pouring coffee from silver pots into delicate china cups for daintily sipping ladies. Catching sight of herself in a sparkling mirror she saw that in spite of her interior chaos, her exterior appeared calm and controlled. Lifting her chin and forcing one foot to follow the other Caroline walked into the room where the event was taking place.

The hum of rampant gossip assaulted her ears as thirty five young women who hadn't seen each other for three years caught up with each other's lives.

"And you know something else? She was three months gone when she got married...!"

"You're not serious, Valerie! And she was such a Holy Mary!"

Well, Val hadn't changed, Caroline thought. Still dishing the dirt. Swallowing hard she took a glass of wine from a bored-looking waiter and edged her way to the far side of the room. Nobody had recognised her yet and she was content just to listen.

"Isn't Pamela a walking bitch? Imagine doing a thing like that on her best friend. I couldn't believe it."

Caroline was agog! What had Pamela done on Thérèse? It was obvious they weren't talking. Thérèse was on the other side of the room with her back pointedly turned on her former best friend. Caroline moved towards the window, passing another little knot of chattering young women.

"Would you look at Deirdre? Did you ever see anything like the hair? You can see the black roots from here. It's dreadfully tarty! And did you hear about Nuala? She's over there by the door. She's living with Aileen. They're gay! Imagine!"

There was a ripple of excitement at this piece of information.

"You mean that utter snob Aileen Corey? Crikey, I wonder what they make of that in her 'cultural backwater'?" A gale of laughter followed that biting remark. Caroline tried to suppress a grin. She remembered Aileen Corey very well. A most pretentious girl who, when asked where she lived, answered coolly. "Dunboyne, a cultural backwater." There was much sniggering in the class at this remark which was quite unoriginal, having been lifted from an interview with an Irish writer. It was typical of Aileen, always out to try and impress. So Nuala and Aileen were living together. Well, it wasn't really anybody's business. Their personal lives were their own affair. The idea of their gayness did not offend Caroline as it did some of the others. For all Caroline's introverted shyness, there was a maturity and tolerance about her that made her a most non-judgemental person.

"I hear Moira and Michelle have emigrated. Honest to God, if I have to go to one more farewell party I'll cry," she heard a soft voice say. Caroline smiled. The soft voice belonged to Anne Morrell, one of the few girls in the class who had ever passed the time of day with her, but she was too shy to go over to her and it was obvious no one recognised her. So Moira and Michelle had emigrated. It wasn't surprising. With mass-unemployment it was the only option many young people had, and most families had been touched by the spectre of emigration. Even Declan, her own brother, had been one of the thousands who had applied for one of the precious American visas allocated to Ireland. What she would do if she didn't get a job herself Caroline did not dare think about. She'd have to go on the dole.

A voice to her right caught her attention and she felt the old familiar dread as she recognised the harsh nasal tones of Ruth Saunders. Ruth had been the notice-box of the class, always hogging the limelight with her sharp sarcastic wit that had often flicked Caroline on the raw. Ruth had been her malicious tormentor every Valentine's day. She had taken a sarcastic delight in embarrassing her and for a moment Caroline almost felt as if she was back in the big airy classroom on the green corridor in Eccles Street.

"I don't see any sign of Nellie the Elephant, do you?" she was saying derisively. "She's probably entered the convent."

Anger surged through Caroline. The miserable bitch, standing there so arrogant, smirking and flaunting her pregnant belly as if to say "Well I've got a man—so there!" How dare she assume that Caroline was only capable of retiring to the religious life and anyway, what was wrong with the religious life? Some of the nuns who taught her had been the most fulfilled and happy women she had met. Many of them had been far better educated and seen far more of life and the world than she or Ruth Saunders ever would.

Taking a deep calming breath Caroline turned to face her old tormentor.

"I think it's a case of the kettle calling the pot black," she drawled coolly. "How are you Ruth?"

The horrified amazement, the ugly flush of embarrassment that mottled the other girl's puffy face were a sweet revenge for Caroline.

"Are you...I...I mean you can't be Caroline Stacey," she stuttered.

"I assure you I am," Caroline responded lightly. Gosh, this wasn't so bad after all, she thought, as her quaking subsided.

Deriving an immense amount of pleasure from the other girl's mortification she decided to press home her psychological triumph. After her years of misery it felt so good to be the cause of her adversary's discomfort. She observed casually, "I see you're married, Ruth. When is the happy event?"

Ruth's little pig eyes glowed in delighted superiority over her spinster sister. She gave a shrill little giggle. "Oh, Peter swept me off my feet. You remember Peter?"

Caroline nodded drily. Peter was as quiet as Ruth was sharp and bossy and there was no doubt who wore the pants in that marriage.

"The baby's due in two months' time. Are you dating yourself?

Their eyes met through the curtain of their mutual antagonism.

"Oh yes," Caroline responded airily. "My boyfriend Mark is in Saudi at the moment. He's a nuclear physicist. I may go out myself later in the year to join him. Who knows?" She gave Ruth a cold smile. "I do want to pursue my own career. I think it's very important for a woman to excel in her own field, don't you?"

"Oh very," echoed Ruth, completely deflated.

Caroline drained her glass and placed it on a convenient table. Every hunger pang she had suffered during her diet had been worth it for this glorious moment of pleasure. She could now leave her class reunion with her head held high.

"I really must be off, I'm meeting someone later, it was nice renewing old acquaintances." Giving a casual wave she sauntered through the crowd, aware that the noise level had dropped as the others had eavesdropped avidly on their conversation. She would be the topic of conversation when she left but she didn't care. Let them talk! She felt compensated for all her years of fat misery. Ruth had envied her...it was there in her eyes and that had been the sweetest thing of all.

With her head held high she walked through the door of the function room, across the foyer and out on to O'Connell Street and the blessedly cool night air.

There was always an air of electricity about Dublin's main street at night. Couples, happy in each other's company, strolled hand in hand or gazed through jeweller's windows at sparkling engagement rings. Caroline passed under Clery's clock, a traditional meeting place for lovers, and observed several people waiting for their dates. Some were discreetly looking at their watches, little anxious frowns beginning to mar their made-up features. Others stared fixedly ahead at the GPO as if it were the most fascinating piece of architecture they had ever set eyes on. Two young itinerants taunted a girl who had obviously been waiting a while. "Hey Missus, has yer fella stood ya up? Hard cheese!" The girl blushed bright pink and Caroline felt for her. She knew only too well the pain of being stood up. One young man tried vainly to conceal the large bunch of flowers he carried. He looked utterly uncomfortable. Typical Irishman, thought Caroline glumly, never having been the recipient of a bunch of flowers from a man, typically Irish or not. Her high had begun to dissipate as she was once again confronted by her manless state.

What was this mysterious quality other girls had that could attract men? Even piggy-eyed sharp-tongued Ruth had secured one of these illustrious creatures and flaunted a wide gold wedding band on her left hand. Caroline's thumb rubbed the soft skin of her naked ringless finger. Sometimes she wore her mother's wedding ring for a while to pretend she was a married woman, holding her fingers up to the light to watch the band of glittering gold. To be left on the shelf was the biggest dread of her life. There was still such a stigma attached to being unmarried. And what horrible terms people used. "Old maid" and "spinster" sounded so barren and shameful. Her aunt and Mrs Canning, her next door neighbour, were always on at her. "And when are you going to give us a day out?" Or worse: "Are you courtin yet?" She was seriously contemplating going to a fortune teller. Devlin had been to one and had been informed that she would marry a wealthy man and bear him three children. Only the fear of being told she might never marry kept Caroline from going. Imagine! To be told you would never marry. She'd drown herself.

She shivered as she left the shelter of O'Connell Street to catch her bus on the quays and a breeze as sharp as Ruth's tongue blew around her ankles. Sighing, she paused for a moment to look down the winding moonlit river. Across Butt Bridge a Dart train was snaking lazily towards Amiens Street, its illuminated carriages glittering in the distance. Down the river a ship's horn moaned a long low wailing sound and it brought a stab of loneliness to Caroline's heart. There was something so melancholy about that sound. Starting to walk on, she passed several young itinerants listless and glassy-eyed from glue sniffing.

"Got any coppers Missus?" A child who couldn't have been more than nine or ten stretched out a beseeching hand. She was thin, ragged and obviously malnourished. Her eyes had a defeated acceptance of her plight that shamed Caroline out of her self-indulgent despondency. At least she had a decent home to go to, which was more than many unfortunate people had. Giving the child fifty pence which she knew would probably be taken by her parents for drink, she carried on walking towards her bus stop. Just ahead of her an old wino lay curled up in a doorway, his weatherbeaten crumpled old face set in lines of desolate despair. Their eyes met and each recognised the loneliness of the other.

Swiftly she passed him but had only taken a few steps when her fingers curled around the fiver in her jacket pocket. Not stopping to think she turned back, walked the few paces to where he was sitting, bent down and pressed the money into his filthy hand.

"It's all I have, but it will buy you a meal," she whispered half afraid that he was really scuttered. Caroline had never in her life spoken to someone like him before. Tired old eyes that had their own dignity looked at her and the old man said, slurring his words only slightly.

"You're a good lassie and thank ye kindly. May ye always have a roof over yer head and someone to keep ye warm."

"Thank you. Goodbye," Caroline murmured inadequately as she straightened up and moved away.

"A kind hearted lassie," she heard him mutter as he stood up and staggered off in the direction she had come from. Maybe he would buy more drink, she thought, sadly watching the sad pathetic figure, his old coat flapping around his ankles as he disappeared off into O'Connell

Street. It must be awful to be homeless, she reflected, trying to imagine what circumstances had forced the wheezing elderly man on to the streets. Well she had given him and the begging child her last penny and now she had to walk home. As she walked along the shadowed streets, keeping a wary eye open for drunks and potential muggers, she decided unhappily that Dublin, despite its charm, could be a mean and savage city. A decade ago a murder or rape could be talked about for days. Now such events were commonplace, rating only a column or two in the papers, and muggings and handbag snatches were two a penny. It was with a sigh of great relief that she reached the familiar security of her own front door in Marino an hour later.

Caroline often wondered what had happened to the old wino as she walked to her bus stop every day after work. While waiting for answers to all her applications she had secured a temporary job in one of the big burger restaurants on O'Connell Street. Each day, dressed in her brown striped uniform and peaked hat, she dispensed tons of fast food to the rushed and hungry citizenry of the Capital. At first she had been utterly self-conscious in her striped uniform and cap but it gradually dawned on her that people didn't even see her as they waited for their burgers and chips, being absorbed in their own thoughts and worries. Often she wondered why she had spent three years killing herself studying but any job was better than no job and at least she wasn't one of thousands on the dole. She was going to apply for some Fás training courses if she didn't get a job soon, she decided. She had her name on file in all the employment agencies; somebody somewhere must have a job for an honours student who could speak two continental languages.

Her graduation day had been a day of pride for Caroline. For once in her life she felt she had achieved something and as she stood in her cap and gown to receive her parchment she caught sight of her father and Devlin smiling broadly at her. She had even gone to the booze-up after with Devlin in tow and had enjoyed it until one of her class mates had made a drunken pass at her. When she recoiled in disgust he had announced loudly that she was a real "frigid Bridget."

"Take no notice of that pissed bastard," Devlin had instructed firmly. "If he was sober you wouldn't hear a squeak from him, the creepy little weed." Nevertheless it made her even more wary of men.

seven

Caroline first encountered Richard Yates through a complete twist of fate—or so she thought afterwards. She had managed to secure a temporary position in a large firm of auctioneers to replace a girl on maternity leave. She worked in a section that dealt almost exclusively with apartment sales but because she was the most junior person in the office she was never actively involved in the selling of them. One weekend she got a call from her supervisor to say that Linda, one of the reps, was out sick and there was no one around to replace her. Caroline would have to take over for the day. They were selling an exclusive complex of apartments on the north side of the city and she would have to give details to prospective buyers. She would earn commission on any apartments she sold.

Caroline was excited and a little daunted by the prospect. Linda was much more self-confident and sophisticated than she was but she didn't want to be stuck in the office forever and this might be her chance to be taken on permanently. If she was lucky she might become part of the team that sold apartments in Spain and the Canaries who often had to fly out with clients. This was her chance.

She dressed carefully in a smart pinstriped navy suit with a crisp white high-necked blouse, informed her father and brothers that they would have to cook their own dinners and set out jauntily. Twenty minutes later, irritated beyond belief by the non-appearance of two scheduled buses, she retraced her steps home and asked her brother for a lift to the office. Caroline had often asked him to teach her to drive but he wouldn't hear of it. Some day, she told herself, she was going to get private lessons and just drive up to the front door and savour the expression of amazement on their faces.

Fortunately Declan was in a good humour so she didn't have too much of a job persuading him to give her a lift. When she finally got to the show flat, having collected all the necessary literature from the office, there were several people waiting and she didn't have time to be nervous. Some of them were young married couples, others elderly people contemplating their retirement and some young professional singles investing in their first home. To all she gave the information required and found herself enjoying the afternoon.

"You're the only one so far, dear, who didn't try to avoid the negative side of apartment living," one elderly but obviously well off couple told her.

"If there's one thing that puts me right off, it's

people who ram the idea of buying down your neck," the wife confided as her husband did some mental arithmetic. "I think we'll be buying. Aren't they gorgeous?"

Caroline was delighted with herself. There was no way she could compete with her colleague Linda for drive and sophistication but so far she had seen twenty people and five were seriously interested. By four thirty she was exhausted but happy. Everyone was gone and she didn't expect anyone else to call but the show apartment was open until five so she decided to make herself a cup of tea.

Caroline had just sat down when a tall tawny-haired man in his early thirties walked in. Dressed in a well-cut grey business suit, he looked rather suave and Caroline decided he was a doctor or accountant. He smiled pleasantly, showing even white teeth and said in a deep cultured voice. "I'd like to look around if I may?"

"Of course," Caroline replied politely, beginning to clear away her tea things.

He noticed and said easily, "Please finish your tea. I'm sure you've had a busy afternoon. Have you sold many?"

Caroline smiled, a glow of triumph lightening up her brown eyes. "Well I've three definites and two mights."

The man nodded agreeably. "I think apartment living is here to stay. In Europe and the States they are the predominant means of housing." He smiled again and said crisply, "Apart from that it never hurts to have a prestigious address. Don't you think?"

"Oh never," she agreed, thinking he was a real dish as she watched him inspecting the apartment and as he did so, throwing questions at her. He must be pretty loaded if he's thinking of buying one of these. Even the one-bedroomed ones were pricy enough, she mused, as she observed him discreetly.

"So there's a jacuzzi, swimming pool and floodlit tennis courts as well as a launderette and lifts to all floors," he read from the brochure. "It sounds very promising. Ideal for entertaining business clients, wouldn't you think?"

"Oh indeed," Caroline agreed enthusiastically, wishing she could afford the luxury of buying one. She had been thinking of moving out from home but could never quite bring herself to make the break.

The man moved out to the flower-bedecked balcony to survey the view of Dublin Bay. Turning to Caroline he said reflectively, "I can't pretend I wouldn't prefer if these were on the southside," he said. A flash of irritation ignited in Caroline. Honestly the ridiculous snobbery some people had about preferring to live south of the Liffey galled her, it was so silly.

"You'd pay a lot more if they were," she responded a little tartly and added, "On the Northside you have the advantage of being nearer the airport and the car ferry terminals and just up the road you have direct access to the East Link

Toll Bridge which will link you with the city centre and the southside within minutes. Or alternatively you could take the Dart." Thank God for the new rapid rail transit system. She was sure it had swayed some of her buyers to buy in the suburbs.

"Mmmm, I hadn't thought of that at all." He smiled a charming smile. "May I have your name; you've been most helpful. I must say I've seen other properties but this one does suit my needs."

Caroline smiled back shyly. "I'm Caroline Stacey and of course I do hope you end up buying here. They are beautiful apartments but they're being snapped up like hot cakes so you wouldn't want to leave it too long to make your decision."

"Of course," he agreed suavely. "I'll make a provisional booking if I may. I particularly like the penthouse in the middle block."

Wow! The penthouse! Caroline thought in surprise as she pencilled in his name on the master plan and stuck a red strip across it. Richard Yates. That sounds nice, I wonder what he does? As if reading her thoughts, the man handed her a business card: "In case you need to get in touch," he said casually.

Richard B. Yates & Co Solicitors, it read, with a business address in Leeson Street. So her guess had been wrong. No wonder he knew all about first time grants and tax relief on mortgages. She had read somewhere in a newspaper report on the highest earners in the country that many solicitors earned more than surgeons, accountants or government ministers and obviously here was the proof. For someone so young—she judged him to be in his early thirties—he must have a very successful practice. Everything about him pointed to success and wealth: his superbly cut suit, expensive leather shoes, gold watch and tie pin. He wasn't wearing a wedding ring but then lots of men didn't. Though surely if he was married his wife would have come along with him. No doubt he had a glamorous girlfriend on the scene. He stood back to allow her into the foyer before him and his manners impressed her. Thanking her once more, he strode to the lift and she was alone. Caroline did not expect to see him again but she knew it would be a great feather in her cap if she sold one of the penthouses.

He did in fact buy the penthouse and her three "committeds" and one of her "mights" also purchased, a fact that did not go unnoticed by her superiors. From then on she frequently had to act as a rep and her confidence and self-esteem increased with every sale she made, especially as she became permanent on the staff after three months.

Devlin was now also working and had decided to move into a flat. She urged Caroline to come with her, telling her it was about time she started to stand on her own two feet. Devlin always made it sound so easy. But Caroline's heart would flutter in panic at the thoughts of leaving home. Not that she was particularly happy there. Her father and brothers, all with their own lives, were content to leave her to cook and clean even though she too was working. Yet there was security of a sort and any change in her lifestyle always seemed vaguely threatening to her, not like the big adventure it was to Devlin.

"Come on Caro, it will be great fun," her friend enthused and so she had been persuaded. Their first flat had been an out-and-out disaster and they had only stayed in it a month but the flat in Sandymount suited them perfectly and life with Devlin was fun. She was such a free spirit, doing things on the spur of the moment, like hopping on the Dart and going out to the fun fair at Bray just because she felt like having some candy-floss. Caroline went to discos and night-clubs with her, although on the night she found herself dancing with a guy who insisted on holding on to his pint through out the dance and who told her he was "on his second time round," Caroline wondered why she bothered. She went on several dates but because of her shyness found it some-what of a strain to keep the conversation going and then at the end of the evening, an even bigger strain to avoid the roving hand syndrome. Was it just her, she wondered, or did other girls ever feel as she did? Still she was able to say with some pride to her aunt and neighbour and to the girls in the office that she was dating. It made her feel one of them.

At first the girls in the office had taken her

reserved shyness for aloofness and when she began to do well in sales there had been some jealousy, but gradually she settled down in her job and they got used to her. Most of them were married and their talk centred around their homes, their husbands and in some cases their pregnancies. Caroline envied them enormously as she heard how "Hugh always brings me a cup of tea in the morning" or that "Donald was so supportive during the birth" or that "Paul and Dermot booked a surprise dinner for us at the Shelbourne. Aren't they pets?" Why couldn't she meet a Donald or Hugh or Paul or Dermot? She would observe these loving husbands and boyfriends collecting her self-assured colleagues after work and feel like an outsider on the edge of a privileged circle. More and more she longed for someone to fall in love and marry her, to remove from her forever the stigma of spinsterhood. Seeing Devlin with men lining up to ask her out Caroline could not understand how her friend had not the slightest interest in marriage, while she, who was quite manless, longed with all her heart for the day when she would walk up the aisle and say to the world: "I am loved...I am no longer alone!" It seemed to Caroline that people expected her to marry. Her father and brothers constantly dropped hints about her "getting over the hill" and her aunt was in an agony of dismay over the fact that she was not yet sporting a diamond. Years later she would look back at her own insecurity and realise that she had been her own worst enemy.

One evening Devlin persuaded her to go to an Opening Night at the Gaiety. Dressed stylishly in well-cut black trousers and a scarlet silk blouse that emphasised the slenderness of her figure, she was quite unaware that she was the object of scrutiny of a tawny-haired man. Nursing her drink at the interval, she waited for Devlin who had gone to the loo. Quietly Caroline observed the first-nighters, recognising many prominent faces as they crowded around the bar gossiping and airing their views. Dublin was such a sociable city, she mused. There was always something on or something to do! Who would have thought that she, "Nellie the Elephant" of yore, would actually be sitting only feet away from a government minister and a TV personality, not to talk about a famous playwright, and a well known gossip columnist, who were all animatedly chatting and laughing and mingling self-confidently. A little glow spread through her as she caught sight of her reflection in a gilt edged mirror. Thin! She was thin and able to fit into size ten trousers with no trouble. It was the biggest triumph of her life and she thanked God for sending Devlin, her friend and mentor, to her. It was she who had got tickets for the show. Her parents were supposed to have gone but Lydia was unwell so her father had given her the tickets. "Drinking again!" Devlin had confided with a deep sigh.

"How nice to see you again!" A deep voice

spoke from above the region of her left ear, interrupting her reverie. Startled, Caroline looked up to find Richard Yates, hand extended, smiling down at her.

"Oh hello," she murmured politely, thinking how dishy he looked in his smart navy suit. His hand clasp was firm and the unusual green eyes that surveyed her were warm and friendly.

"Are you enjoying the revue? Bitingly topical wouldn't you say?"

Caroline laughed. "I'm glad I'm not a politician, the sketches are so pointed, but it's going down well isn't it?"

"It certainly is," he agreed, smiling down into her brown eyes so big and expressive under her feather-cut hairstyle.

"Have you settled in to the penthouse?" she inquired lightly. Richard laughed.

"I have. I must say you were right; it didn't take long for you to sell all the apartments there. I think most of them are occupied."

Caroline nodded. "That's right, they were practically sold out after only two weeks on the market. Developments as exclusive as that will always sell fast because they are aimed at people with plenty of money."

She couldn't believe herself, carrying on a conversation with this charming handsome man. They chatted casually for several more minutes. He offered to buy her another drink but she refused the offer and he did not press it. Caroline noticed a tall distinguished man observing them from the bar but she paid no heed until two stunning looking girls came from the ladies and made a bee-line for Richard and he detached himself from the crowded bar and strode over to where she and Richard were standing.

"Richard, I think it's time we took our seats. The girls are here and I'm sure the curtain will be going up shortly." His tone was low, aristocratic, his eyes cold as they stared at Caroline.

"Fine," said the younger man coolly and turning to Caroline he said pleasantly, "Won't you excuse me. It's been nice talking to you again." She watched the four of them stroll through the foyer, radiating an air of wealth and sophistication that made people turn and give them a second glance.

"My God, that place was jam-packed!" Devlin arrived back breathless and gulped down a large mouthful of her Black Velvet.

"Oooh that's nice!" She was currently into Black Velvets, a mixture of rich creamy Guinness and champagne. Caroline sipped some of her less exotic Bacardi and coke.

"Who was that dish you were chatting up?"

Caroline blushed. "I wasn't chatting him up Dev!" she expostulated.

"Ah go on!" Devlin grinned.

"I wasn't. He's the guy who bought the penthouse. His name is Richard Yates."

"I heard that name before." Devlin said reflectively, a small frown creasing her brow. "Oh yeah, he's a big noise lawyer isn't he?" And he's into politics. I heard Dad talking about him. Did you see who he was with? Mandy Mitchell and DeeDee O'Neill. They're the highest paid models around. I wish I had their figures."

One thing about Devlin was that she wasn't the slightest bit vain, Caroline thought in amusement, as she surveyed her friend's curves which were every bit as good as the two models'. They joined the other patrons en route to their seats and although Caroline enjoyed the rest of the evening she was very conscious of Richard and his party several rows in front of her.

A week later when she was sitting disconsolately in the office watching the rain dripping relentlessly from the branches of a large oak tree, her phone rang.

"Hello, Caroline Stacey speaking. May I help you?" she said with automatic politeness in her best office telephone manner.

"Hello Caroline." A vaguely familiar voice sounded in her ear. Deep, cultured. Where had she heard it before? "It's Richard Yates here, you've probably forgotten all about me."

Her eyes widened in surprise. "Oh! Oh...not at all. How are you?" she managed to respond.

"Oh, I'm fine. And you?"

"Oh, I'm fine too," she echoed inanely, wondering what on earth he was ringing her for.

"The thing is," he said crisply, "I happen to have two tickets for the National Concert Hall. Bernadette Greevy is giving a recital. I was wondering if you would be interested in coming with me?" He paused discreetly before adding. "Of course if you have a boyfriend who would object I quite understand."

Caroline swallowed hard. Twice. "Yes...No, I mean I would like to go," she stammered. "There is no one on the scene at the moment to object." Managing to compose her voice she noticed that her palms were wet with perspiration and she was sure she had an attack of the blotches. Just as well he couldn't see her! She thought she detected a note of relief in his voice as he said firmly:

"I'll certainly be looking forward to that. Shall I pick you up on Saturday evening then?"

"Fine," Caroline agreed giving him the address. She'd have to make sure the flat was tidy, she thought as she gently replaced the receiver in its cradle, annoyed to find that her hands were shaking. How she longed for poise. Still, who could believe that Richard Yates had actually phoned her? Pity the reunion was over. A high-flying handsome solicitor was even more acceptable than a nuclear physicist!

Devlin and Maggie, the girl who lived in the flat upstairs from them, were delighted with her news. Maggie, a nurse, was already living in the Sandymount house when the girls moved in and from the start she had made them welcome and been a good neighbour to them. Although she was several years older than Caroline and Devlin she was lively and vivacious and before

long they started socialising together. Maggie, a
tall athletic sexy redhead was the most natural
down to earth person Caroline had ever met and
yet there was a motherly quality about the older
girl that drew Caroline to her. One Sunday
evening, when Devlin was away for a weekend,
Caroline had arrived back to the flat feeling
lonely and upset. She had attended the annual
blessing of the graves where her mother was
buried and all the old sadness had come back to
her as she stood at the graveside with her father
and brothers. Maggie had met her on the stairs
and seeing the distress on the younger girl's face
had asked her if everything was all right.
Caroline, never good at hiding her emotions,
assured her that everything was fine but
Maggie, instinctively guessing that something
had upset her, insisted that she come up to her
flat for a cup of tea, whereupon Caroline had
burst into tears and ended up confiding her woes
to Maggie. The older girl had been most sympathetic and supportive and over the following
months their friendship had developed. As well
as Devlin, Caroline now had Maggie as a friend.

"What will I wear?" she asked the two other
girls when she got home from work that evening.

"If I were you," said Maggie reflectively, "I'd
wear a little black number with just a touch of
gold at the throat. Elegant but subtle."

"I don't have a touch of gold, Maggie!" wailed
Caroline.

"Don't panic!" her friend soothed. "You can

have something of mine. Now what do you think
of this for a honeymoon negligee?" Holding up a
black silky wisp of nightgown, she laughed at the
expression on the faces of her two friends.

"Do you think this will get Terry going?"
Seeing Caroline blushing she reproved her lightly. "Now Caro, stop blushing. It won't be long
until this Richard guy will be pressing his attention on you, so you'd better be prepared. Men are
all the same, girl, and always will be."

Caroline couldn't help but envy Maggie, who
had no sexual hangups whatsoever and had been
sleeping with her fiancé for over a year. Sometimes she shocked Caroline with her frankness.
Maggie was the kind of person who didn't give a
hoot about what other people thought of her.
Either you liked her as she was or you didn't like
her. Most people couldn't help liking her and
men flocked to her like moths to the flame,
attracted by her generous open personality.

Maggie did a little twirl with her black wisp
and grinned at her friends. "Must be off, I'm
meeting Ma-in-law for dinner. Yuck! Yuck! She
calls me 'Margaret' for crying out loud! I think I'll
put on me real Howya Dublin accent." A sharp
ring on the doorbell caused her face to fall.
"Jeepers, is it that time already! Terry'll kill me.
Devlin, go and use your charm on him until I'm
dressed. Caro, anything you need for your date,
feel free to borrow. I'll see you both later." Striding out of the room, her thick auburn hair flowing gloriously behind her, Maggie looked like an

advert for a health magazine. There was a sensuality and earthiness about her that was completely unfeigned, something Caroline wished she had a little of. All she wanted out of life was one man to appreciate her charms. Maybe Richard was the answer to her prayers. Knowing that Saint Jude was the patron saint of hopeless cases she decided she would do a novena to him.

The next day during lunch hour she slipped into the Pro-Cathedral and earnestly begged the saint's help in securing a husband. Preferably someone as handsome as Richard. She had done the novena for a week and somehow in the massive vaulted cathedral, always crowded with lunchtime prayers like herself, old Dublin women murmuring their rosaries, their beads slipping silently through careworn fingers, old winos snoring quietly and men and women just sitting lost in thought, Caroline felt her prayer would be heard. When Richard Yates rang her again to confirm their date, she felt it was an omen, a sign from God!

By the night of her Big Date she was a nervous wreck. Knowing that Devlin's mother sometimes took valium, Caroline begged Devlin to sneak her one. "Just this once, Dev, please. I don't want to be a babbling idiot for the evening and he's so self-assured."

Devlin hadn't been at all happy about the idea but she had given her friend the valium, knowing how much this date meant to her. If only she could make Caroline realise how attractive she was now, compared to that awful dumpy silent person she had been. Caroline still went to her Unislim classes, even though she had long ago reached her target weight and was now so slim and so small-boned as to appear almost fragile. She ate very sensibly, loads of salads and fruit, and having received her target weight certificate and been loudly cheered by the other slimmers, she remained even more determined to keep her figure. Now she had an added reason to remain slender. Richard!

When she was giving Caroline the valium, Devlin insisted, "They're only crutches Caro, you don't need them." But Caroline wanted so badly to make an impression on this date, she needed to be relaxed. She promised Devlin she would never ask her for one again.

The three of them had gone in to town on the Saturday morning to buy The Dress. It had been a gloriously sunny day and Grafton Street was buzzing and vibrant. They had a giggly fun-filled few hours trying on and discarding dozens of outfits before deciding on a black jersey silk with ruched waist and a deep plunging V-back. It was demure in the front and highly sensual at the back and Caroline loved it. Sheer black tights, some sexy underwear, high heeled patent shoes and an elegant clutch bag completed the spending spree and then it was time to get her hair done before rushing home to get dressed up.

When Caroline was dressed, Maggie arrived with a gold chain and matching earrings and the total effect was one of subtle elegance.

"Much better than those two tarty models," commented Devlin approvingly, as she brushed on some toning gold eyeshadow over the darker brown undercoat. When she mascaraed them her friend's eyes looked deep and enormously mysterious, almost Eastern. She laughed: "It's a pity I'm not a man, I could almost ravish you myself," she remarked, surveying her handiwork.

"I wonder will he kiss me? I wonder will my lipstick come off on his face?" Caroline murmured agitatedly.

Now that she was actually ready, she almost wished that she wasn't going. Honestly she couldn't understand herself. For years she had been praying for something like this to happen and look at her, a bag of nerves.

"For heaven's sake, Caro, take the valium and relax, just let things happen as they happen," Devlin advised her. Sometimes she found it hard to believe that Caroline was two years older than her with a college degree to boot.

Half an hour later the door bell shrilled. By this time the valium had taken effect and Caroline noticed that her anxiety had been noticeably blunted. Now she felt quite tranquil. Really! she thought, these things are pretty good! She felt a little tingle of anticipation as she opened the door to find Richard, looking very suave holding a rose and a box of chocolates which he presented to her with a smile. Slightly flustered, Caroline made the introductions and Richard made some polite small-talk to the girls and then they were on their way. Maybe she was being extra sensitive, she told herself, but somehow she sensed that Devlin hadn't taken to Richard. Don't be ridiculous, she told herself, as he held the door for her and she eased herself into the front seat of his snazzy BMW.

Caroline sat in the luxurious front seat observing Richard's hands on the steering wheel, so clean, his nails manicured perfectly. What a change from some of the dirty-nailed fingers of various men of her acquaintance, most notably her father who always managed to have an accumulation of chalk dust under his nails. They drove along sedately and Richard began to talk on a variety of subjects. Because she read the papers and listened to the news and had a quick mind when it was not clogged up by shyness, Caroline found herself responding to him. He was going out of his way to make her feel comfortable and gradually she began to relax. She thoroughly enjoyed the recital in the Concert Hall, the purity of Bernadette Greevy's voice, the soaring notes invading her spirit, uplifting her. She hardly noticed Richard yawning discreetly behind his programme as his eyes roved the audience in search of familiar faces.

Later they mingled with several of his acquaintances and friends and she was introduced to a district justice, a barrister and a gynaecologist with a double-barrelled name whom she recognised with a slight sense of shock as Devlin's employer. Accompanying him was his charming and very glamorous wife. After a few moments of light chat Richard then took her arm and presented her to a well-known politician. Richard seemed to know an awful lot of people, she reflected a little breathlessly, as he steered her through various groups. It was obvious that he was well known himself and also that he was a very ambitious young man. Why on earth had he decided to ask her out? Fortunately the preconcert drinks they had sipped in O'Dwyer's, and her genuine enjoyment of the recital, had relaxed her and she did not dwell on the notion.

They had their photographs taken for one of the social and personal columns of a newspaper and then they were driving off to Caspar and Guimbini's for a meal which she could hardly eat because she was so happy. When he left her home he said easily: "May I see you again? I had such an enjoyable evening."

Caroline nodded, eyes aglow, and he told her he would ring. To her relief, yet disappointment, he did not kiss her on the lips but took her hand and gently kissed her fingers. She stood almost spellbound on the steps as she watched him drive away and knew without doubt that she had never been so exquisitely happy. Then she floated upstairs to where Devlin was waiting patiently as she herself had so often waited, to hear all the gory details. Patting the bed Devlin said lightly, "Quick! I want to hear everything and don't leave one iota out."

The next day they rushed out to buy the evening paper and there in all her glory was "Caroline Stacey accompanied by well known legal eagle Richard Yates at a recital in the National Concert Hall."

"Ruth, eat your horrible heart out," Caroline sang. This was compensation indeed for all those dreadful tormented years of the past. In black and white for everyone to see: Ruth, her aunt, her next door neighbour. At long long last she had a boyfriend.

eight

From their first date on, Caroline's life changed
utterly. Richard took her out regularly, sometimes three or four times a week, and it seemed
as though her life had become one long round of
eating, dancing and socialising. Timmermans,
Buck Whaley's, Legs, Suesey Street, The Pink
Elephant, the list was endless. Although she
developed a certain outward poise, there were
times her insides quivered like jelly and she
wished she was a hundred miles away from the
ritzy set with which Richard associated. Now she
was the one envied by her colleagues as they
listened to her accounts of where he had taken
her the previous night.

Yet she and Richard never seemed to be alone
and although Caroline understood the need for
him to keep a high profile for business sake, she
longed secretly for him to take her on some long
romantic walks around Howth or Killiney where
they could watch a sunset and be alone, just the
two of them with no friends or acquaintances to
intrude upon them. She would chide herself for
such ungrateful thoughts because to her he was
unfailingly charming, presenting her with

flowers and chocolates despite her protestations. Yet Caroline wondered would she ever get to know the real Richard, the private Richard. All she knew was the social Richard.

He kissed her on their second date and although she found the experience pleasant she waited in vain for her heart to start pounding and her insides to turn to molten liquid as she had read in so many romantic novels. But it never happened, to her secret dismay. She wondered unhappily if she really was frigid.

They attended Maggie's wedding together and that night, after drinking many glasses of champagne she returned his kisses ardently, wishing she could make him want her as she wanted him, aching for him to touch her breasts, but he kept his hands frustratingly resting on her hipbones, his eyes closed almost in concentration.

Although she was sexually innocent Caroline knew instinctively that she did not arouse him but she was far too shy and insecure about their relationship to discuss the matter with him, and he never brought up the subject. He kept dating her and invited her to meet his mother, his father having died while he was still in college.

Sarah Yates almost ignored Caroline for the duration of their visit, concentrating her energies on criticizing her only son as they sat in the darkly formal and gloomy Victorian sitting room of her large red-bricked house. Caroline found Mrs Yates to be a cold domineering person and she could understand where Richard got his reserve. Although he was charming and polite he was not at all demonstrative or affectionate to her and having lacked physical affection for a good part of her life, Caroline did not dwell too much on what was obviously not to be. But sometimes, secretly, she longed for him to lose control and make passionate love to her. Lately, she found sex was constantly on her mind and wondered anxiously if she was odd. Not even with Devlin did she feel able to discuss the problem and besides Devlin was very preoccupied with her new boss and was developing an immense infatuation for him. It was all: "Colin said this" or "Colin thinks that..." Caroline found it very worrying indeed. Sometimes Devlin was so impulsive, going head first into something, never stopping to think of the consequences. She could be as daft as a brush. Maybe their forthcoming holiday abroad would make her forget this suave married man with the very glamorous wife. Caroline certainly hoped so. She could only see trouble in store for her friend if she continued to indulge herself in her infatuation.

Richard had not been happy when Caroline told him that she was going abroad with Devlin and two other girls who lived upstairs from them. An icy mask descended on his face and he had been cold and almost rude for the evening. It was the first time she had seen him in a mood and it chilled her. That night, upset and indecisive, she had told Devlin that she was thinking of not going with them. The younger girl had been furious.

"Are you crazy, Caroline?" She demanded. "Why shouldn't you go and enjoy yourself, for crying out loud? Just who does he think he is?" She had wagged a warning finger. "Don't start letting him order you around, Caroline, because you'll be sorry in the long run! For goodness sake stand up to *him* at least. You know you won't stand up to your father and the boys, so don't make the same mistake with Richard or he'll treat you like a doormat. Honest to God, Caro, you've got to start standing up for yourself 'cos no one else will!"

Miserable, she hadn't slept a wink. It was all right for Devlin to tell her to stand up for herself, Richard might very well decide not to see her again and she would be alone. What was a girl to do? The following day Richard rang her at the office, something he rarely did, and apologised for his behaviour. He put it down to pressure of work, telling her he had lost a court case the day before. "Go and enjoy yourself. Don't mind about me," he had instructed in a faintly martyred tone of voice. Obviously she wasn't being sent off with his full blessing. She suffered excruciating pangs of guilt in the weeks preceding her holiday as he complained of overwork and about how he couldn't leave his practice to have his holiday because of the number of cases he was handling. He moaned that he hadn't taken a holiday in the last two years. "It must be great to be able to take off as the fancy takes you...one of the great advantages to being employed as opposed to being self-employed like me." Caroline miserably agreed, forgetting his long weekends away to France, Scotland, and Wales for the rugby matches and his few days at Cheltenham.

Between Richard and her father, who never stopped moaning about having to wash and iron his own clothes, and make his dinners, her holiday was becoming more of a burden each day. Patiently she told her father that she would make up extra dinners and put them in the freezer for him. Even though she was long since living in her flat, it was expected of her that she still do housekeeping for her father. Usually she went home twice a week to wash and iron her father's clothes, and to hoover and polish the house. She never got much thanks for her efforts, her father and the boys taking it as their due. After all she was the woman of the family.

By the time they boarded the plane she was a nervous wreck. Devlin could barely hide her impatience as they sat waiting to take off. It was Caroline's first flight but all the excitement in her had been killed by the cold kiss Richard had bestowed on her at the airport. Devlin had been so annoyed by his behaviour that she had glared at him and he had returned the glare. Now Devlin was sitting beside her on the plane and from the expression on her face Caroline knew she was going to be the recipient of a lecture. Noeleen and Ailish, their companions, were utterly unaware of the tension, having downed several large brandies to relax themselves.

Caroline caught her friend's eye and knew that Devlin wouldn't be able to restrain herself for much longer. Devlin had only so much patience and then she would let fly. Sitting in her window seat she felt taut and harassed. The engines roared and Caroline couldn't suppress a little gasp as the Jumbo thundered down the runway and lifted its immense bulk smoothly off the ground. She found herself leaning forward in her seat as if to help the aircraft to stay airborne and heard Devlin laugh beside her. "Relax, Caro, it's not going to fall back down." They looked at each other and Devlin said gently: "Now listen, I'm not going to nark but for the next two weeks the only person you are to think about is yourself. Right?"

"Right," Caroline echoed meekly.

"Look! You deserve this holiday. If Richard can't have one that's tough cheese. I mean it's not as if he can't afford it. We're going to have two blissful weeks of fun starting from now."

Devlin grinned at her friend. And to her surprise, Caroline felt her anxieties float away from her, felt herself becoming more relaxed and happy with every mile that separated them from Dublin. The air of gaiety and anticipation that pervaded the jetliner as two hundred and fifty holidaymakers prepared for their hard-earned two weeks of sun and fun was highly infectious and Caroline surprised herself by actually joining in a sing-song.

She surprised herself several times on holiday, in fact. After an initially demure start on the beach, feeling shy in her bikini, she soon realised that everyone was far too concerned about getting their own tan to notice her and at Devlin's urging, she discarded her bikini top and luxuriated in the sensual kiss of the sun's rays on her small pink-tipped breasts.

Noeleen and Ailish were a revelation to her! It seemed as if every ounce of inhibition had been shed as soon as they landed on Portuguese soil. They would parade around the apartment quite naked and their behaviour with the men they met each night in the disco shocked Caroline. They asked men to dance, they kissed and fondled them quite openly and sometimes they brought them back to the apartment and slept with them in their own room, leaving Devlin and herself to try and ignore the sounds of passion that issued forth from the second bedroom. Even Devlin was moved to comment on their behaviour but her warnings on AIDS and the risk of infection went cheerfully unheeded.

"We're on holidays and for goodness sake don't start acting the Mother Superior, Dev," Noeleen had ordered firmly, so Devlin had said no more. Caroline and she had met two Portuguese medical students earning their university fees by working as waiters for the summer and while Noeleen and Ailish found someone new each night, they were content to stay with the young men for the fortnight.

Caroline knew that Devlin was not particularly interested in Vitor, her escort, having her mind full of thoughts of her boss, but Caroline found Paulo, her friend, great fun and excitingly sexy. He was twenty five, very tall and well built and quite the opposite to Richard in personality. His dark brown eyes would glitter with laughter as he did his utmost to seduce her. She made Devlin promise not to leave her alone with him so everything they did was done as a foursome.

The young men took them to small villages off the beaten track where they sampled true Portuguese cooking and experienced the warmth and friendliness of the Portuguese race. On their last night Devlin was stricken with a dose of Spanish tummy and Paulo begged Caroline to take a walk along the beach with him. Half-excited, half-afraid, she let herself be persuaded.

Throughout the fortnight he had kissed her often, kisses that had left her breathless, warm and excited...feelings she had never experienced with Richard. Strange and unfamiliar desires assailed her and she wished she could free herself from the fetters of her shy inhibited nature to enjoy the sensuality of her body that cried out for passion and warmth and giving and taking. That night on the beach with Paulo she knew that she certainly was not a frigid woman. As Paulo gently and experiencedly caressed her she felt her sensuality reveal itself as she caressed the tanned muscular body that lay so intimately

against her. She told him that she wanted to stay
a virgin for her husband and Paulo, staring down
at her with smiling passionate eyes, whispered
seductively, "There are other ways, my Caroline.
Let me show you..."

They spent a wonderful night beneath the
glittering stars with the moonlight shimmering
radiantly on the sea, the sound of the surging
tide adding to their pleasure. Caressing and
kissing, tasting and touching, she experienced
for the first time a deeply sensual pleasure. Deep
down she knew she would never experience such
physical pleasure with Richard, who was not a
sensual man, but she buried the thought in her
mind. That was a choice she might have to make
in the future but now was not the time to think
about it. For that last lovely night Caroline
revelled in her sensuality and her memories of
Paulo often saved her sanity in years to come.

Richard's welcoming kiss, cool and reserved
as ever, gave her no pleasure and for the first
time in her life she deliberately lied to someone,
avoiding his questions about the holidays, fear-
ful that if he ever found out about Paulo he would
finish with her. Now that she was back home all
her old panics and inhibitions were as bad as
ever and her fear of being left on the shelf became
even more pronounced when the office junior
arrived in one morning flourishing a particularly
vulgar looking diamond cluster on her left hand.

Lord, she's only eighteen! Caroline mused
miserably as she tried on the ring and made the

traditional wish. You were not allowed to wish for a man—it wouldn't come true if you did—but wishing for Mrs Yates as her mother-in-law solved that little problem!

Soon after her return from holidays Richard asked her to go to Galway to visit some friends for a long weekend and, happily, she agreed to go. Maybe away from the pressures of his work he might become a warm and loving person. At least the fact that he had asked her showed that their relationship was taking a more serious turn. Caroline felt a little glow of happiness. Maybe he was afraid he would lose control and shock her by his demands, she reflected dreamily. She would just gently let him know that she wouldn't be the slightest bit shocked...would in fact welcome his advances. Bidding Devlin a happy farewell she noticed momentarily that her friend seemed unhappy and tense. Devlin had been in quite bad form lately and Caroline had a feeling that it had something to do with Colin Cantrell-King.

Richard didn't really care for Devlin. Caroline had mentioned as they drove towards Galway that Devlin was unhappy about something. "Is she?" he answered coolly. "You know, Caroline, I don't like the way that girl bosses you around. She's too sure of herself, if you ask me."

For the first time in their relationship she answered sharply. "Devlin never bosses me around, she's the best friend a girl could have. Only I know what she's done for me so please don't criticise her to me!"

Her voice had been a little shaky but she stared him down, noting the tightening of his thin mouth.

"Very well," he said tightly and they had driven along in strained silence. Eventually her nerve broke.

"Richard! Please don't be mad," she pleaded. "It will ruin the weekend. I mean it's the first time we've been away together." She met his gaze shyly. "Let's try to get to know each other a little better." They had stopped on a lay-by to take a rest and impulsively she reached over and kissed him on the mouth. She felt him tense up, felt rebuffed and drew away. Richard stared at her for a moment with a strange, almost sad, look in his eyes.

His hand reached out to caress her face and he said quietly, "I don't deserve you. Do I?"

"Oh Richard!" she murmured not knowing what to say. He reached into his breast pocket and drew forth a small package and handed it to her.

"What is it? she asked intrigued.

"Open it," he said smiling. Caroline's eyes widened as she removed the wrapping paper and opened the box to find a pair of exquisite sapphire ear rings reposing in a bed of black velvet.

"Oh Richard! For me?" He nodded and leaned over and kissed her on the cheek. "I hope you like them."

"I do," she assured him, wishing he had kissed

her on the mouth.

Several times over the weekend she met Charles Stokes, the man she had first met in Richard's company that first evening at the theatre. Subsequently she met him several times when they had been out at functions and it was obvious he was a great and trusted friend of Richard's. In his early fifties and unmarried he was an eminent barrister and Richard confided that he had been most helpful in assisting him to set up in business. Richard felt a deep sense of gratitude towards the older man and Caroline thought that in him he was finding the father figure so missing from his life since his father had died. Charles never had much to say to her, just the usual social chit-chat. When she saw Charles in Galway her heart sank to her boots. She knew there was no way this was going to be a nice secluded week-end alone with Richard as she had hoped. They might as well have stayed in Dublin. They stayed with friends of Richard's, a married couple who made her feel welcome and teased her about how nice it was to see Richard at last looking as though he was starting to settle down.

"You know, this is the longest Richard has ever dated a girl. All the women in Dublin must be broken-hearted. Every time he went somewhere he had a different girl on his arm. The Playboy of the Western World has nothing on our Richard!" Caroline laughed. It never ceased to amaze her that of all the sophisticated beautiful women she knew Richard had dated, she was the one who seemed to have lasted the longest. If only they could break down the physical barriers that seemed to exist between them. Maybe it was because she was that much younger than him. After all he was thirty-two, and with years of experience of women, and maybe he felt he would be taking advantage of her innocence. It was so frustrating! She knew seventeen year olds who were no longer virgins. If only she could get Richard to realise that she would welcome intimacy, but she had her own bedroom in Galway and there was little opportunity for them to be alone together. Frustrated, she went to bed each night with only memories of her encounters with Paulo sustaining her like old friends.

A few days after her return she arrived home one evening to find Devlin sobbing her heart out. She was horrified to find the so strong and usually so self-reliant Devlin crying and swiftly put her arms around her friend to comfort her.

When Devlin told her about her pregnancy Caroline was stunned. How could Devlin, who was usually so full of commonsense, have been so foolish? Shocked, she had listened while Devlin told her of her illegitimacy and adoption and felt such pity and love for the younger girl that she wanted to sit hugging her tightly. For the first time in her life she was needed and the sensation made her feel strong and decisive. She badly wanted to go to London with Devlin to be with her for the abortion. Her mind shrank from the word but still if Devlin felt it was the right thing to do she wasn't going to make her feel even more guilty by voicing her dismay at the idea. If she were in Devlin's shoes, expecting a baby, even out of wedlock, she'd be secretly thrilled. Banishing the sinful thought she had made pot after pot of tea. They talked and confided in each other as they had never done before.

Watching Devlin disappear through the departure doors at the airport, Caroline knew with certainty that whatever happened to either of them, their friendship was a bond which would never be broken. Not even Richard would come between herself and Devlin. When Devlin rang her to tell her that she was going to have the baby, she was so relieved. The thoughts of the abortion had preyed on her mind. What a despicable bastard Cantrell-King was! She wondered uneasily what Richard would have done in the same position. Not that there was much danger of that, she thought sadly.

Devlin's departure left Caroline extremely lonely. And with Maggie gone to Saudi to live with her new husband, she found herself without her two best friends. And so she turned to Richard more and more. Their relationship left her feeling vaguely dissatisfied, yet she was not strong enough to end it or, more importantly, to talk about it with him. Richard seemed happy enough the way things were between them. She guessed that he was glad that Devlin had gone from the scene. He welcomed her growing emotional dependence on him and after a while Caroline had almost persuaded herself that she was truly in love with him.

When he proposed marriage one evening just before Christmas, she accepted, but to her intense dismay, instead of feeling that she was exquisitely happy, as she should have been on reaching her life's ambition, Caroline could only feel a strange deadness like champagne that's been left too long and has gone flat. But the feel of the elegant solitaire on the third finger of her left hand brought her a sense of comfort and solace that almost made up for her lack of excitement and watching it glinting under the lights of the Christmas tree near which she sat with Richard's arm protectively around her, she thought how strange it was that now, when she had what she had always wanted, it wasn't quite enough. Was that always the way with life? Well it was what she had chosen and it was up to her to make Richard a good and loving wife.

Later they went for drinks in O'Dwyers but the frenetic gaiety of the Christmas season seemed only to depress her. For some reason she felt lonely despite the crowds surrounding them, offering their congratulations. She excused herself to go to the ladies, and had just closed the cubicle door when she heard two voices outside. Unaware of her presence, one woman said to the other.

"What do you think of Richard getting

hitched, the bastard? I dated him a couple of times and I was crazy about him, but he just kept on seeing other women. What has little Miss Prim and Proper got that we haven't got?"

The other voice said dryly: "Probably a Swiss bank account. You know, I gave that swine so much business through recommending clients to him, thousands of pounds worth. When I got his firm to handle my purchase of DESIGNER, the shit charged me down to the last penny. If you ask me he overcharged! I wish her joy of him, the penny-pinching skinflint! Anyway, he always loved having young girls fall for him. He wouldn't be able to handle a mature relationship with a woman of his own age. That's why it's not you or I that's flashing the diamond tonight, Elaine!"

Caroline's eyes were on stalks at this display of bitchiness, as she remained hidden in her cubicle. She remembered Richard telling her that the well-known business woman Joyce Jordan was buying a fabulous new boutique and that his firm was handling the sale, but imagine him not giving her a discount! She knew that Richard was careful with his money but still, if she had given him so much business he could have been a little bit generous! And who was this Elaine who had dated her husband-to-be? Oh well, he had dated many women, yet the remark about "mature relationships" stung. She wondered if Richard had slept with Elaine? What a pity she hadn't the nerve to walk out and mortify them.

Caroline waited until they had finished their business and gone, before leaving and walking back to her seat. Richard was up at the bar and she met Charles Stokes's inscrutable gaze. Thinking that perhaps he might feel that marriage might put constraints on Richard's socialising with him she leaned over and said shyly, "You'll always be welcome to visit when we are married."

"Thank you," he said, but didn't meet her eyes.

Caroline sighed. If he wanted to sulk that was his business. She wasn't going to whisk Richard off and never let him meet his friends, for God's sake! Honestly this should be the happiest day of her entire life. To hell with Elaine and Joyce and Charles Stokes! Surreptitiously her thumb caressed her engagement ring. She should be thanking God that she was not condemned to a life of spinsterhood. She was on the edge of that special magic circle. Soon she'd be one of them, a fully fledged married woman at last! Caroline took a long satisfying drink of her Guinness and blackcurrant. Tomorrow the engagement would be announced in *The Irish Times* for all the world and Ruth Saunders to see.

"For business purposes," Richard said when Caroline told him that she thought such announcements the height of pretentiousness, but she didn't quite believe him. Still if it made him happy. Maybe she would get pregnant straight away. Richard wanted a son, he had told her, and the thought of having a baby thrilled her, especially as Devlin and Maggie were now pregnant.

Smiling at the thought she sat among the throngs, her mind full of happy anticipatory thoughts. "Mrs Caroline Yates"—how perfect it sounded! She took another sip of her drink and began to feel more relaxed. Everything would be fine, she told herself. And she was truly the luckiest girl in the world.

Maggie's Story I

nine

Maggie Ryan murdered a fly with an unnecessary amount of violence and slumped wearily on to the sofa, part of the furniture that had been included in the apartment supplied with Terry's job in Saudi Arabia. At the moment the air-conditioning was into its third day of being out of order and if Terry didn't get it seen to rapidly, she was going to get on the next available flight to London. For heaven's sake there had to be at least ten thousand engineers in this God-forsaken hole of a country. Surely one of them could fix the air conditioning!

Rivulets of sweat ran down between her breasts; her hair clung damply to her neck and with a sigh of exasperation she walked into the white tiled bathroom and sat in the bath, turning on the cold shower. Later, when the heat of the day had died down a little, she would go over to the compound, meet some of the other bored wives, and maybe go for a swim. Life in a Saudi compound had begun to pall somewhat though at first it had been so exciting. There were people of all nationalities living in the huge foreign compound that was as least as big as the whole of Dun Laoire. There were parties morning, noon and night and on the compound itself, the social life was terrific. Had she been footloose and fancy-free she could have had a ball, she wrote and told Caroline and Devlin.

In the beginning she had enjoyed it so much, the trips to the souk, the scuba diving, the crack. But after six months, the excitement and newness of it had worn off. The restrictions began to get the independent Maggie down. Having to wear the black abbaya that covered her from head to toe when she left the compound, not being allowed to drive because she was a woman, not being allowed to be driven by a man unless he was her husband. It was a man's world in Saudi; women were definitely second-class citizens. Terry, her husband, was enjoying every minute of it. And then there was the heat. The harsh unrelenting sun was as oppressive as the religious laws that currently ruled her life. Still, the money was good!

Her hands slid down over her swollen belly and she felt the child inside her kick vigorously. Terry assured her that it had to be a boy and she hoped for his sake that he wasn't going to be disappointed. He had taken some getting used to the fact that she was pregnant, and if she was completely honest, she had taken some getting used to the idea herself. It hadn't been planned. But when had things ever worked out according to plan?

Because she had been so sick during the

pregnancy she had had to stop working as a nurse in one of Riyadh's biggest medical centres, and she was bored out of her mind. The days seemed to drag on interminably. They had lived in Riyadh since their marriage eighteen months before and had already made enough money to buy a house and help Terry set up his own accountancy firm at home. His financial experience here and in the States would be of great help as he intended specialising in foreign investment accounts.

They had gone home on one of their holiday breaks to start getting things set up and to attend Caroline's wedding. The feel of the soft Irish mist that had caressed Maggie's face when she arrived at Dublin airport had been heavenly and she had stood gulping in great lungfuls of fresh blustery Dublin air. She had never been so glad of anything as she was of the overcast misty sky that had blotted out every trace of the red ball of heat that she had become heartily sick of.

What she would give now to feel a soft Irish mist on her face! Even the humidity in New York hadn't made her feel like this. It must be because of her pregnancy. How different she felt now from the day she had walked radiantly down the aisle on Terry's arm, ready to face their adventurous new life abroad. She got out of the bath, wrapped a towel around herself and went into their bedroom. Pulling her wedding album from the wardrobe, she sprawled across the bed and began lazily to turn the pages. Observing the glowing vital person that she was then, she wondered if she was now the same girl at all. There was something about this country that sapped your energy and dried you out. Maggie felt like a grape that had shrivelled up into a wrinkled old raisin.

She looked at a picture of her husband with a big pissed grin on his face as he cut his wedding cake. The life here suited him. He would have stayed another five years if she let him, so maybe the pregnancy was a blessing in disguise. She was certainly not going to raise a child in Saudi. A picture of herself smiling proudly in her virginal white caught her eye. She had worn white despite the fact that she and Terry had become lovers within three months of their first meeting. Terry hadn't been the first either. Her eyes glazed over, and she could almost smell the fresh sweet hay, the musky masculine scent of Joe Conway as he brought her voluptuous seventeen-year-old body to its first magnificent orgasm. It had been a hot August day, the sky a vivid azure with little white clouds scudding along in the warm sensual breeze that had rippled through her hair and across her young, tanned, naked, excited body.

She would always remember seeing those little scudding clouds as she lay in the soft hay cradling Joe's body on top of her, as he panted harshly, sweat moistening his lean muscular body, then groaned with pleasure as he felt himself becoming aroused again by the luscious

Maggie who was seven years younger than him.

She was by no means his first woman, she knew that. Joe Conway owned land as far as the eye could see and was considered the catch of the county. Yet, until he met Maggie with her open natural honesty he had never considered marrying. He had seen her around the village dressed in shorts and a teeshirt, her long shapely limbs and slim-hipped firm-breasted young figure causing many of the men to admit to impure thoughts in the confessional.

However, Maggie was completely unaware of her own beauty, innocence adding to her vibrant sensuality. One day Joe had given her a lift in his landrover to the meadows where her father was gathering in his hay, helping her to carry the large basket of food and the cool bottles of beer for the men at work. Her sparkling green eyes, clear and glowing with good health, had met his directly and for her age she was amazingly self-possessed with none of the giggling coy ways of her peers. Maggie for her part, had felt her body tingle with reaction the first time Joe Conway had looked hard at her with warm, admiring black eyes.

Joe Conway was a hard-muscled lean young man in the prime of life. He reminded her of a powerful stallion biting at the bit, eager for challenge and adventure. When he had taken over his father's huge dairy farm he had completely modernised it, introduced a battery of new technology and after two years was on his way to being the biggest dairy farmer in the county. What he wanted he took, and he wanted Maggie. And she wanted him. The teachings of the nuns, the warnings of her mother, the sermons at Sunday mass, had not made one whit of difference to Maggie's views on sex. She had an open uncomplicated view of sex and sexuality. To her it was the most natural thing in the world and when she felt the warm excited tinglings that occurred when she was with Joe she wanted more and, even at seventeen and unlike her peers, she was quite untroubled by any feelings of guilt.

Something as nice as making love couldn't be wrong. She wasn't going to be a hypocrite, not like half the creepin jesuses of the village who went to mass daily, and then proceeded to pass the time gossip-mongering, and taking away people's characters.

"I'd swear that young lassie deliberately got pregnant so he'd have to marry her! Isn't it a shame for her?"

"She's only marrying that ould yoke because she's afraid of being left. He's sixty if he's a day and she won't see thirty-five again and she's no oil painting!"

"Young Neil Doyle has been up fixin the Widda Mullan's central heating! I'd say it's more than the central heating he's fixin, meself."

The hypocrisy of people sickened Maggie, as she watched certain individuals claiming social welfare who weren't entitled to a penny of it, and saw others making fortunes at the expense of their neighbours. The village publican was selling drink to all those who would buy it, whether they were under age or not. He didn't care that half the men of the village went home pissed out of their skulls more often than not, and that many was the wife who was left short of money for her family's needs, money that lined his till. And then there was the doctor, who made more visits than were strictly necessary and who made patients come to his surgery to get their test results rather than give them over the phone. Phone calls couldn't be charged to a medical card! And what about the sergeant, who owned three houses in the area, and who had them let and never declared a penny for tax? But then, of course, nobody reported him, because the sergeant was great for turning a blind eye if there was a bit of after-hours drinking, or someone's car wasn't covered by tax and insurance. And the priest in his big house, looked after by the nuns from the nearby convent, fed the best of food and wine, able to afford foreign holidays and a big fancy car and membership of the select golf club—although she had to admit he worked hard for his luxuries.

These upright, Godfearing self-righteous members of the community would have branded Maggie a loose woman if they had known that several weeks after their first meeting she had lost her virginity in glorious abandon to Joe Conway. She had been out riding, savouring the

smell of the new mown hay and inhaling deeply
the warm flower scented breeze. As she rode
along happily, she saw Joe standing by his Landrover at the edge of the meadow and cantered
over to him. He held out his arms to help her
dismount and it seemed the most natural thing
in the world to meet the firm sensual mouth that
was so close to her own. They walked over, arms
entwined, to a soft rick of new-mown hay, and,
miles from anywhere, in the scorching heat of the
afternoon had made passionate and utterly
uninhibited love. It had been the mercy of God
she hadn't got pregnant, she often thought later,
and from then on she told Joe he'd have to wear
a condom. Maggie liked making love but she was
not irresponsible.

When she was eighteen Joe proposed to her,
but Maggie turned him down. She wanted to see
the world and had grown tired of the restrictive
tapestry of village life. Having secured a place in
a teaching hospital in Dublin, she was anxious to
go and become a nurse. It was a bitter man who
watched her reject a life that many girls would
have given their eye-teeth for. As the wife of the
biggest cattle-exporter in County Wicklow she
would have rubbed shoulders with the landed
gentry of Ireland, had her own yearling to run in
the Curragh, taken trips to Paris on Concorde to
watch her horse race at Longchamps, mixed with
the Smurfits and the Sangsters, the O'Briens
and the O'Reillys, drunk champagne and eaten
strawberries at Epsom. Joe couldn't believe his

ears when she told him that it all sounded dreadfully boring and that her mind was made up.

Her parents hadn't spoken to her for a month, unable to believe the chance she was turning down to marry into the Conway family, one of the richest and best-known in the south-east. None of them had understood, not one of them; the only person who supported her decision was Marian.

In the scorching heat in Saudi, Maggie sighed deeply as she pulled out an old photo of Marian Gilhooley from the back of her album. Sadness came into her eyes as she stared at the blonde curly-haired blue-eyed girl with the laughing face who stared back at her out of the photograph.

Where was Marian now? Had she too married? Had she any children yet? If anyone had told Maggie that her best friend would not grow old with her, Maggie would have told them they were mad. Marian, who was closer to her than any sister could ever have been. Marian the sharer of all the joys and traumas of growing up. Marian who had ended their friendship so abruptly and for reasons Maggie could still not understand. Even after all these years, Maggie found herself shaking her head in bewilderment.

***

They had met at school, two spotty gawky schoolgirls of thirteen, Maggie the tomboy, and

Marian the effervescent extrovert. Maggie grinned as she remembered their first meeting. How well she recalled sneaking into the toilet to have a fag. Peering under the dividing walls she saw no trace of white-stockinged legs or brown-brogued legs. Some of the girls at school were right little tattle-tales. Only the previous week there had been drama:

"Oh Sister! Sister! There's smoke coming out of one of the toilets. Come *quick*! It might be on fire."

Poor Annie Mary Worley had been hauled out of the cubicle, smoke almost coming out of her ears, her lovely comforting fag smouldering ignominiously down the toilet bowl. Sister Mairead's eyes behind their thick-lensed old-fashioned glasses had been two slits of ice-cold anger.

"I should have known, Madam Worley!" she hissed dramatically, her wimple quivering with indignation.

"I was gaspin Sister!" said the unabashed Worley, who had already been caught in such a crime.

"I'll have you gaspin before I'm finished with you, Miss!" exclaimed Sister Mairead ominously, as she hauled the hapless Annie Mary, who in spite of her predicament had begun to giggle at the horrified expressions on the faces of her friends, up to the front parlour to be interviewed by The Head.

Sister Concepta, the headmistress of the

convent school, decreed that Annie Mary be brought forth before assembly to confess her awful crime to the whole school. She then had to break her remaining cigarettes one by one into little pieces. Sister Mairead had been ecstatic at this punishment; she loved to see people humiliated, and her sly shortsighted eyes couldn't hide their pleasure as she watched Sister Concepta march her pupil up the steps of the stage in the assembly hall.

In silence the whole school had watched as Annie Mary had lovingly stroked each "Occasion of sin" before defiantly breaking it into bits. What Sisters Concepta and Mairead, didn't know, however, was that Annie Mary had managed to conceal two fags down her cleavage, which she duly smoked before a thrilled and admiring audience in the dorm that night. Overnight the school had a new heroine.

Maggie, however, had no desire to be a heroine. She didn't want Sister "Never Got It," the nickname given by the incorrigible Worley to Sister Mairead, to catch her smoking. If her father found out she'd be killed, and Sister Mairead would be the first one to tattle-tale if she caught Maggie at it. Hence the caution as she made sure the loos were vacant. Closing the door of the cubicle behind her, she hopped up, a foot on each rim of the toilet, and lit up. Ooh the joy of it! Silently she exhaled a long thin stream of smoke, waving her arms to dissipate it. She had just begun to take another long drag when she thought she heard a muffled cough. Surprise caused the smoke to go the wrong way and she began to splutter. She had been so sure there had been no one else in the loos. Tears streaming down her cheeks, she coughed and choked and gasped and wheezed and in her distress lost her balance and one leg plunged into the wet ceramic depths of the toilet bowl. A wail of dismay echoed through the dim dark-green-tiled den of iniquity.

"Jesus Mary and Joseph! What are you doin' in there?" A vaguely familiar voice asked, as a blonde head poked over the top of the cubicle. Maggie, extricating herself from the toilet, looked up to find Marian Gilhooley, a girl in her new class, peering down at her.

"How did you get in without me hearing you?" Maggie demanded.

"I was already in here standing on the loo," grinned the other girl, taking a pull out of her own cigarette. "I thought you were friggin 'Never Got It.' I nearly died, Maggie!" Catching sight of Maggie's very wet shoe and sock Marian said matter-of-factly, "you'd better borrow a pair of my shoes and socks or you'll be in trouble. Come on."

Marian was a boarder, Maggie was not, and it was with a great sense of adventure that she followed her new friend up to the mysterious dorm, which was well and truly out of bounds to the day pupils.

And so a friendship was born. Marian, who

lived in Cork, but whose mother had gone to school at the convent and wanted her daughter to do the same, became the sister Maggie never had. At weekends Marian would get a special pass from the nuns to stay at Maggie's home and in time she became as much a daughter to Maggie's parents as Maggie was herself. She would breeze in the door, throw her arms around Maggie's mother and say, "Hi folks! Anyone for tea?" every Friday evening, except for the rare occasion that she went home.

When Marian went to the local hospital to have her tonsils removed it was Maggie's parents who were at her bedside when she woke up and they had visited every day, bringing chocolates and fruit and magazines.

"Your parents are too good to me," Marian told Maggie.

"Sure they love you as much as they love me," Maggie laughed. Her brothers, too, had taken to Marian's lively outgoing personality and after a while Maggie couldn't remember what life had been like without Marian.

They went through school together in a whirlwind of giggling adventures, each shared experience binding the knot of friendship tighter. Maggie had gone to visit Marian's home in Cork and found her family to be a warm close-knit one and her mother particularly nice. It was as though she had known them all her life, and she felt immediately at home. It was to Maggie that Marian confided her troubles and dreams, and vice versa and people in the village got used to seeing the pair of them together.

"Where's your other half?" Ma Clancy the postmistress would say if ever Maggie went into the post office alone. And that's exactly what Marian was, Maggie's other half. Marian had been most enthusiastic about Maggie's romance with Joe Conway but she had understood more than anybody why the independent-minded Maggie had not wanted to settle down to marry. While everyone else reacted with shocked dismay to Maggie's refusal to wed, Marian was staunchly supportive and urged Maggie to stick to her plan to go nursing. All too soon their girlhood were over but before they finally stepped on the road to careers and maturity, Marian to study for a degree at UCD and Maggie to nurse, they decided to treat themselves to a holiday abroad.

They left school in June and arranged for a holiday in August, hoping for a cancellation. Maggie couldn't wait. Although Marian was back home and working for the summer in Cork, and she was in Wicklow working on the farm with her father, they phoned each other and wrote regularly. Marian had got herself a new boyfriend, and she bubbled enthusiastically about him to Maggie, who understood perfectly: after all, hadn't she been the same when she first met Joe.

Then a slight disaster had befallen Maggie: she broke her leg and was encased in plaster and hobbling around on crutches. Marian had arrived up on a weekend visit and to Maggie's surprise seemed somewhat agitated. Eventually she said, the words coming tumbling out, "Maggie, would you mind very much if we didn't go away on holidays? I...I don't think it would be such a good idea with your broken leg. We wouldn't be able to go dancing and things and it would be a bit of a waste of money, wouldn't it?"

Stunned was the only word to describe how Maggie felt, but on reflection she conceded that Marian was right. It would be a bit of a waste and there would be other times. They decided to travel around the west coast of Ireland for a few days instead just before they both came to Dublin to study.

Marian went back to Cork, having made plans with Maggie for their touring holiday. They would go immediately after Maggie's parents' twenty-fifth wedding anniversary. Marian had been the first to be invited and would be seated at the family table. Maggie was looking forward to it immensely. All the preparations were underway; the local hotel had been booked and there was going to be a great hooley.

Several weeks later, during one of their phone calls, Marian casually mentioned that her boyfriend had asked her to go away with him for a few days. Coincidentally it was to be the week that she and Marian would have been going abroad. "But of course we'll have our own holiday later in the year."

For a moment Maggie couldn't help but wonder whether the plans to go on holiday with the boyfriend had materialised before or after the break-up of their own holiday plans. Instantly the thought was banished. Marian was her best friend, a person of the utmost integrity. She would never be so underhand as to drop Maggie like a hot potato just because a boyfriend had asked her to go holidaying with him. A friend would never do a thing like that...

The summer flew by, the invitations were sent out for the anniversary party and Maggie began to look forward to the forthcoming holiday. She badly needed a break and a few days of fun with Marian was just what she wanted. Maggie rang her friend to finalise the plans as they were to leave the day after her parents' party. Marian seemed surprised to hear from her.

"I've booked a place for us to stay." Maggie always did the booking when they went anywhere.

"Oh...oh!" Marian sounded rather confused. "For when?" she asked.

"Immediately after the party, of course," Maggie laughed. "I've sent a deposit." Honestly, Marian could be so scattered sometimes.

"Oh, you didn't get my letter then?" Marian said, trying to sound casual.

"No, not yet," Maggie replied gaily. It was great to hear Marian again. Roll on the holliers.

They chatted for a few moments before

Marian, always mindful of the phone charges, laughingly said goodbye. "I can't wait for the party and the holiday," Maggie informed her mother who was ironing a pile of shirts in the big friendly kitchen of the farmhouse.

Nelsie McNamara smiled. "Knowing you pair you'll enjoy yourselves, I'm really looking forward to seeing Marian at the party. You'd miss her around the place."

"You sure would," Marian agreed giving her mother a little hug. The following day Marian's letter arrived, chatty and lighthearted in her friend's usual flippant style. Maggie laughed aloud several times as she read it, until she got to the last page where Marian told her that she might be going abroad with her sister and that consequently she would have to cut her holiday with Maggie short. "I know you won't like this, but it's got to be said, so here goes..." she had written.

Maggie re-read the letter. She couldn't believe her eyes. But it was there in black and white. Quietly excusing herself from the breakfast table, she went up to her room.

It wasn't that she minded Marian having her foreign holiday. She didn't. But that was the second time that year that her friend had messed up her holiday plans and she didn't even have the gumption to say it straight to her on the phone. That was the thing that hurt the most. Then Maggie realised that, although Marian might not have been aware of it, she was always making and breaking plans. Like the time Mrs Gilhooley had driven up from Cork to Dublin and had called to visit Marian at school. Marian had assured her that she would bring her mother out to tea at the farm and so Maggie had helped her own mother bake tarts and scones and the like. The whole afternoon they had waited and no sign of the pair. The next day Marian told her airily that they hadn't had time to fit in the visit.

Then there was the time some of the gang they went around with decided to hire a mobile in Brittas Bay for a few days. Five of them were going. At the last minute Marian asked was it OK for her to bring along her current boyfriend.

"I'd like you all to meet him," she told her friends. Maggie was a bit dismayed. If that was the case she could have asked Joe, and Annie Mary could have asked Tom and Julie and Michelle could have asked their boyfriends.

Annie Mary had been most annoyed when Maggie told her of Marian's request. "For cryin' out loud, isn't that just typical. Everything has to be done to suit Gilhooley. What the hell does she want to bring him for? She's only going with him a wet week. He doesn't even know any of us and besides isn't the whole idea to get away from them for a while? Could you imagine the face of Tom if I asked him to come on a holiday with a gang of girls? She just loves to have people running around after her." The others had been equally unimpressed with the idea. But Maggie had calmed them down, and told them not to cause a row. And so, the boyfriend had been invited, and Marian once again had things done her way.

It was a streak in her friend that Maggie was able to overlook because she loved her. After all, no one was perfect. But this latest episode was just taking things a little bit too far. She grimly took out her notepad, sat down at her desk and wrote her friend a letter. It was a very frank letter in which she pointed out that she was not a doormat for Marian to wipe her feet upon when it suited her. She pointed out that twice that year Maggie had made plans for holidays with her and then broken them. As far as Maggie was concerned, that was not the way friends behaved towards each other, especially not best friends. Friendship meant respect. Friends had responsibilities towards each other. Marian had treated Maggie with neither. She signed and sealed her letter. As far as she was now concerned the matter had been dealt with, she had made her point and all she wanted to do was to forget about it. At least Marian would be there for the party and they could talk about it.

Three days later her mother received a regret card from Marian saying that she would not be attending the party. There was no other message, no reason given and no letter for Maggie. Nelsie was stunned but not half as stunned as Maggie, who couldn't believe that Marian could treat her mother in such a rude and hurtful fashion after all the kindness Nelsie had shown her. She might as well have slapped her mother in the face.

Maggie gave her friend a week, then after hearing nothing from her, she rang Cork. Marian wasn't in but her sister assured her that she would give Marian the message and get her to ring back. The call never came.

Maggie could not understand it. Hurt, bitterness, anger, sadness. Maggie didn't know what she felt. But that was that, she swore. She would never contact Marian again. Pride kept her going for a week. She didn't deserve friends, that Marian Gilhooley. What a bitch!

Maggie couldn't sustain the anger. It wasn't in her nature to hold a grudge. Whenever she thought about it, all she could remember were the great times they'd had. The laughs! The secrets they had shared. How could Marian throw away long years of friendship without a thought? It was something Maggie couldn't, wouldn't do.

Again she phoned Marian. They'd get over this belch in their friendship. They'd had a few hiccups before and no doubt they would again. That's what relationships were all about. As the phone rang, Maggie felt a great relief flood through her. Soon everything would be all right between herself and her best friend. Impatiently she waited for the phone to be answered. Marian herself answered.

"Hi, it's me," Maggie said evenly.

"Oh...hello!" Her friend's voice was cold and Maggie's heart sank. God! couldn't she make any effort?

"Why haven't you written or phoned?" Maggie asked quietly.

Then, in tones of frosty indifference that came clearly across the airwaves, Maggie heard Marian say, "I didn't think there was any point!"

After all they had experienced together, Marian "didn't think there was any point!"

Maggie was so shocked that she didn't know what to say. She was silent for a moment and then she said in disbelief, "If I hadn't got in contact with you, would you never have got in contact with me?"

"No!" came the devastatingly cold reply.

Maggie nearly fell out of the phone box. She had phoned from the village to ensure maximum privacy. She remembered thinking, I don't believe this, it must be a bad dream. Friends don't behave like that. But it was no dream; her last fifty pence had been swallowed up by the phone and the pips were going. Regaining her composure, she said to her best friend, "If that's what you want then Marian, take care of yourself."

There had been no anger in her voice; she was not going to end their friendship in anger. Let Marian do that, it wasn't Maggie's way. She could look back with her head held high on the friendship they had shared. She had nothing to apologise for; it had been she who had made a move towards reconciliation and been rejected. There was no shame in that. The pips ended. The line went dead.

ten

A myriad emotions assailed her. Surely Marian wasn't serious? They hadn't even had a proper fight for God's sake! Just a few home truths had been written and what was a few home truths between friends?

Enough to end a friendship obviously! Well, if Marian was going to end every friendship she had because she couldn't take a bit of straight talking, God help her, she'd never have any real friends.

Nelsie hadn't said much when Maggie told her, just hugged her daughter and said gently, "Maybe when Marian grows up a little bit she'll realise what she has lost and get in touch again. If she doesn't, she doesn't and you'll have to accept it as part of life."

It was a lonely Maggie who set off to Dublin to begin her nursing career. Her parents were dead set against the idea, Marian was gone and she began to wonder was she doing the right thing. Maybe she should have married Joe. As she tried to brighten up her spartan room in the nurses' home, the room that would be her home for the next twelve months, she felt uncharacteristically heavy-hearted. She eyed the list of regulations on the back of her door, glumly.

No visitors in the rooms. Visitors to be received in the parlour. Probationers to be in by 11 p.m. Sure the crack would only be starting at 11 p.m! One late pass per week until 2.00 a.m. Big deal! All rooms to be left tidy. Checks carried out twice a week. No jewellery or make up to be worn on duty. God! it was worse than being at school.

Still, the next morning when she donned her probationers uniform for the first time she felt invigorated and full of anticipation. Maggie was a natural for nursing. Her warmth and cheerfulness, her intelligence and quick wit ensued that she encountered no difficulties with her training. The sight of her moving around the wards with her rangy long-limbed stride, tendrils of curly auburn hair escaping from the confines of her starched white cap, her crisp white uniform hugging her lithe voluptuous body, caused many a man, patient and doctor, to pause and take a second long look.

She made friends easily, and kept in contact with Annie Mary her old school pal who was doing law in UCD. It was Annie Mary who told her that she had seen Marian several times in the cafeteria, Marian had made no mention of Maggie or the "row" and Annie Mary couldn't make head nor tail of her. "One bloody minded, stubborn mixed up girl," she said reflectively, as she and Maggie enjoyed a glass of Guinness in

Joxer Daly's.

Coming up to Christmas, Maggie couldn't get Marian out of her mind. Didn't she miss the friendship the way Maggie did? Could she not make any move towards reconciliation? It hurt Maggie that Marian had never contacted her since that awful phone call.

She'd been writing out her Christmas card and had a list as long as her arm, of friends all around the country. In previous years Marian would have been top of the list. Should she send her a card? How would it be received? She didn't know and that was worse than anything. What a shame that such a fine friendship should be reduced to this. With a set to her mouth, she took her purse and went to the phone on the landing. She knew Marian was staying with her aunt in Ranelagh while she was studying. They had stayed with her several times when they were friends and had come up to Dublin for the weekend so Maggie still had the phone number. Dialing the digits she smiled wryly to herself. This was worse than going with a fella. She actually felt nervous! A voice answered, that old familiar well loved voice. "Hello?"

"Hi it's me?" Maggie said, unable to disguise the uncertainty in her voice.

"Oh..Hello..." Marian sounded equally uncertain.

"I...ah...I was writing my Christmas cards and I just wanted so much to wish you a happy Christmas and I really mean it," she blurted out.

"Thanks very much Maggie. I wish the same to you," Marian replied quietly. "How are things?"

"Ah...you know yourself! I'm swotting my brains out at the moment."

"Me too," echoed her friend. And Maggie sensed that she was smiling. They chatted casually for a while, asking after each other's families. It wasn't strained, but it wasn't the same.

Finally Maggie said, "I'd better let you go. Take care!"

"You too," said Marian. "And thanks for ringing!"

"You're welcome," Maggie responded warmly, glad that she had made the gesture. Replacing the receiver she walked back to her room.

It had been so nice to hear Marian's voice again. If only they could get together and talk. Maggie sat at her desk, and a gleam came into her eye. What time was it? Nine thirty. She'd make it to Ranelagh and back before eleven if she put the skids on and if she took a taxi over! Well, it would be worth it. Hastily running a comb through her hair, she grabbed her bag and flew down to the lift. Within minutes, she had secured a taxi from the hospital rank and was on her way to Ranelagh.

"Please God let Aunt Elizabeth be out," she prayed in the back seat. Aunt Elizabeth was out. And Marian's jaw dropped in shock when she saw who was standing at her front door. "You're as bad as Ma Clancy with your mouth open. Aren't you going to ask me in?" Maggie asked lightly.

"Of...of course..." stammered Marian.

They stared at each other. Marian looked weary and Maggie knew that she didn't look much better herself.

"I can't believe you're here," Marian said finally. "After all I've done to you...it must have been a very hard thing."

Maggie sighed. "It wasn't hard at all, Marian. I really miss you. You're the best friend I've ever had and I don't like not talking. When I heard you on the phone tonight I just had to come over and see you. I mean, can't we even talk about it? Isn't that what friends are for?

"I've been some friend," Marian muttered miserably. Maggie gave her a hug.

"Look it's in the past, can't we forget it? For heaven's sake, Mar, would you put the kettle on, I've got to get back to the nurses home by eleven, and I'll have to go soon 'cos I can't afford another taxi so I'll have to get the bus."

They had tea, caught up on some gossip, and arranged to meet after Christmas to talk things over. It had been a rushed visit but as Maggie left she hugged her friend. "I'm really glad I came," she said happily, "I'll see you after Christmas."

Marian's hug was less enthusiastic but Maggie thought no more about it until a letter arrived on her doorstep early in the New Year to say that Marian had thought the matter over and she didn't think things could ever be the same between them. In an almost theatrical vein she had written, "I'll miss the fun and the chats and when you think of me think of the good times. Let's not hurt ourselves anymore than we've been hurt already!" How typical of Marian, melodramatic to the last. She couldn't haver a row like any normal person. No! She had to end the friendship!

"Talk about cutting off your nose to spite your face," said Annie Mary when she heard the latest. "Look, Maggie," she had said firmly, "She's not worth it. Don't waste your time upsetting yourself. I feel sorry for the girl. She's obviously immature, probably the type that never grows up. Forget her!"

Maggie never heard from Marian again. She got over the hurt and sadness, and the irritation at such a needless waste of a friendship, but she never forgot Marian Gilhooley. She threw herself into her studies, came top of her class in her first year and moved into a flat! She had found life in the nurses' home so restrictive that she vowed once first year was finished she was moving out. It might be more expensive, but at least she'd have her independence. God! they were treated like children. Each night, a member of the home staff would open the door to every student's bedroom and check that they were in for the night. Maggie used to sizzle with anger. It was such an invasion of privacy, and it was something she never got used to. The authoritarian regime exercised by hospital management used to have the student nurses fuming. The common room used to be a forum for gripes and discussion.

"For Christ's sake! I'm past the age of consent, I can vote. I know how to act in an emergency. What the hell difference does it make if my tights are the wrong shade? Is the colour of my tights going to affect someone who is in cardiac arrest?" Barbara Reid spat as she told the others how she had been called up in front of the matron for wearing the wrong colour tights with her uniform.

"I think it's something peculiarly Irish," another young nurse said reflectively "My sister works in a library and the wan in charge asked her if she'd obey a direct order if it was given to her. I ask ya? And a queue out the door and this is all that's worrying her! They're obsessed with authority in this country. You're not treated like an adult. Take the divorce referendum. The church orders us to vote no. But for goodness sake, I'm a Catholic, I know I can't have a divorce, but why the hell should I deprive anyone else from having one just because of my beliefs. If you have to be led like sheep it's a poor reflection on the maturity of the individual."

"Here, here," came a rousing chorus.

Maggie grinned at Barbara, "Well, I don't know about you but I'm thirsty. Hey sheep! Anybody like to come for a glass of Guinness?"

Maggie's energy was boundless and after her

hours on the wards she would need only a refreshing shower before she and her friends would hit Dublin's nightlife. Dublin was a joy to her after the sedate pace of life at home which might occasionally be enlivened by the odd little drama such as the time Don Joe O' Mahony's goat had feasted extravagantly on Mary Ellen Flaherty's best pair of bloomers and Mary Ellen had shot him, the goat that is! There had been ructions; it had kept the village going for weeks.

Maggie moved in to a small bedsit at the beginning of her second year. The pleasure of being her own boss was a revelation. How blissful not to have to wash up after her dinner if she didn't feel like it. She would sit looking at her dirty dishes and decide that she was much too tired to wash them this evening. Twenty minutes later she'd be out the door and off to a ballad session in Slattery's pub in Capel Street, her favourite haunt. She thoroughly enjoyed the hot smoky friendly atmosphere where she and her friends would join in singing evocative ballads, tales of Ireland past and present, until they were hoarse and dry-throated. Long draughts of rich creamy Guinness sliding down their throats would restore their vocal chords for the next session. After closing time a ravenous hunger might set in and they would meander over to Baggot Street and devour one of Ishmael's magnificent kebabs, the crisp tasty pitta bread filled to overflowing with a heavenly sauce full of delicious spit-cooked meat. Fortified then for a night of dancing they would hit the nightclubs to bop till the early hours. Maggie lived life to the full, eager to banish the memories of death and illness which were constant reminders to her that life was short and you just had one go at it.

Much as she loved city life, she did not forsake Wicklow entirely. After a hard, draining, exhausting Saturday night on Casualty, Maggie was more than ready for a large dose of tranquillity and some fresh country air. Saturday nights on Casualty were dreaded by all, doctors and nurses alike. The drunks, the drug addicts, the brawlers, the broken-boned, bleeding, puking, roaring and raving would arrive after the pubs closed while Maggie and her colleagues were trying to take care of the real emergencies, the heart attacks, the car crash victims, the distraught bewildered relatives. She had seen it all but she never got used to it.

Once when she had pulled a white sheet over a young man who had died in her arms as a result of a motor bike accident, a petulant crabby little man who had broken his wrist while giving his wife a clout snapped crossly, "D'ya have ta die here before ya get any attention?" as Maggie prepared to ring down to the mortuary.

A red mist danced before her eyes and for the first time in her career she lost her temper. With eyes blazing she turned on him and said in a voice that was even more menacing because of its quietness, "If you don't shut your big mouth, you little gurrier, I'll make sure you die roaring without a priest!" Three hours later, though he was still unattended, there wasn't a peep out of him.

Maggie loved nursing. It wasn't all blood and guts and trauma but it was people like him and times like these that made her ask herself why she hadn't married Joe Conway. Almost two years after she qualified, savage health cuts and the loss of eighty beds in the hospital where she worked caused her to become redundant.

A little unwillingly, because the choice was not hers, she joined the emigration trail and went to New York to nurse. Five of her class had gone and secured jobs easily. Irish nurses were in demand world-wide and although Maggie had decided that she would eventually travel the world, having to do so because of redundancy left her with a bitter taste in her mouth. All the years of training and hard work that she had put in had meant nothing to the politicians, nor had the protest marches to the Dail where thousands of health workers and union members had demonstrated their anger and disgust. Maggie and her friends had still found themselves on the outward-bound Jumbo from Shannon and the sad thing was, they were the lucky ones. They at least had jobs to go to and the green card that was more valuable than gold dust for anyone desiring to work in the States.

eleven

Despite herself, Maggie took to New York as a duck takes to water and she gloried in the frenzied pace of life in the city that never sleeps. She loved the lights and the noise and the traffic. It all made her feel gloriously alive and part of the racing thrusting pulse of the city. There was so much to do and so much to see.

At first she had lived in the nurses' home of the hospital where she worked, and how different life was there from the regimented system she had been used to at home. There was no such thing as signing in and signing out. Nobody shone flashlights into your room to check to see if you were in or out. Boyfriends or girlfriends or relatives were allowed to stay the night—in short, people were treated as mature adults and Maggie's independent spirit thrived on such treatment. It was very much teamwork on the wards. Nurses were treated as equals by the doctors and consultants, and their input was judged to have as much importance as that of the doctor. Life as a nurse in City General was challenging, rewarding—and exhausting. If Maggie thought Saturday nights on Casualty in

Dublin were bad, the tidal wave of trauma that confronted her on her first casualty night in New York was unbelievable. Suicides, potential suicides, drug-crazed, wild-eyed addicts, AIDS sufferers, mugging victims, it was endless. Her abilities were stretched to the limit, but she coped and went to bed the following morning bone weary but exhilarated.

After two months she took a small apartment in a renovated brownstone in the Murray Hill area of East Manhattan, sublet by a nurse who was going to work for a year in California. As studios go in New York it was good. She had a small separate kitchen, separate bathroom, and a postage-stamp dining alcove. She had a view of the East River and the Queens Midtown Tunnel and at night, she would sit in her big cane chair with its huge chintz cushions, drinking a beer and watching the never-ending stream of cars winding into the dark-holed entrance of the tunnel on their way to Queens and the posh suburbs of Long Island. Maggie loved hearing the hoots of the ships' sirens and the hum of the engines of the various river boats that steamed up and down the murky river. The rent was high, but Maggie felt it was worth it to get away from the frenetic environs of the hospital. She had liked the nurses' home but living there meant she was never rid of the hospital. At least now that she had her own apartment, she was able to separate her private and working life, and although she enjoyed her work, she was always mighty glad by the time the day was over, to take the subway, or the bus, or if she was not too tired, to walk to her little studio overlooking the river. It was comfortable, nicely decorated in pastel pinks and blues and, most important, it was air conditioned. It also had its own intercom video system which from the security angle was great, as the amount of crime in New York city was staggering. Maggie didn't see much of the rest of the people in the building. The man across the hall from her kept the oddest hours; he must do shiftwork, she decided. The girl in the flat beside her, Jessica, worked in an advertising agency on Madison Ave and she always said hello.

Before long Maggie got her bearings. It was almost impossible to get lost in Manhattan and once she had the grid system worked out, she was fine. The avenues went north to south, the famous Fifth Avenue was the dividing line between East and West Manhattan and the streets and avenues all bisected at right angles. Besides she wasn't far from the UN building; once she had that in sight she was only a few blocks from home.

She decided she was going to explore every inch of the city. But first of all she must explore her own area. She discovered that just a few blocks away in the UN building you could get free tickets to the General Assembly and could have lunch at certain times in the Delegates Dining Room overlooking the superb gardens and the East River. It was something she treated herself to many times.

Food took on a whole new meaning for Maggie while she lived in New York. And if she hadn't used up so much energy on the wards she would have come back to Ireland a very fat lady indeed. She tried everything: hot dogs, bagels, strawberry cheesecake, egg rolls, duck paté with pistachios, beef sukiyaki, southern fried chicken, pumpkin pie. Each day had a new delight!

East Fifty-ninth street was her point of reference. On her day off, she would leave her apartment, walk the few blocks to East Fifty-ninth and carry on from there. Sometimes she would just walk its length until she got to Central Park, or else she would walk to Third Ave, Lexington, Park or Fifth, take a section and explore, going from the Lower East side to the Upper West, as the mood took her. She loved to ramble along Madison Ave, past the famous Maxim's at Sixty-first, right up to Seventy-second street, and stare at the windows of the exclusive boutiques full of Giorgio Armanis and Valentinos and other exclusive designer clothes that she had only ever read about before. She would observe the wealthy leisurely shoppers strolling up one side and down the other, sometimes followed by chauffeured limos whose interiors bulged with dozens of new purchases.

Once, just outside Saks on Park Ave, she had actually seen Jackie Onassis looking stunningly elegant in a grey Burberry, her eyes hidden behind big dark glasses. Maggie had tried not to stare. She remembered President Kennedy's visit to Ireland, though she had been very young at the time, and could still remember that awful November day when her mother, sobbing, had told her of his death in Dallas. It had been such a shock to see her mother cry that it had frightened Maggie.

"Will the bad man come and shoot us?" She had asked anxiously, her heart beginning to pound.

"Ah no, darling, but say a prayer for the soul of John F Kennedy, and for his poor wife and children," her mother had replied, taking out her rosary beads.

Now as Maggie observed this famous woman in the flesh she remembered as a child how fascinated she had been by the big book about the President's life and death, that they had at home in Wicklow. Often when it was raining, Maggie would sit curled up in the huge armchair in front of a roaring fire, turning the pages slowly with Nedser her little dog snoring quietly at her feet. Now she remembered those days with a little pang of homesickness. She could feel the texture of Nedser's soft fur between her fingers, she could hear the soft gentle pitter-patter of rain beating against the window pane, and smell the rich tangy perfume of the pine logs as they crackled and spat in the flames of the fire. How nice it would be just once more to be a little girl again leafing through the big black book with the pictures of a radiant Jackie as First Lady. There was an immense dignity about her now and Maggie, conscious that she was staring, chided herself for her bad manners.

On Sunday afternoons she would browse with friends around the antique stores in Greenwich Village, soaking up the unique ambience that made it one of the most exciting places in New York. They would sit outside O'Henry's on the corner of West Fourth and the Avenue of the Americas, drinking beer eating baked clams flavoured with garlic and watching the world go by. It was all so new, so exciting, so utterly different from home.

Sandra and Jennifer, two of the group of five that had come to America, had moved on to Los Angeles and they often tried to persuade Maggie to move over to the West Coast, but although she liked to spend a few days there, she preferred New York. LA, despite its more laid back atmosphere, held no attraction for Maggie and the lifestyle seemed almost unreal. And the drug scene was something else. She had been to parties where coke and other drugs were freely available and using them was as common as drinking wine. Sandra, she knew, often snorted coke. Jennifer had told Maggie that all Sandra's salary was going on drugs and Maggie could see for herself how her classmate's personality had changed so radically as a result of her habit. She was taking pills to bring her up and others to bring her down from her highs and sometimes she was so spaced out Maggie found it hard to believe she was holding down a job.

Once out of curiosity at a party in Dublin she had smoked a joint, had turned pale green and promptly puked. From then on she stuck to health foods and Guinness, ignoring the urgings of others to try some "stuff." Maggie had seen too many overdose victims to have any desire to experiment. She thought Sandra was crazy to be getting mixed up in the drug scene and told her so forcefully when she caught her snorting coke one weekend she was visiting LA. She'd also seen the telltale needle marks in her veins which meant she had been shooting up.

"You're crazy, Sandra. Get help before it's too late or you'll ruin your life!" Maggie pleaded with the other girl.

"Stay cool, Maggs, you're such a square, you have no fun," was the other girl's doped response and Maggie felt like hitting her for being so dumb and irresponsible.

Six months later, after a frantic call from Jennifer she ended up flying out to LA where she had to identify Sandra's horrifically emaciated body in the city morgue. Weeping almost uncontrollably, Jennifer told Maggie how the dead girl had been sacked from her job and had ended up on the streets of LA as a hooker, desperate to support her craving for drugs. She had been working for a Puerto Rican pimp who had been feeding her addiction on heroin. Eventually she had overdosed and now lay cold as ice on a slab in the morgue. In the end, it was Maggie who took care of the arrangements for having the body flown home and it was she who spoke to Sandra's distraught parents on the phone and tried to console them. Jennifer had fallen to pieces in the crisis, so Maggie made her take a holiday break, and took her to New York to stay with her for two weeks, until the other girl got over the shock.

It was Maggie, too, who had stayed with Jean, another classmate, when she was suicidally depressed, having had an abortion. Her boyfriend had told her he would leave her if she didn't have the abortion so she went ahead and had it. He left her anyway, unable to cope with her feelings of remorse. Maggie had listened to her outpourings, made her go for counselling and privately wondered how two intelligent girls like Sandra and Jean had made such a mess of their lives. Life wasn't all roses in the Big Apple, she mused. As she headed downtown towards the hospital, tiny beads of moisture ran down her back so that her light cotton teeshirt clung damply to her body.

It was mid-August and the temperatures had soared into the nineties, the muggy heat making people short-tempered and aggressive.

"Make up your mind, lady!" an aggressive street vendor growled at her as she tried to decide whether to buy *Cosmo* or the *National Enquirer*.

"Ah, blow it out your proverbial," she snapped

back, deciding to take her custom elsewhere. She grinned to herself—she'd been dying to use that colloquialism since she'd heard one of the nurses say it at the hospital. And it had certainly taken the wind out of Grumpy's sails. He looked positively insulted. Sticking her purse back in her bag, Maggie decided it was too hot to walk, or even wait for a bus. She dived into a subway entrance and clattered briskly down the steps. She had just reached the bottom when a skinny wild-eyed coloured youth stood in front of her and produced a vicious-looking flick knife. She didn't know that Jose Guerreo had been watching her from the moment she had stopped by the kiosk to buy her magazine and that he had noted with satisfaction the nice thick bulge in her wallet. Blithely unaware that Jose Guerreo was mainlining heroin and needed to score fast to feed his addiction, Maggie came to a breathless halt at the base of the subway steps. The youth almost smirked as he instructed her to hand over her money.

Maggie stood, open-mouthed.

"Come on lady, what's keepin ya, d'ya wanna feel my knife in-ya ribs?" he snarled as Maggie stood stock still in shock. My God! She was actually getting robbed in broad daylight and people were just stepping around them, eyes averted. She had heard of people getting mugged so often, had taken care of victims in hospital and now it was happening to her. She couldn't believe it.

"Gimme the money NOW!" The youth made a threatening gesture with the flick knife.

Anger boiled up in her. He couldn't be more than sixteen or seventeen, the little scut! Grimly she rummaged in her bag and found what she was looking for. In a voice that shook with temper and disgust Maggie brandished a scalpel in her attacker's surprised face.

"Listen! You little hoor's ghost. In case you don't know what this is, let me enlighten you. This," she waved the instrument at him furiously, "is a scalpel...a very sharp scalpel...that's used for cutting off the balls of little pricks like you. So unless you want to become a eunuch I'd advise you to fuck off right NOW!"

She thrust the scalpel in the direction of his most treasured possessions and he gave a yelp of horror. Christo! The dame was a nutcase; maybe she was wired too! Hastily Jose Guerreo rethought his strategy. There were plenty of other dames to be ripped off, he decided, as he sheathed his knife and melted into the crowds, leaving Maggie glaring after him.

It really didn't hit her until she sat in the swaying tube as it trundled its way through the city subway. She started to shake. God Almighty! Was she mad? She had seen people die of stab wounds from being mugged on the street by drug addicts who were so high they didn't know what they were doing. He could have been on crack!

"Christ, what a city!" she muttered aloud, her

limbs trembling with reaction. A middle-aged black woman eyed her warily and moved a little away from her. Maggie felt like laughing hysterically. Life wasn't all fun and excitement in the Big Apple.

twelve

Maggie shivered in the scorching heat of Saudi as she remembered the occasion. Even the memory brought a hard knot in her stomach and she remembered the fear that she had continued to experience months after the incident. At least Saudi was relatively crime-free, she thought, as she shifted her weight on the bed and continued flicking through photos, feeling as though the events of the past were somehow unreal. A small coloured snapshot slipped onto the coverlet and she smiled with pleasure as she held it up and stared at the picture of a pleasant handsome man. She had really cared for Leonard. They'd had such good times together despite their in-auspicious first meeting. Maggie smiled broadly at the memory.

***

It was a Monday morning, her day off. Maggie, feeling a sunbeam tickling her cheek, opened her eyes, stretched luxuriously and jumped out of bed. It was great to have the whole day all to herself. She had long been promising herself a trip to the Guggenheim Museum, the Frank Lloyd Wright-designed building which housed a treasure trove of exhibitions and today she was going to immerse herself in culture. She'd had breakfast, made her bed and showered. Humming gaily to herself she dashed off a letter to home, she'd post it en route to the museum. She decided to give the studio a quick dust before she went out, she'd vacuumed yesterday, and that would be her housework done and she wouldn't have to feel guilty about not doing any. Industriously she sprayed her polish around and shone with a vengeance. The studio was a joy to live in, it was really easy to keep clean. The biggest item of furniture was the old piano in the corner by the window. Maggie flexed her long tanned fingers and grinned to herself. It had been years since she played a piano. Energetically she began.

"Doh, a deer, a female deer," she sang lustily as her fingers inexpertly tickled the ivories. Twenty minutes later she had played her entire childhood repertoire and was about to finish with a crescendo when a figure appeared through her doorway causing her to hit several wrong notes. The apparition winced as though in pain and a deep and very irritated voice rasped, "Would you for heaven's sake cut out that infernal racket. I'm trying to sleep!"

Maggie's temper began to ignite as she stared at the intruder, who now stood, legs planted as though they had taken root in her studio, his arms folded across his chest which was barely covered by the bathrobe he wore. His thick black hair was ruffled as though he had just got up, but it was his eyes that caught her attention.

Blue ice cold prisms stared out of a tanned rugged face, his firmly carved mouth drawn in a tight line of barely suppressed anger.

"How dare you barge in here! How did you get through the door? I have a Chubb lock on it! The nerve of you! Get out right this minute," Maggie ordered. Her tone was pure frost and many a drunk in Casualty had quailed when he met the scorn than now flamed in her expressive eyes. Inwardly, she was cursing herself. She must have left her door unlocked. How could she be so careless.

"I dare," he retorted coldly, "because I am very tired and you are disturbing the peace of this building with your caterwauling. So kindly desist."

"Look here, Mister...?"

"Craigie," he scowled.

"I can't help it if you've been out carousing all night so kindly exit this apartment rapidly or I'll call the police!"

"Will you indeed?" he drawled, giving a huge yawn. "Who the hell are you anyway? Frances never told me she was subletting."

"Does Frances need your permission to let her own apartment?" Maggie snapped indignantly, outraged at his arrogance. Just who did he think he was talking to? Some little schoolgirl?

"We had an agreement. I have a key to her apartment, she has a key to mine and we look after each other's when we're away," the tall man informed her.

"Is that so? Well, Frances left quicker than she had planned, and I don't think you were around so that's just tough!" Maggie said crisply and pointed to the door. "Leave..."

Angry blue eyes ringed by long black lashes met equally angry green ones. "It will be a pleasure," he fumed, "but if I hear any more of that rumpus I will personally dismantle that piano."

"If I want to practise, neither you nor anyone else will stop me!" she replied, seething.

"Just try me!" he challenged.

"Do you realise that I'm attending classes and I was doing some extremely difficult finger exercises," Maggie lied through her teeth, determined not to back down in face of the sheer effrontery of his behaviour. "I suggest you insert some earplugs if you can't sleep," she advised him coolly. "I mean it's ten on a Monday morning. It's not as if it were the middle of the night!" What an autocrat! Well, he just wasn't getting away with it.

"Did you say classes?"

"Correct," she answered primly.

His jaw sagged. "Oh God! I'm having a nightmare," he muttered.

They stared at each other and Maggie became aware, as heavy-lidded blue eyes slid over her negligée-covered figure, that she was not dressed. Pink coloured her cheeks as she also became aware of the way she was staring at the dark tangle of hair on his chest revealed by his partly open bathrobe and on a level with her eyes. Memories of Joe flooded back. It had been a long time...

Yawning once more the man turned on his heel and strode towards the door. "I suggest if you are going to 'practise'," the tone was heavily sarcastic, "that you at least close the windows and have some consideration for the rest of your neighbours. And lady..." he glared at her, "I don't carouse."

Sizzling with temper Maggie watched him march across the hall to his own apartment, then, slamming her apartment door, she Chubb-locked it and returned to the piano. Her fingers hovered over the piano keys. No bossy New Yorker was going to tell her what she could and could not do in her own apartment. Defiantly she played "The Last Rose of Summer," the only song she could remember properly, before lowering the lid over the keyboard.

"That might teach him," she muttered as she dressed to go culture-seeking.

She didn't see him again. She toyed with the idea of asking him for his key. But obviously Frances trusted him implicitly and so she didn't bother. She continued out of stubbornness to play inexpertly on the piano when the mood took her but she prudently kept the windows shut and didn't play quite so loudly. If he hadn't been so rude she would have ceased her musical experimentation, but Maggie just could not back down in the face of his impudence.

As they chatted during tea break at work one morning, Sally, one of her colleagues grinned, "I see 'Luscious Leonard' is operating this morning. Just wait until you see him, Maggie. He's divine! Paradise on legs! And he's divorced...da..da..."

Maggie laughed. Sally tended to exaggerate about men. Maggie was doing a three-month stint in theatre nursing so she would see the paragon Sally was referring to. The morning was busy. They had a full list but everything ran smoothly. Maggie had a niggling pain in her right side which she tried to ignore. It had become increasingly troublesome over the previous few days and she thought ruefully that she had better get it seen to.

"Luscious Leonard" was delayed by an emergency in another theatre and so when he did arrive, scrubbed and gowned, Maggie could only see a pair of piercing blue eyes over his mask, and a rather large physique. Her own eyes, all that could be seen of her face behind her mask, studied him as he operated calmly, his fingers sure and deft. Professionally, she anticipated every move of the routine operation and handed him each surgical instrument before he had to ask.

"Excellent work. Thank you," he complimented her when it was over. And Maggie smiled behind her mask. The surgeons in New York always thanked the nurses for their input. At home some of them treated nurses as though they were second class citizens!

The surgeon's blue eyes were staring down at hers, faintly perplexed. There was something vaguely familiar about the deep voice beneath the mask and Maggie almost gasped in horror as he untied it and she saw her "carousing" neighbour full face. No wonder he had been mad. He had probably been up all night at an emergency. Before she could say anything an excruciating pain caused her to crumple up at his feet. Perplexity was replaced by concern in his blue eyes as he leaned over her and removed her mask, assisted by a horrified Sally.

"Good Lord!" she heard him say softly as gentle fingers pressed on her abdomen. White-faced, Maggie gasped as pain hit her again and then she passed out.

A pair of twinkling blue eyes were the first things she focused on when she came to, feeling as though she had been run over by a truck.

"The nurse will give you an injection for the pain," "Luscious Leonard" informed her smiling-ly. "I've removed your appendix, which ruptured in theatre. But..." his eyes crinkled disarmingly as he leaned nearer and murmured, "You'll be glad to know that I've left all your fingers intact. It won't be long until you are playing the piano again."

In spite of herself, and her discomfort, Maggie grinned. At least he had a sense of humour, she thought, as she drifted back to sleep. He arrived on his rounds the following morning and she found herself rather mortified. After all he had been poking around her insides, he'd seen *everything*. Sensing her embarrassment he said easily. "So, Sister MacNamara, did you sleep well? I'm finding it rather difficult to sleep myself. You see I have this neighbour who used to lull me to sleep with her piano playing..."

Their eyes met and they both burst out laughing, to the surprise of Sally, who had popped in to see how Maggie was.

"Get well soon," he said and she watched him go, smiling.

"What was all that about?" her friend demanded. "I've never seen anything so blatant, Maggie MacNamara. Falling at that hunk's feet with appendicitis. I've been trying to get him to notice me for the past six months. Why didn't I pull a stunt like that?"

Maggie laughed and grimaced. "Ouch that hurt! Oh Sally, it's embarrassing...him of all people." She proceeded to tell her friend about her previous encounter with the surgeon.

"You mean he lives across the hall from you!! Trust you to have the luck. Of course Murray Hill is crawling with people from City General. I'll have to move over from The Village." Sally shared a mews in Greenwich Village with four other nurses. "I don't know if he's dating anyone,

I'm sure he is. He got divorced last year, according to the grapevine, but he keeps a low profile."

Maggie yawned and snuggled down into her pillows. "Go back to work, you idle gossip, and let me go asleep. I'm recuperating from surgery, I'll have you know!" Laughing, Sally left her to snooze.

Two days later, he came to visit again.

"Hello, Sister MacNamara," he said pleasantly.

"Hello, Doctor Craigie," Maggie responded a little warily. Watching him as he read her chart she reflected that he really was a good-looking man. She grinned as she remembered Sally's description of him, "paradise on legs."

"You seem to be coming along fine," he remarked and his face creased into a smile as he added disarmingly, "Of course, you were lucky that you just happened to have been operated on by the finest surgeon in New York City."

Maggie laughed. "Modest as well, I see."

"I'm glad you think so. It's one of my most noticeable attributes," he grinned wickedly, "that and my ear for music!"

"I never imagined I lived next door to such a paragon," Maggie grinned back. She was beginning to like him more and more.

"I bet you didn't and aren't you lucky it's such a small world," Leonard said, taking two letters out of his suit pocket and handing them to her.

"I checked your mail box. If you like I'll check

the apartment, I used to do it for Frances when she was away, but I'd prefer to ask you first, I wouldn't wish to invade your privacy." He cleared his throat. "I must apologise for bursting in the other day. I did ring the bell but you couldn't hear. I didn't know Frances was gone. I was in Washington for a while and I didn't realise she had left. I got a letter from her yesterday telling me all about her new job and about subletting to you. I must confess, a quick temper is also one of my attributes—as you discovered!" He held out his hand. "Am I forgiven?

Maggie took his outstretched hand and gave him a firm handshake. "Of course you are. I shouldn't have inflicted my...er...amateurish attempts at piano-playing on you. And I'm sorry you didn't know Frances had sublet to me, but she did have to go in rather a rush. And I'd be delighted if you would check up on the apartment for me," she paused, "oh and, by the way, the name is Maggie.

"How do you do, Maggie?" he said, still holding her hand. "I'm Leonard and I'm very glad to know you." He smiled and continued teasingly, "you had the most charming appendix I've ever seen."

"It was one of my most attractive attributes," she teased back.

They smiled at each other. And Maggie wondered why any woman would divorce some-one who seemed as nice as him. Maybe he was a street angel and a house devil.

"See you at the end of the week," he said as Sally arrived for a quick visit.

"OK, bye," Maggie answered, wishing that Sally had delayed her entrance by a few minutes.

"What a dish!" Sally drooled.

"Hmm," murmured Maggie, non-committally. But she was looking forward to his next visit.

On her last day in the hospital he arrived as promised. "My bill," he said suavely, handing her an envelope.

"Oh yes, of course!" Maggie was a bit taken aback. He wasn't wasting much time about getting his money.

"Well, open it and see if it's too much," he suggested.

"I'm sure it isn't," she murmured.

"Just to please me," he urged, his eyes twinkling.

She opened the envelope and two tickets fell into her lap.

"As you are a pianist yourself, I thought you might enjoy going to a Richard Clayderman concert and of course as your attending physician I shall have to accompany you in case it becomes necessary for me to save your life again," he informed her gravely. "And then, after dinner for two I expect you'll want to do some of your finger exercises." He grinned broadly. "I'm sure I'll enjoy listening to them now that I know what they are. They do have their own rare charm."

Maggie grinned back at him. And so do you, Doctor Leonard Craigie, she thought happily.

If she had enjoyed life in New York before she met Leonard, she enjoyed it twice as much after they became friends and eventually lovers. Leonard took her here, there and everywhere. They went to concerts, exhibitions, they took boat trips on the river, they visited the Bronx Zoo and Long Island. Here she saw the famous Hamptons, elegant suburbs where the moneyed people lived, full of exclusive restaurants where Maggie indulged her love of food to the limit. They had a wonderful time. He took her sailing in Martha's Vineyard at the weekends. Whenever they could both get a free weekend together they would leave the city and make for the beautiful countryside that surrounded New York. She saw Connecticut in the fall. Its display of multi-coloured autumn leaves like a woven tapestry left her speechless. They went skiing in Vermont and rented a log cabin where they spent a romantic weekend together skiing by day, sitting in front of a roaring log fire by night, exchanging confidences and getting to know each other even better.

Leonard told her that he was divorced and his wife had custody of their two children although he had unlimited access and took them for holiday periods. His wife Anya was an ambitious lawyer who worked for a prestigious New York legal firm. She had worked hard for her position but their marriage had suffered. Of their nature his working hours were unsociable and it had been a bone of contention in the marriage that Leonard would not go into private medicine where the money and status was. He preferred working with his public patients, he had several clinic in the various public hospitals and although he earned a generous salary he could have earned five times the amount if he practised privately on Park Avenue. And of course there was no status whatsoever in ministering to the lowly paid of New York City. Eventually Anya had had an affair with the vice-chairman of her company. Leonard had found out about it from a "well meaning" friend of his wife's who was attracted to him. His wife had informed him that she was going upstate to a seminar on company law and of course he believed her. The nanny was taking care of their two little girls and he had arranged to take a day off to be with them. Instead he had gone to the address given to him by the woman and found his wife and her lover in bed.

Disgusted, betrayed, Leonard had given the company vice-chairman a bloody nose, his wife her walking papers, and returned home and contacted his lawyer to begin divorce proceedings. A very honest and direct man, he could not cope with his wife's infidelity and the relationship had been damaged beyond repair. They had agreed, however, that it was better that the children remain with their mother, although it was clear to Maggie that they were the light of Leonard's life. He had moved out of their comfortable Queens home and taken a three-roomed apartment in the house where Maggie lived. He was rarely there, having thrown himself into his work in an effort to get over the trauma of the divorce. It was only since he met Maggie, he told her, that he started to enjoy his leisure time time again.

Maggie found him to be a sensitive, caring man with a wicked sense of humour. She could see how private practice on Park Avenue would hold no attraction for him. Leonard was a born doctor. His patients loved him and he loved his work. Money was not the be-all and end-all of his life. She found herself becoming more and more attracted to him and in her direct and open way welcomed his growing desire for her. They became lovers and the relationship that they shared was the happiest, most trusting one she would ever know. Leaving Leonard and New York had caused her immense unhappiness and even now four years later her mouth tightened at the memory of the letter she found waiting for her one beautiful October day as she arrived at her apartment, red-cheeked from the malicious little autumn wind that was blowing up the East River. She had been on night duty nursing an AIDS patient, a young man of twenty-four who was dying slowly and painfully. Mentally and physically exhausted, she had taken breakfast in the hospital cafeteria with Leonard, who had several operations to perform. Seeing her exhaustion he had told her to go home to bed.

"Good idea," she agreed. There was nothing else in the world that she wanted more than to tumble into her warm welcoming bed. She had pre-set her electric blanket and in weary anticipation of the cosy warmth that was waiting to envelop her aching body she ran up the steps of the brownstone. There was a letter from home in her mailbox and she smiled happily.

Maggie loved getting letters from home. Sometimes she would stick her nose in the envelope and assure herself that she was inhaling good rich healthy Wicklow air. The last time she had been home for a visit was Christmas of the previous year and there were times she really missed her family. She noted with surprise that it was her father's writing on the envelope, and her fingers, cold from the wind, were a little clumsy as she opened the seal.

Strange, she thought. Usually it was her mother who wrote while her father would add a postscript. As she read the contents a myriad emotions assailed her. Guilt. Anger. Frustration. And a bitterness that was completely alien to her nature. Twice, three times, she read the letter in which her father asked her to come home and nurse her mother, who was going to have a hysterectomy. It was not that she minded so much; it was the way her obligations were pointed out to her that hurt.

Her father reminded her that she had never

wanted for anything. That he had supplemented her income generously during her nursing training even though they had been bitterly disappointed when she had refused to marry Joe Conway. As her father had put it, for the last four years she had been off gallivanting in the States. Surely she must feel it was time to come home and settle down? Himself and her mother were getting on and they might need her to take care of them. She should have married Joe Conway when she had the chance and not be messing around with some divorced joker in New York.

Maggie fumed. It was incredible. They still hadn't forgiven her for not marrying Joe. To have married into the wealthy land-owning Conway family would have conferred a kind of prestige on her family. People would have pointed her mother out as she shopped in the village, or outside Mass on Sunday.

"That's Nelsie MacNamara now. Her only daughter Maggie is married to Joe Conway! She did well for herself didn't she now?"

"By gor of heaven didn't she just. They won't be short of a penny!"

Her mother would have loved it! Only a son entering the priesthood could equal the importance of marrying a Conway in the village. And Maggie had deprived her parents of their moment of glory and just taken off to Dublin to nurse without as much as a by-your-leave.

"Ah shit! It's not fair," she muttered, flinging the letter away from her. Why did her parents feel they owned her? God knows she had sent home money every month, and clothes and sheets and things. She was a good daughter! Some of the girls she worked with never contacted their parents from one Christmas to the next. Why did they have to make her feel so guilty? Maggie wondered wryly if her father had written to her younger brother Patrick, who was training as a chef in Switzerland, to come home and cook for their mother. She doubted it. Always it had been Maggie who had to make the sacrifices. The boys were treated like little Gods.

"Get up and make Patrick his tea, Maggie!" or "Maggie run down to the village," which was a mile and a half away, "and get a nice few rashers for Tony; he doesn't like fish."

If she was watching something on TV and the boys wanted to watch sport the channel was changed without a thought. Oh yes indeed! The notion of equality among the sexes was a very foreign concept to many Irish men even in the Eighties and in many cases it was because of the way the mothers had raised their darling sons. Women were their own worst enemies. Had Maggie been a son, that letter would never have been written!

Unable to sleep after several futile hours of tossing and turning, Maggie dressed in jeans and a thick chunky jumper. Throwing on her parka she went walking. It was a lovely fresh autumn day. The air was crisp and sharp, the sky a deep cobalt blue unmarred by smog. Rambling through Central Park, ankle deep in crunchy red gold leaves, she sighed deeply. To think that this eight hundred and fifty acres of park, carved out of the vast concrete jungle that surrounded her, was the only countryside that many New Yorkers had ever known. At home too the leaves in her native forests would be turning to rust and catching the breeze fluttering here and there. All along she had intended returning home if an opportunity arose that suited her. But she had wanted to go back when she was ready. Not like this! Not when she was enjoying her life so much.

Dodging skateboard riders and joggers and Walkman-deafened students and ghetto-blasting youths, Maggie walked on, trying to think of a solution. There was none! If she didn't return home to look after her mother she would never be forgiven. No use in pointing out that millions of women survive hysterectomy without requiring someone to give them twenty-four-hour attention. She was a daughter who was a nurse and her father saw it as her duty to give up her job and her independent life to come home and nurse her mother for at least six months after the surgery. Maggie would willingly have taken leave and gone home for six months, but she knew this would be unacceptable to her parents. Frances had stayed in California and Maggie had continued living in her studio, but Frances might not like the idea of the apartment being empty for six months and besides there was no possibility that Maggie could afford to continue paying the rent if she wasn't working. She'd just have to go home and that was it.

At home the neighbours would say, "Isn't she the grand girl? Nelsie, you're lucky to have such a devoted daughter." And her mother would lap it up delightedly.

Oh she'd have to go...she knew, because if she didn't, grown mature woman that she was, she'd feel guilty to her dying day. Defeated, Maggie thrust her hands deep into her pockets and headed towards the nearest hot chestnut vendor. It might be her last chance to indulge. There was no such thing as hot chestnut sellers at home...

***

Within three weeks she was seated in a huge green and silver Aer Lingus Jumbo, winging her way across the Atlantic to home. Leonard had been stunned by her decision.

"Can't you go for six months and come back? You can always move in with me." He smiled at her. "I've got used to having you around, I guess."

"Me too," Maggie said. She knew that Leonard, scarred by his first marriage, was not anxious to marry again. He had been quite straight about it and she was under no illusions about their relationship. Maggie would have been happy to marry him; she loved and cared for him deeply but realised that financially and emotionally Leonard was a long way from remarriage. It was this realisation that helped her part from him less painfully than if there was total commitment on his part. Maggie was nothing if not a realist. Although when they parted at the airport she had buried her face in his coat and cried like a baby.

"I love you," she whispered.

"I love you too, Maggie. I'll never find a woman like you again. Think about coming back."

"We'll see," she told him, but somehow she knew that she'd never go back to New York. Later she would think it had all been fate because it was on that transatlantic flight that she met Terry Ryan, the man who would woo and wed her.

thirteen

In the heat of her non-air-conditioned apartment, Maggie looked at the wide gold wedding
band that circled her finger. Terry had courted
her with a persistence that had taken her breath
away. Sitting up on the crumpled bed, she leaned
across to her bedside locker on which reposed a
photograph of her husband. She traced the
outline of his handsome face, her finger lingering
on the heavy-lashed black eyes which he used
with such effect when chatting up women. She
had often seen him in action at a party. He would
corner the most beautiful woman in the room, his
eyes would work overtime, his head bent
attentively to catch what was being said to him
as if no one else existed in the room except the
pair of them.

Maggie had become used to it. She never
lacked attention herself and sometimes while he
was chatting up the women he would wink boyishly at her and she would laugh. He was very
lovable really. It was his brash boyish optimism
that had attracted her in the beginning as she sat
next to him on the plane, depressed and lonely at
leaving New York.

"You don't seem very happy to be returning to the ould sod," he remarked cheerfully as they fastened their seat belts for take off. Maggie's heart sank. Just her luck to be seated beside a chatterbox when all she wanted to do was to nurse her broken heart and feel sorry for herself. She ignored the comment, hoping that he would take the hint. No such luck!

"The name's Terry Ryan," the irritating personage said, holding out a hand.

"Maggie MacNamara," she replied, unenthusiastically returning the handclasp.

"Aren't you looking forward to going home?" he asked curiously.

Maggie glared at him. "Frankly no!"

Terry laughed. "Well I can tell you one thing, Maggie MacNamara. I can't wait to murder a pint of Guinness in Mulligans. They serve the best pint in the world."

Despite herself Maggie laughed and by the time he had finished telling her how he was looking forward to a feast of bacon and cabbage and home-made brown bread and a decent cup of tea, her own mouth was watering and the future didn't seem quite so gloomy. She listened to him as he told her that he had just spent three years as a broker in New York and how he wanted to set up as a tax and investment consultant in Dublin.

"There's plenty of rich boyos there looking for tax havens and ways of investing their goodies and I'm the one who'll show 'em," he proclaimed.

Terry thought she was mad to give up her career in the States to go home and nurse her mother. "Couldn't your Da hire a nurse?" he asked incredulously, not believing she could leave so much behind her and go home to nothing. He told her that he came from an impoverished family from the west of Ireland where he had worked all hours of the day and night to put himself through University in Galway. There he had taken an honours degree in Commerce and then gone to Dublin to continue his studies. He had firmly and unemotionally put his past behind him and he told Maggie that he rarely went home. She guessed that despite his brash self-confident ways he would never quite erase the memory of his childhood poverty and that it would be those memories that would spur him on in his career.

They talked about everything on that long journey home as others slumbered around them in the dimly-lit cabin of the 747. When they landed, stiff and red-eyed in Dublin at breakfast time, he helped her with her luggage and as they were waiting to clear customs he asked if he could see her again.

Maggie laughed, telling him that her home was nearly fifty miles from Dublin. He had taken her address and phone number nevertheless. She hadn't really expected to hear from him again, and she wasn't too pushed, her mind still full of thoughts of Leonard. They had got separated as the other passengers, anxious to see loved ones, poured out of the passageway to the arrivals hall, and as Maggie was greeted by her father she caught her last glimpse of her travelling companion with his arm around a stunning blonde. Smiling wryly, she thought: men! they're all the same!

***

After a month in Wicklow it seemed to Maggie that she had never been away from home. Her mother had her womb removed and came home from hospital to languish in bed despite her doctor telling her she would be flying around and feeling much better after a few weeks.

"By gor of heaven!" she declared, "But that doctor had the impudence to tell me I'd be flying around an' me after havin half me insides removed. Them young fellas are just in it for the money, Maggie! If only Doctor Roche were still alive. He'd know how to treat me."

Maggie sent a brief prayer of thanks heavenwards that Doctor Roche had gone to a better life because if he had been there to treat her mother, Nelsie would still be in bed this day next year. Doctor Roche had been God's gift to the hypochondriac and Nelsie MacNamara and half the women of the parish had loudly mourned his passing.

"You know," her mother continued mournfully, "I can't take to that Doctor Lyne at all. Do you know what he had the nerve to say to me one day when I went to visit him?"

"What?" said Maggie, trying to suppress a smile. She knew Doctor Lyne, a lively no-nonsense man with an outrageous sense of humour which often had her in kinks of laughter but which sometimes passed over the permed heads of his more staid patients.

Nelsie's nostrils flared at the memory and her mouth tightened. "Well, I went in and told him about all my complaints." God help him, thought her daughter unsympathetically. "And do you know what that...upstart...said to me?" Maggie bit her lip. She could just imagine Frank Lyne listening to her mother's litany. "He gave me a cheeky grin and asked me did I ever think of being put down!" Maggie guffawed. She couldn't help it.

"Maggie!" Her mother was outraged. A sense of humour was not Nelsie's greatest characteristic. "Well really, Maggie! I'm surprised at you. And you being a nurse! Do you know that fella doesn't even wear a white coat. He's no more like a doctor than the man in the moon and if you are going to sit laughing at me I'll thank you to leave me alone." The older woman gave a huffy sniff.

"Ah Ma, don't be so cranky. Lie down there now for a while and I'll bring you a nice cup of tea," her daughter said briskly.

And so it went on. Old routines were resumed and life itself became one long routine. Up early to make breakfast for her father and Tony before they went off to do the milking. Then her mother's breakfast had to be prepared. Maggie's mother was perfect martyr material. Nothing was ever said directly, just hinted at obliquely. It seemed to Maggie that she could do nothing right.

"That's not the way I do it but you do it your own way," or, "Don't mind me sitting here after me operation, go off and enjoy yourself." This came usually on a Saturday night when, after a hard week's grind, Maggie would borrow the old runabout and drive up to Dublin to stay with friends. She would grit her teeth and fume all the way to Dublin. Was her mother blind? Did she not see her doing the washing and ironing, the cleaning, the cooking! Three big meals a day for men hungry from working outdoors. By nine at night she was more wrecked than she would have been after doing a double shift at City General.

One evening, just after tea, there was a phone call for her. Now who was that, she wondered? Annie Mary, with whom she had resumed contact, had rung earlier in the day to make arrangements for the weekend and she wasn't expecting anyone else.

"Hello?"

"Hello, Maggie MacNamara. It's Terry Ryan. I'm ringing from Fagin's Pub. If you've nothing better to do how would you like to join me for a drink?"

"From Fagin's in the village?" Maggie's eyes widened with surprise.

"That's right. If you give me directions I'll collect you if you like, or else I'll wait for you here. The Guinness is pretty good."

Maggie laughed. "Stay where you are, I'll see you in ten minutes." She ran up to her bedroom, brushed her hair, washed her face, changed her dress, and put on a bit of lipstick. Imagine Terry Ryan ringing her from Fagin's. She'd forgotten all about him. Her spirits lifted and she found herself looking forward to seeing him again. Although Leonard wrote and phoned telling her that he missed her and giving her all the news from City General, Maggie knew that she would not be returning to New York. It was time to move on. Once she had taken care of her mother she would resume her career and her independent lifestyle. Meanwhile, she was going out for a jar in Fagin's and she was looking forward to it.

She'd forgotten how good-looking Terry was, and how attractive his black twinkling eyes that were now smiling appreciatively into her own.

"Well, you're a sight for sore eyes," he greeted her. "Excuse me for not getting in touch before now like I said I would, but I was no sooner back than I had to go to London on business and I haven't had a minute to myself."

"Don't worry about it," she smiled. "I was so busy myself I never gave it a thought."

Terry's face fell in mock dismay. "You mean you weren't pining by the telephone. What a shock for my ego!"

Maggie laughed "I'm sure your ego is well

massaged if your reception at the airport is anything to go by."

Terry laughed. "That's what I like about you, Maggie. You're a straight talking woman. Now, where's the best place hereabouts to go for dinner?"

He took her to dinner in Arklow and she enjoyed his company immensely. It had been so good to get out and do something out of the ordinary that she had readily agreed to his suggestion that they meet again. She began to look forward to their dates, which took her out of the monotony of her domestic lifestyle. Terry provided an ear to listen to her moans and usually after being with him for ten minutes she was laughing and light-hearted, ready and eager for fun. And fun they had. Terry knew how to give a girl a good time. He wined her, dined her and she never knew where he was going to bring her. It was always a surprise. Although he could and did act the successful young businessman around town there was a boyishness about Terry that Maggie loved. They didn't go in much for the sophisticated night club scene. Instead, he would bring her to the Zoo or sometimes they would go out to Greystones where they would fish from the beach, Terry yelling at her when she got the lines all tangled up in knots while all she did was laugh. At Christmas he took her to Funderland and Maggie felt like a child again. They went on all the rides and swings, gasping in delight as they sat on top of the big wheel and saw the lights of Dublin sparkling in the velvet night beneath them. Screeching with laughter, they shot down the big curving slide together and for a while she felt carefree and happy with no worries or cares to burden her.

Terry had that effect on her. He had a knack of making everything seem like a big adventure and he made her return to Ireland much more bearable. Maggie knew that he fancied her like crazy and she was flattered. She had told him all about Leonard, and said that she wasn't sure she was ready for another relationship but he brushed aside her excuses.

"I'll make you forget that boyo," Terry assured her and Maggie had to laugh at him.

There was an openness of spirit, a naturalness and honesty about Maggie that men adored, and Terry was no exception. She didn't place men on pedestals. They were human and fallible as she was and she never held high or false expectations having seen and experienced so much of human nature, especially during her years of nursing. Watching Terry with other women she knew that he was no Leonard. Fidelity would not come easy to Terry. She knew he saw other girls when she was stuck deep in the country but somehow, when he was with her at the weekend, she could push it all to the back of her mind and enjoy her time with him.

Three months into their relationship they started to sleep together and the long lustful nights she spent with him seemed to recharge her for the week of dreary ordinariness that left her limp and drained and ready to scream with boredom. She felt so smothered after her life in New York. Even her love of nature seemed to be failing her and the long punishing walks she took with her dog could not comfort her as they once did.

One day she was striding along, swinging an old bit of a bush she had found by the side of the road. It was early summer. Everything was fresh, the hedgerows and trees growing more voluptuously green each day. Passing a field of blazing yellow rape Maggie paused to gaze at it. A light breeze ruffled the crop and it looked like a rippling golden lake surrounded by fields of emerald green. There she stayed for a long time trying to quieten her restless spirit. Then her dog became impatient and with a deep sigh Maggie resumed her walk, her legs long and tanned in her denim shorts, her burnished copper hair blowing behind her in the breeze. A car drove past, stopped and reversed.

Maggie had almost gasped aloud in disbelief as she recognised the man who got out of the car. In the years that had passed since she had last seen him, Joe Conway had become gross and florid. His eyes were red and bloodshot and although it was only mid-morning she could get the whiff of whiskey off his breath. Maggie was horrified when he took her in his arms and tried to kiss her. She recoiled sharply and told him to remember that he was married. In truth she pitied the unfortunate girl who was his wife. Maggie had seen enough of drink-related problems and heard enough gossip to know that Joe was an alcoholic.

He had been furious at her rejection of him. "You stuck up whore!" he roared after her as he staggered back to the car. "You think you're great don't ya? You always thought you were better than us, even though yer Dad's only a penny halfpenny farmer. You're a big headed bitch!"

Watching the car weave its way down the road Maggie felt unutterably sad at what had become of her former lover. He'd had everything going for him and it looked as if he was letting it slip through his fingers. Who would have foreseen that Joe Conway, the catch of the county, would end up like this. The encounter disturbed her, made her think and assess her own life. Where was she going? What was she doing? She had paid her dues, she told herself firmly. It was time to take up the reins of her own life and get moving.

fourteen

Two months later, six months after her return to
Ireland, with her mother well on the road to
recovery, Maggie gently but firmly told the
family that she was going back to nursing in
Dublin. Her father could well afford to get a
woman in to help for a couple of hours a day and
her mother was a fine healthy woman. She told
them that she would visit them often but it was
time for her to start working again. They had
protested but Maggie was determined. Despite
the health cutbacks, she had been lucky to
secure a good job in her old training hospital and
it seemed as though her years in New York and
her time at home were all a dream.

She found a nice flat in Sandymount and
settled back to life in Dublin and it was during
this period of her life that she made friends with
Devlin and Caroline, friendships that would
endure with women whose lives would
intertwine with hers in the future. She remembered so well the night they were moving
into the flat below her. Maggie had lived in the
house for about three months and the elderly
woman in the flat below her was a real dipso-

maniac. Maggie had once come in from hanging out clothes on the line to find her swigging the Bacardi Terry had brought her on his last trip to London. From then on she never left her door unlocked. For a while Mrs Ford would be fine and when she was sober she was an elegant cultured lady. But when she went on one of her batters she became slovenly and foul mouthed. She had a family, two sons and a daughter, and once, after a particularly bad binge, she had knocked herself out by falling against the fridge. Hearing the thud, Maggie had gone to investigate and found the poor woman unconscious, a lump as big as a golf ball rising on her forehead. She got her in to hospital, informed the eldest son of what had occurred and the following evening the son called on Maggie to say that the family were putting the mother in a nursing home and that the landlord would be letting the flat again. Maggie had been on tenterhooks wondering who would arrive next. After her experiences with Mrs Ford she was quite wary.

She returned home from work to find a friendly blonde girl and a quiet brown-eyed girl struggling through the front door with an assorted array of black plastic sacks full of all their bits and pieces. The blonde girl was cursing beneath her breath as the bottom fell out of one of the sacks and half a dozen saucepans, and a frying pan and kettle spilled out on to the floor. The brown-eyed girl, catching Maggie's amused eye, had taken a fit of the giggles at the expression on her friend's face and eventually they all ended up laughing. Maggie had offered to help them carry in their stuff and had introduced herself, delighted that they were the two girls who were moving in underneath her.

Devlin and Caroline were their names and by the time she had helped them move in and brought them upstairs to her own flat for a cup of tea she knew that they were all going to get along fine.

And get along fine they did. The extrovert Devlin and the shy Caroline took to Maggie as she took to them. This was their first attempt at living away from home, their first flat, apart from a disastrous place where they had stayed for a few weeks in Rathmines. And soon it seemed that they had known each other for years. Maggie, being older, was the one they turned to for advice, which she always gave readily, and for the first time since Marian Gilhooly she enjoyed a sense of comradeship with the girls, as they became friends and began to share each other's lives.

Her relationship with Terry developed and deepened too. He had such great enthusiasm for life and living that he often carried her away on a tide of ebullient daydreams. He asked her to marry him. When she reflected on it later on, she sometimes felt that it was his dreams of travel and adventure and making a fortune in a foreign land that influenced her to accept. He wanted to work in Saudi and being a wanderer at heart,

like him, she thought it seemed like the perfect
match. As well as which, she thought philosophically, she was heading for the big Three O
and her biological clock was ticking slowly but
surely away. It was time she thought of making
a commitment. She had sowed her wild oats and
enjoyed every moment of it, had no apologies or
regrets, but marriage would be a new phase in
her life, a turning point.

Maggie was excited about her wedding.
Between them Terry and she had many friends
and they had hired a bus to bring them all down
from Dublin to the farm in Wicklow. In a little
country church with rainbow-coloured sun-
beams dancing through the stained-glass
windows, the altar wreathed in honeysuckle and
hibiscus, they had plighted their troth, surrounded by families and friends.

Far away in hot dusty Saudi Arabia, Maggie
smiled as she remembered. After the ceremony
they had gone back to the big white and pink
marquee that had been erected in one of the
luscious green meadows near the house. They
had served a buffet and her mouth watered as
she remembered the huge hams baked in honey
and decorated with cloves, the turkey, duck, and
pheasant slices laid out on big platters, the
loaves of fresh homemade bread, the dozens of
different salads. The tables had been covered
with crisp snowy white tablecloths and decorated with sprays of dusky pink roses that grew in
wild profusion on the farm. The weather had

been kind and it had been a happy carefree day which even her mother's little protestations of exhaustion did not spoil. Leonard had sent a telegram wishing her joy and happiness and a gift of the finest table-linen. Maggie was delighted at the genuine good wishes of her old lover. Terry and she had spent their honeymoon in a tiny whitewashed villa in Rhodes before flying out to Saudi to start their new life.

Maggie had been very happy the first year of their married life. Both of them were working. Life with the other Europeans and Americans seemed to be one big round of parties and barbecues. She had learned how to scuba dive and spent many happy hours exploring the warm underwater attractions of the reefs in the Gulf. Then she had got pregnant. Her husband had blamed her entirely for the pregnancy, which made Maggie sizzle with rage. He never wanted to be worried about contraception, leaving all the worrying to her. He hated using condoms, preferring Maggie to take the pill. And of course, she had forgotten to take it one night. They'd been at a party where some delightful illicit alcohol had flowed freely and by the time she got home, the pill was the last thing on her mind as she eagerly returned her husband's passionate kisses. They had made love and fallen asleep and it was only the following night that Maggie realised what had happened. Unfortunately the damage was done, and Maggie was well and truly pregnant. They had got over the shock but Maggie found it hard to forgive her husband's attitude when he found out that she was so unexpectedly pregnant.

She was having such a difficult pregnancy too. She'd hated having to give up work but she had to because of the constant nausea and sickness. Even after the usual three months the sickness had not abated, much to her dismay, and as well as feeling miserable she found the days long and soul-destroyingly boring. The servants wouldn't allow her to lift a finger and indeed would become quite annoyed should she even attempt to tidy up.

She was a stranger in her own kitchen. Mehemed, the cook, would shoo her from the room with much lamentation and eye rolling should she even try to make herself tea and toast. Needless to say Terry loved it all. He couldn't get enough of it, the pampering, the fussing. Maggie wondered how he would adjust to life without servants when they finally decided to return home. One thing was sure: she was certainly not going to treat him like a lord. Domestic duties would be shared, she had told him jokingly on several occasions, but somehow she didn't feel that he was taking her seriously.

Hunger gnawed at her stomach. Maggie sat straight up on the bed. Dammit! I'm going to make an omelette, she told herself firmly. Throwing on a loose cotton wrap she marched into the kitchen, all cool white tiles. Under the eagle eye of her cook, the house boy was polishing the huge copper pots and pans so that they gleamed spotless. Ignoring the hurt soulful cocker-spaniel eyes of Mehemed she proceeded to cook for herself a delicious savoury omelette. Her mouth watered as she sat down to eat it. If only she could get the idea of corned beef and cabbage out of her head. It was such a strong craving sometimes. Still her creation looked delicious. She was about half way through it when nausea overtook her. Tears of self-pity stung her eyes as she deposited her lovely fluffy creation down the toilet. Retching miserably, she vowed she would never become pregnant again.

Glumly she made her way to the lounge and caught sight of Mehemed hovering around wearing his best "I told you so expression" as he offered her a glass of water. It's a pity I didn't puke all over him. That would knock the superior smirk off his face, she thought nastily, as she studiously ignored him. Changing her mind she marched into the bedroom and slammed the door, knowing she was being childish. It wasn't the cook's fault that she was so miserably pregnant. She felt so frustrated and full of anger. It was OK for Terry—he didn't have to put up with Mehemed, he was out working day and night. Nor did he have to listen to the inane yap of the other wives. Waves of resentment surged through her. It was a man's world, of that there was no doubt. All she could do at present was either vegetate in the apartment or, worse, sit listening to the gossip down at the pool.

Maggie hated the backbiting and bitchiness that was part of life on the compound. She was too direct a person to enjoy the subtle innuendoes and snide character assassination that some women indulged in. She couldn't care less if so and so was having an affair with such and such. It was none of her business what other people got up to. Let them lead their own lives and she would lead hers. It was the hypocrisy that really sickened her. She had seen them being so nice, so charming to some poor unfortunate and then five minutes later when she was gone, the venom would come out and every aspect of her life would be torn to shreds.

"Dreadful figure! Shouldn't wear those awful bermudas. Husband's an alcoholic, you know. Mark fancies her! Don't ask me what he sees in her." It went on and on. Oh, she couldn't face going down there. God knows what they said about her behind her back.

Opening her dressing table drawer she pulled out a large red notebook, sat down and read the previous day's entry. Giving a deep sigh she started to write. Maggie liked writing her thoughts down. She had kept a diary for as long as she could remember. In it she could pour out all her rage and frustration, although it seemed lately that these emotions were the only ones in her life. Her diary in New York had been so lively and exhilarating. Head bent, soft auburn hair tumbling around her shoulders, Maggie wrote until her fingers were stiff. Catching sight of herself in the mirror she grinned. She certainly looked like a demented novelist. A thought struck her, leaving her open mouthed. Well she certainly had the time to try writing a novel... She could write one about life on the compound! All human life was there. The sex! Drama! Intrigue! It couldn't be rivalled by Hollywood. And those Saudi Arabian sheiks!

What a lark it would be. She could just see it all now, the wives reading her novel around the pool, wondering just who was meant to be who? Maggie felt a surge of energy and the cloud of depression lifted. Turning over some blank pages she bent her head and began to write furiously. Life was what you make it. If she wanted to sit at home and be bored she could do it or else get off her butt and stop feeling sorry for herself and do something about it.

Three hours later she lifted her head. Her wrist was aching, her cheeks were flushed, her eyes sparkled with their old lively vitality. She was no longer bored out of her mind, in fact she felt invigorated.

Smiling to herself, Maggie read what she had written.

Devlin's Story II

fifteen

Devlin observed her two year old daughter sleeping in her arms, the long sooty lashes fanning her pink little cheeks, her halo of fine golden curls soft and silky against Devlin's tanned arm. It was the first time in months that the baby had looked so well and healthy.

The week in Rosslare had got rid of the pinched unhealthy pallor, the legacy of high-rise living, from both mother and child. Devlin wanted to kiss her baby fiercely, this precious little bundle that had been the cause of so much heartbreak and joy for her. Regretfully she decided against waking her. Lynn was quite a handful when awake and they still had a fair bit to travel.

Catching Kate's eye in the mirror she smiled at her aunt. If it hadn't been for Kate she would never have pulled herself out of the mire of hardship and depression she had been in. For the first time in three years the burden of anxiety was lifted from her shoulders and she sank into the comfort of the back seat of the Peugeot station wagon, relaxing in the warm sunshine. They were driving to Wexford, to a new life, a healthy life in the rich sea air where her daughter's lungs, which had been such a source of anxiety when they lived in Ballymun, would not be affected by the smog-laden air of the city or by the unhealthy heating system that they had to live with in their high-rise flat.

Mind you, it hadn't been all hardship living in "Ballier"; Devlin had made some good friends there and, more important, had discovered reserves in herself and a strength of character that she hadn't realised she had. In Ballymun she had left behind forever the last vestiges of carefree girlhood. In Ballymun Devlin Delaney had become a strong determined woman and now this woman was starting out yet again to make a new life for herself.

It was a relief to be moving away from the city of her birth although she felt a little pang at the thought of leaving Caroline and Maggie. What friends they had proved to be; utterly supportive, lifting her out of the black moods of depression that sometimes enveloped her, although it hadn't been all gloom. They had also had great moments of fun and laughter, shoulder-shaking, rib-tickling, hearty laughter just like the old days. Friends were so important; great friendships something to be nurtured and treasured. Devlin knew that in Caroline and Maggie she had the best. Time and trauma had proved it over and over. They hadn't slipped by the wayside when the going got rough. They had been right there with her and always would be, accepting her for what and who she was. With them there were no barriers. But apart from Caroline and Maggie there was nothing else to keep her in Dublin—nothing at all.

As the miles slipped by, distancing her from the city and her old life, her thoughts wandered back over the past three years. They had been three years of experience, that was for sure. Smiling, she remembered the early months of her pregnancy and how she had got a job in an exclusive health centre in Kensington through sheer neck. It must have been desperation that had given her such courage. She grinned broadly as she remembered how it happened.

***

After Devlin left the abortion clinic, she had hailed a taxi, booked a room in the London Tara, ate a huge breakfast and then gone shopping. Kensington had fantastic shops and boutiques and it hadn't taken Devlin long to select a chic white linen suit. The skirt was pencil-straight but the well-cut jacket had slightly padded shoulders and three quarter length sleeves. She wouldn't have to wear anything under the jacket and it complemented her tan beautifully. A pair of white high heeled shoes, a clutch bag, her gold chain at her neck, some perfume and she was right. It was a sophisticated vision that stared back at her from the mirror. She had had her hair done in the hotel salon and she knew without vanity that she looked perfectly groomed and classy...just the right person for the job as a receptionist in The Capital, the most exclusive health and fitness centre in London.

Devlin had seen the job advertised in a health magazine she had picked up at the clinic and decided that it would suit her fine until her baby was born. "Don't bother interviewing anybody else; I'm perfect for the job," she had informed the astonished personnel manager whom she had demanded to see, without an appointment. Listing off her impressive qualifications for the job, she had given Colin's name for a reference. Having asked the woman to ring her at the Tara with her decision, Devlin had spent the following day sitting by the phone, sick with nervous tension, uncomfortably aware that staying at a top class hotel, and splashing out on her expensive suit had made a sizeable dent into her finances. She had almost given up hope of hearing anything when the phone rang and Mrs Arnott, the manageress of the health centre, told her grandly that on receipt of her references they would be happy to employ her. Limp with relief, Devlin rang Colin, told him that she was resigning and said the only thing she expected or wanted from him was a good reference, which she had earned.

Coldly he asked for the address to send it to. He never mentioned her pregnancy or the abortion and Devlin had been as calm and cold as he. How little integrity he had. He was the ultimate in selfishness, an utterly shallow person, and she had fooled herself into thinking she was in love with him! Well that was one episode in her life that had taught her a lesson and she wouldn't make the same mistake again.

Two weeks later, Devlin was installed behind the reception desk, surrounded by the cool marbled walls of the luxurious Capital centre. It was exclusive all right: only the very rich were able to afford its great range of health, beauty and slimming aids. It had its own hair salon, beauty therapists, nutritionists, aerobic instructors and health personnel. Many people from abroad came to avail of its services while staying in London and she recognised several well-known personalities who signed in to be pampered and petted.

It was an enjoyable job that suited her outgoing personality and the tranquil surroundings helped to calm her sometimes frazzled nerves. Luckily she had found a fairly reasonable bedsit which wasn't too far from work. Her salary was excellent but she saved most of it, because in just a few months she would have another mouth to feed.

Between getting the job and starting work, Devlin had returned home. When Lydia discovered that she hadn't after all had an abortion and that she was planning on keeping the baby and living in London, there had been a horrific row. "What are you keeping it for? All right, have the baby in London but for goodness sake, child, have it adopted!"

"I don't want to have it adopted!" Devlin shrieked, at the end of her tether. "I don't want it to end up like me wondering about its real mother and father, feeling guilty like I do because I'm not yours and I feel I've let you down." Her face was scarlet with emotion, her hands clenched in two tight fists.

"Jesus Mary and Joseph! Will you keep your voice down, Devlin, the whole street will hear you," Lydia snapped.

"Fuck the neighbours, do you hear me? I don't give a shit what the fucking neighbours think. They can go to hell for all I care!" Devlin was shouting now as bitterness and resentment battled with hurt and despair inside her.

"Devlin Delaney!" Her mother's exclamation and the swift sharp slap of her palm against Devlin's cheek were simultaneous.

"Oh!" Devlin's voice became a shocked whisper.

"I won't have that gutter language in my house, Miss. Is this the thanks you give your father and me after all we've done for you? You wanted for nothing Devlin, nothing!"

"That's where you're wrong, Mum," Devlin was calm now. She knew it was pointless to argue with Lydia. Her mother's vision was so narrow that she couldn't see beyond the bounds of what people would say and the gossip about her pregnancy.

Two bright spots appeared on Lydia's cheeks.

"What on earth are you talking about? Look at the standard of living you've grown up with. Gerry bought you a car for your eighteenth birthday. You've had foreign holidays, the best of education. What more could you want?"

Devlin looked at the elegant woman standing before her, her perfectly made up face puzzled and angry. There was no harshness in the younger girl's voice, only a sad wistfulness, as she said quietly. "I wanted someone to love me. I wanted a mother to kiss and cuddle me and make me feel special. And I'm going to do that for my child."

Lydia's gaze faltered. Then she turned and walked towards the lounge door. "I'm not that kind of woman, Devlin, I did the best I could," she said stiffly. "And if you keep this child will it live on kisses and cuddles alone. There's much more to life than that. It's got to be fed and clothed. What do you tell it when it asks about its father? How do you think you're going to afford to give it the kind of raising you had? You always were headstrong, you always will be. I just wash my hands of the whole affair." She gave Devlin a strange look. "You're exactly like your mother, if that's any comfort to you," she said before leaving the room.

Devlin sat down in the tasteful apricot and cream lounge of her home. So that was that, then! Lydia washed her hands of the whole affair. There was no point in staying there, she decided glumly. With a determined thrust to her jaw Devlin closed the front door behind her and drove out to Sandymount. She rang her father and arranged to have lunch with him, over which she quietly told him of her plans.

"Please stay in Dublin, I'll support you, pet," he pleaded.

"I can't do that, Dad. I have to stand on my own two feet. Don't worry—you know I'll make the best of things, and besides I think I'm really going to like London." Poor Gerry! Caught between Lydia and herself, wanting to do the best for both. He made her promise to keep in touch and then swiftly wrote out a cheque and handed it to her.

"I can't, Dad!" Devlin protested, stunned at the amount. It was for three thousand pounds.

"You can and you will." Gerry's tone was quite firm. "A father can give his daughter whatever he likes and don't ever be short of money, darling. I'm glad you've decided to keep the baby. I hope it gives you as much joy as you've given me."

"Oh Dad!" Devlin couldn't speak. The lump in her throat was as big as a tennis ball. He hugged her hard and then he was gone back to the bank and Devlin didn't feel quite so alone.

Caroline too was utterly relieved that she was keeping the baby. "You're doing the right thing, Dev, I know you are. It will all work out for the best—you'll see."

"I don't know. I hope so, Caro. I feel kind of scared," Devlin confessed. With Caroline she didn't have to put on a brave face as she had done with her father. Now that she had finally burned her bridges she was beginning to feel very vulnerable.

"You're never scared of anything, Devlin!" Caroline declared stoutly but her hug was extra warm and her cheeks were wet.

By the time Devlin had sold her car and stereo, packed her clothes, books and dearest possessions and got her flight back to London organised, she hadn't had a minute to think about the future—which was just as well. She arrived in Heathrow on the Sunday night, went back to the bedsit, made herself a cup of tea and went straight to bed. She started work at nine the next morning.

Devlin had not told her employers that she was pregnant and she worried that if they found out they might ask her to leave. She consoled herself with the thought that winter would soon be upon them and she could wear big chunky sweaters to hide her condition. Pregnancy suited her: she was glowing and radiant, her skin and eyes clear and bright, her hair shining with health. Mrs Arnott told her one day that she was an excellent advertisement for the centre and that they were very pleased with her. Devlin was delighted. Her work always took her mind off her problems, and it helped to ease the awful loneliness she experienced. London was so big and impersonal, any city was, so she decided to act positively and do something about it. She might need friends when the time came for her to give birth.

She had enrolled in a business studies course at night and gradually after her initial shyness had worn off she had become friendly with a girl called Doreen, a bright, extrovert, articulate West Indian girl. Doreen hadn't been able to afford to go to college after leaving school but she was determined to further her education. She worked in a travel agency and had taken the course with a view to starting up her own business. Her determination and ambition had surprised Devlin. She had not taken the course with any eye to the future; she had taken it because it sounded interesting, the times of the classes suited her, and she wished to meet people, but as she studied more and listened to Doreen she began to have ideas about setting up a business of her own in the future. After all, she would have a child to support, so it was something to think about.

About three months later, Doreen mentioned to Devlin that her flatmate was leaving to get married and asked her if she would like to share with her. Devlin was thrilled. Living on her own in the strange noisy exciting city was lonely and because she was saving hard she didn't go out much, except perhaps for an occasional meal with some of the girls from work she had got friendly with.

Doreen was the only one who knew about her pregnancy and the fact that she had still asked her to share meant a lot to Devlin. Her self esteem, which had taken such a battering, began to recover and as the baby kicked lustily against her gently-swelling stomach she even began to look forward to the birth. Sometimes she talked to the child inside her, her hands gently caressing the bulge. So far she had been lucky. By clever dressing she had been able to conceal her thickening figure, but this would not be possible for much longer.

Devlin decided to tell Mrs Arnott. After all they had been very good to her and she felt it wasn't fair to betray their trust. Though she knew that she was legally entitled to keep her job despite her pregnancy, she would not want to stay on if by doing so she caused problems at the club. The manageress was taken aback and gave Devlin's figure a close scrutiny. "Well, dear, I'm glad you told me. Let me think about it," she said kindly and Devlin had spent the day and night taut with tension, awaiting her decision. The following morning, she got a call from Mrs Arnott asking her to drop into her office. Her hands were damp with perspiration as she sat down in front of the manageress's desk, trying to look composed. Mrs Arnott had smiled comfortingly at her.

"Relax, Devlin! You don't have to worry. We've decided to keep you on. After all, your work is excellent and our clients like you. As long as you do your work, dress smartly and look your best there is no reason to let you go." She met Devlin's eyes. "There is one thing, dear. I'm sorry

I have to ask this of you but could you wear a ring on your finger? It might be easier on yourself." Devlin blushed, pink with embarrassment. Nodding her head mutely she left the office, cursing Colin but most of all cursing herself for allowing herself to be in the position she was in. How stupid and silly she had been.

Well, she had made one big mistake in her life and she'd be exceptionally careful not to make another. At least they aren't sacking me, she thought. The prospect of her salary helped her to swallow the bitter pill of humiliation.

Christmas was the worst. Doreen had invited her home with her but Devlin had been reluctant to impose herself and had decided to stay in the flat. Her father rang and asked her to come and stay in a hotel in Dublin at his expense. Obviously Lydia was determined not to allow her home. It didn't really surprise Devlin that her mother's fear of what the neighbours would say overrode all other considerations. She pitied her father, torn between his love for her and his love for his wife. She gently refused his offer and hung up in the pits of depression.

Tears stung her face in the biting wind as she walked home to the flat. All around her was evidence of the festive season but she kept her eyes averted from the gaily decorated shops, the magical brightly lit Christmas trees. It was hard to ignore the evocative Christmas music that tugged at her heartstrings bringing memories of happier Christmases in the past when all she had to worry about who was bringing her to the New Year's Ball, and which dress would cause the biggest sensation.

The day before Christmas Eve, Caroline rang and asked her to come and stay with the family. Devlin was touched. Caroline was always there for her in her own quiet understated way. Again she refused but they talked for a while and when the call was finished she didn't feel quite so alone. Caroline told her about her forthcoming engagement and Devlin tried to infuse some enthusiasm into her voice as she congratulated her friend. Why she could not take to Richard she did not know, but if he made Caroline happy that was all she cared about and God knows all Caroline had ever wanted was to be married.

When she got home to the flat a big parcel awaited her and also an airmail letter with a Saudi stamp. Eagerly she ripped open the paper and found a huge furry dressing gown with matching slippers in a beautiful shade of pink. A bottle of her favourite perfume fell out of the sleeve and tears welled up in her eyes at Caroline's kindness. The letter from Maggie was warm and full of encouragement and again Devlin couldn't prevent a lump rising in her throat.

God, I'm turning into a right weeping willow, she chided herself as she tried on the dressing gown. A snow shower had just started and she watched the snowflakes whirling hither and thither, blocking out everything in sight, imposing their own authority on the landscape. If only she could blot out her past so easily and start afresh, how simple life would be. Shivering, she lit the gas fire and made herself some tea and toast. Having done enough shopping to last her for three days, she intended not setting foot outside the door for the remainder of the week. The sooner Christmas was over the better. She comforted herself with the thought that she was no longer in her lonely basement bedsit. The flat she shared with Doreen was small and compact but very cosy and bright. Deciding resolutely to treat her few days off like an ordinary weekend she tried to forget the depression that had settled leechlike on her shoulders. She wondered why Kate had not written. It was most unusual, for her aunt wrote faithfully each week. The disappointment of not getting a letter or even a Christmas card nagged at her. It seemed to Devlin that the smallest thing could upset her these days and blaming it on her rioting hormones she settled down with a deep sigh to escape reality in front of the TV

For the next two days she slept late, didn't bother dressing but just sat wrapped up in her new warm furry dressing gown in front of the gas fire, flicking TV channels when programmes got too sentimental. Not once did she allow her thoughts to dwell on past Christmases or thoughts of home and although the days dragged somewhat it wasn't as bad as she had feared. Her body caught up on some much needed rest and it was a treat not to have to get up for work. Catching sight of herself in the mirror, hair unbrushed, face naked of make-up, enveloped in her big pink robe, Devlin decided she looked like a big pink bear in hibernation. Boxing Day found her depressed and listless. Dragging herself out of bed around noon she found herself unable to face another day of non-stop TV viewing. Outside it was bitterly cold and she gazed out at the deserted street, her thumb nail idly making patterns in the frosty tracery on the window pane.

sixteen

She had to get out of the flat! It was driving her mad. She was feeling decidedly claustrophobic. Passing through her tiny kitchen she eyed the sink, full to the brim with dirty dishes. A look of distaste crossed her face. Normally a tidy person, for the last few days she had just taken clean crockery from the press, dumping it into the sink as she finished with it. Pieces of soggy burnt toast and a sticky marmalade-smeared knife lay on a crumb covered table. She gave a grimace of horror and muttered aloud, "God I'm turning into a slut." Squaring her shoulders she rolled up her sleeves and wished heartily that Nanette Newman and her mild green fairy liquid would materialise in her dirty little kitchen.

She had just finished drying the last glass and was surveying with some dismay her reddened and wrinkled hands when her doorbell rang. Puzzled, because she was not expecting Doreen back for another few days, she went to the intercom and said warily, "Yes?"

"Guess who?" said a voice that was instantly recognisable in spite of the tinny distorted sound. On winged feet Devlin flew down the stairs and flung open the door, to be met by the beaming loving face of her aunt.

Kate stayed a week, having paid a man to take care of the farm while she was away. Devlin's blues disappeared and they went shopping for baby clothes and maternity dresses with great gusto. They caught a few shows, had meals out and generally had a good time. Devlin, in spite of her now obvious bulk, was blessed with the constitution of an ox, and apart from the occasional bout of heartburn, and some lower back pain, was sailing through her pregnancy like a stately galleon. Together she and Kate choose some beautiful maternity dresses that were superbly cut, flowing gracefully over Devlin's greatly expanded figure. It was an enormous relief to escape from the figure-flattening panty girdle she had been wearing to try to camouflage the bulge. Kate promised she would try to get over for the birth and Devlin experienced a surge of love and gratitude for the small slim elfin woman who had given her more love and support than Lydia ever had.

She missed Kate badly when she had returned home to Wexford but Doreen was there and she did her best to keep Devlin's heart up. She sometimes felt as though the nine months were nine years and found herself becoming restless and edgy as she went into her eighth month of pregnancy. Her one big fear was that her waters would break while she was at work and that she would saturate the elegant deep-pile carpet in the foyer. She had nightmares that she was in labour and that everybody just kept ignoring her, continuing with their aerobics and body-building while she begged in vain for help.

Having attended pre-natal classes, Devlin often practised her breathing exercises with Doreen who assured her that she would stay at the hospital for the birth, although she couldn't face actually being present at birth because she had a mortal dread of blood. Several nights later, Devlin woke from a restless sleep and felt an unfamiliar warm dampness in her lower regions. A sharp pain in her back pierced her drowsiness.

Oh Jesus, I've wet myself, she thought in dismay, hauling herself into a sitting position. Another stronger little pain gripped her and she came instantly awake. "Oh my God! Doreen, QUICK! I think I've started," she yelled frantic-ally at her sleeping flatmate down the hall. Scrambling out of bed, her sodden nightdress clinging to her, she rushed into Doreen's bedroom, her heart thumping. She shook her friend hard. "Quick, Doreen, I think I'd better go to the hospital, I think it's coming."

Doreen gave a startled yelp. "Ooooh Dev! Oh, girl, what will I do?" She jumped out of bed and started rooting in the hot press.

"What in the name of God are you doing?" Devlin asked, astounded,

"I'm getting towels, girl. They always ask for towels and boiling water," Doreen retorted.

In spite of her discomfort, Devlin had to

laugh. "You goose, it won't happen for ages yet. Just help me to get ready and call a taxi. OK?" she said reassuringly. It was obvious that Doreen was completely rattled so, taking a deep breath, Devlin ordered her to the kitchen to make tea while she phoned the hospital to tell them what happened. Calmly the nurse told her what to bring and as she concentrated her mind on her packing a strange fatalism overcame her. It was time for the big event. This time next day it would all be over and she would have her baby. A new phase in her life would start and one thing she had discovered about herself was a strength she hadn't known she possessed. Having got through the eight and a half months of her pregnancy through sheer grit and willpower she assured herself that the same willpower would get her through the next few hours.

For Devlin the memory of the birth of her daughter would always be a blur of dismayed pain. Had she been hoaxed all along? Childbirth was supposed to be a woman's ultimate experience. True fulfilment was supposed to be the reward, if all she had read and been led to believe was true. No one had ever told her about the reality. For Devlin, it was a painful, messy, even humiliating experience as she was prodded and poked in the labour ward and later in the delivery room, coldly but professionally told when and when not to push. In her most desperate moments she even called out Colin's name and the look of superior pity the nurse flashed her almost broke her spirit.

"Hush now, like a good girl. Don't make a fuss," the Indian doctor said crisply and authoritatively in his clipped half-English accent. Devlin sensed that he was annoyed at being called out to deliver her premature baby. She was the only one in the labour ward and her sense of isolation increased. All of the films she had seen had shown supportive husbands or sisters or friends holding and giving encouragement to excited fulfilled women, yet here she was alone with all these strangers, going through the most painful and frightening experience of her life.

Once, when the doctor rather sharply instructed her to push, she raised her head from the pillows and glared angrily at him. "Oh push yourself, you big bully!"

"Now now, Devlin!" the nurse had murmured but she'd had to hide a grin.

It was a long and difficult birth and when it was finally over Devlin felt a limp relief. All she wanted to do was sleep and to her despair she wasn't able to muster up an awful lot of enthusiasm when they placed the tiny red wrinkled bundle in her arms. Guilt overcame her as she was wheeled back to the ward, as she had heard all about bonding and rejection. She begged them to let her see the baby again but they just murmured soothing words and told her to relax.

Doreen had peeped in at her, pretending to smoke a huge fat cigar, and Devlin grinned weakly and gave her a hug before sinking into oblivion as healing sleep renewed her battered body. She slept until six the following morning and her first waking thought was, this time yesterday I was going through it. Thank God it's all over. I'll never get pregnant again. They brought the baby to her and as she held the fragile tiny being, her eyes screwed tightly shut, little wisps of fine red tufts of hair sticking up, her perfectly formed miniature fingers curled tightly, Devlin felt all her resentment and bitterness evaporate as a tide of protective love surged through her. She held the baby close, crooning softly to her. "I'm sorry you had such an awful introduction into this world. I'll make it up to you, darling," she whispered contritely.

Even though she was three weeks premature the baby was five pounds in weight and after both of them had mastered the art of breastfeeding she suckled contentedly at Devlin's breast. As she gave herself up to the physical pleasure of nursing her baby, Devlin knew that there was no earthly way she could hand her up for adoption. All through her pregnancy, Lydia's words had haunted her, causing her immense worry. What would she tell her child about her father? Where would she get enough money to give her even a few little luxuries? Her salary would just about cover rent, food and clothing and the baby-minder. Would it be fairer to her daughter to offer her for adoption? Devlin had spent many sleepless nights tossing the pros and cons around.

The first time she fed the baby she knew her answer. Her father had flown over when she rang him to tell him the news, and Devlin felt a surge of love for the grey-haired tired-looking man, who sat by her bed holding her hand in one of his and the baby in his other arm. With Gerry she had always felt loved and even though she now knew that she was not his natural daughter, somehow it didn't seem to matter.

"Won't you come home, Devlin?" he urged.

But she was determined. "Honest, Dad," she told him, "I have a great job with a very good salary." She embroidered the figures a little for his benefit. "And I've a lovely flat and a real good friend." She told him all about Doreen.

"Well if ever you need anything, let me know immediately, now won't you?" he made her promise. She had promised and he left for home after a couple of days, a little more at ease about her circumstances.

Before he left, Devlin arranged to have her baby baptised and christened. In a small intimate ceremony, with Doreen and her boyfriend Stevie as godparents, Devlin and her father smiled at each other as Lynn Kate Delaney gave a lusty roar when the waters of baptism trickled over her forehead. Gerry treated them all to a champagne lunch which Devlin thoroughly enjoyed, delighted that her pregnancy was finally over.

She was lonely when her father left. When he

had been there, she felt she could face anything but, alone in her bedroom, with Lynn ensconced in the cot beside her she felt anything but brave. Straining to hear her child breathing, she decided to make extra sure that the baby was alright and for the third time that night she got out of bed and held a mirror up to the baby's little lips. Reassured once more that Lynn was not the victim of cot death, Devlin's biggest worry, she settled down to get some sleep, only to be awakened by a hungry howl, it seemed like minutes later. As she fed her, Devlin marvelled at the tiny perfection of her daughter. Her minute fingers were curved around one of Devlin's forefingers, her little toes wriggling as she hungrily suckled at her mother's breast. Downy red gold wisps of hair touched Devlin's skin where the baby's head was cradled in her arms and Devlin bent her head and kissed the top of her daughter's head inhaling with pleasure that unique scent possessed only by babies.

She spent hours watching her daughter as the bond between them grew and that first magical moment when Lynn really focused her big cornflower blue eyes on her mother and smiled at her was something Devlin would never forget. The weeks of her maternity leave when Devlin was able to give total attention to her baby, forgetting all outside worries and considerations, were not exactly relaxing. The baby demanded constant attention as most newborn babies tend to do, but compared to what was to come, life was easy.

Before going back to work Devlin had secured the services of a well-recommended child minder. One of the women she worked with assured Devlin that she was excellent and very capable. Devlin liked Miriam on sight and shortly before she was due to go back to work, began taking the baby to the woman's house so that she should get used to her.

Although she charged a high rate, Devlin knew a good childminder was her biggest priority. She would never forget her first day back at work, as she tried desperately to concentrate on what she was doing, trying to ignore her swollen breasts that were crying out for Lynn's little rosebud mouth to empty them of their milk.

Was she awake or asleep? She'd had a touch of diarrhoea that morning. Was it any worse? Her hand stretched out to ring Miriam's number. Stop it! she told herself miserably. This would be her third call and Miriam might get annoyed. She wondered if her daughter was fretting as much as she was. Somehow she got through the day, and almost broke her neck to get to the childminder's to reclaim her precious child, whom she found sleeping contentedly, quite unaware of the trauma her mother was going through.

Unfortunately this happy state of affairs did not last. The baby got a wheezy cough that developed into chronic bronchitis. Torn between the demands of her job and the needs of her baby.

Devlin worried herself sick. She was constantly taking time off to be with the child, or to bring her to the hospital and though Mrs Arnott was sympathetic to her plight, Devlin knew it was a situation that could not last.

Many times, Devlin was sorely tempted to ring her father but that would have been giving in, taking the easy way out, and she had vowed to support herself and the baby. Gerry had given her more than enough and all she had given him was worry. A leech she would not be! But there were many times that she was sorely tempted when she held her baby daughter in her arms and watched the little face getting redder and redder after a coughing bout.

As the weeks turned into months and Devlin was forced to take more and more time off work, she knew it was only a matter of time before Mrs Arnott would call her into the office and ask her to leave. When it did happen, she could not blame them in the Centre. They had treated her exceptionally well during her time there and she knew herself that things could not go on as they were.

The loss of her job meant she had to dip into her precious nest-egg to supplement her DHSS welfare payments. She, who had never known what it was to scrimp and save, became an expert at making mince last three days. She knew down to the last penny how much she could spend and she knew all about the cheaper cuts and the own brand labels. Her rent took a huge chunk out of her weekly income and without her salary,

Devlin began to find it an increasing struggle to make ends meet.

Doreen helped as much as she could. She was so utterly good-natured and reliable that it touched Devlin but she felt awfully guilty in the pre-dawn hours as Lynn howled in her arms and Doreen, her sleep interrupted almost as much as Devlin's, insisted on making Devlin tea.

Eventually, as her savings dwindled and life seemed to get more difficult, Devlin made the decision to return to Dublin. Unwilling to impose on Doreen any longer, she felt it would be easier to raise a child alone in Dublin than in London. Living there had become impossibly expensive. At least Caroline, and Maggie, who was back home with twins, would be there. It was the memory of Maggie's words that made her finally decide to go home.

Her friend had written faithfully each week, and when the letter came telling Devlin that Maggie was leaving Saudi for good and would be stopping over in London, en route to Dublin, Devlin had been in a tizzy of excitement. They had made arrangements for Maggie and her twins to stay at the flat for the night and Devlin couldn't wait to see them all. When she saw the familiar redhead, beaming broadly as she emerged from customs, two sleepy babies in her arms, Devlin couldn't stop the tears. "Oh Maggs! Maggs it's so good to see you. I've missed you and Caro so much," she whispered, as she enveloped mother and twins in as much of a hug as her own bump would allow.

"I know! I know! I was really lonely in Saudi when I had to give up work," Maggie was half-laughing, half-crying herself. She stepped back and said admiringly, "Dev, you look fantastic. Obviously impending motherhood suits you. You should have seen me. The mother of sorrows had nothing on me."

Devlin laughed as she took one of the babies from her friend. In fact she had never seen Maggie look so haggard. Deep circles surrounded her friend's eyes and she looked unusually pale. It was more than jet lag. Devlin knew Maggie had had a difficult pregnancy. Obviously she hadn't gotten over it yet. Terry shouldn't have let her make the journey with the babies alone. But as Maggie explained, he still had a month of his contract to run and she had to arrange accommodation for them.

Despite the fact that she had put in such a long flight, Maggie got her second wind once she had settled her children for the night, and it was well after midnight after hours of laughter and chat and a truly satisfying gossip that only the best of friends can indulge in, that Devlin persuaded her to get to bed.

"Why won't you come back too?" Maggie had queried "Just think, Dev, our children would be friends for each other. They could grow up together. If you had a little girl, she and Michelle would be bosom buddies just like us."

At the time Devlin, enjoying the security of

her weekly salary, contented with her flat and Doreen's friendship and liking the anonymity of London wouldn't entertain the thought. But as her life took on a different hue and things didn't work out as she had planned, Maggie's words came back to her night after night as she lay awake worrying, tossing the pros and cons around in her mind until she felt she was going to crack up. Listening to Lynn wheezing, she cried tears of anger and frustration. If only the baby wasn't so afflicted she would have managed in London, but the reality was that she was now finding it harder and harder to cope and going home was the only answer. Things couldn't be any worse over there and at least she would have the girls to fall back on for moral support. And Gerry too.

As she boarded the boat train at Euston and saw the tears in Doreen's eyes, she felt an enormous sense of regret to be leaving the city that had been a haven to her. Doreen embraced her warmly. It would be hard for Devlin to find as good a friend as Doreen had been through the months in London and they promised to keep in close touch, a promise that was kept throughout their lives.

seventeen

Standing on the deck of the gently rolling ship as she sailed into Dublin, the sun's rays painting the early morning sky, Devlin felt a strange mixture of emotions. It seemed like an eternity ago that she had been going in the opposite direction, a lot less mature, a lot more self-centred than she was today. Today all her orientation was towards the sleeping child in her arms. Devlin smiled down at the white-bonneted head. Obviously the sea suited her daughter as she had slept for most of the journey.

The ship glided serenely past the emerald and mauve heather-covered Howth Head. In the distance she could see the distinctive twin red and white ESB chimneys stark against the vivid early morning sky. Her heart gave a funny little lurch as they sailed into the curve of Dublin bay and they made their way majestically past the Poolbeg and North Bull lighthouses that guarded the entrance to the river Liffey. Up then between the South Wall and the Bull Wall that stretched out like two long welcoming arms drawing them towards their journey's end. She was coming home to the city of her birth with her own daughter, a city that despite its faintly decayed air, its crime and ugliness, always tugged at the heartstrings of those who left it.

Lifting her head to catch the gentle salt-laden breeze, she breathed deeply the air of home. Kate was at the quays to meet them, a relieved and delighted Kate, glad to see both of them on home soil. She begged Devlin to come and live with her but her niece was adamant. She'd stay with Kate until she got a flat in Dublin but she was determined to stand on her own two feet. It wouldn't be fair to have Kate made a target of idle gossip in the village and besides she had no intention of burdening her with more problems. God knows, Kate had had enough hardship nursing her husband through his long and fatal illness.

No! she thought briskly. She had to take responsibility for her own life and Lynn's. After all it had been her irresponsibility and selfishness that had caused her problems in the first place. Kate hadn't pressed her; there was time enough for that. At least her beloved niece was home where Kate could visit her occasionally. It did her heart good to see the strength of character and new maturity so evident in Devlin. Before, she had been a lovable but immature girl, slightly selfish, always used to getting her own way. Now Kate saw a determined and thoughtful young woman ready to make her own way in life. Devlin and Lynn were coming down to the farm for a week or two before settling back into city life. A fresh healthy Rosslare breeze was just what both of them needed to get that pinched white look out of their faces. Once Kate made up her mind about something there was no changing her mind, and in a way Devlin was glad she didn't immediately have to face the task of finding accommodation.

Devlin hadn't yet told her father of her plans to come home. She'd wait until she was settled somewhere and then ring him. For now she was just content to surrender herself to Kate's delightful pampering. What bliss it was to wake up in Kate's so comfortable bed where she slept, burrowed down into soft feather pillows on lavender scented snowy sheets, arms and legs spread extravagantly. So different from her small divan in London. Lynn too had slept well, a rare event. It must be the sea air, her mother surmised thankfully, sticking her head out the window and breathing in deep lungfuls of that rich sea-scented air.

Gazing out at the panorama of blue sky, green fields and aquamarine water, Devlin felt herself really relax for the first time since she had become pregnant. She watched a ferry make a graceful sweeping arc of the bay below her as it prepared to dock at the pier. As a child it had been her great delight to watch the boats coming and going. Her big treat was to be allowed to stay up until the lights came on at night when the great curve of the pier and viaduct would be magically illuminated like a sparkling glittering

necklace in the velvet night. The lights of
Wexford would start twinkling across the bay,
the late train would rumble past, an immense
glowworm casting shadows from its illuminated
carriages on the softly swaying bushes that ran
along the railway line that traversed Kate's
farm.

Then the magic moment: two mournful howls
from the ship's sirens, a belch of smoke and she
was moving away from the pier with all her
lights aglow, a floating Christmas tree. The
young Devlin would watch until the last light
was swallowed up by the night. Eyes drooping,
her last memory would be of Kate tucking her up
with a kiss and a cuddle that would send her to
sleep smiling.

Even now she was an adult, the magic was
still there. She had watched the ship before
going to bed, watched the sweeping yellow beam
of Tuskar lighthouse rhythmically patrol the sky
and sea and even as she lay in bed its beam was
still faintly caressing the picture of the Virgin
Mary hanging over her bed, every sixty seconds.
She fell asleep looking forward to the time when
Lynn would be old enough to be entranced.

Some things never changed, she thought
happily the next morning, breathing air untaint-
ed by smog. She had slept soundly and felt ready
for anything. From her bedroom window she
could see the men at work gathering the hay.
Later she would bring Lynn down to the fields for
her first viewing of the countryside. The mouth-

watering aroma of sizzling bacon wafted up the stairs and Devlin needed no second invitation. Before long she was tucking into a breakfast of rashers, sausages, black and white puddings, tomatoes and fresh mushrooms as well as crusty homemade brown bread smothered in creamy butter. To hell with cholesterol, she thought—she had died and gone to heaven.

It was an idyllic two weeks of long walks in the rambling winding lanes, or down by the water's edge playing with her daughter who would gurgle delightedly as the foamy surging surf covered her toes. Devlin would spend hours looking at her baby. She still found it hard to believe that this small wriggling bundle of energy was of her body, her own flesh and blood. Her tiny little fingers would grip Devlin's as she fed her and once, thinking of Lydia, Devlin felt a sense of pity overcome her bitterness. Maybe if Lydia had held a child of her own in her arms she might have been a different woman.

All too soon it was time to face reality again. Devlin took the train to Dublin, leaving the baby in her aunt's care. With intensely mixed feelings she went to the relevant social welfare department and explained that she was an unmarried mother with no means and no housing. As she filled out the necessary forms Devlin felt truly stigmatised. Labelled. Red-cheeked, she left the building feeling almost furtive. The girl behind the counter had been very nice indeed but filling out the form to claim her unmarried mother's allowance had been almost soul destroying.

Devlin knew that many people, including one very prominent lady politician, believed that girls deliberately got pregnant so as to be in receipt of the allowance. It was a view that was frequently aired on the radio with superior self-righteousness. How smug they were, how condemnatory!

Devlin knew, as she filled out that form, that she would never judge a person again. "Cast not the first stone" would be her motto as long as she lived.

She had been referred to a hostel for unmarried mothers by the welfare people and had been informed that if she stayed there for a while she would be housed fairly quickly by the Corporation. She had gone to the address given, made her arrangements, gone back to Rosslare and collected Lynn. They took up residence the following evening. Several times in the few weeks she spent in the hostel, she felt like eating her pride and taking Kate up on her offer. Although the rambling old hostel was clean and functional, the lack of privacy and its institutional air almost drove Devlin crazy. To escape, she would get up early feed and dress herself and the baby and walk town all day, feeding Lynn in hotel washrooms when necessary. She hadn't got in touch with Caroline or Maggie, preferring to wait until she was settled, because she knew in her heart and soul that Maggie would insist on her staying with them, and she might not have the strength of will to resist. If she ended up staying with Maggie, it would take her longer to get housed, as she would no longer be considered homeless.

One afternoon, pushing her buggy around her old haunts of girlhood, Grafton Street and Wicklow Street, Devlin almost bumped into a young woman coming in the opposite direction. The other girl was so busy talking to her friend she hadn't been looking where she was going. "For goodness sake! Would you ever watch where you are going!"

There was something vaguely familiar about the strident affected voice and Devlin curbed the retort that sprang to her lips. It couldn't be! It was! Oh God, why her, of all people?

Instinctively Devlin thrust her left hand into her jacket pocket. She had never been able to stand Jeraldine Ryan who was so affected she spelt her name with a "J" rather than a "G." A loud, brash, opinionated girl of limited intelligence, she had undoubtedly been the most unpopular girl in the class. Although the clothes she wore were wildly expensive, Jeraldine had absolutely no sense of style, Devlin had sometimes wondered if the girl was colour-blind. Their set had had many a giggle as she appeared in the most outrageous colour schemes. She had a thing about mohair and must have had about twenty multi-coloured jumpers that she wore to dazzling effect. Once, hearing Jeraldine announce loudly that she was going to buy an expensive bikini for her forthcoming Greek holiday, Ginette, a friend and classmate of Devlin's had muttered caustically,"Mohair no doubt!" causing Devlin to burst into uncontrollable giggles.

She had been blonde the last time Devlin had seen her, but her hair had now a peculiar reddish orangish hue, which was why Devlin had not immediately recognised her. How would Devlin explain about Lynn? This was the first time she had met someone she knew since she became pregnant. Should she have stayed in London after all, to spare herself this kind of trauma? All these thoughts flashed through her mind as she stared at the hard, heavily made-up face of the other girl.

Jeraldine looked right through her! Almost as though she didn't exist. "Excuse me!" she snapped, brushing past and once again launching into oratory. Devlin stood open-mouthed. She hadn't recognised her! A wry smile crossed her lips. All the heart thumping for nothing. She, the jean-clad, Devlin of now, hair pulled back in a pony tail was not the expensively-dressed fashion-conscious Devlin who had gone to school with Jeraldine. She had changed...Jeraldine hadn't...

"As I said to Alexandra, I envisage making policy decisions that will affect..." came floating back on the breeze and Devlin grinned in spite of herself. Same old Jeraldine, same old bullshit,

I...I...I...it had always been 'I'. She watched the other girl in her wine taffeta blouse and peach skirt swan into the hallowed portals of Brown Thomas. Devlin had noticed she was wearing a wedding ring. Was it the tall skinny dark haired guy she used to date? The class wit had christened them Worzel Gummidge and Sally and it suited them!

eighteen

The encounter left her feeling a little shaken and vulnerable. Was this how she would react when she met other people she knew? She was annoyed with herself for feeling like this. I don't have to justify myself to anybody. Anyone can make a mistake, she told herself fiercely, but from then on she confined her rambles to the north side of the city. There was less likelihood of meeting any of the old crowd shopping in Henry Street or Moore Street. She grew to like this unfamiliar part of the city. It was friendlier, livelier, than its posher, more elegant counterpart across the Liffey.

"That's a lovely chisler ye got there luv. D'ya want ta buy a few apples 'n' oranges?" one of the women behind the stalls asked her one day. The apples looked lovely, big, bright, green, luscious globes that made Devlin's mouth water. She hadn't tasted a crisp juicy Granny Smiths for years.

"I'll have a Granny Smith," she said taking out her purse. To her absolute mortification, she was five pence short, literally down to her last few coppers. It was the day before payday.

Scarlet, she murmured, "I don't seem to have enough. Maybe tomorrow." Anxious to leave, she hastily shoved the buggy back towards Henry Street.

"Wait a minute Missus!" Devlin heard the woman call after her and, turning, she saw her putting apples and oranges into a bag. "Here luv, take 'em. It's getting late an' I won't be able sell 'em all, an' sure what good will dey be doin me rottin away an' all?" She saw Devlin hesitating. "G'wan luv, take 'em an enjoy 'em."

"Th..thanks very much," stuttered Devlin.

"Yer very welcome," said the kindly old lady, smiling as she chucked Lynn under the chin. They were the nicest Granny Smiths Devlin had ever eaten, and she munched her way through two of them before reaching the hostel. Some people were really kind, she told Mairead, another unmarried mother who lived in the hostel.

"Hmm...they are few and far between, believe me," the other girl replied cynically but she smiled as she took one of the oranges Devlin offered her.

There were girls from all backgrounds in the hostel but the turnover was constant as they either left or were rehoused. If only the precious letter would arrive to tell her she had a flat, she wouldn't feel so unsettled. Anything had to be better than life in a hostel. Her father was still under the impression she was in London, but after her first week in the hostel, Devlin rang

Caroline, making her promise not to tell Maggie that she was back until she had her flat.

Excitedly they arranged to meet. Caroline had been married since early spring and they were living in Richard's apartment in Clontarf. She had written regularly to Devlin and had been terribly upset that Devlin couldn't make it to the wedding. Devlin had been distressed and felt that she was letting her friend down but there was nothing she could do about it; she simply couldn't afford it. It was well over a year since they had last seen each other and Devlin was dying to meet her. They had so much news and gossip to catch up on. When they did meet, Devlin was surprised at the change in her friend.

Even more slender and petite, dressed in a superbly cut pair of soft leather trousers with a gorgeous Italian knit jumper, gold discreetly displayed at ears and wrists, Caroline exuded an air of affluence and sophistication that was quite amazing. She also exuded an air of unhappy tension and Devlin was dismayed to see dark circles underneath her eyes. After they hugged each other warmly, Caroline took Lynn from her and cuddled her lovingly.

"Oh Devlin, she's beautiful! Look at her eyes—they're just like yours! Oh I wish..." She didn't finish what she was going to say, just smiled and hugged Devlin again.

"Oh Dev, it's so good to have you home. I've missed you so much! Let's go and and get something to eat and settle down to a good natter." They went to a quiet but inexpensive restaurant, thoughtfully chosen by Caroline who remembered Devlin's fiercely independent nature and had guessed quite rightly that she would not allow her to pay for lunch.

They talked for hours but Devlin sensed that Caroline was holding back something concerning herself and Richard. It was patently obvious that her marriage wasn't making her deliriously happy and Devlin felt an immense pity for her friend. Of all people, Caroline had truly longed to be married and now things didn't seem to be working out. At least she was single and free even if she had Lynn. Caroline was tied to Richard as once she had been tied to her father and brothers. It was obvious that she was bored and lonely. Richard had insisted that she give up work and he wouldn't let her drive. It seemed to Devlin that he wanted Caroline to be dependent on him for everything. She knew that Caroline was shocked that she was living in a hostel, although being her usual kind self she had made no comment.

Knowing Caroline as she did, she did not mind telling her the truth, but when Caroline invited her to visit the apartment, Devlin demurred, inwardly cringing at the thought of Richard's suave superiority.

"As soon as I've got a place of my own," she promised. They arranged to meet once a week and to phone every other day. It was the one event Devlin looked forward to. For the rest of the time she walked the legs off herself in preference to spending all day in the hostel, her self-esteem sinking lower and lower.

By the time the letter came from the housing department, she almost didn't care, so great was the depression that had descended on her. They offered her a flat in Ballymun, and her heart sank. Ballymun, the only high-rise complex in Dublin, housed twenty thousand families, nine thousand of whom lived in high-rise flats. It was located on the north side of the city and Devlin had driven through it when taking the back route to the airport. She had pitied anyone living there and now she was going to live in its depressed greyness herself.

The next day, she surveyed her new environment from her balcony eight storeys up. Grey seemed to be the predominant colour, the grey tall buildings merging into the damp grey fog that hung like a dirty lace shawl from the sky. She remembered having read that there was a high incidence of respiratory illness in the area. It did not surprise her. The flat was a one-bedroomed unit with a sitting room and kitchen combined. A bathroom and small hallway completed it.

The wallpaper had peeled off the walls, the floorcovering was lifting in places and it was obvious that the previous tenant had not been house-proud. There was an unceasing clamour about the block that set Devlin's already overwrought nerves on edge, a mixture of child-

ren playing and screaming and dogs barking.
She had never seen so many dogs! They roamed
in packs all over the vast estate, huge alsatians,
dobermans, and a variety of mongrels. The man
next door to her kept pigeons and their cooing
added to the cacophony of sound.

"My God! Is this what I'm reduced to!" she said
aloud as she sat on her suitcase and listened to
her daughter screaming to be fed. Fear gripped
her and she started to shake. She could be here
for years and years, she thought wildly. She'd
have to go crawling on her hands and knees to
Lydia. This enormous wilderness scared her.
She'd noticed two young girls of about fourteen
draped on the stairway, obviously spaced out on
something. Gently she bared her breast for Lynn
and fed her baby, jumping nervously at every
sound.

They had told her in the hostel that she could
stay for a few days longer until she got some
furniture together, and later, as she stood
waiting for one of the graffiti-ed lifts to bring her
down to ground level she felt as though the hostel
was arcadian compared to Ballymun.

"Lift's broken, Missus. D'ya wan a hand?" a
gruff voice said beside her and she turned to see
two teenage boys observing her. Cold fingers of
terror gripped her insides. She had heard about
getting mugged. Maybe these were two gurriers.
Devlin almost fainted as the pair of them lifted
the buggy with Lynn in it and began to march
down interminable flights of stairs.

"Yer new, Missus, aren't yer?" the gruff one with the spiky hairstyle and purple streaks was saying over his shoulder.

"Yes that's right," Devlin agreed faintly.

"Me and Rog live next door to ya. Me ma 'll be delighted to have someone new beside us. We had squatters an all, they were awful druggies too!"

"Oh!" responded Devlin inadequately, as they reached the exit. They gently lowered the gurgling baby who had thoroughly enjoyed the experience.

"See ya Missus," they said cheerfully as they strolled off to the shops.

"Thanks very much," Devlin shouted after them, belatedly remembering her manners. They waved again and as she pushed the buggy towards the bus stop she marvelled at how prejudiced she had been, immediately suspecting them of intending to rob her just because they were tough-looking young lads and she was in Ballymun. She felt ashamed and was to feel ashamed many times in the future as one by one her narrow social prejudices were demolished and she learned while living there that there is good and bad everywhere. For the first time in her life Devlin realised that it wasn't where you lived and what you worked at that mattered. It was the kind of person you were that was important.

Standing in the bus queue with other young mothers and their babies she thought longingly about her Ford Fiesta that she had taken so much for granted. How free she had been then. Bus queues had been for others. Now she was one of those people she had unconsciously looked down her nose at. Now she was also a person dependent on welfare the same as many others. What a turn her life had taken. Caroline had done much better for herself. Even Maggie with her twins had someone to cherish and take care of her. Wait until she told them where she was living! God, wouldn't they pity her. She looked at her blue-eyed daughter grinning happily at her and felt an awful fear in the pit of her stomach. Would she be able take care of her and provide for her? How would she manage to give her the childhood that Devlin had taken so unquestioningly for granted, the music lessons, the horse riding, the school trips to the Continent? "I can't even afford to buy a bed," she muttered in despair.

Her pride at rock bottom, she rang Caroline and asked her to meet her the following day. As they sat sipping their coffee, she looked at her friend straight in the eye and said quietly, "Caro, I'm in a bad way for money and you are the only person I could bring myself to ask." Swallowing hard she continued, "I've got to buy a bed and some cups and plates and something to cook on. Could you lend me some money? I swear I'll pay you back." Lowering her head, she whispered. "Oh God, Caroline, look what I'm reduced to! Please don't tell Richard."

Wordlessly Caroline opened her expensive Gucci bag, took out her cheque book and a slim gold pen and swiftly wrote out a cheque. Passing it over to Devlin she said firmly. "Take this, Dev, it's my own. Money I saved from when I was working. No one except the two of us will ever know about it and if it takes you until you are fifty to pay me back I don't care," she said defiantly.

Devlin's eyes widened as she saw the amount of the cheque. "Five hundred! Caroline, I can't!" she said, almost in tears at her friends generosity.

"You can and you will!" Caroline retorted. "You were always there when I needed you. Please let me do the same for you." She looked at Devlin, her lovely brown eyes earnest. "Please Dev, let me do this. Nobody has ever needed me before, let me help you pick yourself up out of this mess. Don't waste your time feeling sorry for yourself. You've got to think of your future and Lynn's." She chucked the baby under the chin. "I'm not going to let you bury yourself for ever out in Ballymun, but while you are there you might as well have the bare necessities." She grinned, "Now finish your coffee and let's go shopping and then I want you to give me your new address. I have a surprise for you tomorrow."

Devlin sat back open-mouthed. Caroline's attitude astounded her. She was right: she had been giving in to self pity, feeling that she had a lot to be sorry for. But Caroline was having none of it, and she sounded so determined! Usually it was Devlin who led and Caroline followed. Much to her surprise she found herself saying meekly, "Yes, Caroline" as she followed her friend out of the cafe. They headed to a discount store and again Devlin watched in amazement as the other girl swiftly loaded up a trolley with cups, plates, tea towels, knives, forks, and other household wares.

"I know these are cheap and not great quality but they will do until you are in better financial circumstances," Caroline was saying, in a brisk matter-of-fact tone.

"Crikey, Caroline," Devlin said three hours later when a small divan, a second hand sofa and a plain kitchen table had been purchased and they were sitting over another cup of coffee. "You've changed so much!"

Caroline smiled at her. "Maybe I have," she agreed wryly. "But so have you." When they parted, Caroline to rendezvous with Richard, Devlin to spend her last night in the hostel, they hugged warmly. "Don't forget now, Devlin. Chin up and think positive."

"OK," Devlin promised. How their roles had been reversed. "Thanks Caroline, I'll never forget what you did for me."

"And I haven't forgotten what you did for me either. Now bring that child home and put her to bed and then get your thinking cap on. See you tomorrow with my surprise."

The following morning Devlin was up at the

crack of dawn. She packed the rest of her
belongings in the hostel and stripped her bed,
leaving the clothes neatly folded in a pile. The
other girls wished her well and she was warmed
by their sincerity. After all they were all in the
same boat. Extravagantly she ordered a taxi,
knowing it was the last time she would be able to
indulge in such a luxury and as it sped towards
the northside suburb she decided yet again to
close the door on one phase of her life and begin
another.

Making a pact with herself not to look back
and think of the past, she turned her thoughts to
the future. Caroline was right: she was not going
to turn into a whimpering whinging welfare
dependent. Lynn was going to have her music
and horse riding lessons just as she had. She sat
up straight in the back of the taxi, her jaw set and
determined.

The sun was shining, the thick damp grey fog
of her previous visit had evaporated and in the
distance she could see the sharp outline of the
seven high rise towers of the flats. They did not
seem so bad when the sun was shining: they even
had their own stark attractiveness, she thought.
To her left she noticed a single storey redbrick
building surrounded by trees and shrubs and a
rich lawn, a green oasis in the concrete jungle.
Noticing some adults and children leaving the
building with books under their arms she
mentally tucked the the information at the back
of her mind. The library would come in handy

until she could afford a television and at least it was free, she thought briskly. To think that she, Devlin Delaney, belle of many a ball, was reduced to going to a library for entertainment! Impatiently she banished the thought. She had vowed not to look back but as the taxi drew to a halt outside her towerblock and she saw the litter-filled graffiti-decorated entrance she knew it would be hard going.

nineteen

Two hours later, as Devlin determinedly scrubbed out her tiny kitchen, there was a knock on the door. Expecting it to be the furniture, she dried her hands, tucked a limp strand of blonde hair behind her ear and didn't bother to remove her apron. She opened the solid wooden door and her mouth formed an "O" of surprise as she discovered a grinning Maggie, rubber gloves already on, and a similarly rubber-gloved Caroline beside her.

"Why didn't you tell me you were in Dublin? I'll murder you," Maggie exclaimed.

"We've come to help you settle in, Dev," Caroline explained. Indicating a large box at her feet she said cheerfully, "there's another one in Maggie's car but don't ask me to get it yet; I couldn't face those stairs for a while!" Devlin stood almost speechless as a tide of emotion surged through her. Here were her two best friends, both affluent married women and here she was an unmarried mother, living in poverty, looking a mess, with a hole in her jeans.

Oh God, what must they think of her. She couldn't bear the thought of their pity. Her thoughts were mirrored in her eyes and Maggie, instantly aware of what was going through the younger woman's mind, put her arms around her and said gently, "Stop it, Dev, it's us! Your best buddies! Don't feel defensive with us, for heaven's sake! All for one and one for all. Remember?" Devlin smiled at their old catch-phrase. Maggie was right, she was far too defensive. Look at the way she had felt about Jeraldine. Really! It was time she got her act together.

"Come on Dev," Caroline urged, waving a litre bottle of duty-free wine. "Get the glasses and let's get pissed for old time's sake!" Not knowing whether to laugh or cry and on the verge of both, Devlin stood back and let them in. Maggie instantly made for Lynn's cot and Devlin noted in surprise that her friend had put up some weight and that the radiant *joie de vivre* that had been so characteristic of her seemed somewhat diminished. Marriage and motherhood had certainly taken their toll of the effervescent Maggs.

Several mugs of wine later and they were all laughing as they scrubbed out the flat. The furniture had been delivered in the meantime and the place had lost its cold bare unlived-in look and was beginning to have a more homely aura. Maggie had brought a chicken casserole and after they had hung up a pair of old but clean curtains that she had found somewhere, they heated it up and settled down to eat, ravenously hungry after their exertions. It was a happy meal, one of many they were to have in the ten months Devlin was to spend in Ballymun. Her friends' support and encouragement got Devlin through those hardship-filled months during which she discovered resources within herself that made her battle on, determined to make a life for herself and her child.

Her other source of comfort and support was Mollie O' Brien, mother of four, and her husband Eddie who were her next-door neighbours. A warm motherly Dublin woman, Mollie had come calling with a freshly baked apple tart the first week Devlin was in the flat. "Howya luv, me name is Mollie, I hope yer settlin. I brought ya a tart just te introduce meself like," were her first words to the astonished Devlin.

"Oh! Oh that's very kind of you. Would you like to come in and have a cup of tea?" Devlin responded, delighted by the other woman's warmth and neighbourliness.

"Oh I'd only love a cuppa cha. Dere's nuttin like eh," Mollie beamed, stepping into the flat. "Janey! Aren't ye after doin a grand job on the place all the same. That other crowd a gurriers left it like a feckin pigsty," she exclaimed, casting an experienced eye around the place. "Now luv if dere's ever anything ya need don't be shy about knocking on me door. Right?"

"Right," agreed Devlin happily. Maybe she wasn't going to be too lonely after all.

With four grown sons, including teenagers Roger and Rayo, the pair who had helped Devlin with the buggy on her first visit to the flat, Mollie obviously missed not having a daughter and in no time Devlin and Lynn were taken under her motherly wing. Mollie's flat was immaculate and beautifully decorated and the balcony, a south facing suntrap painted white, was where Devlin spent many a happy afternoon listening to Mollie tell stories of life in the Liberties, where she had been reared. In turn Devlin told her about her life, her pregnancy, and her non-existent relationship with her mother. It was so easy to talk to Mollie, the down-to-earth Dublin woman was always giving her helpful hints about Lynn, and knowing she was next door and so dependable was an enormous help to the younger girl.

Mollie explained that she and her husband were on the waiting list for one of the new houses being built in the Liberties. "But I'll miss Ballymun all de same," she sighed "Dere's some awful nice people here. Bernie now, ye met her, she lives just below ye. Well, ye couldn't meet a nicer neighbour. She'd give ye the shirt off her back."

Devlin smiled. She had indeed met Bernie a few days after moving in. A good-natured cheerful woman, Bernie knew anything and everything about living in Ballymun. When Devlin wanted to find out about getting a leaking pipe fixed, Bernie told her who to contact. She personally brought her to the Health Centre when Devlin inquired of its whereabouts and sat with her, introducing her to other mothers until

Lynn and Devlin were called into the doctor.

"My Margaret will babysit for ya if ye need her," Bernie assured her as they walked back to their block, and she sent her young son up every day to see if Devlin needed any messages from the shops. It was an eye-opener to Devlin the way the women of the flats supported each other. So different from the self-contained anonymity of the exclusive suburb she had grown up in. If it hadn't been for Mollie and Bernie, Devlin knew she would never have stuck it out. No matter how down she was, just hearing Bernie's infectious guffaw would lift her spirits.

"You'd make a bleedin fortune hauntin houses!" Mollie told Bernie one day as the other woman laughed heartily in her distinctive fashion at the sight of a local garda chasing after his cap that had been caught by a gust of wind. Devlin burst into giggles. Mollie's caustic Dublin wit was a source of constant amusement to her. Eddie, Mollie's husband, was a carpenter by trade, a tall, quiet, unassuming man, who would knock on her door now and again with shelves, and presses he "just happened to have lying around" and would she be "bothered" with them. Within weeks of Devlin getting to know them, Lynn was presented with her very own hand crafted cot and Devlin marvelled at her neighbours' kindness.

Despite their outwardly tough image Rog and Rayo were good lads and would often call and keep her up to date with all the gossip on their block, while playing with the delighted Lynn. "Bridie upstairs is preggers again, worse luck! Betcha we'll hear a few barneys on the landing, it's always the bleedin same when she has a bun in the oven," Rayo informed her gloomily one day.

Devlin had encountered Bridie several times, a small fat hard-faced woman with brassy blonde hair who seemed to be in her late thirties. On several occasions she had made audible remarks about whores and sluts getting money from the state which, by rights should be given to her legitimate children and not to fatherless bastards.

"Thank God I'm a good Catholic mother, not like some young wans around here!" she said another day to nobody in particular as Mollie and Devlin stood waiting for the lift. Devlin blushed, and Mollie bristled, the light of battle flashing in her eyes.

"Feck off outa that you, ya cheeky scrubber ya an don't be annoyin the neighbours. It 'id match ya better if ya practised bein' a Catholic steda preachin about it."

Bridie gave a shriek of outrage. "Jaysus! De nerve a you talkin ta me like dat! Youse think yer the bees knees don'tcha with yer mahogany shelves an all. Boastin an braggin about that gurrier o' yours out in the Levenland!"

Mollie's oldest son Jimmy was a soldier and serving with the U.N. in Lebanon. He was his mother's pride and joy. "It's the Lebanon ye ignorant biddy an yer only jealous, Bridie, yer always the same, causin trouble in the block. G'wan out o' that and don't be bothrin dacent people."

"I'll get my Les down after youse, ye hussey ye!" roared Bridie furiously.

"Ah Janey! I'm all a tremble!" Mollie retorted drily, marching into the lift and leaving the other woman arms akimbo, speechless.

Devlin, slightly horrified at the exchange, had paled.

"Wouldja look at ya, you've dripped!" Mollie exclaimed in dismay. "Don't mind her luv, I think she's a bit unhinged myself. An as for dat husband o' hers…" she continued grimly. "He's a right little bastard! Dere's a pair of 'em in it. Tinkers the two of 'em! This is her seventh and she always takes it out on the neighbours God preserve us an' save us from all harm." She gave a wicked chuckle. "If I was married to dat little rat I'd tie his balls around his neck for him that's for sure an certain."

Devlin grinned at Mollie's earthy humour. She had often heard Bridie fighting with her husband, sometimes so loudly that poor Eddie would be forced to go out on the landing and bellow at them to be quiet and give the neighbours a bit of peace.

Gradually Devlin began to settle down a little bit. Religiously once a week Caroline came over, and Maggie too if she could manage it. If the weather was fine they went out and forgot their troubles, if not they stayed in and made pot after pot of tea, chatting endlessly. Devlin's heart bled for Caro. That she was not happy was obvious and although sometimes she herself would be feeling fed up and depressed she always made an effort to be cheerful for her friends. It was the happiest time of the week for her when they would visit, a time to lay down the burdens of life, a time for fun, a time for friendship.

Meeting her father once a week was another treat that got her out of the flat. For this occasion she would always wear one of her old snazzy outfits. He had no idea that she was living in Ballymun, existing on the unmarried mother's allowance. Devlin hating to lie but knowing that he would only worry himself sick if he knew the truth, had led him to believe that she was living in a flat in Drumcondra and was working as a doctor's receptionist. Wednesday, the day she met him for lunch, was her day off. Poor Gerry, he wanted to buy her a car but she wouldn't let him, although it would have given her such pleasure and made life so much easier. But there was no way she could afford a car on her allowance, so regretfully she declined his offer, gently but firmly. Of Lydia they never spoke, as if by mutual consent, but although time had eased the bitterness for Devlin, the hurt was still there. Gerry adored his granddaughter and spoilt her as much as Devlin would allow, bringing presents each time they met on her "day off."

The nights were the loneliest. Sometimes

Mollie would drag her to bingo while Rog or Rayo babysat and to her surprise she would enjoy herself listening to the chitchat and gossip and humour of the other women. There were many unmarried mothers like herself living on the vast estate and Devlin became friendly with a few of them. One girl from Galway, Helen, had a seven year old son. A quiet-spoken gentle person, she was firm in her resolve to get out of Ballymun eventually. She told Devlin that she was doing her Leaving Certificate as a mature student and had every intention of going on to university. It was Helen who had told Devlin where to get in touch with the Relieving Officer when she had difficulty paying an ESB bill and it was Helen who encouraged her to start thinking about what she was going to do with her life.

She too would get out of Ballymun, she swore one night, as she listened to Les and Bridie fighting in the flat above her hurling abuse, their loud raucous screeching mingling with the noise of barking dogs, slamming doors, singing drunks, and crying babies that made up the night time sound of Ballymun. Often, unable to sleep, she would stand at her window and look out at the thousand twinkling lights and wonder if she would ever get out of there. At night the velvety darkness hid the ugliness and it could look quite beautiful. It reminded her of the skyscrapers of London or even New York, lit up against the star-studded sky, but the dawn gliding inexorably from the east would bring back reality...and despair. Listening to Lynn wheezing from the dampness that seeped through the walls of the flat, Devlin knew she would have to get somewhere else to live.

On Helen's advice, she had enrolled in night classes in the local comprehensive, taking an accounts class to supplement the business studies course she had taken in London. Mollie, or Margaret, Bernie's daughter, babysat for her while she studied hard, dreaming of getting enough money to set up her own business. It was a daydream that kept her going and often in the warmth of the local library with Lynn dozing in the buggy beside her, she would pore over books that gave advice on setting up in business. Devlin had taken to visiting the library daily, enjoying its warm bright atmosphere as she sat reading in one of the comfortable armchairs that were dotted around. She would watch the girls who served behind the big issue desk as they joked and laughed, thinking that she too had once been a working girl with her own flat and car and a lifestyle that others had envied.

Nobody would envy her now, she thought wryly, engrossing herself in her business books, determined to get out of her rut. Apart from the few times Maggie and Terry had invited her over to their dinner parties, and insisted on her staying overnight with Lynn, occasions she had really enjoyed, she never went anywhere. Caroline had never asked her to visit again and Devlin sensed that all was not well in her marriage, but she did not pry. She knew Caroline of old, knew how loyal she would be to Richard and knew that eventually Caro would confide in her about whatever was troubling her.

With dismay, she realised that Caroline was beginning to drink quite heavily and guessed, knowing her friend, that she was using it as a crutch. If only Caroline could accept herself as she was. The marriage she had so longed for certainly hadn't improved her self-image. Still, if Caroline ever needed help or a shoulder to cry on, she'd have herself and Maggie. Staunch friends counted for a lot, Devlin could testify to that.

And so the months went by and Devlin found herself adapting to her new lifestyle, though not always cheerfully. One Sunday evening in early autumn, Mollie and she took Lynn out for a walk in her buggy. Because she was teething she was whingy and cranky all day and Devlin had begun to feel extremely irritated and short-tempered. Mollie must have sensed her desperation because in her kindly Dublin tones she had suggested, "C'mon luv, let's go for a bit of a ramble, dere's nuttin like a bit of fresh air to lift the ould spirits. We'll leggit up to the back of the airport to watch a few planes."

Within five minutes of walking they had left behind the stark grey towers blocks of the vast estate and were walking past the little church of St Pappin, up then to the Meatpackers' hill and out into the countryside with the vast complex of the airport to the right of them, rich rolling farmland to their left. It was one of the things about Dublin that Devlin loved the most, how swiftly one could get to the country or seaside and away from the noise and the grime of the city streets. Although she was a city girl at heart, Devlin had a keen appreciation of the country.

Because it was Sunday evening the airport was very busy with holiday charters and as Devlin sat on the grass with her baby in her arms and watched the widebellied jets taking off and landing she remembered how she too had once been a carefree jetsetter. Tears came rolling down her cheeks and for the first time since she became pregnant so long ago she gave way to self pity and howled.

"That's right luv. Get it out of your system. There's no use in bottlin' all that lot up inside ya. Many's the little weep I do have meself an ye feel only great after it."

"Th...thanks Mollie," Devlin sniffed. "I don't know what I'd do without you."

"Ya know somethin, Devlin," Mollie said thoughtfully. "I think you should think about goin an livin with your aunt in Wexford. This is no life for a young wan like ya or the chisler."

"Oh I don't know, Mollie," Devlin had answered doubtfully. "It seems unfair to burden Kate with my troubles."

"Kate might like the company," Mollie remarked quietly. It was something Devlin had never thought of. She had been too busy thinking of her own reasons for not going to give any thought to the reason behind Kate's constant invitations. God knows Kate was always at her to come and live in the Harbour. They had always got on exceptionally well and Devlin knew that she was terribly lonely since her husband had died. During the cold damp winter that followed Devlin was to consider the option many times.

Once again she found it necessary to go to the Welfare Officer to help make ends meet, although Caroline and Maggie would have willingly loaned her the money had they known she was in need. But Devlin still had her pride, a fierce determined pride that had given her strength all along. She was responsible for her own actions, she told herself often enough when the money was gone at the end of the week and she knew all she had to do was to ask the girls for the loan of a tenner. They were so unobtrusively kind. Whenever Maggie came to visit she brought a mouthwatering casserole or an apple tart and Caroline was always bringing clothes for Lynn. When Devlin remonstrated with her, she said so sadly that Devlin almost cried for her, "Please let me Dev. She's such a beautiful baby. I wish I could be so lucky and blessed."

It was Maggie, though, who convinced Devlin to move to Wexford with the baby. One winter's evening she invited Devlin and Lynn to stay the night and as she held the little girl in her arms and heard her wheezing after a coughing-bout Maggie said very firmly and with a faint trace of anger, "You know Dev I really think you should go to Kate's. I know you have your pride but Lynn deserves to grow up healthy. And as long as you bury yourself out in Ballymun acting the martyr there's no way her chest is ever going to be right."

"I am not acting the martyr!" Devlin retorted, stung by her friend's accusation.

"Oh come off it, Dev. There's no need for you to to be living out there existing on a pittance. There are plenty of single parents holding down jobs and rearing children. You've got a good brain in your head. You'd get a job no problem in Rosslare. I mean it's the third busiest port in the country!"

"You don't realise that my daughter needs me to look after her when she's sick. That's why I came home from London," Devlin snapped angrily, not liking what Maggie had to say one little bit.

"Well, maybe she wouldn't be sick if she was living in a healthier environment," Maggie said more gently, knowing that she had upset her friend by her blunt talking, but determined to stick to her guns.

There was a long silence as Devlin digested this. Was what Maggie was saying true? Was she acting the martyr and letting her pride stand in the way of having a decent future? Maggie's points were very true. Lynn would never get better in smog-filled Dublin, but the fresh sea air would be a godsend to her. The village itself had a quiet easy-going charm and it was a lovely place to rear a child. Equally true was the fact that the ferryport was expanding at a great rate and a job would not be hard to come by. How nice it would be to earn her own living again.

She looked Maggie squarely in the eye.

"Thanks Maggs. I needed that. I haven't been acting very positively, have I?" she said ruefully.

"I think you just couldn't see the wood for the trees, Dev. I was hoping you'd come to your senses a bit sooner. I've been holding this back for a long time but really, enough is enough."

They grinned at each other and Devlin felt incredibly light-hearted. It was like the light at the end of the proverbial tunnel. It had always been there only she had been too stubborn to see it. Her pride, which at times was one of her greatest strengths, was also one of her greatest flaws.

"You know what I like about us, Dev," Maggie remarked as they sat later, having put the children to bed.

"What?" asked Devlin stretching luxuriously in front of a roaring fire and sipping creamy hot chocolate laced with brandy.

"We can say what we like to each other and not get huffy."

Devlin laughed. "You can say that again! Maggie you're the straightest person I know. Acting the martyr indeed!"

"You know me, Dev. If I've something to say I say it and that's it, all forgotten about then. That's what real friends are all about. Believe me, I know."

"I wouldn't have it any other way, Maggs," Devlin replied, giving her friend a warm hug that was just as warmly returned.

twenty

A few months later Devlin had made the move. Once she had made her decision, she seemed like a new person. Her old positive way of thinking took over and she sloughed off the careworn anxiety that had engulfed her since Lynn's birth.

Things would turn out all right. Single parenthood was not easy—there was no arguing about that—but thousands of others had coped: widows, widowers, married people and unmarrieds. It was only her negative thinking and stubborn pride that had enmeshed her in a prison of her own making. Thank God Maggie and Mollie had made her see reason.

Paradoxically, she felt a sense of regret as she closed the door of her Ballymun flat behind her. Mollie and Bernie had been terribly good neighbours. She would miss Mollie's reassuring presence next door and Bernie's constant good humour. She had got to know many of the people in her block and when word got out that she was going to live in Wexford, Bernie, Mollie and some of the other women had organised a little going away "do" for her. The laughs and crack had been mighty and Devlin had left Ballymun with the good wishes of her neighbours ringing in her ears as they waved her goodbye.

Her father was delighted when she told him she was going to live with Kate. His eyes lit up and his hug was tight when she told him the news at their Wednesday lunch. "Ah Devlin, that's great news!" he exclaimed. "It will be great for Lynn growing up, and Kate must be beside herself with pleasure."

Devlin laughed. "She certainly is, Dad, she can't wait. She's going to spoil my daughter dreadfully, I'm afraid."

"Let her!" Gerry ordered, smiling. "A bit of spoiling never did anyone any harm."

She would miss her weekly date with her father but he promised he would visit often. When he once again wrote Devlin a cheque for three thousand pounds "to get her going," as he said himself, she had been tempted to refuse it. But Maggie's words came back to her and she took the money graciously, knowing that it made him happy. She might open a little craft shop or bookshop to cater for the hundreds of tourists who came to the village in Wexford each summer. The possibilities were endless and she felt excited at the thought of the life that lay ahead. It was great to feel she was in control again, and how wonderful it would be to earn her own money and be independent once more.

She kept her goodbyes to Caroline and Maggie short and sweet. It wasn't that she wouldn't see them again, she told herself, as she tried unsuccessfully to swallow the lump in her throat when they had gone out for a farewell drink a few days before she finally said goodbye to city life. It would be strange not seeing them each week, but they had all kept in contact by letter before and Rosslare was only a two-and-a-half-hour trip from Dublin. The girls could come down for long weekends and she could come up and visit them.

Kate was thrilled to bits that Devlin had at last decided to come and live with her. They sat gabbing for hours the first few days, after the arrival of Devlin and Lynn, making plans for Devlin's future. They decided that leasing a premises to open a craft- and book-shop would be the ideal thing for Devlin. Her father's three thousand pounds plus the same amount from Kate would be more than enough to start a small business in which Kate and Devlin would be partners. But first her aunt insisted that Devlin take a holiday for a few weeks, doing nothing but relaxing in the glorious sunshine. Each morning Kate would pack her a picnic lunch and send her and Lynn off down to the beach below the house.

Lying on the golden sand watching fluffy little clouds drifting by and listening to the gentle lapping of the waves against the shore Devlin felt months of accumulated tension slowly melt into the sand beneath her. Each day she became more relaxed as the tight coil of apprehension that seemed to have become part of her, slowly loosened and life, which had become such a burden, became a new and invigorating challenge. The change in her daughter was even more gratifying. Each night, having played on the beach beside her mother all day, Lynn would sleep like a log, the rich ionised sea air stronger than the most powerful sleeping pill. Even Devlin would find herself yawning hugely by ten thirty. Most nights she couldn't remember her head hitting the pillow. But then, Rosslare air had always had that effect on her. Both of them were eating like horses and it gave Kate the greatest of satisfaction to watch her niece and grandniece gain much needed pounds. Tanned shapely curves replaced Devlin's gaunt appearance and Lynn soon had chubby pink cheeks that made her mother so glad she had made the decision to move. It was one of the happiest times of Devlin's life and her letters to Gerry, Caroline and Maggie bubbled with an enthusiasm they hadn't seen in her since before Lynn was born.

Kate and Devlin drove in to Wexford with Lynn one day to speak to a solicitor about leasing a premises that had been offered to Devlin in Rosslare. It was all fairly straightforward and the solicitor assured Devlin that she could go ahead and start ordering the stock for the new shop.

In celebration they went to White's Hotel and treated themselves to a magnificent meal as they decided what exactly they would buy. They were still engrossed in their discussion as Kate drove the twelve miles home from Wexford. So

engrossed were they that Devlin wasn't aware of
the huge juggernaut thundering along behind
them as it sped towards the French ferry. As it
overtook them at speed it skidded on black oil
and caught the car a glancing blow, sending it
careering into the ditch. All Devlin remembered
was the sickening thud and her own screams
before she was knocked into oblivion.

twenty-one

A month later, her baby daughter and Kate dead and buried, Devlin sat in a wheelchair in the warm early autumn sun in the grounds of a Dublin private hospital. A nurse walked across the grass and checked her drip before handing her her medication. Obediently Devlin swallowed the pills.

"Is everything all right, Devlin? Would you like a cup of tea sent out; it's afternoon tea time?" the nurse asked cheerfully.

"No thank you, I'm fine."

"Are you warm enough? Do you want another rug?" The nurse patted the plaid rug around Devlin's knees.

For God's sake would you just leave me alone, Devlin wanted to scream at the white-uniformed woman standing in front of her. There was no peace for her, they were always at her. Doctors poking, nurses waking her up to take her temperature, physiotherapists making her exercise, radiographers taking X-rays, priests murmuring words of compassion and comfort at her bedside. Why couldn't they all leave her alone?

She knew the nurse was only doing her job,

and so was everybody else. The staff of the hospital were very kind to her but Devlin, completely traumatised by the horrific accident and the deaths of Lynn and Kate, found their attentions irksome.

She once again heavily assured the nurse that she was fine and mercifully the woman moved on to another patient. Thoughts flooded back. Devlin had been in a coma for a week, during which time her daughter and aunt had been buried side by side in the quiet little harbour graveyard at Rosslare. Devlin was brought to Dublin by ambulance and admitted to a neurological unit in a city hospital and she regained consciousness to find Lydia and Gerry at her bedside.

When they told her, she turned her head away but did not cry. She couldn't. Even now, weeks later, she could not let her sorrow express itself. Night and day she asked herself *why*? After all the hardship and heartbreak, the decision not to have the abortion, the struggle that had followed, and now just as life had taken a turn for the better for both of them, God had let this happen to them. Lynn and Kate, the most precious people in the world for her, were gone and she was left. Worst of all was the numbness. Devlin felt that she should show grief, but all she felt was this strange unreal numbness.

Devlin suddenly became aware that a man was standing in front of her blocking the sunlight. She raised her head, expecting it to be her father or one of the doctors. A deep, faintly familiar voice asked quietly, "It's Devlin Delaney isn't it?" Surprised, she squinted in the sunlight and recognised Luke Reilly, who was obviously unable to mask his surprise and shock at the sight of her. She supposed she looked a sight but her appearance had ceased to cost her a thought. She wore the filmy negligées Lydia brought her and allowed the nurses to brush her hair, but apart from that, she took no interest in how she looked. Sometimes she would catch sight of herself in the mirror and see a thin gaunt hollow-eyed woman. But she did not care.

"Hello." Her response was automatic. Why did he have to stand there staring? Why couldn't he just go and leave her alone?

Luke Reilly knew he was staring but couldn't help it. My God! What has she gone through, he found himself wondering, as he noted her extreme pallor, the deep dark circles around the eyes that had lost their sparkle, the blonde hair once shining and bouncy, now so dull and limp. What shocked him most was the suffering that was evident in her blue eyes, now huge pools of sadness that made him catch his breath. Awkwardly he stood in front of her, not knowing what to say. Then he cleared his throat: "I'm sorry to see you like this, Devlin. I hope it won't be long until you are recovered."

"Thanks," she murmured, surprised at the gentleness of his tone. At least he had the sensitivity to realise that she wanted to be left alone.

She watched his broad figure stride across the grass and wondered briefly what he was doing at the hospital, but soon forgot him as the cloud of misery descended on her once again.

Two days later they met again. This time she was on crutches, the nurses having insisted that she was no longer sick enough for the wheelchair. "Hello, Devlin," he said crisply.

"Hello," Her tone was guarded. She remembered she hadn't taken to him the first time she had met him at her parents' house nearly three years before. He had seemed so overpowering, yet there was a strength about him that was strangely attractive.

"You seem to be making progress," he smiled at her, and she noted the strong even white teeth and the nice way his eyes crinkled up at the sides.

"I suppose you could say that." Her tone was uncharacteristically bitter.

"These things take time but at least you've plenty of that," he said, and she caught a note of sadness in his voice. He said goodbye and she found herself wondering who he was visiting. A wife, maybe? She must ask him the next time she saw him. Although Maggie and Caroline visited often and tried to cheer her up, she felt in the few moments she had spent with him that he had understood her grief although he could have known nothing of what had happened to her.

It was a week before she saw him again. He looked tired, deep lines running down the sides of his mouth but he smiled when he saw her.

"Hello." This time she greeted him first.

Good, he thought to himself. She's getting better. "How are you?"

"Well, at least I'm getting the hang of these things." She indicated her crutches. They walked along the hospital corridor, he matching his pace to hers.

"Are you visiting someone?" Devlin inquired.

He turned and his amber eyes clouded. "It's my father," he explained quietly. "He's dying."

"Oh...Oh, I'm sorry," she murmured inadequately.

"He had a good life, and a very full one," Luke said half to himself. "He's slipping in and out of a coma. I try to get here as often as I can. I have a lot of business commitments in London." He sighed. "It's not easy."

For the first time since her accident Devlin felt some emotion for another human being. Having been so wrapped up in herself she hadn't taken much notice of the other sick people around her. She heard herself asking, "Does your wife never come over?"

They stood staring at each other and she blushed at her impertinence. "Oh excuse me," she stammered. "That was very rude of me."

"I'm not married," he said quietly, his heavy-lidded amber eyes staring down at her, a strange look in their attractive depths.

"Oh." Devlin felt a flicker of surprise at this piece of information.

Luke smiled at her. "My poor old Dad was always on at me every time I came home. 'Any sign yet?' he'd say to me." He rubbed a hand wearily along his jaw. "It was a bit of a disappointment to him, I suppose. He always wanted me to come home and settle down. I don't think he liked Nola. "

It was as though he had forgotten she was there. And she wondered who the disliked Nola was.

He shook his head slightly. "Excuse me, Devlin. Of course this means nothing to you. I didn't mean to keep you standing so long."

"That's OK. I've nothing much else to do anyway." Then a thought struck her. "If you like," she said a little hesitantly, realising that she wasn't the only person in the world to suffer trauma, "I'll sit with your father sometimes, when you aren't here."

He stared at her. "Would you really, Devlin? That's extremely kind of you. I know the nursing staff here are excellent but they can't be there all the time and I hate to think of him being alone." He smiled down at her and it warmed her. "I'd be very grateful."

"You'd better show me his room," Devlin murmured, half sorry she had offered. What on earth had possessed her? Hadn't she enough problems of her own without getting involved with anyone else's?

He showed her to a private room similar to her own, and as she watched Luke take the limp hand of the waxen-faced old man who lay so frail and ill in the bed she was glad she had made her impulsive offer. It was obvious that there was a strong bond between them and she found it touching to see the way Luke cared for his father.

She was discovering that there were many sides to Luke's character and gradually, over the weeks that followed, she found herself growing closer to him. She told him of her accident and about her aunt's death but she couldn't bring herself to talk about the baby. That was her secret, forever to be buried in her past. Lynn was gone and she was left and the only way she could deal with her grief was to push the memory of her daughter into the furthest recesses of her mind.

Luke had been very interested when she told him that she and Kate had planned to start up in business together. Briefly she told him a little of her time in London, omitting all reference to Lynn, and he was fascinated to hear that she had taken a night course in business studies.

"Brains *and* beauty," he teased her. And she gave a rare smile.

"Will you carry on with your business plan in Rosslare?" he inquired

Devlin swallowed and shook her head. "There's nothing down there for me now," she said tightly, and turned her head away from him so he wouldn't see the tears that glittered in her eyes.

"I understand."

When she had composed herself she turned to

face him. "I would still like to go into business for myself. Perhaps you might advise me on an idea I have."

"Of course I will. It's the least I can do to try and repay your kindness. But it will have to be next week. Here's Agnes to throw me out and I'm flying to London first thing in the morning." Luke smiled at Agnes, their favourite night nurse, who would always bring him a cup of tea along with Devlin's.

"Go on with you, Luke Reilly," Agnes smiled at the handsome man in front of her. "You should have been gone an hour ago."

"Ah Agnes, under that tough exterior lies the softest heart in Dublin. You can't fool me. Look after Devlin for me, I'll just go and look in on Dad." He smiled at the nurse, touched Devlin's cheek with a gentle finger and then he was gone and the room seemed suddenly empty.

"That's one nice man," Agnes said approvingly as she gave Devlin her medication and settled her bed for the night. "Good night, pet. If you need me ring the bell and if you can't sleep I'll make you some hot milk later on."

"Thanks, Agnes."

The door closed quietly behind her and Devlin was alone with her thoughts.

What would Luke think of her idea when she told him about it? Would it work? She couldn't think why not. To keep herself from going crazy with thoughts of Lynn and Kate during the long pain-filled nights, she had developed this idea.

An idea that returned constantly to her and which gave her something to hold on to. Something to sustain her. She wanted to open an exclusive health centre in Dublin, to cater to the wealthy who had the money to throw around. It would be something on the lines of the one she had worked in in London. Devlin was convinced that it would take off. The market was there and as far as she was aware, it hadn't yet been tapped. True there were health and fitness clubs in the city, but nothing *Exclusive*.

Kate had willed her the farm and a substantial amount of money and her father's solicitor had told her she could expect a very large settlement in damages for her own injuries. It was with this money that she would set up her own business.

twenty-two

One evening they sat outside Luke's father's room, while the nurses were caring for him. The subject of Devlin's business venture at last came up for discussion. From what Luke had told her, he was obviously a sound businessman with an instinctive flair for a good opportunity. Self-made, he had left school at seventeen and gone to sea. For several years he had travelled the world and made enough money to invest in land and property. He had then gone to London, invested in several profitable business ventures and never looked back. He commuted regularly between London and Dublin and still owned several properties around Dublin.

When Devlin told him of her idea he was intrigued and they spent hours discussing the project. "You know," he said thoughtfully, "as well as catering to the wealthy trendsetter lot, I think you should cater for the young 'upwardly mobile' woman executives who put in a hard day at the office and need a place to relax, unwind, keep fit or whatever. There's a lot of them around. Nola used to go to one in London all the time."

Who is this Nola, she wondered. This was the second time he had mentioned her. "Hmmm...You're right there." She smiled at him. "That's a very good idea, Luke. In fact I was just reading an article the other day that said the very same thing. The hotel business is just beginning to cater for these American Express-waving women. Maybe it's just what the city needs. We could cater for both types and maybe I'll just open a club specifically for women, you know, like The Sanctuary in London."

Luke felt a strange sense of achievement as he watched a faint hint of pink banish the dreadful pallor from Devlin's face. There was a spark of animation in her expressive blue eyes as she discussed this dream of hers and slowly but surely he was beginning to inch his way through that reserve that she so successfully hid behind.

Luke had never met a woman who interested him as much as Devlin. He couldn't explain it. He hadn't been joking when he had told her she had brains as well as beauty. She had a sharp intelligent mind and they could talk business for hours, but when the subject became personal she retreated behind her guard and the old unhappy look would reappear. He had a powerful longing to make her laugh, to banish the pain from her eyes. Many nights he lay awake wondering how he, man of the world Reilly, could be so obsessed by her. For him it was a new experience and a disturbing one. He hadn't planned on getting involved with anyone for a while after the break up of his relationship with Nola Hanlon, a personnel manager in a large London building society. Nola's hard, driving ambition had ultimately wrecked their love affair. It wasn't that Luke didn't understand his lover's drive to succeed. He did. He, of all people, knew what it was like to have goals and ambitions, and he had encouraged and advised her as much as he could, but it seemed to him that as she stepped higher up the ladder of success, she became harder, more ruthless.

"They think I'm a bitch at work," she often moaned to him and in a way he felt sorry for her. She was in a position of power over people and she gloried in it. She could transfer staff from one building society branch to another, all over London, something she did with great frequency, not caring that personal lives could be affected drastically. Flats would have to be changed, longer distances spent commuting. To her, the staff were pawns on a chessboard, not people with feelings.

"It's good for them, keeps them on their toes, Luke," she argued when he pointed these things out to her. "You're much too soft. I don't know how you succeeded in business."

"I succeeded," he said evenly, "because I have a very loyal highly-motivated staff who work hard for me because I look after them and treat them with respect."

"Oh shut up!" she retorted.

"If you don't like my opinions, don't ask for

them," Luke responded curtly. Their arguments had become more frequent, Nola was promoted yet again and spent more and more time in the office. Work dominated her waking time completely and they spent less and less time together. What had attracted him in the first place—her drive, her energy, her will to succeed—was eventually the cause of their splitting up. He had the same traits himself, but he also had a caring quality that Nola, with all her success and achievement, completely lacked. He knew their relationship would never be her number one priority until she had achieved everything she had aimed for in her career and he had to admire her singlemindedness. There were many businessmen he knew who were less singleminded than she. But he needed more from the relationship than she could give and so they parted. Now here was Devlin Delaney who not only had Nola's intelligence and ambition but a vulnerability and compassion that his former lover would never possess. She intrigued him like no other woman he had ever met.

An idea began forming in Luke's mind one evening as he sat on a 737 winging its way across the Irish Sea. One long tanned finger rubbed his dark evening-shadowed jaw in reflection. Oblivious to the admiration in the eyes of the attractive air hostess as she handed him his drink, he murmured a polite thanks as facts and figures raced through his quick brain. A slow smile curved his firm mouth. Lucky girl! thought the air hostess enviously, accepting defeat as she watched him take a pad and paper from his briefcase and begin writing.

His father had neither improved nor disimproved and he sat patiently beside the hospital bed holding the thin old hand in his. Devlin had been there when he arrived, sitting beside his father, a great sadness in her eyes as she wiped the sweat from the old man's face. Their eyes had met and Luke had felt a surge of gratitude—and something else—for the frail girl with the huge luminous aquamarine eyes that smiled when she saw him.

"I'll see you later," she whispered, leaving him alone with his dad.

Later, when Devlin's own visitors had left and the night nurse began pulling the curtains and bringing supper around, they sat in her room and she told him that she was to be discharged in another week or so. Her physical injuries had healed well, whatever about her emotional wounds.

"I'm going looking for a loan. Do you think I'll be successful?" she asked. Luke said nothing for a while and then he said steadily, "Well, Devlin, from what you've told me, you've certainly got acceptable collateral in the property your aunt left you as well as the settlement you'll get from the insurance company." He smiled. "You know as well as I do that for the business you hope to start and for the clientele you hope to attract you are going to need a good central property and a hell of an amount of cash to stock, staff and decorate it. Your overheads will be big and frankly..." he paused, as if unsure of what to say next.

"Go on."

"Don't think I'm patronising you, Devlin. I assure you I'm not, but I don't know if you have enough experience to convince a bank manager to give you the amount you are going to need. That's if you really want to have the best of everything, and in my view, for the business you envisage, nothing but the best will do."

Devlin looked at him glumly. She didn't think he was being in the slightest bit patronising. He was just being perfectly straight with her, which was one thing she liked about him. Besides, she had had the same thought herself. Luke cleared his throat. "Listen, Devlin, you know the old saying 'two heads are better than one?' As it happens I think yours is a great business idea and I'll certainly understand if you want to go it alone. But if you'd like to accept me as a partner, I have a property in Stephen's Green that might be ideal."

He stood up, his broad-shouldered body impressive in a black leather jacket, neatly pressed grey pants hugging his long legs. Beside him Devlin felt like a pygmy. "Think about it," he said easily and walked from the room. She watched how he walked, like a panther. There was something so solid and dependable about Luke, she mused. How mistaken she had been about him at their first meeting. It must have been her hormones. Her mind weighed the pros and cons of the idea. What he said was true and his business experience would be invaluable. The idea of property on the Green was enticing. Right beside one of the most trendy shopping areas in Dublin, it could not but attract the moneyed citizens of the capital. From listening to how he visualised it, and from her own experience in London, she knew he was right about the amount of money that would have to be spent. Devlin also knew that Luke would not have made such an offer if he hadn't thought it was going to work. They would have to get the best of everything to appeal to those who could afford it. It would have to become an *in* place to be seen at—that took money.

Excitement rose within her. Instinct told her it was going to work and she decided to accept Luke's proposal. Impatiently she waited to see him the following day. Devlin had grown to look forward to his visits. His ideas excited her and she could understand how he had made his fortune. There was always a slight air of impatience about him, as if he was straining at some invisible leash and ready to explode into action.

When he finally did come and stood at the door late on the following evening, her heart went out to him as she saw the taut grimness of his face. He didn't have to tell her his father had died. It was written all over his face. Devlin swallowed hard. She didn't want to think about it, didn't want to bring back all her own misery, misery that she had savagely suppressed these last few weeks. But he was suffering and needed comfort as she had needed it. Wordlessly she held out her arms to him and felt him bury his face in her hair. She held him tightly for a long while, her heart aching for both of them, her thoughts turning to Lynn whom she would never hold in her arms again. Grimly, frantically she struggled to control herself, afraid to release the emotion she had never expressed over her bereavements. She couldn't add to his grief. If she started to cry now she would never stop. She managed, just about, and a little later he drew away from her and managed a brief smile.

"Thank you, Devlin. You've helped me more than you could know...I've got to go and make funeral arrangements. I'll see you when it's over."

Three days later he strode into the ward with three dozen red roses. He looked tired: his craggy lean face seemed to have aged and the touch of grey at his temples seemed more pronounced but he smiled warmly at her. Devlin smiled back, a blush tinting her cheeks as she accepted the flowers. "For a caring generous lady," he said softly. "I really appreciate what you did for my father. Thank you."

"Not at all, Luke. Honestly, there was no need for you to take this trouble when you have so many other things to do right now," Devlin said, slightly embarrassed, yet touched by his gesture. She looked him straight in the eye. "You'd want to start saving your money if we are going into business together. To staff, stock and decorate *it*, you're going to need lots and lots of cash!" There was a wicked glint in her blue eyes.

A broad grin spread across Luke's face as her words sank in. He could feel the adrenalin begin to rush through his body as it always did at the start of a new venture. He knew they were on to a winner. Maybe he could make Devlin feel attracted to him as he was to her. He knew it would be a long slow process. She had been hurt, and hurt badly by something or someone. Luke squared his broad shoulders. He had never backed down from a challenge and she was the biggest he had ever encountered. He wouldn't rush things, though. Reaching into his briefcase he said crisply. "Don't just sit there grinning, Miss, we've got plenty of work to do!" Handing her a pen and some blank pages he said, smiling at her, "Let's get down to business, pardner!"

twenty-three

For Devlin the next six months were a hectic but exhilarating time. She worked tirelessly, throwing herself into the preparations despite Luke's admonitions that she take things easy. Physically she was recovered. She wanted to keep herself busy every minute she could, to try to smother the feelings of guilt and grief that consumed her. If she hadn't decided to go and live in Wexford, Kate and the baby might still be alive today. Her heart felt like a vast lead weight and every time a thought of Lynn came into her head it was frantically banished. Don't think about it! Don't think about it, she ordered herself a thousand times a day. Live for now, this minute, don't think about the past. It got her through the days but the nights were torture.

She knew Maggie and Caroline couldn't understand her seeming lack of grief, but not even with them could she talk about it. For the first time in her life she couldn't let the girls help her, although she had listened and comforted Caroline when she told her about her treatment for alcoholism. Devlin couldn't bring herself to share her grief and let go because she was afraid of the torrents of emotion any giving into it would unleash.

Bitterly she told Lydia that she wanted nothing to do with her and the other woman had not come to the hospital again. Nor had she seen her since her discharge, although she met her father several times a week.

Luke would sometimes look at her, a perplexed look in his eyes as she kept pace with him step for step in the development of the club, bouncing her ideas off him, learning from his suggestions and gaining confidence in herself and the venture as everything began to slot into place. They could talk about anything concerning the business and talk they did, but with any hint of the talk turning personal, Devlin clammed up, politely but very firmly, steering the topic around to business matters again.

Don't push, he told himself a thousand times, but no matter how gently he tried to get behind her reserve he wasn't having much luck. Even the odd deliberate reference to Nola elicited no queries as he had expected it to. He could have sworn she had been surprised when he told her he wasn't married but obviously he had read more into her response than was there. Was it just that she wasn't interested in him? Or was she getting over an unhappy love affair? If only he had some line to go on. The woman was driving him crazy.

Devlin knew her behaviour puzzled her

partner, but she couldn't help it. Her new health
club consumed her. It was all she cared about. It
filled her mind and kept her thoughts from other
painful things and that was the way it was going
to be. Luke had insisted that she visit similar
clubs in London, Paris and the States and she
had spent ten long informative days in a plush
resort in Florida where many rich and famous
celebrities came to relax and fight the flab and
make the body beautiful. The treatments she
herself received had left her glowing and
refreshed, she had even gained some of the
weight that had fallen off her in hospital and she
had come back to Dublin bursting with ideas for
their place. Luke had flown over from London
later in the week following her return and his
heart lifted at the sight of her. She looked so
tanned and vital, almost like the Devlin he had
first seen so long ago, but catching her in an
unguarded moment staring down at some children going to feed the ducks in the Green he had
cursed beneath his breath at the awful lonely
sadness in her eyes. If only she would tell him
what had caused that pain he might have been
able to give her some comfort. It had to be more
than grief for her aunt, he knew they had been
close but surely time would have started healing
the sadness. He considered asking Gerry but
decided against it. That would be an invasion of
her privacy. If Devlin wanted to tell him what
was troubling her, she would, and if and when
she did, he knew he would have moved a big step

forward in their relationship. Better to know her crisp and businesslike than not to know her at all.

Devlin decided to call the club CITY GIRL and Luke liked the name. It had a snazzy uptown ring to it and the interest that was already being shown gave a good indication that they were on to a winner. Caroline and Maggie were as excited as Devlin and there were endless discussions about the decor. The building, which had previously housed offices, was gutted from top to bottom, the elegant Georgian facade cleaned and painted. With the help of the designer of the Florida resort, the interior of the building was transformed into a luxurious haven.

"Get the best," said Luke, and she did. Only the plushest of furniture was used, enormous cane sofas and chairs with soft plump cushions lay dotted around the lounging areas, which were decorated in soft pastel colours, muted pinks and greys and pale greens. The relaxing ambience exuded a subtle air of wealth, tinged with unmistakable sophistication It was the perfect place for a busy business woman or rich wife to relax with friends.

Professional staff was recruited. CITY GIRL had its own doctor, nurse, beauty consultants, as well as masseurs, hairdressers, aerobics instructors and a host of other personnel. The rooftop swimming pool, jacuzzis and saunas were surrounded by vivid, lush tropical plants and enclosed under a huge glass dome. It was a rich green paradise at artificial temperatures. There were two intimate restaurants, and an attractive Spanish-tiled shopping mall which sold wildly expensive goods. There was a small library where the weary city girl could relax over the daily newspapers, or read a few chapters of the latest on the best sellers list. If she wished she could take a linguaphone course while having a pedicure, or perhaps, dictate a business letter while having her manicure, to a top class secretary who would have it ready for her departure.

Visiting business executives from other countries could avail of CITY GIRL's exclusive services. And there was wide corporate interest in the club which generated enormous business. Membership of CITY GIRL became one of the tantalising perks that corporate employers used to headhunt the best. As Luke had foretold, membership of the club became a status symbol and even women from other parts of the country who visited the capital two or three times a month availed of a special membership of the club.

The venture was succeeding beyond Devlin's wildest dreams but even so, she didn't forget old friends. She asked Eddie, Mollie's husband, to take charge of the carpentry and Rog and Rayo were sent to do a course in lifesaving with a view to becoming pool attendants. The boys had noticed that Devlin couldn't bear to talk about Lynn or the accident, so by unspoken agreement it was a taboo topic. To all intents and purposes, her secret past life had never happened. Only with Mollie would Devlin make a passing reference to the past, when lonely, tormented, unable to face the thoughts of an evening alone she would drive out to her friend's lovely new corporation house in the Liberties, and spend a few hours with the kind motherly woman.

Devlin's lifestyle had changed dramatically. She was now the managing director of a fantastically successful company, CITY GIRL Ltd, and earning a large salary. When she had protested about the amount, Luke said firmly, "Devlin, you'll earn every penny of it. There's no point in living on a pittance. You'll be entertaining potential clients, you'll need your expense account. You need a place to live that's going to be relaxing and comfortable for you after the ten- or twelve-hour day you'll be putting in. The first rule of good business is pay a decent salary and you and I are employees just like the others. They deserve their salaries; so do we." He grinned at her. "Don't worry, if we are in danger of going bankrupt you'll be the first to know."

He was right of course. And there was not the slightest fear of them going bankrupt. The figures were very firmly in the black.

Devlin bought an apartment in the same complex as Caroline, although it seemed as if she was never there. Luke was right: she was earning every penny of her salary. The new club excited enormous media interest and the opening day was something Devlin would never forget. A PR firm worked flat out to ensure that it was one of the biggest social events of the year. Devlin spent the day being interviewed by the press, radio, and TV and in the process became something of a celebrity.

She was invited to opening nights, galas, and a host of other functions, which she went to, realising that by maintaining a high profile she would generate more business for the club. It was a strategy that worked. Women were clamouring for membership, not the least deterred by the hefty yearly fees. To be a member of CITY GIRL was a must for the socially conscious woman.

Devlin's life was full. Yet the emptiness inside would not go away. She couldn't bear to be alone, yet she longed sometimes for solitude at the height of a hectic party or in her plush office at the club where there was a constant stream of people requiring her attention. For the first time in their friendship she couldn't talk to Caroline and Maggie about her feelings. They too were emotionally wounded, Caroline by her alcoholism and by something else, something that affected her marriage that she could not talk about either. Maggie, deeply hurt by Terry's affair, was pouring all her bitter feelings into the novel she was writing. Devlin had read what she had written and the raw pain in some of the writing had made her want to cry as she identified with it. Poor Maggie was so giving and yet

Terry, the fool, couldn't see what he was losing. She could almost understand Caroline turning to drink because of being married to Richard, but Terry cheating on Maggie? That she couldn't credit. They all had such problems, and they couldn't talk to each other. It wasn't that their friendship was under strain. Devlin decided that the reason she didn't want to talk to her friends about her emotional state was because they had enough troubles of their own, without her burdening them with hers. Although she didn't realise it, that was the exact reason the other girls had for not telling her their troubles.

Sometimes she longed to confide in Luke. If only she could bring herself to. He had the most calming way about him and could see straight to the heart of a problem and take quick decisive measures to solve it. She had seen him in action so many times during the build up to the opening of CITY GIRL. Calm, totally in control, he had time to talk to anybody who needed to talk to him. He treated his staff with the utmost respect and they loved him for it. Devlin had learned a lot from Luke Reilly. She made frequent trips to London to keep him informed of progress. He left most of the day-to-day running of the complex in her capable hands but major decisions they made together. He was always so glad to see her, always so pleased by the great success of their joint venture.

The first time she went to London, she had stayed at her old haunt, the Tara. At dinner later that evening. Luke had said teasingly, "You know I do have a three-bedroomed apartment overlooking the Thames. Think of what you could save the company by staying there instead of using your expense account on hotel accommodation."

Devlin laughed. She loved Luke's sense of humour. It made her feel young and a little carefree again. Sometimes his dry asides during long intense company meetings would set her off into fits of giggles. It was a bit daft, her staying in a hotel when they had so much to discuss, so the next time she flew over she stayed in his luxurious but homely apartment. He cooked the most magnificent meal for her and they stayed talking until the early hours. He was so supportive that it touched her deeply and she always flew home after her time with him feeling more invigorated and alive, her unhappiness forgotten for a while.

She realised that he had more than a business interest in her although he had never pushed or made any mention of it. Had things been different in her life, had she been able to scale the huge wall of her grief, it was something she would have welcomed. Men like Luke Reilly were few and far between. But to love was to be hurt—that was a lesson life had taught her. Lynn, Kate, Lydia, even Colin. All she had was the pain of love. She would never allow herself to care for someone deeply again. CITY GIRL was all she needed.

twenty-four

Several months after the opening, Luke flew over to Dublin, something he did regularly. He took Devlin to dinner as usual but noticed that she was uncharacteristically subdued. His heart sank. He decided he was definitely losing his touch with women. He seemed no nearer to penetrating her reserve whenever matters turned personal. She was completely engrossed in the business and while he was delighted with the club's success he often cursed it for taking her away from him. Was this a repeat of his earlier experiences?

No! there was no comparison between Nola's naked ambition and hunger to succeed, and Devlin's total absorption with CITY GIRL. She was immersing herself in the business because she was trying to forget someone or something and it seemed there was nothing he could do about it.

Studying her discreetly in the soft lamplight of the restaurant, he sighed. A cap of shining blonde hair fell in a soft silky curtain to frame her beautiful heart-shaped face. Perfect wing-tipped eyebrows arched delicately over her darkly lashed aquamarine eyes that were, tonight, gazing with a sad faraway expression into the space behind him. Her beautiful soft tender lips, which he dreamed constantly of kissing, taunted him with their unapproachableness and he groaned inwardly. He couldn't take much more of this! She was driving him nuts. He noticed her toying with her food. She had hardly eaten a mouthful all evening.

"Don't eat it if you don't want it!" He spoke sharply, his frustration making him abrupt. Startled, she came back to earth.

"I'm sorry," Devlin said. "I'm not hungry."

"Well, that's obvious," he remarked dryly. "Why don't you tell me what's the matter?"

"Nothing's the matter," she retorted coolly, her lips tightening.

"Come off it Devlin!" Luke snapped, more angry with himself than with her. "You haven't spoken two words all evening. Is something going wrong at CITY GIRL?"

"CITY GIRL is fine." Devlin spoke back just as sharply, surprised at his tone. Catching his angry stare she saw a muscle jerking in the side of his jaw. Just lately there seemed to be a vague tension between them when they were outside the business environment and tonight she was not up to it. "I think I'd like to go home."

"Fine."

In silence he paid the bill, held her coat for her and walked towards the car. Grimly polite, he held the door open for her and slammed his own with more force than was necessary. They drove to her apartment without speaking. When they got there Luke said coldly, "I thought we were more than business partners. I thought we were friends, but obviously I was wrong. I'm sorry. Goodnight Devlin." His eyes were hard flints of amber and his anger chilled her. She had never seen him like this. Pain darkened her blue eyes and she turned her head away to hide the tears that sparkled in them. Without answering, because she was afraid she would cry, she got out of the car and ran up the steps. Hearing the angry rev of the engine, she saw the car disappear down the drive in a cloud of dust. The tears that had been welling up inside exploded down her cheeks and when she got into her apartment she leaned her head against the hard cold plane of the door and let them fall silently, warmly, wetly down her face. Oh God, if only she could have told him! She wanted to tell him more than anything and now it was too late...

The doorbell, shrill and abrupt, intruded on her distress. Devlin heard his voice, deep and resonant through the intercom. "Let me in, Devlin!" Luke ordered.

Devlin knew she could fight herself no longer and she needed badly to talk to someone. She couldn't carry it alone any more and she needed him to know, wanted him to know. She pressed the button and moments later heard the lift come purring up to her landing. Opening the door she turned away from him so he could not see her tears but he swung her around to face him and muttered an imprecation as he saw the expression on her ravaged face. "Ah Devlin, what's wrong? Can't you tell me?" he said, horrified by the haunted pain in her eyes.

Devlin buried her face against his chest. "Oh Luke, help me...I can't cope with it any more. I...I can't bear it!" She was crying now, racking sobs shaking her body.

"Can't bear what, sweetheart? Tell me so I can help," he murmured, drawing her down beside him as he sat on the sofa and holding her tightly.

His kindness was the key that unlocked the grief that had been imprisoned in her heart throught all those eventful months since the accident. And the words came rushing out of her.

"Oh Luke, Luke...the accident...I...I...my baby died a year ago today."

Devlin heard his sharp indrawn breath and went to draw away from him, sure that he was shocked, but his arms tightened around her and as she wept openly against his shoulder his hand gently stroked her hair. All the grief she had suppressed so long poured out of her and she cried bitterly as she told him everything.

Later, he made tea for them after wiping her tear-stained face with a facecloth, as gently as a mother would her child. They talked for hours with no more reserve between them until pink slashes of dawn began to streak the eastern sky.

"Go to bed, Devlin. I'll be here when you wake up," he said, knowing instinctively that it was what she wanted. Her fingers rested briefly against his cheek.

"Thank you, Luke. I can't tell you how much you've help..."

"Hush." He didn't let her finish. "That's what friends are for and you and I are friends. Never forget that! Now try and sleep!"

As he sat on her sofa pondering all that she had told him, from the child's conception, her own adoption and estrangement from Lydia, to her life over the past few years he realised why she had been so guarded and reserved.

Luke knew without doubt that he was falling in love with Devlin. Nothing she had told him had changed that. If anything, he admired her all the more for all she had gone through. If he could help her get through this maybe she could put her past behind her and look to the future. A future that held him. The fact that she had told him everything, held nothing back, was a step in the right direction. She had even asked him about Nola! And he had thought she hadn't even noticed his deliberate name-dropping. Luke smiled to himself. He had cared deeply for Nola when they were together but it was nothing compared to what he felt for Devlin. At last she had taken the first real trusting step in their relationship. Patience was a virtue he knew little of, but because of her he would learn. He fell asleep on the sofa, vowing to make her happy.

He awoke before her and he showered and dressed quickly. He had met her straight from the airport so his luggage was still in his car and he was able to get a change of clothes. Luke knew there was something Devlin must do before she could accept the past. He rang Gerry, gave him a brief outline of his plan and listened carefully to the older man on the phone. Then, moving around her well-equipped kitchen he deftly prepared a tasty breakfast and brought it to her on a tray. Snuggled deep in the bedclothes with one hand under her cheek like a child, Devlin was sleeping soundly for the first time in a year. A deep untroubled sleep. He decided not to wake her and was halfway to the door when her heard her murmur, "Hi Luke."

"Hello, Devlin."

They smiled at each other. Later, when she had eaten, he said. "I want you to come somewhere with me today. Just trust me. OK?"

Devlin met his steady gaze. She trusted him implicitly and without question she dressed and got into the car with him. "Why are we going to Wexford?" she asked, a little shocked, as she recognised the route they were taking. Devlin hadn't been to Wexford since the accident. Despite herself she shivered at the memory. She had instructed her solicitor to employ someone to take care of the farmhouse that Kate had willed to her. She had sold the farm but couldn't bear to part with the house, so twice a week a local woman came in to clean and air it.

Seeing the tension in her face Luke reached out a strong firm hand to squeeze hers gently.

"Take it easy Dev. Trust me. I know what I'm doing. Now sit back and relax."

To her surprise she found that as the miles slid smoothly by she was quite calm and relaxed. It was as if after the exorcism of her grief, a huge burden had been lifted from her and although she paled at the spot where the accident had occurred, she was quite composed until Luke made a right turn instead of going to the harbour. He saw her tense, her hands clenched in her lap. His phone call to Gerry that morning while Devlin was still asleep had been to elicit directions to the graveyard.

It was a beautiful summer's day. The song of the skylarks filled the air and as he pulled over to the entrance of the cemetery he saw her bite her lip to stop it trembling.

"Come on, love," he said firmly as he opened the car door for her.

"Luke...I...I can't. I've never come to visit."

Bending down, he drew her out, pity and understanding in his voice. "It helps, Devlin, I promise you. I know what it was like with my dad. You can't go on forever pretending it didn't happen. You've got to let go. Come on, I'll be with you."

With one arm supportively around her shoulder Luke walked her slowly through the gateway of the peaceful and well-kept cemetery. Devlin knew where her uncle's grave was and walked hesitantly in that direction. Luke gave her a quick hug. "Good girl," he whispered encouragingly.

Tears streamed down Devlin's face as she read the brief inscription. "Here lie Robert and Kate Seymore and their baby grand-niece, Lynn Delaney. May God cherish and protect them in Heaven forever more."

Crying quietly Devlin bent to touch the clay. "Oh Lynn darling! Oh Kate, I miss you,"she sobbed over and over again. Eventually her weeping ceased and she noticed through her tears that the grave was well cared for and covered with a profusion of small colourful bedding plants. Her grief eased and Devlin became conscious of the birdsong and the incredible serenity that enveloped this holy place. A kind of peace descended upon her and she stood just letting the healing balm of acceptance wash over her, knowing that when she was ready, Luke would be waiting for her.

Later he took her to lunch in one of the delightful hotels overlooking the picturesque harbour. They talked quietly, free from strain, enjoying each other's company. "Would you like to see the most beautiful place on earth?" Devlin asked the tall broad-shouldered man with the kind amber eyes who was seated across the table from her.

Luke reached over and took her hand. "If you're bringing me, I'd like that very much," he said and a hint of a blush coloured her cheeks at the expression in his eyes.

They drove, Devlin directing him, through the

narrow winding roads to a long and lovely swathe of beach lapped by whitecrested waves, its solitude broken only by the magnificent symphony of birdsong. The sun sparkled on the glittering blue water, the lush green and gold patchwork of the fields behind them making a striking contrast. It was deserted because few knew of its whereabouts. Slowly they walked its length, hand in hand, for mile after golden mile.

The comfort of his strong firm handclasp warmed her more than she had thought possible as Devlin heard him say, "I think you should try and make your peace with Lydia, I know you've the capacity to forgive her and it would mean so much to your father."

Devlin stared into his warm heavy-lidded eyes noticing how they crinkled so attractively when he smiled, and the deep laughter lines chiselled into his tanned skin. Slowly she lifted her finger and softly traced the outline of his firm sensual mouth.

"Luke Reilly," she said matter-of-factly. "I think you are a very nice man."

They stared at each other.

"May I kiss you?" he asked quietly.

Again she met his eyes, so warm and steady and comforting. Luke had told her it was time to make a new beginning. Smiling she raised her lips to his.

Caroline's Story II

twenty-five

His first blow sent her reeling against the sofa and knocked the breath from her body. At first she felt no pain, so shocked was she by the unexpectedness of the assault.

"Bitch! Bitch! Bitch!" he grated, as his clenched fists battered her ribs and breasts. As suddenly as he started, he stopped. His eyes glacial, his fingers cruelly gripping her arms, he hissed at her, "Don't ever do anything like that again without my permission. I don't want you next or near that tramp. Don't ever visit her in Ballymun again. I won't have my wife seen in a place like that! Do you hear me, Caroline?"

Too shocked to say anything, she could just stare back at him through pain-filled eyes.

Walking over to the door he said coldly, "Dominic Carter is opening a new wine bar in town, I told him we'd put in an appearance tonight. Be ready for eight thirty." Then, as if nothing had happened, Richard picked up his briefcase and left for work. They had been married just six months.

How long Caroline sat there she couldn't remember, but eventually she dragged herself into the bathroom and eased her negligée from her bruised and battered body. Every intake of breath caused her pain but it was nothing to the mental anguish she was suffering. Nothing had prepared her for this! How could she have been so wrong about someone, she asked herself over and over. Had her great desire to be married blinded her to his true character? If she had looked hard enough would she have found any indications that would have given her an idea of what was to come? Horrified, she wiped the blood from her ribs where his wedding ring had torn her skin. Her wisp of a negligee had not been much protection against the ferocity of the beating. She climbed into the bath, wincing as the warm water made contact with her wounds.

Why did he hate Devlin so much? He had never liked her, probably because she was not impressed with his status and position in life as people usually were upon meeting him. When he heard she was pregnant he was disgusted. Richard could be so prim. When he heard she was going to live in Ballymun he ordered his wife not to see her again. She cursed herself for leaving her cheque book lying around the bedroom. It had been all there on the stub. Pay Ms Devlin Delaney five hundred pounds. Standing in front of her, furiously angry, his skin mottled red with temper, he had roared at her, "What did I tell you?"

"But it's my own money!" she had protested heatedly. Then he had hit her.

What had she done to deserve such unhappiness? Her marriage had been a disaster from the start. Bitterly she massaged the baby oil into her bruised skin remembering the horror of her wedding night.

Caroline had been so happy, anticipating the night of rapturous love that would be hers, when she finally became a woman, equal to Devlin, Maggie, the obnoxious Ruth and millions of others. Having spent a small fortune on her Janet Reger lingerie she felt beautiful, slim and even sexy for the first time in her life. They were honeymooning in Paris and she longed to explore its treasures with her new husband. Paris was supposed to be for lovers and it was springtime. If the wedding had been a bit of a disappointment she was certain the honeymoon would make up for it.

Surprisingly, for such a social person, Richard had informed her that he would prefer a small intimate wedding. "Your mother and my father are both dead, darling, and I think it would be easier on our parents don't you?" When he put it like that, what could Caroline say? Then, Devlin wouldn't be there, a source of great disappointment to Caroline, who had longed for her friend to be her bridesmaid. But she quite understood how Devlin, having just given birth, could not make it. Fortunately, Maggie and Terry were back in Ireland to make preparations for their final return and Caroline had fixed the date for when they were home, so that they could attend.

There had been a family row about who was going to be bridesmaid. Her aunt wanted her to choose her daughter Rita, Caroline's cousin, when she heard that Devlin couldn't make it. But Caroline was adamant. Rita never had time to talk to Caroline when Caroline had been living at home and been fat and dumpy, but since Caroline had started dating Richard and begun to move in yuppie circles, Rita had become much more friendly, always angling for an invitation to join Richard and Caroline on a night out.

"Wouldn't it be a great way to introduce Rita to some nice well-off solicitor. I'm sure Richard must know plenty of them," her aunt would say, not a bit backwards about coming forwards. It was so sickening! Caroline knew she was being used, and for once put her foot down. And besides just because you were a solicitor didn't mean you were the perfect catch, Caroline felt like telling her aunt. Paulo, had been a waiter when she met him in Portugal, he had little money, no social position to speak of, although he was studying to be a doctor. Yet he had made her feel more alive and sensual and womanly in the two weeks she had been with him than Richard had in their entire courtship— despite his BCL! There were times when her aunt and cousin really irritated her. But it was partly, she had to admit to herself, that their behaviour made her question her own. Was she marrying Richard because he was considered a great catch? Or because she truly loved him? Or because she was afraid she would be left on the shelf?

God, why was life so complicated? Did all brides have these problems and self doubts? Did all brides have families who seemed bent on upsetting their most important day?

"I'm not wearing bloody tails. It's not a god-dammed circus we're going to," her father had fumed, when Caroline told him that Richard was insisting on top hat and tails.

"Please Dad," she pleaded "Couldn't you just do this one thing for me?"

"I'll feel like a right eejit! It's far from bloomin' top hats and tails you were reared, miss, so don't go getting any notions about yourself," he had grumbled. Privately she had to agree with him. When she heard Richard saying he was wearing top hat and tails, and expected her dad and the boys to wear the same, her heart sank. Richard could be such a snob! Those ridiculous hats looked so silly on men, and the tails always reminded her of penguins. Of course, he was getting the whole thing on video. And when they came back from their honeymoon, they were going to throw a big bash for all their set. Big weddings seemingly were not the "in" thing. But a small wedding and a big bash afterwards for the friends and acquaintances meant that you could invite as many as you liked and still get decent presents.

"We'll get the caterers in; it's much cheaper than having a big reception but the effect is just as good! And it will be much less of a worry to you," Richard had explained to Caroline when they were making their plans. Was it true what Joyce Jordan had accused him of? Was he a "penny pinching skinflint?" Or was he just being thoughtful, thinking of the feelings of their widowed parents as well as their own?

There were times when she felt like calling the whole thing off. Only the feel of the ring on the third finger of her left hand kept her going. Soon she would be a Mrs and all her troubles would be behind her.

It had been so good to hug Maggie when she met her in town a few weeks before the wedding. Maggie had managed to calm her down and had been delighted at being asked to be her Matron of Honour. It had been a bit of a rush getting a dress for her, but eventually they had selected a beautiful lavender silk outfit that had made the gorgeous redhead look a million dollars. Caroline was wearing a creation of satin and lace and she looked, as Maggie admiringly put it, "A real classy knock out."

Her aunt and Rita had been extremely cool. Her father had indeed looked like a little fat penguin in his top hat and tails and had a face on him that would turn milk sour. Her mother-in-law had sat throughout the ceremony and the meal that followed with an expression that suggested she had nothing to do with the whole affair; the boys were bored out of their minds. Richard's aunt was deaf and everything had to be repeated at least three times and the urbane Charles Stokes who was Richard's best man had got quietly pissed.

Thank God for Terry and Maggie and her uncle who had laughed and chatted gaily and kept her mind off the rest of them. Because of them her wedding wasn't a total fiasco. "Look at Ma Yates; she looks as though she's got a poker stuck up her arse!" the irrepressible Maggie had whispered to Caroline as the photographer fussed around seating them in various poses for the wedding photographs. In spite of herself Caroline took a fit of the giggles, causing Richard to look at her with eyebrows raised. He, to her surprise, had been quite tense throughout the day, fussing over this and that. He had been much more nervous than she at the wedding ceremony, his fingers shaking as he placed the wedding band on her finger. Caroline had been amazed at him. She had got to the stage where she just wished the whole ordeal was over and they were alone together. It was such a different wedding from Maggie's and Terry's joyful celebration.

Finally it had been time for them to leave for the airport and she had never been so glad of anything as she was at the sight of the 737 awaiting them on the tarmac. The thoughts of being alone in Paris with her new husband were sinfully delightful.

By the time they got to Orly Airport it was after eight, so they had driven straight to the hotel and ordered dinner. Then they had gone for a short stroll along the banks of the Seine, as they tried to relax after the tensions of the day. They didn't talk much, just walked hand in hand, and she had been so happy when Richard had put his arm around her and kissed her tenderly under the lamplight. "You're the least complaining person I know, Mrs Yates," he said smiling at her.

"I've nothing to complain about," she smiled happily. Mrs Yates, how good it sounded. She had undressed for bed in glorious anticipation.

For over three quarters of an hour Richard had skulked in the bathroom and when he finally did come out, dressed in a maroon silk dressing gown over his chocolate brown pyjamas, he had merely brushed her forehead with his lips, saying that he was sure she was exhausted as he was, and wishing her a good night's sleep. With that he had got into the other double bed, leaving her twisting her wedding ring forlornly around her finger.

She was too shy to assure him she was far from exhausted, that thoughts of tonight were what had kept her going all day and as she lay in the dark, lonely and frustrated, she thought how ironic it was, that here she was, ready and willing to lose her virginity and Devlin would give anything to reverse the loss of hers. Was she doomed to a lifetime of celibacy in spite of herself?

After sleeping fitfully, Caroline awoke

around dawn, desperate for the comfort of a loving touch. Plucking up her fading courage she crept into bed beside her husband, fitting her body to the curve of his. "Richard?" she whispered.

"Caroline!" He sounded faintly shocked.

"Please, Richard," she whispered tremulously. "Make love to me."

There was a strained silence and then he turned and put his arm around her, turning her away from him. Gingerly, he eased his body against her. Caroline tried to turn and face him but he whispered "Please, Caroline let me do it like this." His hands lifted up her nightdress as he pressed against her slim hips. Before she realised what he was doing he had entered her from behind, causing her to gasp in surprised dismay. This wasn't what she had expected at all! She felt him move rapidly against her and then it was all over and he drew away from her. Caroline could still remember the scalding tears that slid down her cheeks on to the pillow in which she buried her face.

"Go back to sleep, Caroline," Richard muttered miserably, and she could feel him lying tense beside her.

In the morning he treated her as though nothing had happened between them, urging her to dress quickly so that they could see as much of Paris as possible, and avoiding her distressed eyes. He had shown her the sights of Paris, had been a caring and considerate companion but at night he slept in his bed and she slept in hers.

Things did not improve on their return to Dublin. They never discussed sex. It was something that rarely happened between them and always when it did, it was the same as the first time. She never saw her husband's face when he made love to her. Caroline blamed herself, of course. It had to be her, she reasoned. It was quite obvious she was not a sexually attractive woman capable of giving pleasure to her husband. Had she made love to Paulo, he would probably have been disappointed too. It certainly couldn't be Richard's fault. Women were mad about him. At parties he was the centre of attention with women of all ages giving him the eye and flirting madly, attracted beyond measure by the suave sophisticated charm he exuded and by his finely chiselled handsome features. That she was envied by other women was obvious. She could see it in their eyes when she entered a room on his lightly supportive arm. He was always extremely courteous and protective when they were out. The perfect husband!

As her self-esteem disappeared Caroline found the social scene beginning to get on top of her. They were always going somewhere. A week after the return from their honeymoon, they had given a party for all of their friends and acquaintances who had not been to the wedding. The video of the wedding ceremony had been shown and Caroline, watching herself wide-eyed and full of anticipation in her exquisite wedding gown, felt a hundred years older. She remembered Devlin confiding that she had been most disappointed with her first time with Colin. Maybe sex wasn't such a big deal, although she had certainly enjoyed her interlude with Paulo and Maggie was living proof that some women had a great love life. Maybe it would get better with time, she tried to console herself. In the meantime her life was one big social whirl and she was getting tired of it.

All her fond notions of quiet candle-lit dinners for two at home had gone with the wind. If anything, now that they were married, Richard and she led an even more hectic social life. All the big events were on his social calendar: The Horse Show, The Royal Dublin Carrolls Open, The Galway Races, The People of the Year Award. She had even met Jerry Hall, and "Blake Carrington" from *Dynasty*, at the Budweiser Derby...the list of events she attended was endless.

Then there were Richard's political meetings. His interest in politics stemmed not fron the fact that he was particularly passionate about his party's policies, but from the fact that there was business to be made from all the contacts. You scratch my back and I'll scratch yours, was Richard's motto, as he confided to his wife. And so, while he attended branch meetings and strategy meetings, Caroline attended fashion shows for every conceivable charitable organisation and owned more clothes than she knew what to do with. Richard insisted that she bought expensive clothes and would frequently go shopping with her, commenting authoritatively on how he wished to see her dressed. They mixed in affluent circles where The Label was of the utmost importance.

"Darling, is that an Ib Jorgensen? Isn't it divine? Have you seen the new Pat Crowley collection yet? And darling you simply must get something from Ton Sur Ton. They're absolutely terrific!"

Once she went to a diplomatic do wearing a silky black skirt that swirled softly around her shapely legs. The compliments amused her no end. "Caroline, it's fabulous. Where did you buy? Do tell? Is it a Bruce Oldfield?"

Had she told them the truth, that she had bought it in Dunne's for less than thirty pounds, they would have been genuinely horrified. And so would Richard. One didn't buy clothes in Dunne's, for heaven's sake. A chain store! So she had murmured something about a little place she knew and gone to get another drink.

She had started to drink much more than before. At first it was to bolster her spirits when they were going to a function she had no interest in. Although she disliked the taste of it, vodka relaxed her the best and there was no tell-tale smell. Usually she would down a quick double before leaving the apartment, that same apartment she had sold Richard so long ago. Now

Caroline hated it with a vengeance. Everything was so perfect.

She was never at home in the place, always feeling that she was just another decorative object like one of his paintings or pieces of sculpture. When he bought it, Richard had commissioned an interior designer to decorate the penthouse. The result was a sterile high-tech effect with harsh geometric lines, stark white walls and highly polished parquet floors covered by black rugs. Gleaming chrome and glass furniture highlighted his growing collection of objets d'art, each piece selected for maximum impact. It was an impressive showplace but not a home, and the more unhappy Caroline felt there, the more she drank, until after a while it was unthinkable for her to go anywhere or do anything without a stiff vodka.

twenty-six

As she sat in her luxuriously appointed bathroom nursing her wounds, Caroline knew again that she needed a drink. The thought frightened her a little. It was only nine in the morning but as she wrapped a soft fluffy towel around her aching body she knew that by five past nine she would have had her first drink of the day. Swallowing her second, Caroline eyed herself wryly in the mirror. "Cheers!" she said raising her glass in bitter self-mockery. "It's not every day a girl becomes a battered housewife."

By lunch time the pain in her body had become almost unbearable and by searching the yellow pages she managed to locate a doctor who lived in the area. He lived close by and held afternoon surgeries, so dressed in the most loose-fitting clothes she could find, she walked stiffly towards the address.

Caroline sat in the antiseptic waiting room fighting a strong urge to leave. What in the name of God was she going to tell the doctor? A whinging child who hadn't stopped fighting with his sister since they had come in with their harassed mother aimed a toy and hurled it at his sister. It missed but caught Caroline square in the ribs. Giving an agonised gasp of pain she crumpled up in a heap on the floor. When she came to, the doctor was kneeling beside her on the floor, his fingers on her pulse. Through a giddy mist she could see the rest of the patients watching in fascinated horror. Distressed, she tried to rise.

"Gently now," murmured the doctor kindly, as he eased her up into a sitting position. The pain in her ribs was excruciating but nothing compared to her mortified embarrassment. Her one thought was to get away as fast as she could. The doctor and his receptionist were helping her to her feet and leading her through to his surgery. "I'm going to examine you now," he said. "Can you manage to remove your dress?

"I...I...yes." Caroline wished she was a million miles away as she slipped painfully out of her dress. Her cheeks flamed when she saw the bruises, but no expression crossed his face as he examined her thoroughly.

"I fell down the stairs," she said faintly.

"I see," was all he said. When he was finished and she was dressed he told her to sit down and began to write on a form his receptionist had handed to him.

"Mrs Yates?"

She nodded.

"You've never been here before, isn't that right?"

"That's right," she agreed miserably. He was

about fifty, a grey-haired fatherly man with a lined rugged face. Noting her address, he remarked evenly. "Don't they have lifts in those apartments?"

"Yes. Of course," Caroline answered in surprise, too late, remembering her excuse for being injured.

"Is this the first time you've been battered?" he asked in the same even tone.

She couldn't answer, just nodded her head mutely.

"I see..." he paused a moment and then said crisply, "I don't think you've sustained any cracked ribs, it's more bruising and internal contusions but I would like you to go for an X-ray just to make sure."

"No." Caroline shook her head in determination. She just couldn't go through the whole ordeal again.

The doctor eyed her steadily. "My advice to you is to go to the hospital and the next time your husband beats you go to the Gardai or your solicitor. If you wish I can give you the address of the battered wives' hostel."

Caroline almost laughed at the irony. Go to your solicitor. Ha! "Please, just give me something for the pain," she asked.

The doctor raised a weary eyebrow. "Well if you won't take my advice, you'd better take these" he retorted dryly, handing her a a sachet that contained four capsules. He bent his head and wrote on a pad, tore off the page and handed it to her. "I've just given you some painkillers and here's a prescription for some more. They're pretty strong. Take two every four hours and if the pain persists, call me." He stood up to see her out.

"For what it's worth, I'm always here if you ever feel the need to talk," he assured her, wishing he could have five minutes alone with the bastard of a husband who had battered her. He knew she would be back again. He had seen too many battered wives in his day to delude himself that it was a once-off thing. They always said the same thing too. It was always the stairs. He felt a great pity for this young girl who had just had her illusions about marriage shattered into pieces. As he walked her to the front door he said, "Mrs Yates, I wouldn't drink while taking those tablets. It could be very dangerous."

Caroline felt her face go scarlet. "Of course not," she murmured, highly embarrassed that he realised she had been drinking so early in the day.

"Go home and rest," he instructed her, giving her a fatherly pat on the shoulder. Caroline smiled wryly. "I've nothing else to do, thank you, doctor."

He nodded understandingly. "If the pain persists, come back, and you know where the surgery is if you need to talk."

"Thanks." She was almost in tears at his kindness. If she didn't get out the door soon she'd disgrace herself by sobbing her heart out.

Managing to compose herself, she paid the receptionist and left the surgery.

As she walked down the tree-lined suburban road with its expensive Victorian red-bricked houses she wondered if there were any other women living behind the white lace curtains who were in the same position as she was. Devlin had told her about her upstairs neighbours where the husband engaged in frequent physical violence against his wife. She had never given the subject much thought, being sure it could never happen to her. How wrong she had been. Richard had turned on her with a viciousness she hadn't thought possible. Usually he was so contained and reserved. The only time he ever let himself go was when he was in Charles's company and they were discussing the merits of some case or other, then he could become quite animated and they would spend ages in legal arguments, forgetting about her completely.

With her, Richard was never less than charming and attentive when she was doing what she was told. He lavished compliments and jewellery on her and was always greatly pleased if their pictures appeared in the social and personal columns. But the closeness and love she had hoped would be hers when she married had not happened between them. Their relationship was still the same as when they had been dating. Caroline saw herself as no more than a decorative social asset on his path to success.

This was the first time she had seen the

darker side of her husband's personality. He was not the suave reserved person she knew. A violently abusive almost bitter man had surfaced and she couldn't forget the look of wild despair on his face as he had lashed out at her. Maybe he was under pressure at work, she thought miserably, trying to make excuses for him. If only he would share his worries with her, it would mean far more to her than all the clothes and jewellery he gave her.

She knew the nature of his job frequently put him under intense pressure. Since she had first known him he had become even more successful. His practice had expanded so that he now had two other solicitors, a secretary and two typists working for him. It was almost, she felt, as though he was driven by some force to be the biggest and best there was. When he lost a court action he would brood for days, taking it as a personal insult. Not that his firm lost many. He had gained the reputation of a solicitor who got results and was much admired in the legal field.

When he heard that his most detested rival was celebrating the birth of a son, he sat down with Caroline and worked out her fertile period. Every month since he would make love to her, always in the same manner, on the days she was ovulating. Once she had asked him if they could do it from the front and he had glumly agreed. It had been a disaster. As he lay on top of her she felt his erection wilting against her. Her confidence had evaporated until there was even less of it than his erection and she had burst into tears of dismay and frustration. Richard had stalked out of the bedroom, his face like a thunder-cloud, his naked buttocks pale with lost dignity.

Oh God, why could she not arouse him? Was she now too thin where once she had been obese? Why couldn't she be normal like other women? She could never be normal, she decided in despair. She must be some kind of freak! Why had he ever married her? Caroline had no answers. She began to dread the monthly acts of messy misery, feeling an intense pressure to conceive and bear him the son he so badly wanted to inherit his firm. Maybe parenthood would bring them together as marriage had not. The obvious annoyance he felt when her periods arrived would cause her immense misery. She was such a failure that she couldn't even conceive. He had found out this morning that once again she had failed in her womanly role. Maybe it was his frustration that had made him beat her so savagely.

As Caroline let herself into the apartment that bore the hallmarks of Richard's personality—restrained and impersonal, lacking warmth or comfort of any description—she remembered the doctor's advice about resting. She smiled scornfully at herself in the mirror. What else had she done since her marriage? What a fool she had been to allow Richard to persuade her to give up her job. "I don't want my wife to work. I'll support us, darling. Take life easy, go shopping with the girls, maybe you could get involved with a charity or two, you know, the Central Remedial Clinic or something. I don't want you to be too tired to go out with me. It will be nice knowing that you are waiting here when I get home."

This had been said two weeks before her wedding and the girls at work, who though they were married were unable for financial reasons to give up their jobs, thought Caroline was so lucky to have a husband who could support them both and in such style.

The idea of not having to get up in the morning, of being able to swim in the complex's pool and maybe do a spot of exercise in the gym and then take a sauna before having breakfast on her secluded balcony overlooking Dublin Bay appealed to her enormously. It would be a completely different lifestyle to what she had been used to. Like something out of a TV programme. Caroline was an avid watcher of the American soaps. Pam, Sue Ellen, Alexis, Maggie Giobertti, were to her the ultimate women. So self-confident, powerful and assertive, everything that she was not but would like to be. After watching them, she would escape into fantasy, imagining herself head of the biggest auctioneering firm in the country, jetting off to Europe to sell properties in Marbella, the Algarve, the French Riviera. When Richard suggested she give up work, she hadn't been too keen as she enjoyed her job very much. But she was now a married

woman with a husband to think about and so her
fantasies took another turn. Like her heroines,
she could just imagine herself after her morning
swim and workout, going shopping, having
coffee mornings, lunching with friends, and then
having cosy intimate candle lit dinners with
Richard. It would be a lovely lifestyle, after all
the years of hard work. Giving up her job would
be no hardship at all!

The reality had been somewhat different to
her imaginings. Perversely, once she did not
have to get up in the morning she no longer felt
like turning over and going back to sleep.
Richard kept on his daily help so there was
precious little housework to be done. True, she
swam and worked out in the mornings and
indulged in social chit-chat with the other wives
who lived in the complex but she had nothing
really in common with them as most of them
were older than her.

As for her friends, Maggie, caught up in child-
rearing, found her young twins a handful and
had little free time. Devlin had been in London
for the early months of her marriage, so Caroline
was quite lonely. She continued to visit her
father and brothers and to do their cleaning and
washing on her weekly visit. But apart from
that, time hung heavy on her hands.

As for intimate dinners with her husband,
they rarely ate alone, in or out. There was the
invariable social function to attend and the rare
nights they were at home and not entertaining

themselves, Richard usually worked on his briefs until the early hours. She found herself becoming excruciatingly and stultifyingly bored.

Her only real pleasure was the couple of hours she spent on Tuesdays and Thursdays doing Meals on Wheels at the nearby senior citizens complex. Caroline enjoyed the company of the elderly people who were always ready for a chat and a bit of a laugh. Well most of them were, there was the odd moaner who never had a good word for anybody or anything. Mrs Newton was a holy terror! "You call this chicken? It tasted like a shuttle cock! There wasn't a bit of meat on it and tell them over in the kitchen that I said so!" These had been her first words to Caroline the first time she had called to collect her dinner plate. Her ingratitude always left Caroline speechless but amused and she never managed to have the last word no matter how hard she tried. One day she had entered with a steaming plate of roast beef, carrots, and creamed potatoes, a bowl of soup and a dish of fruit and ice cream.

"I'm sayin me rosaries!" Mrs Newton informed her in a tone that dripped icicles, as if she had just been interrupted while on her personal hot line to heaven. She had three rosary beads and a stack of prayer leaflets and missals around her.

"Sorry," said Caroline cheerfully, "but your dinner will go cold if you don't eat it now."

"Huh! You call that dinner!" was the sarcastic

retort, nevertheless her old fingers quickly lifted the lid off the plate to see what was on offer and she began to eat hungrily.

When Caroline had called back for the dishes and the small charge she had said pleasantly, "You can carry on with your prayers now and say one for me."

Mrs Newton had raised one deeply unimpressed eyebrow. "I pray for ALL sinners."

The other women had roared with laughter when Caroline told them. "The hypocritical old bitch," Mrs Molloy said. "You know she's loaded. She could well afford to live in a private nursing home but she's too bloody tight. She's so mean she dries out her teabags and uses them again."

"Ah go on!" Caroline couldn't believe her.

"It's true. Just have a look on her kitchen window the next time you call." Caroline laughed. She'd believe anything of Mrs Newton. But not all of them were cranky and crotchety. There were some lovely old people that Caroline became very friendly with. She would sit listening to their reminiscences of the past, wide eyed. One old lady knew Maud Gonne MacBride, another one had been a gun runner in the civil war and had an uncle who ended up in a workhouse. The tales were fascinating. One incorrigible old lady, Mrs Knowles, who read "hot" books brought by the library girl, told Caroline about her last heart attack. She'd had about ten, and was in her eighties, but had a mind as sharp as a razor and a wonderful sense of humour.

"Dere I was, on the flat of me back in the amblance, an' this fine thing wuz holdin me hand an I sez to him, 'If I faint ye can give me the kiss of life.'

'It's the priest I'm getting for you, Missus,' he told me, roarin' laughin. Anyways true to his word when I gets to the hospital in arrives this priest, a real dry ould stick. 'I'm on me last legs, Father,' sez I. 'I better make me last confession.' "

Mrs Knowles paused and drew a deep breath, her blue eyes twinkling. "Well I told him everythin an then I remembered. The dirty books! 'I forget ta tell ya Father,' sez I. 'I'm always askin the library girl ta bring me hot books, an when she brings 'em, I enjoys 'em. I wuz readin one when I had me attack.' 'Is that so!' sez the priest. 'Well don't worry about it, and when you're finished with the book ye can give it to me!' "

"Well Caroline, luv, I nearly had another heart attack there an then." Mrs Knowles chuckled heartily at the memory as Caroline guffawed. She always left the old lady's flat laughing at her witticisms. Caroline enjoyed the camaraderie of the group of volunteers who cooked and served the meals. It was hard work, but at least she felt she was doing something worthwhile and it was a time in the week that she really looked forward to.

Richard had not been impressed when she informed him that she was doing Meals on Wheels; it was hardly a glamour charity.

Caroline was determined, her stubborn streak making a rare appearance, so apart from a few dry comments about cooking for geriatrics, he left her to it.

twenty-seven

By the time their first anniversary arrived Caroline had been the recipient of several severe beatings. Concerned as always about public appearances, Richard would never mark her face, but the rest of her body was fair game and she would have to drag herself to Doctor Cole's surgery on each occasion.

She tried to analyse what triggered off the beatings, but could come up with no pattern, although the arrival of her period would always leave him tense and edgy. Richard brought her to see a gynaecologist who assured her that there was no physical reason why she could not conceive and to give herself time. Richard refused to have tests himself. There was nothing wrong with him, he told her brusquely.

"For Christ's sake, Caroline!" he said in exasperation one day. "Thousands of women conceive every day. Why can't you?"

"Maybe if I had a husband who loved me and made love to me, as opposed to having a five-minute quickie every so often, I'd succeed," she retorted.

His face reddened and he turned away from

her, his hands clenched. "I do love you," he said tonelessly.

"Well, you have a very funny way of showing it," Caroline murmured.

"I'm sorry, Caroline. You don't understand..."

"Why won't you try and let me? For God's sake Richard, I'm your wife, not some stranger." She was almost crying, frantic to try and understand his true feelings towards her. He sighed deeply, his back to her.

"Please, Richard!" she pleaded. "Doesn't our marriage mean anything to you?"

"Oh for God's sake, Caroline!" His voice had a strangely despairing tone that caught at her heartstrings. "Caroline, I..."

The phone rang, its harsh shrill tone piercing the fragile moment of communication between them. They stared at each other and Caroline knew instinctively that the moment was lost. He had been going to tell her something, something that might explain their unhappy relationship. She cursed the caller at the other end of the line. It was Charles Stokes. Silently Caroline handed the receiver to her husband. Since their marriage Charles had not taken up her invitation to visit them and the only time she ever saw him was at the various functions they attended. He never seemed entirely comfortable in her company and their conversations were stilted awkward occasions.

Once, after Richard had given Caroline a beating, they had been in O'Dwyers for a few drinks after a concert. The place had been packed and they had had to stand. Caroline had been wearing a loose chiffon top with long sleeves to conceal her bruised arms. Richard had left her with Charles as he made his way through the crush to order another round and as they stood, making polite conversation someone brushed against her, drawing her sleeve up over her elbow. Caroline, wincing, had quickly covered the ugly yellow and purple bruises on her forearm, but Charles had seen them and given a smothered exclamation.

"I fell," she lied quickly.

"Are you sure?" he queried intently, his blue eyes staring into hers.

"Of...of course," she stammered, flustered.

"Did Richard do that to you?"

His directness and perception stunned her. Instinctively she knew that he, knowing Richard better than she did, even though she had been married to him for over a year, guessed he was capable of battering his wife.

"Please, Charles! I don't want to talk about it," she said miserably, knowing that it was pointless to lie. From what she had heard her husband say about his friend, she realised that Charles knew her husband better than anybody. Maybe he had even confided in Charles about the beatings.

"Do you want me to talk to Richard about it?" he said gruffly, but there was kindness in his voice.

So Richard hadn't confided in his friend.

"No! No please don't! He might..."

"All right," Charles agreed hastily, seeing her husband battling his way towards them.

"But please, if ever you...you are afraid of getting another beating, ring me."

"Oh!" His response surprised her as up to this she had felt that Charles rather disliked her. "Thank you," she murmured, "Maybe it won't happen again."

"Well, please...if you need help ring me," he repeated earnestly as Richard arrived with the drinks.

Needless to say her husband had beaten her again but she hadn't rung Charles, nor could she bring herself to confide in Devlin, who was back in Dublin, or in Maggie. She just couldn't tell them about the failure of her marriage. How she longed to have the guts to walk out of their sterile marriage. But she was afraid to.

Materially Caroline lacked for nothing and was the envy of many. Her long years of drudgery at home with her family were over. She lived in a luxurious penthouse with all the modern conveniences any woman could wish for. To the outside world she had the perfect marriage. How could she just walk away from it all? If she had to stand on her own two feet and support herself, how would she manage? Everyone would know that she had failed at marriage too, and separation was nearly as big a stigma as spinsterhood.

Life was so difficult, she would decide,

downing another double vodka and watching yet another video. Her consumption of alcohol at home had increased, much to her husband's dismay. "You're drinking too much, Caroline. It's not good for you. Some day you're going to get drunk in front of our friends and disgrace us!"

"That's all you're worried about, isn't it? Don't worry, Richard, I won't let you down in public," she snapped, her tone bitter. Despite Richard's ruling that she should no longer meet Devlin, Caroline religiously spent one day of every week with her, telling her husband that she was visiting her aunt or family. He never questioned her further, utterly confident that she would not have the nerve to go against his wishes.

With Devlin, Caroline was able to forget her troubles for a few hours and it had given her a measure of self-esteem to lend her friend the money she so badly needed. After all the years of support and friendly guidance from Devlin, she felt as if some of the debt was being repaid. Devlin never probed, but Caroline knew that she sensed that all was not well with her marriage. Devlin had her own problems, she reflected; she wasn't going to burden her with hers as well. Caroline pitied her living in her high-rise one-bedroomed flat struggling on a pittance, yet she envied her friend's complete independence and especially her sense of pride. Nobody told Devlin where to go and what to do! God, Richard was so domineering, he wouldn't even let her learn to drive.

"You drink too much. I wouldn't have a minute's peace worrying about you." This was his response when she broached the subject. He had a point, she supposed, but it was only because of him that she was drinking in the first place. If only she could conceive and have a baby. At least, then, she would have some reason to exist. With secret envy she watched Maggie, who was pregnant again, and Devlin, both engrossed with their offspring. Sometimes she held Devlin's baby, pretending it was hers. She would never forget Lynn's first footsteps. It had been so exciting to watch the first tentative and finally triumphant moves. The pride on Devlin's face had surprised Caroline. She had never thought of her friend as maternal but Devlin had certainly changed a lot since becoming a mother. Her old cocky self-confidence had been toned down and there was a vulnerability about her now that Caroline found very endearing. She would never forget the look on her friend's face when Maggie and she had arrived to help her settle in.

When she saw Devlin's circumstances, her plans for walking out on her marriage would recede like the ebbing tide only to resurface the next time Richard assaulted her. Once, as she lay at his feet crying in pain and begging him to stop, he had fallen on his knees beside her and started to cry. "I'm sorry, Caroline! I'm sorry! I don't know what comes over me. What am I doing to you? Oh Caroline, I hate myself. If only you knew..."

His harsh dry sobbing shocked her in spite of herself and in spite of the beating he had just inflicted on her. She said faintly, "Richard...I think you need some kind of help, some counselling. Please let me get help for you."

Composing himself, he said, "There's nothing wrong with me. I...it won't happen again!"

It was the only time she had ever seen him express remorse for what he was doing and as their marriage descended into a morass of misery and despair, her drinking worsened. Nothing went right for her. As if she hadn't enough to worry about, she was walking from the bus stop one night after her weekly visit to Devlin when two youths had jumped out from behind a shrubbery and demanded that she give them the leather jacket that she was wearing. Stunned she stood motionless, her mouth open. This was Clontarf for heaven's sake, not Sean MacDermott Street. People didn't get mugged in Clontarf!

"C'mon give us the bleedin jacket, ya stupid bitch!" One of them was grabbing her by the arm and pulling the jacket off her. It was over in seconds, seconds that remained etched in her memory for months and caused her to have nightmares. She knew that Dublin, like other capital cities, was crime-ridden but somehow crimes always happened to other people. Now she was a crime statistic as well as everything else!

"It's the latest thing now," the world-weary

sergeant had told Richard as, stunned and
shaken, she had made her statement. "Leather
is the fashion now. We get incidents like this
every night of the week. We'll look into it, Ma'am.
Go home and have a cup of tea and try and forget
about it," he said kindly, patting her arm.

Caroline had gone on a drinking batter that
lasted for three days.

twenty-eight

A visit to London with her husband marked the nadir of Caroline's existence. Richard liked to do his Christmas shopping in London. Like an Arab sheik, Caroline thought, unimpressed. She dreaded it. He always made out lists and would spend hours searching for exactly what he was looking for. This year his mother had decided to come, and between the pair of them she was almost demented. She disliked her mother-in-law intensely. Sarah Yates ignored Caroline and treated her son as though he was six years old. "Don't argue with me Richard, I'm still your mother," was her constant refrain and Caroline felt like telling her to shut up and let him alone. Sometimes she felt that Richard had never grown up in his relationship with his mother and he was constantly seeking her approval—approval that was always withheld.

"I won an important case today, Mother" he would inform her proudly.

"I should think so," would be the response. "Your father would expect it of you. *He* never lost in court." Only by the grim tightening of Richard's lips would Caroline know how much this annoyed her husband.

She would feel like yelling, "You stupid old bat! Why can't you say well done for once and give him his moment of pleasure and glory?" But she never did and so it went on.

Now she had to put up with Sarah coming to London with them. It was a horrific week-end. Sarah had criticized everything, from the flight to their hotel accommodation, her haughty nasal voice grating on Caroline's already taut nerves. She needed a drink badly but Richard had refused to let her drink at the airport or on the flight. He was afraid that it might start a binge and even more afraid of what his mother would say if she caught her daughter-in-law knocking back the vodkas.

They had spent the day shopping, pushing their way through the pre-Christmas throngs until Caroline was exhausted. Sarah thrived on it; she had come to London to shop and shop she would. If she had to go into every store twice until she was satisfied with her purchases, so be it. By the time they got back to their hotel, Caroline had visibly wilted. They were supposed to be going out to dinner and a show that Richard had managed to get tickets for, but all Caroline wanted to do was to have a drink and go to bed. Wearily informing them that she was too tired to go, she sank into an armchair and kicked off her high heels. She shouldn't have worn the bloody things, they were murder on her feet.

Richard was furious. She could see it in the

coldness of his eyes. Ah to hell with him, she thought tiredly, she'd had enough. Let him go with his mother so she could have a few blissful hours alone.

"I've bought the tickets, Caroline, and they were dammed expensive and hard to get," Richard snapped. "Mother will be terribly disappointed if you don't come."

"No she won't, Richard!" Caroline retorted tartly "And I'm not going and that's final."

Richard's mouth dropped open. Caroline *never* answered him back and she always yielded to his wishes. Caroline could see his surprise. Well this time she was doing what *she* wanted. Her stubborn streak came to the fore as he persisted.

"Go on and get ready," he insisted.

"No, Richard, I told you I'm too tired to go."

"You'll enjoy it." He changed his tack and started wheedling. "It's the show everyone is talking about. Martin and his wife were over last week and they raved about it and Shaun O'Rourke was mad because he couldn't get tickets for it."

"Richard, for the last time I'm too tired and I'm not going. Give Shaun O'Rourke my ticket when we get home," she said irritably.

"I just don't know what gets into you, Caroline. You can be most ungrateful. We were lucky to get those tickets. Lots of people would give their eye teeth for them." He angrily shed his suit, which was still immaculate despite the travel and shopping.

"Bully for them!" Caroline muttered dryly, observing her husband's bony knees. Richard's legs were not his most attractive feature. Grim-faced he marched into the bathroom and Caroline reflected wryly that in all the time they were married, she had never seen her husband completely naked, except for the time she had seen his bare buttocks when he had left the room in disgust after their disastrous attempt at normal lovemaking. Richard was such a prude as regards appearing naked in front of her. It was hard enough to get him to wear something casual instead of his perennial suits. She heard of a guy she knew who was so addicted to suits he even wanted to bring one to Cyprus on holiday until his girlfriend got her hands on it. She should introduce Richard to him; they'd be well...suited! Smiling at her little private joke, she heard a smart rap on the door and knew it was Sarah Yates. It was no wonder Richard was the way he was with a mother like her.

When her mother-in-law saw that she wasn't ready, she frowned. "Aren't you changing? You'd want to hurry—we'll be late!" she remonstrated.

"I'm not going. I'm too tired," Caroline informed her crisply.

"Oh come on now, Caroline. You'll feel much better when you're showered and dressed," Sarah said authoritatively.

"I don't think so." Caroline's tone was quietly firm. She'd had enough of the Yates family for one day.

"Well really!" expostulated Sarah huffily. "Richard's gone to a lot of trouble to get these tickets for you. The least you could do is come with us."

That's right—start trying to make me feel guilty. Well tonight I just don't care. I just want to be alone...I just want a drink, Caroline thought determinedly. She was dying for a drink. She hadn't had one all day and if they didn't go soon, she didn't care, she was going to have one sent up from the bar.

Finally, with freezingly polite goodbyes, they went and she was deliciously, delightfully alone. Ordering a bottle of vodka from room service, she ran a hot bubble-bath. Her clothes were stuck to her skin after the long day of travel and shopping. It was so good to get out of them. Her vodka arrived and, clutching it to her bosom, she slid gratefully into the bath. It was pure bliss. As she lay in the warm sudsy water sipping her third drink she realised with surprise that she was hungry. The vodka had started to work; she no longer felt tense and strung out so she decided to make the most of her precious few hours of freedom. A peaceful meal was just what she needed.

Dressing in a soft baby-pink angora dress that clung to her slender figure like a glove, she lightly made up her face, sprayed some *White Linen* on her neck and wrists, had another drink and glided down to the dining room, untroubled—thanks to the vodka—by any feelings of guilt about missing the show. The dining room of the luxurious hotel was quite full but the head waiter showed her to a table in a discreet alcove. The meal was delicious: melon with Sauternes followed by poached salmon in a creamy chervil sauce and crisp lightly-cooked vegetables. This banquet was concluded with the most deliciously sinful mouthwatering chocolate gateau she had ever eaten. Everything was washed down with a carafe of light sparkling wine.

Utterly relaxed, Caroline strolled past the bar on her way to the elevator and on impulse decided to have a nightcap. She didn't want to go back to her lonely room. To hell with it! Everyone else was enjoying the season that was in it. So would she!

Caroline ordered a double brandy, enjoying its comfort, enjoying the soothing hum of conversation that rippled around her, oblivious of the many admiring glances that were coming her way. A tall distinguished-looking man who had been drinking alone at the bar came over and offered to buy her a drink.

"Why not?" she said gaily, her inhibitions completely overcome by the alcohol she had already consumed. He was Spanish and his accent was vaguely reminiscent of Paulo, her Portuguese boyfriend of so long ago. The way his black glittering eyes admired her sent delicious tingles of longing through her body. Since her marriage to Richard she had begun to feel almost sexless.

"What is a beautiful woman like you doing all alone in a big bad city like London?" her Spanish admirer wanted to know as he handed her the brandy she had ordered.

"I'm a business woman, Señor...?

"Forgive me, I did not introduce myself. I am Ramon Santander Rameriez. And you?"

Caroline smiled at the handsome man sitting beside her. He was just gorgeous, she decided. So dark and Latin, virile-looking, warm, admiring, everything her husband was not.

"I'm Caroline Stacey," she said, giving her maiden name, "and I work selling holiday properties all over Europe for an auctioneering firm. That's why I'm in London at the moment." She gave a little giggle at her fibs. Well it sounded much more interesting than saying she was a stuck-at-home housewife.

"How fascinating," Ramon murmured, his black eyes observing her admiringly.

"What do you do?" she asked, staring right back at him.

"Oh I'm a diplomat. I'm en route to the UN. I had some meetings in London," he informed her lightly. Caroline loved his sexily accented voice and the way he looked at her with such warmth.

"That must be very exciting," she responded, smiling back with just as much admiration herself.

"To a degree," he said and raised a dark

eyebrow, "but you know yourself, a life of travel is a very lonely one."

"Oh very," she agreed, believing her own fantasy in her intoxicated state. Recklessly she consumed the next brandy he ordered for her, basking in his admiration as her mood became even more gay and lighthearted, and her head a little light.

He was the most entertaining man she had ever met and she laughed and flirted with him quite uninhibitedly. By the time he had asked her back to his room, she was more than willing, excited by the desire in his heavy-lidded eyes. "To hell with Richard and frustration," she muttered, her words slurring.

Ramon laughed. "I'll drink to that, Carolina mia. Let's have some fun." He led her along the hotel corridor; they were giggling and laughing as they went. She hoped his room was over theirs. Tonight she was going to get royally laid and right at this moment she couldn't care less if Richard was kept awake by the rattling of the bedsprings.

Her memories of the night were a blurry haze of pleasure. For the second time in her life she realised she had intense feelings below her neckline. The throbbings and tinglings of pure pleasure that she experienced made her want more, and she kissed and caressed uninhibitedly, much to her lover's delight. He was an experienced man and brought her to several powerful orgasms, each time making her cry aloud with pleasure as years of frustration were wiped away and she realised all that she had been missing. They drank more brandy and made love in the shower, and on the floor and once again in bed where she finally passed out in a satiated stupor.

When Caroline awoke her head felt like a ton of bricks and she was alone. A note pinned to the pillow next to her said "Gracias, Cara mia; you were the best lover I've known. If ever you are in my part of the world, contact me. Yours with gratitude, Ramon." He left a number.

Oh God Almighty, what did I do? she thought weakly, trying to put the night's events back into focus. Memories came flooding back and she blushed as she remembered her wanton behaviour. Her fingers holding the note trembled. A thought struck her. Maybe she was pregnant! He hadn't used a condom. An even worse thought came to mind. Oh God! Just say she had contracted AIDS! He most certainly had slept around. Just one act of unprotected intercourse could cause a person to become infected. She'd seen the ads on TV. What on earth was she going to do? She made her way to the bathroom and another thought struck her. Caroline stared at herself in the mirror. She looked wild-eyed and frantic, her face pale and hungover. She wasn't in her own room. How was she going to explain her absence to Richard? He'd wallop the daylights out of her. A vicious hammering at her temples made her groan. She couldn't think about all this now—

she'd have a shower first. She must try and gather her wits about her. Assuming that the room was paid for until midday she wrapped a sheet around her naked body and swiftly hung the Do not Disturb sign on the outside of the door. Heart in her mouth, her hands shaking, she stood under the steaming jets of water. She'd have to have a drink before facing Richard.

She only meant to have one drink, one to give her courage, but an hour later she had polished off the remainder of the brandy and was quite drunk again as she finally made her way to Richard's room. Caroline gave a delicate little hiccup as she eased the bedroom door open. In the bed, Richard stirred and his arctic eyes flew open.

"Where the...?"

"I spent the night with a man," she informed him airily, cutting off his tirade before he had a chance to begin. She was feeling no pain—the brandy had been a life saver. Richard's stubble-lined jaw sagged in amazement.

"Yesh Rhichard a real man. And you know shomthing?" She hiccupped again. "Ish was a real pleasure..."

"Jesus Christ!" Richard flew out of bed. "You're as drunk as a skunk. If mother sees you...!"

Caroline giggled, went to sit on the bed, missed and landed on the floor.

"Thash all you're worried about...your Mammie."

"Shut up, you stupid bitch," he hissed, but she was too drunk to care. All she wanted to do was to sleep. Dragging her up from the floor, Richard pushed her under the bedclothes, pulled off her shoes and stood glaring at her. "Stay there and sleep it off. I'll tell Mother you've a migraine."

"Tell her what you like," mumbled Caroline and passed out. There she stayed all that day with Richard hopping in and out every so often like a cat on a hot tin roof. Later, she undressed and got into bed properly, sinking back into oblivion in the warm comfort of the bed. By evening she had recovered somewhat and was able to eat a little dry toast and drink some tea. The fumes of brandy emanating from her pores decided Richard that his mother could not come in and see her. Not that she particularly wanted to see Sarah Yates.

She couldn't think straight. Richard hadn't spoken one word to her apart from asking her if she wanted something to eat. And so she lay in her bed, hungover and frantic with worry about what might result from her night of debauchery. To think that she had allowed herself to be picked up in a bar by a stranger, albeit a very charming sexy stranger. Or, had she picked him up? Either way she had behaved very badly, even if she *had* enjoyed every minute of it.

Richard did not refer to the subject at all. All he wanted to do was to get home. He was petrified that Sarah might find out about Caroline's drinking problem. Maybe she was dreaming but

Caroline thought she heard him ringing Charles Stokes as she passed in and out of her drunken stupor. "She's back but she's in the fuckin' horrors again, Charles. What the hell am I going to do?" she thought she heard him say. But she must have been imagining it. Richard never used bad language!

They flew home the next day with Sarah complaining bitterly about all they had missed doing because of Caroline's migraine. Richard was so harassed he actually told his mother to hush up. And the look of outraged horror on her mother-in-law's face gave Caroline a brief moment of pleasure. They deposited Sarah in strained silence at her front door and declined her invitation to stay for tea. Then they drove in silence to the penthouse.

"Richard, I...I just don't know what to say." Now that she was sober, remorse had set in.

"Just say nothing," he said shortly. "I don't want to hear any of it."

"Oh God, Richard!" she burst out. "I just can't stand this. We haven't got a marriage. You've never made love to me. Is it me? Why did you marry me? Why?" She was almost incoherent.

"Be quiet! Be quiet. I can't think straight, damn it!" he swore, his hands gripping the steering wheel.

Caroline was crying now, shuddering sobs that shook her slender body.

"Stop! stop it, for God's sake, Caroline. Someone will see," he muttered miserably.

"I don't care, Richard! I just don't care any more."

"Well, I do. I don't want people talking about us," her husband said tightly as he parked the car.

"Oh you and your image. Your goddam bloody image. That's all you care about!" Caroline spat bitterly as she rooted in her bag for a tissue. Blowing her nose and wiping her eyes, she said quietly, "What happened in London would never have happened if you had ever shown me one moment of loving tenderness. I'm only human, Richard."

His lips tightened. "I've given you a damned sight more than Maggie's or any of your friend's husbands have given them."

Caroline laughed scornfully. "Grow up, Richard. Material things mean nothing. I supposed beating the shit out of me is a sign of your great love for me. I wish to God I had never met you."

He reddened. "I...I...oh, what's the use. Just get out and leave me alone," he muttered inadequately, unable to meet her eyes.

"Where are you going?" she asked dully.

"I...I have to go over and discuss some briefs with Charles."

"Charles! he sees more of you than I do. But don't, for heaven's sake, let our little marital crisis interfere with your briefs."

"Leave Charles out of it," Richard growled. "And for Christ's sake keep away from the drink while I'm gone. If you're not careful you're going to have a big problem."

"And that wouldn't be good for your image, darling, would it?"

"Shut up Caroline, I'm warning you!"

She was shaking now. Never before had they fought or argued like this. She realised just how bitter she felt and it was as if it was all spilling out like lava from a volcano. "Go to hell!" she swore, getting out of the car and slamming the door.

twenty-nine

Caroline had told her husband to go to hell that night but it was as though she had descended into its Godforsaken pits herself. The next months were the most lonely and frightening of her existence. The strain of their unhappy marriage caused her such mental anguish and depression that she began to have frequent panic attacks and she would lie in her lonely bed, her heart pounding so loudly that she could hear nothing else. Shaking, she would retrace every step of their relationship, her thoughts racing, unable to sleep, wide-eyed with worry and fear. Would this be the way her life would be from now on? Had she developed AIDS? What would happen if she left her husband? Would she end up in Ballymun like Devlin? Was her heart going to explode?

Questions, questions, questions. She had no answers. Each morning she would awake and the cloud of fear would settle on her and the thought of getting up and facing the ordeal of another day would be unbearable. Drinking didn't help, it only made the fear worse, so in desperation she went to Doctor Cole and begged him to give her valium.

"Caroline, you need treatment for your drinking and for your mental state. Valium is not the answer."

"Please, Doctor Cole. I'm afraid."

"Afraid of what? Are you afraid of Richard beating you up?"

Caroline shook her head. How could she explain all her fears to this kind harassed man?

"You can't go on like this," he reasoned. "Let me send you to a nursing home for treatment and a rest and you can think about your future. There has to be more to your life than this. Don't start depending on valium. Stop depending on drink. They're only crutches for a while, then they collapse under you." He smiled kindly at her. "How about trying to depend on yourself for a change. In the end you know the only person you can truly depend upon is yourself, but don't make the mistake many people make. Depending on yourself doesn't mean that you're alone. You've got Devlin and Maggie and I'm here. Now go and confront your problems and make some decisions about your life. It's the only one you've got, you know."

She knew what he was saying was the truth but she wasn't ready to face it. Eventually after several more visits where she refused outright to see anyone else or go to to a nursing home, he had written the prescription she had asked for.

The valium helped a little. She managed to keep herself calm for her weekly visits to Devlin and sometimes she felt that if it wasn't for Devlin and Maggie she would go completely insane. Both of them had asked her outright what was wrong with her. Stubbornly, she refused to confide in them. She couldn't bear for them to know of the failure of her marriage, and of the shameful event that had occurred in London. Both of them seemed to be able to handle their own not inconsiderable problems; she'd just have to handle hers. Caroline knew they were worried about her. She worried about them too but this was something that not even Devlin and Maggie could help her with; so on the days she visited she tried to keep the best side up and with them she was able for a while to forget the misery of her empty existence.

She and Devlin would sometimes take the baby and go off for the day if the weather was fine. "Let's go for a jaunt," Devlin would say and Caroline would laugh. Since she had gone to live in Ballymun Devlin had picked up some really colourful colloquialisms which she loved to try out on Caroline. They would usually go to Howth, their favourite destination. Caroline loved Howth. It made her feel as though she was abroad. They would explore the village and around it, wandering along narrow winding roads that were dotted with magnificent houses and a great variety of pubs and restaurants, all with beautiful views of the harbour and Ireland's Eye. The trawlers sailing in and out, the seagulls circling and screaming as the catches of the day were unloaded, reminded her of the fishing villages of Portugal and she would sit and close her eyes and pretend she was a million miles away.

She had often dined with Richard in Howth, and now that he had been accepted as a member of the yacht club she expected to be socialising in the peculiar new building that had been erected in the marina. The thought thrilled her not one whit! She was much happier to be out with Devlin and the baby, dressed in a pair of jeans and a teeshirt and exploring the beauty of Balscadden Bay and having a picnic after the exhilarating climb to the summit. Devlin was like her life-support system. Some day she would tell her about her marriage and her drinking but not now.

When Devlin told her that she was going to live in Rosslare, Caroline felt as if her world was falling apart. With her best friend gone, she'd be drifting like flotsam in the murky tide of her pitiful marriage. She'd have no weekly visits to look forward to, no lifting of the soul-destroying burden she bore. Trying her best to think of Devlin's happiness, she assured her friend that she was doing the right thing in making a new start. How she wished she had the guts to do the same herself. In spite of her brave words, she was crying along with Devlin when they hugged and said goodbye a few days before Devlin left.

"You can come down anytime you want. It will be a break for you and we'll have fun. Rosslare is beautiful and think of the tan you'll get," Devlin had reassured her, giving a childlike sniff as she wiped the tears from her cheeks with the back of her hand.

"I know...I know." Caroline tried to compose herself, knowing full well that because of the way Richard felt about Devlin she would never be able to go and stay with her. If he ever suspected that she had been visiting Devlin every week, she'd be in real trouble. She sat on the bus into town and decided that her life was an out-and-out disaster and that she, Caroline Stacey Yates, was the only one to blame. Doctor Cole was right. Only she could change it and she just didn't have the gumption to do it. Devlin always had loads of guts while she hadn't an ounce. On impulse she stayed on the bus as it passed her stop and carried on until she got to the stop near the Bull Wall. Alighting, she crossed the road and began to walk towards the huge plinth which held a statue of Our Lady, who seemed to be watching protectively over Dublin Bay.

Her high heels clicked rhythmically along the wooden causeway and it seemed to her that they were saying, "Alone, alone, alone, alone, alone." That's exactly what she was, now that Devlin was going away. Utterly alone. What a sad bitter word "alone" was.

Reaching one of the quaint pastel-painted ladies' bathing shelters Caroline slipped inside and sat down on the cold cement resting place.

There was no other person to disturb her solitude, only the sound of the small white-capped waves as they lapped idly against the steps that led into the sea.

It was a beautiful summer's evening. The rays of the sun as they slanted over the Dublin Mountains across the curve of the bay, made her little shelter glow with a warm caressing light. In the distance she could see the big B+I ship gliding gracefully across the glassy sun-dappled water to enter the haven of the Liffey estuary and home. How elegant she looked in her white and blue, moving slowly, majestically past the red and white ESB towers, past Ringsend and the Shelly banks towards her berth.

Caroline stared across the water towards the southside of the city. How happy she and Devlin had been in their little flat in Sandymount. Why hadn't she realised it at the time? She'd been too busy worrying about being left manless. Well, she had a man...and what happiness had it brought her? None! Restlessly she got up and began walking again, passing couples hand in hand, trying to swallow the bitterness inside her as she compared their obvious happiness to her desperate unhappiness. She and Richard had walked this very pathway hand in hand on an evening such as this during their courtship. How deliriously happy she had been then. How had it all gone so badly wrong? Since their return from London, over six months ago, they had hardly spoken, except when they were in company.

They could have got Oscars for their acting abilities then. Her husband immersed himself in his work and seemed oblivious to the fact that her mental state was precariously fragile. He never again referred to what had occurred in London, and he no longer had sex with her in an effort to conceive a child. She wasn't sorry. After her experiences with Ramon she didn't want him to touch her. She still worried dreadfully that she had contacted a disease or infection from her one-night stand. But she couldn't possibly tell Doctor Cole about what had occurred. He'd be shocked, she knew he would.

Caroline reached the statue on its triangular plinth. When darkness fell it would be illuminated, a guide for seafarers to bring them safely home. Would it help to guide her also out of the darkness of her misery? Was there really someone who was the mother of them all? God! How she missed her own mother.

"Oh Holy Mother of God, help me please," she whispered forlornly. Sighing deeply she turned her face into the warm salt laden breeze and began her walk home.

"Where were you?" her husband said grumpily when she got back to the apartment. Caroline's heart sank. He had a frown on his handsome features and a pile of law tomes in front of him.

"I went for a walk." She made her voice deliberately light. She couldn't face a fight.

"It's well for some," he muttered. He looked

tired and harassed and impulsively she lay her arm lightly around his shoulders and gave him a little hug. He tensed and she drew back, rebuffed.

"Why don't you put those away for a while? It's such a lovely evening and we could go for a walk along the Bull Island." Caroline tried to keep the hurt out of her voice. Why could she never learn?

"I've to call over to Charles. I need his advice on a case," her husband informed her flatly.

"Why don't you get him to come over here? He's never visited since we married," Caroline suggested, desperate not to have to spend the evening alone. Richard gave her the strangest look.

"It's been arranged," he said brusquely. "I think Shaun O'Rourke is dropping by to Charles's house as well. It's a hell of a case we're working on."

"OK," she replied, defeated.

The morning that Devlin was leaving Dublin she rang Caroline. They spoke a while and as Caroline gently laid the receiver back on its cradle her heart began to pound rapidly as a panic attack engulfed her. She was going to faint, she felt sick. Where were her valium? She needed a drink. It was an awful day!

thirty

Caroline never thought that things could get worse but as long as she lived she would never forget picking up the morning paper and reading the details of Devlin's accident. This couldn't be happening! It had to be a nightmare. Her fingers shaking, she rang Lydia, although she knew that she and Devlin were estranged. The other woman told her that Devlin was in a coma and that Kate and Lynn were dead. Caroline sat stunned and motionless and then with a determined set to her mouth she dressed and went to the nearest off-licence. Since her drinking had got worse, Richard kept the drinks in the house under lock and key. Caroline didn't care who saw her in the off-licence or who saw her with her brown-bagged purchases. Let the whole lot of them be damned. She couldn't care less, she was going to get plastered. Pissed out of her skull. If Richard wanted to go to the function in the yacht club he would have to go without her.

Richard arrived home that evening to find her in the horrors. "Jesus Christ, Caroline, I'm going to get you committed," he yelled in desperation.

"I don't care!" she sobbed. "Oh Devlin. Poor

poor Devlin!"

"What the hell is wrong with her?" snapped Richard as he started to make black coffee.

"She moved to Wexford and her aunt's car crashed and the baby's dead," Caroline moaned, rocking backwards and forwards on the sofa.

"How do you know all this? Have you been seeing her after what I told you?" Richard roared in outrage, as he surveyed the mess of the lounge and the empty bottles beside her.

Drunk, not caring what he would do to her, Caroline laughed hysterically as she informed her horrified husband that she had visited Devlin in Ballymun once a week for the ten months she had been living there, and that she had phoned Wexford twice weekly since Devlin had moved and had, in fact only been speaking to her two days before.

"And don't take that tone with me," she screamed at him. "Don't forget I've seen you with your underpants down and I'm not impressed."

Richard was so shocked by his drunken screaming virago of a wife that he was speechless. Contemptuously she lifted the bottle of vodka to her lips and took a long drunken swig. When he moved to take it from her she glared at him in such wild fury that he stepped back.

"Fuck off, Richard," she cursed him viciously before putting the bottle to her lips again. In a misty haze she saw him lift the telephone and dial a number.

Was he going to get her committed? What the

hell did she care? And anyway, he wouldn't have the nerve. The scandal it would cause among their set would be horrific for him, he who was so almighty concerned about his image. He was talking now. It was an effort for Caroline to concentrate on what he was saying.

"Charles! For God's sake, get over here fast, I need your help," she heard her husband pleading on the phone.

Huh! Charles. She should have known Richard couldn't even take a pee without consulting poor old Charles. Caroline started to laugh and then she started to sob and it was in this state that Charles found her as he arrived at their apartment sometime later.

"Ah Charles! welcome," she slurred from her half-sitting position on the floor. She'd fallen off the sofa.

Richard looked on helplessly. "I can't do anything with her."

"Have a drink, Charlie," she invited kindly, trying to focus on the other man's face.

"Well, maybe one," the older man said gently as his fingers loosened her fingers that were clutching the neck of the vodka bottle in a vice-like grip. He smelt of tobacco and tweeds as he knelt over her and for a moment, despite her drunkenness, Caroline was reminded of her father, the father who had forgotten about her when her mother died. She began to cry again.

"Oh for God's sake, don't start off again," her husband said in mortified desperation.

"Shush Richard! You didn't hit her again, did you?" Charles said anxiously.

Richard reddened. "No!"

"He hits me and he won't make love to me. Nobody loves me, Charles. Why? Devlin was the only one and she's dying and I'm so frightened. Charles, why am I like this? What's wrong with me?" It was all rushing out of her in a torrent of words that wouldn't stop.

"I wish I was dead," she sobbed wildly. "I think I've got AIDS and what does he care?" She pointed a shaking finger at her husband. "He doesn't give a fucking damn. I slept with a man in London and he didn't give a shit. What kind of a rotten bastard of a husband have I got? All he cares about is making money."

Richard was deathly pale, horrified by the gutter language his wife was using.

"It's all right, Caroline. You'll be all right now," Charles was soothing her as he tried to help her to her feet.

"Come on now, pet, let's get you to bed for a while and we'll talk about it when you feel better." Caroline swayed on her feet, supported by his arm

"You know something? I didn't like you. But you're kind," she whispered before passing out.

Later she woke, undressed to her underwear and in her bed. Her head was throbbing, her mouth dry and tasting vile. Painfully turning her head, she saw that Richard's bed was unslept in and that it was twelve thirty by her alarm

clock. She wondered wearily if Richard and
Charles had gone to the yacht club do. As
memories of the evening came back she blushed
scarlet in her darkened room. How could she face
Charles Stokes again? Richard would murder
her, and she really couldn't really blame him.
She had disgraced him in front of the man he
most admired. It was strange how kind Charles
had been. How wrong she had been to think of
him as cold and unfriendly. He had been most
comforting and human, unlike her own husband.

She was bursting to go to the loo, so she slowly
edged her way out of bed and made her way to the
bathroom. When she was finished she looked at
herself in the mirror. God! What a sight! Her
eyes, red and dazed, were sunk deep into her pale
face, which was framed by lack-lustre fronds of
black hair. She looked like a zombie out of a
horror movie. Licking her parched lips, Caroline
decided to fill a jug of iced water and drink as
much of it as she could. It might help her de-
hydration. As she walked past the lounge on her
way to the kitchen she saw a low shaft of light
and heard the murmur of voices. The door was
ajar and she decided that now was as good a time
as any to apologise to Richard and Charles for
her behaviour. She drew her wrap tighter
around her and in barefoot silence she slipped
into the room.

She'd often heard people saying that time
stood still and never understood what it meant
until she stood there frozen to the spot at the

sight that met her eyes. Her husband was lying cradled in his friend's arms and was, with the most exquisite tenderness, caressing Charles's face, an expression of such love on his face that Caroline almost cried out in pain. She would have died a thousand deaths to have her husband look at her like that even once. She heard him say softly, "I love you, Charles. I always will. You were right—I should never have married Caroline. I've ruined her life as well as my own. I've turned her into a drunkard because I can't give her what she wants. I've treated her dreadfully. I've treated you dreadfully. What the hell am I going to do?"

"Oh God Almighty!"

Caroline turned and ran from the room, not even seeing the expressions of shocked dismay on their faces. So that was it! What a stupid blind fool she had been all along, so desperate to be married that she had ignored the many tell-tale little signals that Richard had unknowingly given her. His reluctance, indeed distaste for physical contact. His intense dependence on Charles. She had thought they were good friends because of their legal business together. How wrong she had been!

It was obvious why Richard had married her. In his profession respectability was everything. To be homosexual in Ireland was nothing to shout from the roof tops. She had heard of the queer-bashing that went on. Even her own brothers were so hostile and intolerant of gays.

Poofs! Faggots! Pansys! Nancy Boys! That's what they called them. And she was married to one.

She had to leave this place. She had to get away. Devlin! Yes! she'd go and stay with Devlin. Suddenly Caroline remembered that Devlin was lying critically ill in hospital. "Oh Christ, what will I do?" she moaned, reaching the bedroom. Stumbling into the bathroom she located her valium and shoved a handful of tablets into her mouth but couldn't keep them down and started to retch.

God, she couldn't even commit suicide properly. She dragged herself into the bedroom and pulled out a drawer full of delicate expensive underwear and found a Baby Power kept for emergencies. Shaking and sweating she uncapped the whiskey. Her heart was pounding in her ears and she could hear nothing else. Was this all a horrible drink-induced nightmare?

You can't run away from it. It's happening to you. Face up to it, her mind cried out and she knew the more she ran away from the truth the harder it would be to face it. Caroline had made a career out of running away from the truth. And look where it had got her.

She was a drunk married to a wife-beating homosexual in a nightmare of a marriage. Where could she go? Who could she turn to? Oh God! she just wanted to die.

Again she swallowed a handful of valium and this time the tablets stayed down, washed by a mouthful of whiskey. Shivering violently, Caroline got into bed just as Charles knocked quietly on the door and came into her room.

"Caroline, I..." His gaze fell on the empty whisky bottle and the tablet jar.

"You didn't...Jesus, Caroline! How many tablets did you take?"

She gave a half-laugh, half-sob. "What do you care anyway? Wouldn't it suit the two of you down to the ground?" Her voice was slurred and she felt very tired. Her eyes began to droop.

"Richard! Richard!" Caroline was vaguely aware of the frantic note in Charles's voice as the older man yelled for her husband. He was shaking her, slapping her cheeks when Richard arrived.

"Get an ambulance quick! She's overdosed."

Why wouldn't they leave her alone? All she wanted to do was sleep...She was having a nightmare. A weird terrifying dream of naked men hurling abuse at her as she lay trapped and drowning in a huge vodka bottle. "Help me," she tried to scream but the words wouldn't come. Strange men were around her, men in blue, then harsh bright lights and men in white coats who were putting tubes down her neck and trying to suffocate her.

thirty-one

Caroline opened her eyes and saw Charles, grey
-faced and haggard, peering at her anxiously.

"It's all right, Caroline. You're all right now,
you're in hospital," he assured her.

Flashes of memory came drifting back and,
closing her eyes, she felt the sting of bitter tears.

"Please don't cry!" The misery in his voice
made her feel even worse. She wanted to hate
him but she couldn't. Her tears were for him as
much as herself. What a sad triangle they made.
She, Richard and this wretched man at her
bedside. Trust her! Other men had affairs with
women. Her husband was in love with a man.
Who else would it happen to but her? Drained,
emotionally and physically, she lay in her
hospital bed weeping.

Charles tentatively took her hand, half afraid
she would snatch it back. But she didn't. She felt
strangely comforted by the warm handclasp. She
was vaguely aware of Richard arriving, felt her
other hand being held and opened her eyes
briefly to meet her husband's troubled stare. "I'm
sorry, Caroline!"

He looked awful. His face was ashen, his eyes

red-rimmed as though he had been crying.
Despite herself she felt sorry for him. In some
ways Richard was such a little boy.

"I'm sorry too," she murmured before drifting
off to sleep. For the next week or so Caroline
slept, heavily sedated. Richard had had her
transferred to a private hospital where she had
been tested for AIDS and other venereal diseases
after her episode in London. All tests had proved
negative. She was also drying out and being
weaned off valium. It was the most painful,
frightening lonely time of her life and yet it
marked a turning point for Caroline as she confronted reality for the first time.

It was so true what Doctor Cole had said. She
had never depended on herself at all. There had
been food, then Devlin, then Richard, then
alcohol and valium. Only she could change the
pattern of her life and though the thought
frightened her, Caroline knew she had been
through the mill and come out of it a stronger and
more determined person.

It wasn't easy. She craved alcohol badly and
begged Richard and Charles to bring some on
their visits. She trembled and shook as her
system was cleared of its impurities but she
found herself for the first time beginning really
to get to know her husband as he tried in his own
way to help her with her battle.

At first she had been bitter and almost abusive. "Why did you do it to me, Richard? Do you
know what torment I've put myself through?

Thinking that I was a complete failure as a woman, thinking that it was my fault that you weren't sexually attracted to me. Oh, you bastard, you lying bastard. I don't hate you because you're gay. I hate you because you lied to me! You used me, Richard, in the worst possible way."

Her husband had sat with his head in his hands listening to her in silence. "Do you want me to go?" he said eventually. Caroline looked at him. Now that she had verbalised the hurt, the pain, the grief, she felt drained. She couldn't sustain the hate; she just wasn't that kind of person. To tell the truth she couldn't help feeling sorry for her husband. In her own way she loved him despite what he had done to her. Materially he had given her everything she wanted and more. Maybe he *had* felt something for her.

"I'd better go," he said dully.

"Would you get me just a tiny drop of vodka?" Her voice showed her desperation.

"Caroline, I can't." He was miserable. "You've got to stay off it. For your own sake."

"I know... I know," she muttered dry-mouthed. "It's hard."

He took her hand and squeezed it. "Don't think about it. Try and think about something nice..." Caroline gave a small laugh. "I just can't think of anything nice right now!" But she lay back on her pillows and drifted into sleep still holding his hand.

It was Charles who had given her some

insight into the secret misery of her husband's life as a homosexual. Pushed by his cold ambitious mother into a career as a solicitor, starved of affection, he had realised from an early age that he was gay. He had been terrified. Desperate to hide it he had thrown himself into his studies, and eventually his business. He had had some furtive sexual experiences but the fear of being found out caused him dreadful anxiety and as his business took off, he dated many women in an effort to deny his true sexuality.

"You see, Caroline, unlike me Richard is ashamed of his gayness," Charles told her frankly. "He can't cope with it because of the pressure society puts on him to conform. I knew early in life that I was homosexual. I didn't fight it. It's me, it's part of what I am and if people don't like that they can lump it. People are so judgemental. A person's sexuality is his or her own business as long as it doesn't hurt anyone else. That's why I fought so hard with him to try and prevent your marriage. I knew it would end in disaster. I know Richard inside out. We were lovers for many years but once he married you we stopped making love." He paused to smile at her. "Whatever you may think of me, I don't sleep with married men! Try not to be too hard on him, although you have every right to be. He thought it would work out. And in his own way he cares for you very much although you might not believe it. Richard can be selfish and immature but I can tell you one thing. He's grown up these last few days—and not before time."

Caroline sighed. "So have I, Charles, believe me, I'm as much to blame for the disaster of our marriage as Richard is. I knew from the start that something wasn't right, but I wouldn't let myself see it. I was so desperate to be married, to be Mrs someone or other, I deluded myself that everything between us was fine. Richard and I deserve each other!"

Charles leaned over and took her hand. "Stop punishing yourself, Caroline. We all make mistakes in life but fresh starts can always be made." Caroline found Charles to be a surprisingly warm humane man under his suave cultured facade and he seemed to understand her fears and terrors as no one else had done. How ironic, she mused, that the one man in her life with whom she felt comfortable and able to be herself, was her husband's lover.

Gradually, as Richard began to realise that his wife was not repelled by his homosexuality, and that her anger towards him had dissipated somewhat, and seeing her so comforted by Charles, he began to relax with her. Deeply shocked by what had happened, he tried in his own reserved way to support her through her painful detoxification treatment. One night she was suffering severe withdrawal symptoms.

"Will I get a doctor?" he asked anxiously as she began to shake.

"No, no. I'll be OK after a while," she whispered. Parched, she asked him for a glass of water.

Her hands were trembling so much she couldn't hold the glass and Richard gently held it to her mouth, cradling her head in his arms. It grieved her that it was only in this situation that he should be so tender and concerned. If only he could have been like that during their marriage...

Something of her thoughts must have shown in her face because he drew away from her and said flatly, "You must hate me for what I've done!" They stared at each other across the bed, his words falling like bitter droplets into the futile void of their marriage.

Caroline swallowed. "I don't hate you Richard," she gave a wry smile. "I wanted so badly to be married that I just closed my eyes to everything that was wrong in our relationship. It's not all your fault! Why did you marry me?"

Richard awkwardly jammed his hands into his pockets: "When I first met you, you were so shy and unsure. You kind of reminded me of myself except that I was much better at hiding it. And as I got to know you better I liked you very much, you were... are... such an undemanding person. I thought I could put my past behind me and make a go of it. Be a 'normal' person like everyone else. I just kept denying what and who I was. That's why I used to date all those other women. I was a man about town. I'd date them for a while and drop them so I wouldn't have to get into a relationship with them." He smiled at his wife. "It was incredible, women threw themselves at me, and I wasn't the slightest bit interested but no one, not one person, ever guessed that I was gay and eventually I started believing myself that I wasn't. I told myself I was bisexual. I wouldn't listen to Charles, I told myself he was only jealous. I knew the night of our honeymoon that I'd made a horrible mistake. It was too late then. Wasn't it? I treated you both very badly. All I can say is that I'm sorry."

After years of unhappy experiences caused wittingly and unwittingly by others, Caroline's capacity for tolerance was enormous. She couldn't bring herself to hate her husband. She understood far more than he guessed the reasons he had married her. In a way they were very similar. Once she got used to the idea, his homosexuality did not offend her. She had seen how much he and Charles cared for each other and envied them. It was a hard world to live in, God knows, and a loving relationship was a precious gift no matter what gender you were. If only she and Richard had not been so desperate, she to avoid what she thought was the misery of spinsterhood, he to avoid what he percieved as the stigma of homosexuality, they might not be in the sorry mess they were in now.

Paradoxically, now that Caroline knew the truth about their marriage she no longer felt under pressure. A burden had somehow lifted. It had not been her fault. She was not unlovable or unsexy or the womanly failure that she had tortured herself about, and in a faltering yet exhilarating way she knew that if she came through this experience, she could face anything.

"Do you want me to leave?" Richard's voice intruded on her thoughts.

"Not unless you want to," she replied.

"Oh!" he said, taken aback. He had expected her to say "yes."

"Do you know what I did before our first date?" she was smiling faintly.

Richard cleared his throat, There were times when Caroline really surprised him. "What did you do?"

"I took a valium!"

They stared at each other and then in spite of themselves burst out laughing. They were still laughing when Charles joined them.

***

After five weeks Caroline was ready to leave the hospital. Drink- and drug-free for the first time in almost two years, she was about to take her first faltering steps towards a new life. A life where she would depend on herself first and foremost, no longer concerned about what people thought.

"Are you going to leave me? Could we work something out between us?" Richard asked her tentatively.

"We'll see, Richard." She was gentle with him. They would never have a proper marriage, she knew that, and although their relationship had improved enormously now that all their secrets had been bared she didn't know if she could cope with the idea of a permanently sexless relationship. She too had her needs, as Doctor Cole reminded her when she confided all that had happened to him.

"You have your life to lead as well as Richard," he warned "If you think you would be better off leaving him, for God's sake do so. Don't sacrifice your life, Caroline." He had smiled warmly at her. "It does me good to see you like this, my dear. I hope everything works out for you and don't forget I'm always here if you need to chat."

Almost light-hearted Caroline walked out of the surgery. How silly she had been to think she had been alone. Doctor Cole had been so good to her, as had her father and the boys, She had phoned them from the hospital and told them frankly that she was having treatment for alcohol and drug abuse. She hadn't told them about Richard. That was nobody's business except hers, Richard's and Charles's. She knew that in time, when Devlin was fully recovered, she would tell her and Maggie. Their friendship was so strong and they had no secrets up until now. Why, Maggie had confided in her about Terry's affair and how it had pained her and as Caroline hugged her in the hospital where she had come to visit her, she realised that everyone had their share of unhappiness. She, Caroline Stacey, was not, as she had so self-pityingly thought, the only miserable person in the world.

For the first time in years, her father had reached out to her, shocked out of his self-absorption by the sight of his gaunt traumatised daughter. Shyly, awkwardly they had talked about many things during her stay in hospital as they tentatively began to re-establish that most precious relationship that only a father and daughter can have. When her two brothers arrived in to see her with a huge furry teddy bear she didn't know whether to laugh or cry and ended up doing both.

"Ah don't drown the poor thing," Declan joked sympathetically as she buried her face in the soft cuddly toy. Handing her a handkerchief he gave her hand a squeeze.

"Honest Caro, why didn't you tell me and Damien about the old drinking? We might have been able to help," he said gruffly.

Caroline blew her nose and grinned at her brothers. Despite their gruffness they had always been quite protective about her in their own way. "Huh!" Her voice was still a bit shaky. "If I remember rightly, I had to put the pair of you to bed once or twice when I lived at home."

Damien laughed. "Give us back me Teddy this minute, I told him he was going to live with a nice young lady and here she is impugning our characters!"

"What characters?" She laughed but she clung tightly to them when they hugged her goodbye and promised to visit her again. They had been as good as their word, and even when she had left hospital they had both begun to keep in touch, phoning her regularly or even paying the occasional visit, something they had never done before.

Immediately she left hospital, she asked Richard to bring her to visit Devlin. He had in fact suggested it himself one day he was visiting her. He had told her that he had been in touch with Maggie and that Devlin was out of her coma and beginning to recover. Caroline had been quite stunned that Richard had gone to the trouble of making the enquiry. Especially because the first beating she had received at his hands had been because she had disobeyed him and gone visiting her.

"I know she's your best friend. I was always jealous of your friendship. I always felt Devlin didn't like me either. She's a very astute lady and I was afraid she would find out about me," he confessed shamefacedly as they sat in the grounds of the hospital one evening.

Impulsively Caroline reached out and gave her husband a brief hug. For the first time in their relationship he did not draw away but warmly returned the pressure of her arms. "I can't believe the way you are behaving towards me," he whispered, trying to swallow the lump in his throat. "I thought you wouldn't want to see me, wouldn't want to touch me."

"Oh Richard! After all we've been through! Surely we can at least be friends." Caroline spoke quietly, meaning every word.

Her husband stared at her. She looked so frail and waiflike after all she had been through, but the warmth in her steadfast gaze, her brown eyes so kind and unreproachful made him feel such a bastard. She was comforting him. He who had beaten the daylights out of her and made her life a misery. No wonder Devlin and Maggie thought the world of her. People like Caroline were rare.

"More than anything I'd like to be your friend, Caroline," he managed to say and then he was crying, holding her tightly as he said brokenly, "I'm sorry...I'm really sorry about the beatings and everything. If you want an annulment I'll co-operate. You won't have any difficulty getting one, I promise."

Caroline held him, shocked by his words, My God, if she were to go for an annulment he'd have to confess his homosexuality. She felt a surge of love for him. If he would do that for her he had to have some feelings for her. Maybe their relationship wasn't a total disaster after all.

"What does Charles think?" she asked him gently.

Richard swallowed hard and managed to regain some composure. "Charles loves me, Caroline, you know that. And I love him. But," he met her eyes squarely. "I love you too in my own way. As long as you forgive me and we can stay friends I'll be happy."

"Well I *do* forgive you and I *am* your friend,"

Caroline assured him. She looked at him questioningly.

"Do you want me to get an annulment immediately? I was thinking of going away for a week or two on my own just to think. If you and Charles want to resume your relationship, that's OK by me. I won't feel betrayed and I think he deserves some consideration too."

"But...don't you... I mean aren't you upset by the idea?" Richard stammered.

"Oh Richard!" she laughed. "Now that I know, I can face it. If I could stay in the apartment until I get myself organised?"

"Caroline, of course you can," Richard said earnestly. "I don't want you to leave." He sighed deeply. "Please, please, don't feel you've to go rushing off to get an annulment. Couldn't we leave it for a while, at least until you are on your feet again, and you've got over this. I'd like to be with you and support you. I can't change the way I am, but I promise I'll never lay a finger on you again and I'll always be there for you if you need me."

Caroline smiled at her husband. "Thank you, Richard. Knowing that will help me more than anything to face my future. There are so many things I want to do. I'd like to get a job, learn to drive, travel. I can't believe it...I don't feel afraid any more."

Maggie's Story II

thirty-two

The piercing wail of a baby interrupted Maggie's precious slumber. Snuggling down into the comfortable womb-like hollow of the bed she tried to ignore it. A feeling of desperation enveloped her as the wailing became louder and more demanding. Maggie kept her eyes tightly closed, hoping against hope that Terry might rouse himself and go and attend the baby who was crying. An irate elbow in the ribs shattered her carefully-cultivated illusion.

"Baby's crying, Maggs. For God's sake, do something about it! I've got to get a decent night's sleep, I've got the Goodwin account tomorrow and it's very important to us."

Terry's voice held a note of barely concealed impatience and Maggie had to fight down the impulse to tell him exactly what he could do with the Goodwin account. Having had little or no sleep for the past six months she was at the end of her tether. Sleep was all she could think about these days, craving it like an alcoholic craves a drink or a drug addict a fix. All she wanted was just one night of oblivion to sink into the soothing balm of slumber, undisturbed by crying babies.

Nobody had ever told her that motherhood was like this! When she had discovered that she was pregnant, Maggie had envisaged herself gently rocking her sleepy offspring in her arms for ten minutes or so in the evening before laying it in its delicate wicker basket where it would sleep undisturbed the whole night through. It was a long time since she had worked with newborn babies. Time had dulled her memory and the reality was vastly different. To say that Terry and herself were finding the going a little difficult was more than an understatement.

In the first place they had surprised themselves and everybody else by conceiving twins. Maggie shuddered as she remembered her pregnancy. It had been a nightmare! She had suffered morning noon and night sickness all through her pregnancy, excruciating backache compounded by a bad kidney infection for the last three months and then she had got toxaemia. Things had gone from bad to worse and in the end she'd been induced four weeks early and the babies had had to spend a month in incubators in Saudi. Their plans for coming home had been delayed and it seemed to Maggie that from the moment the twins had been born, she hadn't had a full night's sleep.

On their arrival in the Ryan household the two tiny little beings had taken over her life and it was the rare moment she had to herself, what with feedings, nappy changes and baths...and more feedings. It was one endless cycle. In Saudi it hadn't been too bad because she had domestic help but once she got home to Ireland Maggie found the going tough. Terry did help out occasionally but he had to spend long hours in the office, building up the consultancy firm he had set up on their arrival home from Saudi. She found to her dismay that she was very much alone.

A second wail joined the first and wearily Maggie slipped out of bed and went into the babies' room. Scooping her two bawling treasures from their cots she eased herself into the single bed in the corner. It was cold and unwelcoming, which added to her irritation, and she felt quite sorry for herself. In the next room she could hear her husband snoring loudly and she felt like throttling him. No such thing as equality of the sexes for her darling Terry! Maggie unfastened the top of her nightdress and smiled in spite of herself as two hungry little mouths fastened on her nipples like two ravenous piranhas. At least tomorrow was Friday and she would see Devlin and Caroline. The thought comforted her. She loved their get-togethers. They were imperative to her sanity. How glad she was that she had persuaded Devlin to leave London and come home. At least they had one another to share the delights of child-rearing. The babies suckled contentedly, their downy little heads resting against her breasts and, settling herself more comfortably against the pillows, Maggie gave herself up to the joys of motherhood. She must remember to bring a tart and a casserole for Devlin. Honest to God but there were times when Maggie was sure she was going hungry. Of course Devlin had such pride! There was no room for pride in friendships—that was one lesson that Maggie had learned from hard experience. Pride was a destroyer, a barrier that she had crossed once and which she could safely say would never come between her and anyone.

She suddenly felt sad. Where was Marian now? Had she, too, got married? Did she know the joy of holding a child to her breast? Maggie had written to her once, asking her to reconsider her decision to end their friendship, telling her that she would always be there for Marian and that the door would always be open for her to come back. She never received a reply and had heard nothing from the other girl since. She could be dead, for all Maggie knew. Did she ever think of Maggie? Probably not! Had Marian just used Maggie and her parents while she was at boarding school? They were questions she had asked herself over and over again. She would never know the answers. Time and the friendship of Caroline and Devlin had healed the hurt for Maggie, but not knowing why was something that would always puzzle her.

She sighed, observing the two sleepy little heads nestled close against her. Her children would have to learn for themselves the hard lessons of life. Unfortunately, there were people who would use and abuse others; that was the way of human nature. Her arms tightened their hold on her two feeding babies. What on earth had made her think of Marian Gilhooley after so long? Between Marian and Devlin and Caro there was no comparison. No fairweather friends they. Through thick and thin they had stuck with one another as their lives had changed over the past few years.

Had any of them envisaged how things would turn out? Devlin living in a high-rise flat with her illegitimate daughter. Caroline, wealthy, wanting for nothing yet obviously unhappy in her marriage. And herself...she made a wry grimace. She, who had been the most exuberant of the trio, travelling, living life to the full, had at the age of thirty-one had her wings well and truly clipped. The fetters of wife and motherhood had slipped around her so slyly that she hadn't been aware of them. It was only when she remembered how life had been that she realised quite how dramatically she had changed. Was it worth it, she often wondered, watching her suckling twins.

Maggie knew, no matter how hard she tried to suppress the knowledge, that she was not content with her life as it was. Being a wife and mother were not enough to fulfil her. She missed her job, badly. She was torn between the desire to take up the reins of her career again and the need to be at home for her children. On no account did Terry want her to employ a childminder. But, then, he didn't have to give up his career. He wasn't imprisoned within the four walls of the house with only the babies for company. Yet she knew that if she did go back to work she would worry about the twins. She wouldn't be there to see their first tentative footsteps. Another woman would have that pleasure. Her mother had always been there for Maggie and the boys. She was the first person they saw when they came in from school, standing at the cooker preparing their dinner, ready to listen to all their excited chatter. How much she had taken her mother for granted. Had Nelsie ever got fed up cooking, cleaning, caring? Did Maggie have the right to deny her children the stability of motherhood while she searched for fulfilment? Did they have the right to expect her to give up her own desires? What was fair? What was right? Maggie didn't know and Terry was no help.

The twins were almost asleep, sated, untroubled by worrisome thoughts. She smiled down at them. It was such a pleasure to see them gaining weight. They had been so frail and tiny at their birth that she had feared for their lives. A while later, having winded them and changed them, Maggie dropped into an exhausted sleep noting that it was already six a.m. A howl of outrage shocked her into wakefulness and tears of frustration rose to her eyes. It was only seven! They should have stayed in Saudi, she thought miserably. At least she would have had servants to attend to Terry and the housework.

Her son lay contorted with colic and she did her best to comfort him. Being a nurse she knew the attack would pass but it was distressing for the child and she felt powerless to do anything. Crooning softly to him, she rubbed his back and tummy as she paced the bedroom floor, noticing glumly that it was lashing out of the heavens and that she'd never get her washing dry today. By the time she had the baby settled it was time to get Terry's breakfast and reluctantly, Maggie gave up the notion of getting any more sleep. Bleary eyed, she slapped rashers and sausages on the grill, cut up a grapefruit and burned two pieces of toast.

"Shit!" she cursed as the distinctive smell of burned toast pervaded the orange kitchen. She hated this kitchen! All bright oranges and yellows. They were living in a rented house on a large housing estate in Templeogue and out of it she thought they would never get. She felt so closed in. There were hundreds of young children and teenagers. The noise level was incredible. Maybe the rain was a blessing in disguise; they wouldn't be out kicking ball and screaming and roaring from early morning to after midnight. Many was the night she had tried in vain to get the babies to sleep, even get to sleep herself, but the racket outside made it impossible. Thank God the summer holidays would soon be over and maybe there'd be some respite.

"Are ya trying to set the kitchen on fire,

Maggs?" Terry inquired cheerfully as he noted the little puffs of smoke emanating from the ancient toaster.

"Oh shut up!" She just wasn't in the mood for Terry's humour this morning.

"Jesus, Maggie, but you're becoming a right grouch," her husband informed her indignantly as he stuck his head into his *Irish Times*.

thirty-three

The twins were almost a year old before Maggie began to feel she could cope. Thankfully, after much nagging, Terry bought a house out in Castleknock on the north side of the city, a big detached four-bedroomed house with good gardens front and back. Maggie decorated it in soothing pastel colours and compared to the hideous orange and yellow monstrosity they had inhabited in Templeogue, the new house was a castle. By dint of very hard work, Terry was making a great success of his business, which was expanding rapidly. He expected her to entertain his clients at the drop of a hat. They had many a hot argument about his nasty habit of arriving unexpectedly with some stranger for dinner.

Maggie was a great cook. She was a creative person, and to her cooking was an art, but she liked to have notice that visitors were coming so she could spend time preparing a special meal with all the trimmings. She knew Terry never thought of things like that. Bringing someone home wasn't such a big deal in his eyes. She knew her husband felt that it was up to her to take care of things on the home front just like his mother had. That's what marriage was all about, in his opinion. All he wanted, and was it too much to ask, he inquired testily, when they were having an argument over his attitudes, was to come home after a hard day's work, relax over a drink and have a tasty dinner. If a client came with him what difference did one more mouth make?

"What about what I want?" Maggie demanded. "Do you ever think about that?"

Terry was shocked. Hadn't he given her a lovely home, didn't she have her own cheque book, plenty of food on the table, time to come and go as she pleased while he slaved away to provide for her and the children? What more could she possibly want? He genuinely couldn't understand her attitude. "If my mother had had a tenth of what you have, she would have thought she was in heaven. You know it's no joke at work. The pressure is killing me. All you have to do is take care of the babies and get a dinner. The rest of your time is your own," he said indignantly.

"I am not your mother and these are the Eighties you're living in, Terry. I am your wife, not your housekeeper. And I have a life to lead too and, believe me, I have precious little time to myself," Maggie told him furiously one evening after he complained when he came home with a friend and found her surrounded by talcs and nappies and his dinner not yet cooked.

Another thing they argued about was sex, or rather the lack of it. Maggie was the first to admit that their sex life had suffered since the birth of her twins. Before she'd got pregnant Maggie was always ready to make love. She'd been a wild uninhibited lover and she knew that Terry had never looked at another woman once they'd started to sleep together. But her pregnancy had changed things. As she got bigger and more ungainly she hadn't felt like making love and she had seen Terry looking at other women in the compound with that old familiar light in his eye. He had started working late, leaving her alone with only Mehemed and the house boy for company. And she'd seen that sly bitch Ria Kirby, who lived on the floor below them, flirting with him. She'd tried to ignore it all, hoping that things would sort themselves out when she'd got over the birth and they were back home.

She'd got over the birth, they had come back home, but things didn't improve. Although Terry was eager to resume their active sex life, and she was also, Maggie found that by the end of the day, and with her sleep constantly interrupted, she was exhausted. Making love was the last thing on her mind and Terry just couldn't understand it.

Marriage certainly hadn't been what they had both expected. There was a lot of adjusting to do and it seemed to Maggie that she had to adjust the most. Her life had changed much more than her husband's. Somewhere along the line her identity had disappeared. Now she was Terry's wife, Michelle's and Michael's mother and caring

daughter to her parents who, now that she was
back home in Ireland, expected her to visit
regularly. Once a week she would drive down to
the farm where she would help to hoover and
polish, do the weekly baking as well as take care
of the twins. Then she would drive home, put
them to bed and turn around and make a meal
for herself and Terry. It seemed that everyone
wanted something of her and there was nothing
left for herself.

A few months later she found that she was
pregnant with her third child and well and truly
smothered in her suburban rut. Each day she
would get up, give her husband his breakfast,
feed and bath her infants, do her washing and
housework, bake, mend, garden, it was a never
ending routine that often had her at screaming
point. Even doing the weekly shopping in the
enormous shopping centre ten minutes away
was a break for her. Maggie even found herself
listening to Gay Byrne and enjoying his
programme on the radio like thousands of other
Irish housewives. It was something she had
always vowed she would not do! She would not
become another bored housewife dependent on a
daily radio programme for stimulus and entertainment. When she lived at home her mother
used to drive her mad about Gay Byrne! Nelsie
listened to him religiously each weekday. Well,
her daughter was not going to follow in her
footsteps. Every morning, Maggie would deliberately tune into a pop station immediately

she heard the annoying jingle that preceded the GB Show. One morning though, she had forgotten to do this, and a letter that was being read out over the airwaves caught her attention.

A woman was complaining that now that summer had arrived she would have no peace on the street because of the kids out kicking ball until all hours. She also told Gay that she lived in fear of her life of her windows getting broken and that she hadn't a flower left in her garden. The broadcaster had made light of her complaint, saying hadn't she little to moan about—kids were always bouncing balls and she must be exaggerating. Maggie found herself getting mad. The nerve of him! Wasn't it all right for him living out in secluded splendour out in Howth. He wouldn't be troubled by ball-kicking. Maggie knew *exactly* what that woman was going through. Hadn't she gone through it in Templeogue. Maggie sat down and wrote a letter in support of the other woman's complaint, and to her great satisfaction it was subsequently read out on the programme. From then on she was hooked on the show which covered such a wide range of interesting topics. At least if she was a housewife, she was an informed housewife, she told herself a little wryly. And so the bland routine of coffee mornings, playschool rosters, chore-filled mediocrity that was her existence continued, broken only by her visits to Devlin and Caroline.

With the girls Maggie could escape for a while

from the everlasting routine her life seemed to have turned into. She felt she was neither happy nor unhappy—she was just existing. Where once she had lived life to the full, had crammed every minute with experiences, she now had the sense that the fast-flowing river of life was passing her by and she was stranded, clogged like a reed against a weir and going nowhere. Where once she had chafed against entertaining Terry's clients, she now found herself looking forward eagerly to meeting new people after the stultifying boredom of being alone with two small children day after day.

Invitations to Maggie and Terry's dinner parties were much sought after in their circle. Although she had a tastefully decorated dining room, Maggie much preferred to entertain in her warm spacious kitchen. Not for her the elegance of Cordon Bleu cuisine. Maggie was not a country girl for nothing. Her mouthwatering roasts and casseroles and pies were always devoured by her very appreciative guests who would then relax, elbows on the large circular pine table, sipping from their brandy-filled goblets. The after dinner discussions were always lively and amusing and she made sure to have a good cross section of guests.

Several times she invited Devlin to stay overnight with the baby so she could join the party and it always did her heart good to see her friend dress up and enjoy herself for a few hours. Terry was always especially kind to Devlin and for that she loved him. He never judged people, not like Richard, the bastard, who had been exceedingly cool to Devlin during one of their soirées. Terry had become Richard's investment consultant and although he was doing well for himself, her husband could not help but be impressed by the amount of money Richard and some of his other clients were earning. Richard was making over one hundred thousand pounds a year, he informed Maggie one evening as they were preparing for a dinner party.

In spite of Terry's carefully acquired successful-man-about-town veneer, Maggie knew he had never quite lost his boyhood sense of inferiority. It was this country-boy complex that pushed him on and on. Status and material wealth were important to Terry and it frequently annoyed him that he couldn't match the Yateses' glittering lifestyle. Maggie couldn't have cared less whether she drove a battered old Renault or a Rolls Royce. As long as she got to where she wanted to go she was happy. She dreaded each occasion that Richard presented Caroline with something new. Richard loved to boast and always brought it to Terry's attention. The ear-bashing she would then get would usually end up in a row as Maggie tried to impress upon her husband that she didn't give a fig if Richard had spent three hundred pounds on a leather jacket for Caroline. What her friends or neighbours or anybody else had, meant nothing to Maggie. What Maggie craved more than anything else was time. Time of her own, for herself, when she could do as she pleased. It was the one thing that seemed to elude her. There were the needs of her husband and children to be taken care of. Her family in Wicklow were a constant drain on her time with her mother frequently arriving on her doorstep on a day trip to the city and expecting Maggie to drop everything and escort her around. There were times when the utterly harassed Maggie really envied the childless Caroline and the husbandless Devlin. Now with this new baby on the way she'd have even less time!

Ironically it was her pregnancy that gave her a liberation of sorts. She was in her fifth month and as in the previous pregnancy their love life was suffering. She knew that Terry found pregnancy a sexual turn-off. Maggie accepted this quite philosophically. Terry was solicitous of her comfort and for him, quite caring, especially after the awful pregnancy she had endured before. Although this pregnancy was much easier on her, healthwise, she found taking care of two lively toddlers very tiring. She promised herself that this was going to be her last child. Three were more than enough. Nor was she ever going to take the pill again. She hadn't gone back on it after her first pregnancy because she had been breast feeding for so long, and it hadn't been too much of a shock to her to get pregnant again. She wanted to have her children close together because it was much easier to rear them, but after this one, Terry was going to have to have a vasectomy, or she was getting her tubes tied. No more messing around her internal rhythms with the pill. And there was certainly no way she would consider an IUD, as Terry suggested when she told him she didn't want to go back on the pill. She'd like to see him having his insides mucked about by foreign bodies! It was easy for her husband to suggest she use the pill or the IUD. She wasn't getting any younger, and she had been using contraceptives since her late teens and she was fed up of it. His body wasn't affected and it was either a vasectomy or tied tubes from now on, she informed him firmly, much to his dismay.

It was about ten days after this conversation that she came home to find her husband making love to another woman. To discover that little slut Ria Kirby in her bathroom! In her house! Making love to her husband! This was the most devastating experience of Maggie's life. Nothing that she had ever experienced before had prepared her for the pain and trauma of Terry's betrayal of her and there had been a row to end all rows.

She had always intensely disliked the over-powering self-confident Ria. Their paths had crossed for the first time when they were living in Saudi and Maggie had been pregnant with the twins. Ria, who worked in the Department of Agriculture and had been in the Gulf as part of a team sent to teach animal husbandry to the

Arabs, also hailed from the same part of Galway
as Terry. She lived in the same apartment block
as Terry and Maggie and she was a hard-
drinking hard-living young woman who took
what she wanted and to hell with other people.

Although she was small and on the plumpish
side she had an incredible ego and a loud im-
perious personality. At any party they attended
Ria could be found, her brown eyes sparkling,
her carefully tousled black locks tumbling in
disarray over her plump little shoulders and
invariably decolletée, as she flirted outrageously
with every man in the room.

Maggie judged her to be in her early thirties,
although it was difficult to tell with the amount
of make-up she always wore, and it seemed to her
that beneath the gaiety there was the faintest
hint of desperation about Ria's giggly flirting.
She would often loudly declare for the other
women's benefit that she was strictly a career
girl and that marriage was certainly not on her
agenda at the moment.

"Wash some man's socks! Not me!" she'd
declare. The men were charmed by her! Ria had
taken one look at Terry and the heavily pregnant
Maggie and had made a determined play for him.
One night, having spent the evening sniping
rudely at Maggie, she remarked insultingly,
"You're sooo *tall*, Maggie! I bet your nickname
was beanpole!" She laughed gaily.

Maggie had had enough of her sarcastic
comments. It was bad enough to sit and watch

her flirting cheekily with her husband who was enjoying every minute of it, but to have to listen to her making personal remarks was too much. She was not in the humour to take any more and she snapped coldly, "I'd rather be a beanpole than a fat smart-ass tarty dwarf!"

A stunned silence had descended on their table and then Maggie got up and walked out as Terry tried to laugh it off by saying it was her "condition." From then on out-and-out hostility existed between the two women and it wasn't too long after their exchange that Maggie began to suspect that Terry was seeing Ria behind her back. Maggie never actually caught them, but she knew from the sly triumphant looks that Ria flashed her that something was going on. Terry was out late and Maggie was no fool. When she confronted her husband, he indignantly denied that there was anything between himself and the other woman. And Maggie, because she wanted to believe him, accepted his word. They returned to Ireland and she had put the episode out of her head. Ria had in fact returned to Dublin before the twins were born, and Terry never referred to her again. During her second pregnancy, Terry was so considerate of her welfare that Maggie was totally unprepared for the shock that awaited her.

She had driven down to Wicklow one Friday to see her parents and had told Terry she would be back late in the evening and that his dinner was already prepared in the fridge. Nelsie, for once noticing her daughter's pale and tired appearance, had unexpectedly offered to keep the twins for the week-end. Maggie jumped at the idea, it was so rare, a chance to have time to themselves. Driving home she hummed happily to herself. It was a lovely warm afternoon and maybe she could persuade Terry to leave work early and take her away for the weekend. Noting with some surprise that his car was already in the drive, she was astounded to find that the French doors to the patio were wide open and towels and suntan oil strewn around their well-sheltered lawn. Her mouth tightened. What the hell was going on? Instinctively she knew it was something she wouldn't like.

Heart pounding, she mounted the stairs and walked into their bedroom. She could hear the sound of running water and a female giggle and she didn't have to be Sherlock Holmes to know that her husband was with someone in the bathroom. Opening the door, the steam almost took her breath away and her housewifely pride was annoyed by the fact that they hadn't even bothered to open a window. Flinging aside the shower door she found Terry and that little fat bitch Ria Kirby! Her plump little dimpled bottom was the first thing that Maggie could see through the steam.

Terry's jaw dropped in horror and Ria gave a little squeal of dismay. Maggie's blazing eyes met those of her arch enemy. "Get out of my house, you fat little trollop!" she yelled. "What's wrong? Can't you get a man of your own? Well keep your claws out of mine or you'll be sorry, you vulgar little tart!"

Hustling the startled Ria out of the bathroom she flung her clothes at her and snapped angrily, "Get dressed you or I'll put you out on the street naked." The other girl, scarlet with humiliation, had wasted no time, her fingers fumbling at the fastenings under Maggie's laser stare. Terry remained bashfully in the bathroom until his lover was gone and then came into the bedroom with a sheepish grin on his handsome face.

"Aw, Maggie, don't be mad! I just needed some sex. I know you're not in the humour for it these days. You know it means nothing!"

"You dirty lowdown bastard! Don't use that as an excuse," she shrieked. "Did it have to be with her? Did it? And in my own house? How long has this been going on? Since we came back from Saudi? What do you think I am? A doormat? What about your marriage vows? Don't they mean anything?" she raged, hurt beyond belief.

"Ah come off it, Maggs. You're getting upset over nothing."

"Over *nothing*! Don't insult me, Terry. How would you feel if you caught me with another man? Would *you* think it was *nothing*? Would you even care?" She glared at her husband, hating him. "Let me tell you something Mister, I've just had enough of you! I'm going to stay with Devlin for the weekend and when and if I come back there's going to be some changes in this household—whether you like it or not!"

Slamming the door behind her she left a thoroughly shaken Terry standing dripping on the carpet.

How Maggie got from Castleknock's lush greenness to Ballymun's grey drabness alive she never knew. She drove automatically, her mind full of hurt, anger, bitterness.

Betrayed! Once again she had been betrayed by someone she loved. Just as her best friend Marian had once betrayed her, so too had her husband. The man who had vowed to be faithful all the days of his life. Ha! Faithful! Terry didn't know the meaning of the word. Poor Leonard. Was this how he felt the day he discovered his wife with another man? Leonard would never have done this to her.

Why? why? why? she asked herself over and over again. Did she not give enough love? Was she someone who invited betrayal? Did people think because she was a fairly tolerant person that she had no feelings? Why did the two people in her life who had meant the most to her, hurt her so brutally?

"Bitch! Bastard!" she sobbed, tears blurring her eyes. She was stopped at red lights and she knew that the man in the car beside her was staring. To hell with him, she didn't care. All she cared about was the anger that was bubbling up inside her. First Marian, now Terry! What a pair they would have made. Users! Abusers! They didn't deserve her love. Marian and Terry would have made a perfect couple! Why was she thinking of Marian now? It must be the feelings of pain and hurt that Terry had caused her that had brought back all the old memories so long buried in her heart. The pain of betrayal was the same no matter who caused it.

Well one thing was for sure, from now on *she* would be number one. No longer putting others first as before. From now on Maggie Ryan would do exactly what she wanted to, when and where she wanted to. She would love and raise her children but, by God, she'd teach them to be independent of people. Never would they be hurt as she had been—not if she could help it.

"Love many; trust few; always paddle your own canoe," her mother had advised after Marian rejected her. She should have learned her lesson then. But not Maggie, too generous, and trusting and loving. That was her problem, always believing the best of people. But it was a failing she would guard against in the future and her children would learn from her. This she swore as she drove towards Devlin's grey graffiti-decorated tower block.

Devlin had listened to her sad and sorry tale, eyes wide with dismayed shock. "Is Terry crazy?" she blurted out. Maggie burst out crying. Devlin said nothing else, just put her arms around her friend and let her cry.

"God, I haven't cried for years!" she gulped when it was over.

"Just as well," Devlin smiled, " 'cos it was a

real Niagara and I'm drenched." In spite of herself Maggie laughed as she hugged her friend. "Thanks, Dev, for letting me stay and for letting me bawl all over you and, most of all, for being there."

"Listen!" said Devlin firmly. "Don't give it a second thought! You've always been there for me and I'm more than glad to do the same for you. That's what being friends is all about. I just wish the circumstances were different."

Maggie stared at the slender young woman beside her. How different from the frivolous girl she had first known. Devlin had matured so much since her pregnancy. They had become much closer since they had returned to Dublin, sharing the joys and traumas of motherhood. It was to Devlin that she had instinctively turned in her time of need and as her friend fussed around making tea and toast she realised that Devlin was a far better friend to her than Marian Gilhooley had ever been. There was a steady integrity about Devlin and Maggie knew without a doubt that she could rely on her for anything. The thought comforted her. It was during the bad times that you found out who your real friends were and these were bad times!

Later, they went shopping as Devlin hadn't been expecting visitors and after they had gone back to the flat and Devlin had put the baby to bed, Maggie found herself starting to relax. It was strange not to have to rush out to the kitchen to get a meal for Terry and not to have the twins to watch out for. What was Terry doing now? Was he with Ria? Would she ever learn to trust him again? Did she want to stay married to him? Maggie swallowed the lump that was in her throat. Devlin was putting fresh sheets on the bed and she was alone in the shabby but spotless lounge.

To break up a marriage was a serious thing. Would she cope with two children and another on the way if she decided to leave Terry? Suddenly, she felt lonely for the twins. How were they getting on down with their grandmother? Michael had forgotten his favourite Teddy so he wouldn't be able to go to sleep. And Michelle? Maggie smiled as she thought of her precious little daughter. Always the one to get into mischief first, she was going to grow up exactly like her mother!

Devlin came back into the room, took one look at her friend's exhausted face and packed her off to bed. Maggie felt bad about taking Devlin's bed but her friend had insisted. "For goodness sakes, Maggs, make the most of the weekend. Get as much rest and sleep as you can—you look as though you need it!"

It was ironic. For the first time since the birth of her babies Maggie had time to herself, time to be alone, time to sleep, but her mind kept exploding with memories of the day's events. Just before dawn she stood at the bedroom window and watched a jet gliding gently down on its approach to the airport. It seemed so near that she felt she could reach out and touch it. The twinkling lights disappeared from her sight and she heard the subdued roar of its landing. Silence had descended truce-like after the noisy battles of the day on the vast estate, its tower blocks reminding her a little of New York. Below and above her the lights of Ballymun shimmered and glittered in a losing battle against the glimmering dawn of the eastern sky.

There was so much hardship here it was unbelievable. She took so much for granted. Devlin had told her that sixty-one per cent of its population was unemployed. She had seen the queues of men in the local supermarket doing the shopping. Some of them looked so hopeless and despairing her heart had gone out to them. Even shopping with Devlin had been an eye-opener. Devlin had selected the cheapest brands of every item she had to buy. Coffee was a thing of the past, she confided matter-of-factly, as she purchased special offer teabags and Maggie, knowing better than to offer to buy some, had begun to realise how unaware she was of the poverty that existed in her own city.

As she stood staring out of Devlin's high-rise window she reflected a little ashamedly that she was one of the lucky ones. So her husband had cheated on her! So a friend had let her down in the past! How trivial these problems might seem to many of the people here who were living in grinding poverty with no future to look forward to. At least Maggie knew she could go back to work if she had to. If she left Terry she'd manage—of that there was no doubt!

"Make the most of what you've got and stop whinging, Maggie!" she murmured, easing her pregnant bulk into bed and snuggling down into its comfortable warmth. Minutes later she was asleep. Around midday, having slept soundly for the first time in almost two years, Maggie woke to find Devlin grinning at her, a tray in her hands.

"You'd better give that child inside you some nourishment," her friend smiled warmly. Maggie gave a catlike stretch and an appreciative sniff. Her morning sickness had not lingered beyond three months in this pregnancy and she was hungry. Her eyes surveyed the attractive breakfast on the tray before her.

"It's a 'Cruiser Breakfast'," Devlin grinned.

Maggie grinned back at Devlin's reference to a holiday Caroline, Devlin and she had taken— a cruise on the Shannon—the year before she got married. It had been a fantastic holiday. The three of them had hired a luxury cruiser for the week and sailed from Banagher to Clonmacnoise and then up to Athlone, across Lough Ree and up to Dromod. They had had a ball. The weather had been terrific and at times they had felt they were on the Mediterranean, passing little islands in the lakes, with the sun shimmering and glittering on the water. They had read and fished and giggled and ate. And at night they would pull into a riverside berth, join up with other cruisers and have barbecues and sing-songs until the early hours. The only thing was, they were eating like horses, the healthy fresh river air giving them enormous appetites.

Each morning who ever was on cooks for the day would serve juice, cereal, tea, toast, rashers, sausages, mushrooms, puddings, and crispy fried bread. Having polished off this repast they would then attack the "Sin bag," so called because in it reposed occasions of sin, most injurious to the figure. Yorkies, Crunchies, Twixes, Flakes. The "Sin bag" was replenished at every riverside stop...and was never empty. All three of them had returned to Dublin half a stone heavier!

Maggie smiled at the wonderful memory. "That was a great holiday, wasn't it? We were all so young and carefree and untroubled."

"The best ever! We'll do it again some time!" Devlin agreed, plumping up a pillow at Maggie's back. Maggie surveyed the loaded tray.

God! Devlin must have spent a fortune. Honestly, she was the best in the world.

"Eat up, Maggie," Devlin admonished her "It's great having you here. It's just like old times!"

They spent a lovely day together. They went into town and rambled around the shops, not looking for any thing in particular, just enjoying the freedom of having time together. On their way back to Ballymun, Devlin asked Maggie to stop at the library so she could get some books for the rest of the week-end. As she made her selection, Maggie strolled around the impressive single-storeyed building with eyes wide. Libraries had certainly changed since she was a child, she mused, as she observed scores of children painting, playing chess and Scrabble, or just reading in the brightly decorated airy children's section. As she studied a large well-filled notice board displaying information on a variety of subjects, she thought that maybe when Michelle and Michael were older she would enrol them. She noticed a door that was marked "Community Information Centre." If she decided to leave Terry she'd need the services of such a centre. What on earth would her entitlements be? Fishing in her bag, she took down the times of opening and noted with surprise that the Centre held Free Legal and Financial Advice sessions as well. It was good to know such services existed. Then another notice caught her eye.

"Would you like to write? Join our Writer's group!" Well that was an idea! The memory of a half-written novel came to mind. She should take up her writing again. A writer's workshop would be a great outside interest. She was too consumed with her children and the home. It was time she started discovering her own identity again.

"Ballymun has a nice library," she remarked to Devlin as they drove to the flat in the light drizzling rain.

"I'd be lost without it!" Devlin replied frankly.

"I can go there to borrow a painting, cassettes, magazines, books and I can read the papers too, all for nothing. But Mollie says that because of the cutbacks the services provided have gone down badly; and you could see for yourself the staff on the desks are run off their feet. Did you see that gang of kids? Imagine having to put up with that all day? The kids here love the library but I suppose they'll start charging eventually and for the likes of me and them, that will be disastrous. Believe me Maggie I'm an expert on free entertainment and you won't get much better than this."

"Don't you ever feel bitter?" Maggie asked, sometimes wondering how Devlin, who had had so much, could cope so well with living on the breadline. It annoyed Maggie sometimes, because she felt that if Devlin wasn't so stubborn about letting her father and Kate help her, she could have been out of Ballymun long ago. She was going to say it to her too some day.

Devlin grimaced. "Maggie, sometimes I wake up cursing the day I was born. But," she shrugged her shoulders "It's a mess of my own making. Things could be much worse. I have a beautiful daughter, good friends, an independence of sorts and a roof over my head, and I'll get out of here some day."

You can say that again, if Kate and I have anything to do with it, Maggie thought to herself. She insisted on buying a steak for each of them for dinner plus a bottle of sparkling wine. "My treat!" she said in tones that brooked no argument. She cooked a delicious meal and they enjoyed every morsel. By now there was a full blown gale outside. Yesterday's sun was a memory, and as the rain lashed against the windows, they sat mellowed by wine, giggling at memories of the good times in the past.

That night Maggie went to bed early and slept like a log. She took her leave of Devlin the following day, refreshed in body, determined in mind. She was going to change her life too, she told herself firmly, as she drove along the rain-washed leafy back roads to Castleknock.

She stopped off at a newsagents to buy some chocolate for her craving hormones and the heading of an article in a magazine caught her eye: "See your Novel in Print!" She smiled wryly, remembering the novel started in Saudi. God knows she had enough experience of life there and in the States to write about, and what about Terry and Ria? Maggie grimaced. No Jackie Collins novel had quite prepared her for the shock of finding her husband with another woman. Picking up the magazine, she bought a box of Milk Tray as well. Let Terry go and pick up the children in Wicklow. *She* was going to read her magazine and eat chocolates for the afternoon, she decided. A subdued and abashed Terry agreed to her cool suggestion that he collect the children and when he was gone she settled down to enjoy her afternoon of lazy solitude. When Terry returned with the children, there was no meal ready for him, and so he had put the twins to bed and for the first time she could remember, her husband had cooked dinner.

That night she told him to move in to the guest room, and seeing the expression in her eyes, he didn't argue. There he would stay, she decided, until she was ready to forgive him. That was if she ever forgave him. It had been his choice to play around, she was making her choice now. The following morning before her husband went to work, Maggie informed him that she was going to employ a woman to come every Friday and take care of the twins and do some housework. From now on Fridays were going to be hers completely. Terry was too taken aback at her determined attitude, to protest and when he came home from work and found his dinner not ready, the twins playing with her knitting and Maggie tapping inexpertly but enthusiastically on a new portable typewriter, she could see from the expression on his face that Terry felt that his carefully ordered existence had collapsed!

thirty-four

For months Maggie worked on The Novel. Her diary had sown the seeds when she had been in Saudi and although it had been a long time since she had read what she had written there in that hot dusty country, her pulse had quickened with excitement as ideas began to form and she started to write again.

She would enter the competition in the magazine and see how she got on. Maybe she would win and see her novel in print. What a thought! She decided to base her story on the lives of three wives of very different backgrounds who find themselves becoming friends in the claustrophobic setting of a foreign compound in Saudi. Smiling to herself one day she prepared to introduce a new character.

"Ira Kingston was the kind of woman who wore *Poison*. And it suited her!" she had written. Maggie knew *precisely* who the bitch in the story would be modelled on.

"Ria Kirby, you might help make my fortune yet," she muttered as she tapped away briskly. It was hard going, finding the time to create. Maggie didn't find writing itself difficult. The ideas poured out of her, but finding the time to do it was another thing. She kept at it, sitting at her kitchen table while her children played at her feet, or if the sun was shining, sitting at her patio table with her portable typewriter and her Ballygowan, dressed in the loosest, coolest maternity dress she could find, one eye on her keyboard, the other on the twins. She found that she could shut out all noise and diversion and concentrate on the lives of the women she was writing about.

As in her previous pregnancy, she developed toxaemia and had to go into hospital early to be induced. Again she had a difficult labour but when her baby daughter was placed in her arms Maggie forgot all the hassle and pain as she looked into the big blue eyes that seemed as though they were saying "Well here I am and wasn't it all worth it?"

For a while after her return from hospital, Maggie didn't go near her novel. She just hadn't the time, although Josie, her "Friday Woman," made a great difference to her. Eventually she got into a routine. Her new baby, Fiona, was a quiet contented child, who thankfully slept through the night unlike her siblings at the same age. Maggie would give her her six o' clock feed and then write until it was time to prepare Terry's breakfast. As the pages rolled off the typewriter and the manuscript began to pile up, Maggie came to feel a quiet satisfaction. At last she was doing something creative, something that wasn't connected with her family. She knew she was writing a good story. Surely someone would publish it!

Caroline and Devlin were delighted for her. They would read each instalment, oohing and aahing as they recognised this one and that, and demanding more. Maggie was so pleased that Devlin had decided to go and live in Rosslare. She'd miss her like crazy, but at least she and Lynn would be starting afresh.

When Maggie heard from Caroline about Devlin's accident, she was devastated and guilt-ridden. After all, it was she who had told Devlin to stop acting the martyr and think of Lynn and Kate and go and live in the Harbour. Maybe if she had kept her advice to herself, Kate and Lynn might still be alive and Devlin wouldn't be suffering like she was. Then there was Caroline's breakdown and alcoholism. She should have made Caroline tell her what was troubling her. Maybe she could have eased the younger girl's trauma. What was happening to the three of them? All deeply troubled, unable to help each other as they wanted to.

It had been the hardest thing in the world to walk into the ward where Devlin was lying and face her. They had held each other tightly. Maggie had been unable to hide her tears, but Devlin had remained dry-eyed. "I don't want to talk about it, now or ever," she said to Maggie and Maggie, not knowing what to say or do could only hold her friend in her arms. She visited her daily, but Devlin never spoke about the accident or the death of her aunt and daughter, and Maggie couldn't raise the subject, although she knew that her friend, by not expressing her grief, was letting herself in for trouble.

Caroline too was undergoing a detox programme, and although she seemed to be recovering, and had lost that awful haunted unhappy expression she couldn't talk about the underlying cause of her troubles. She told Maggie that some time she would tell her everything, but not now, not yet.

It was a difficult time for Maggie: both her friends in trauma, her own marriage damaged by Terry's affair with Ria, and the demands of a new baby and two young toddlers to occupy her. But somehow she found the strength to keep going: to visit and be supportive to her two best friends, to look after the needs of her family and even to write.

She drove herself to have the novel finished by the competition closing date. There were times when the last thing she wanted to do was to sit at her typewriter and write. She would find herself making excuses, even doing the ironing—which she hated—rather than sit down in front of her keyboard. But other times she'd make herself do it, and once she got going, and the flow was there, she might write fifteen or twenty pages and end up drained of energy but on a high as the lives of her characters took shape and she began to think of them as almost human. It was with immense relief and the sense of a burden being lifted that she finished her first manuscript on time and posted it off. She collected Caroline, who was now out of hospital and looking much better, and they both went in to see Devlin and toasted her achievement with Lucozade.

Maggie couldn't say that she had really enjoyed writing the novel. The part where Ira Kingston seduced the husband of one of the heroines had been written from the heart, but she had very much enjoyed the reaction of her friends as they read each instalment and clamoured for more.

"Maggie, that's a sweet revenge," Devlin had smiled as she instantly recognised the unmistakable Ria.

Maggie grinned back, unabashed. "That'll teach her to go messing about with other women's husbands!"

Privately she was thanking God that Devlin seemed to be coming out of that frightening shocked depression she had been in since the accident. The new health club idea she was on about was just the thing to take her mind off things. If anybody could make a go of it, Devlin could. Hearing a knock on the door, Maggie saw Devlin's eyes light up a little and knew before he even walked in, that it was Luke Reilly.

Now there was a man and a half! He'd be perfect for the hero in her next novel. What a dish, and so genuinely nice too. Maybe she'd write about them in her next novel and Devlin would recognise herself and take the hint. Taking Caroline by the arm, she smiled and said her goodbyes.

"He's nice isn't he?" remarked Caroline.

"He certainly is," agreed Maggie.

"Let's hope he's not the kind of bastard Colin Cantrell-King was," mused Caroline.

Maggie gave a wry smile. "I wonder if there's any such thing as a faithful husband?

"Ah, Maggie, I'm sorry about you and Terry. I always thought you and he were the perfect couple," her friend said. "If it's any comfort to you I know what you're going through, Richard..." Caroline stopped, unable to continue.

"It's alright, Caro. You don't have to tell me anything," Maggie hastened to reassure her.

Caroline smiled. "I want to tell you, Maggie, and I will, but right now it would take too long to go into and I've got to go for a counselling session. We'll get together soon and really talk."

"Whenever you want to is fine with me," Maggie said, hugging the younger woman. Watching her hail a passing taxi, Maggie reflected that Caroline seemed to have gained a quiet self-assurance and serenity since she had admitted her alcoholism and started getting treatment. That awful wounded unhappiness was no longer evident in the depths of her brown eyes. She seemed to have taken control of her own life somewhat, no longer allowing Richard to dictate to her and they seemed much happier in each other's company. The trouble with Caro was that she kept everything to herself. Maggie knew that Richard had been beating her friend. She had seen the bruises several times when Caroline's guard was down after a few drinks. But when she had brought up the subject, Caroline had clammed up and remained utterly loyal to her husband. If Terry had ever raised a hand to her, he would have regretted it bitterly, Maggie thought, as she unlocked the car and drove in the direction of town.

It was Friday, her day off, although now that she had Fiona to breastfeed she was a bit tied. However she had fed her just before she came out, and she wasn't due a feed for a couple of hours, so she might as well make the most of it. Terry was very grudging about her day of freedom but Maggie was adamant. Being the person she was, she couldn't sustain her anger with Terry about the affair with Ria. They spoke to each other, entertained and socialised. She had even allowed Terry to move back into their bedroom after the baby had been born, but she was through with putting herself last. And she religiously kept Fridays for herself. Sometimes she had nothing specific planned and would just meander about town, enjoying being alone. Terry had thought it was a passing phase, just like the novel-writing, but Maggie had stuck to her guns, determined to re-discover something of her old independent identity. She lived for her Fridays and today she was going to an exhibition she had been looking forward to since she had heard it was coming to Ireland.

Driving south through Phibsboro, past the faded grandeur of the Broadstone and the elegant King's Inns she hummed to herself. It was a lovely autumn day and the sun glittered on the rippling swirls of the Liffey tide as she crossed the Church Street Bridge. Where once the majesty of Christchurch had graced the skyline to her left in towering splendour, the view was now spoiled by a hideous monstrosity of American-style architecture. Maggie frowned, she thought that the architect who designed the Civic Offices had absolutely no sense of history or appreciation of visual beauty. Nor had the people who had given planning permission for the outrage despite widespread protests from the people of Dublin. The historic Wood Quay site of Viking Dublin had been bulldozed and the unsightly office block erected. An act of civic vandalism!

Sighing, she turned right on to cheerful Thomas Street with its street sellers and colourful markets. The Liberties market was a great place for a bargain and Maggie often did some of her Christmas shopping there. It was a nice way to spend a Sunday afternoon and it reminded her of the many afternoons she had spent in The Village in New York. Driving past the imposing gates of Guinness's Brewery, Maggie gave an appreciative sniff. The unique smell of Lops permeated the air, rich and full-bodied, part and parcel of James's Street. Finding a parking space she locked the car and strolled down to the Guinness Hop Store, which was now a vast exhibition centre. It was here that she had first seen the fantastic Norman Rockwell Collection in early summer and she had made a habit of visiting the centre every so often. She clattered across the cobbled street towards the building which had once stored the hops for the brewery but which was now a vast imaginative cultural centre.

It was great! Today she didn't feel a bit guilty about not being at her typewriter. Her novel was posted and winging its way to the magazine and she could dawdle along, secure in the knowledge that she had achieved something again after years of mental inertia. What would she write about next? Maybe she'd call into the ILAC library and get a few books on writing. God, it was great to have a few hours to herself!

An hour and a half later, having thoroughly enjoyed the exhibition, Maggie was rushing up the marble steps to the Central Library in the huge ILAC shopping centre, a great new idea in her head for her new novel. She'd get a few books to research her background material and while she was there she must check to see if Terry Prone's *Write And Get Paid For It* was in. She'd read the review in the paper and decided that it was just the book for her. It covered everything and was just what a beginner like herself needed. The last time she had looked it hadn't been on the shelf, nor had there been anything else covering the subject, and the librarian she spoke to told her that anything about writing was always out. "It's a very popular subject—you've no idea the amount of enquiries we get."

Maggie hoped that all these would be novelists hadn't entered for the same competition as she had. Briskly she walked towards the relevant section. Only one other person was there, a tall good-looking blonde-haired young man, Maggie noted. Rather an Adonis in fact!

Oh Maggie! She chided herself in amusement. He couldn't be more than twenty five. What was getting into her these days? She seemed to be constantly fantasising about men. Sex with Terry seemed almost boring and mechanical, a far cry from the early days of their relationship. Somehow, after Ria, things didn't feel quite the same. It must be all the passion that she was writing about that was causing her hormones to revolt. Sighing she scanned the shelves and saw the slim paperback she was looking for. Great. Reaching up for Terry Prone's book, her fingers clashed with those of the young man beside her, as he too went to select the book.

"Oh!" exclaimed Maggie in surprise, dropping her hand. He must be a would-be novelist too.

"Snap," said a cheerful voice above her left ear and Maggie found herself staring into a pair of smiling hazel eyes.

"Please take it," he said politely.

"But you were here first," Maggie pointed out.

"We're closing now!" an authoritative voice

announced, and the lights started to flicker.

"I'll tell you what," announced the young man firmly. "You take the book this week and you can give it to me next week or the week after. I'm always in here around this time on Fridays."

"Thanks very much," Maggie said, gratified.

"Not at all. We authors must stick together." He winked conspiratorially.

"Oh, do you write too?" It was out before she realised it and she could have kicked herself. Maggie was still a closet writer!

"I've written a few bits and pieces," he responded matter-of-factly.

"Did you ever get published?" she asked eagerly, her embarrassment forgotten at meeting a fellow scribe.

The young man grinned, displayed even white teeth. "*Reader's Digest* published one article and the *Evening Press* another. That's about the extent of it."

"At least it's something!" Maggie replied, impressed.

"Closing now!" came the voice of the authoritative one.

"We'd better go," Maggie said hastily.

"See you next week, then," came the calm rejoinder as the young man strode down the library, leaving her with her book about writing and getting paid for it, and a smile on her face.

***

Two weeks later Maggie marched up the steps towards the library. She wondered would the young man be there. Their encounter had given her such a lift. It was nice to know that other people wrote and were successful. If only she could win that competition what an achievement that would be! She had a quick look around and felt an unaccountable sense of disappointment. He hadn't come!

Really, Maggie, grow up! she rebuked herself, half amused. My God, he was only a baby and she was a married woman in her thirties. Was she taking leave of her senses? She was deeply engrossed in a book about the Art of the American Indians when a deep voice said cheerfully, "Hi! Did you enjoy the book?"

Maggie gave a start and turned to find her Adonis smiling down at her. She herself was a tall woman but he was easily six two. Suddenly her afternoon took on an extra sparkle. "Hello," she smiled feeling ridiculously light-hearted.

"Well are you going to make your fortune?" He indicated *Write and Get Paid for It*.

Maggie laughed "Not a hope! I found out all the things I did wrong, but it's a very informative book. You'll enjoy it. But I'm afraid I won't get my novel published."

"Oh dear!" he said, his hazel eyes twinkling. "What exactly did you do wrong?"

To her surprise she found herself telling him all about the mistakes she had made and in answer to further interested questions, she told him all about her novel. She found him very easy to talk to and both of them were quite shocked when the familiar "Closing Now" interrupted their conversation. It seemed they had only been talking ten minutes, but it was in fact an hour. His name was Adam Dunne. He was an electrician with Telecom Eireann, he was twenty-five and had just bought a small house in Drumcondra. Maggie felt as though she had known him all her life.

"Closing please!" Maggie was beginning to dislike intensely the unseen owner of that bossy voice. She had an accent and tone of voice exactly the same as Sister Mairead, her old teacher. Maybe they were related! Damn the library for closing early on Friday. She had really enjoyed talking to Adam.

"Tell you what," Adam said easily. "If you're around next week I'll show you a book in the reference section called *The Writer's and Artist's Yearbook*. It tells you all you need to know about the mechanics of the manuscript, where to send them, how to present them. Just what Terry Prone's been saying. It's very good. Just what the budding author needs."

This time they left the library together and the boyish smile he gave her as they said goodbye made her feel ten years younger.

That night she as sat in front of her bedroom mirror Maggie studied herself long and hard. She had let herself go a bit, she thought glumly. It was time she took herself in hand. There was nothing she could do about the fine lines etched around her green eyes but the sagging spreading bottom could be toned up and the thighs firmed. The hair was a mess! That was easily remedied. She should be ashamed of herself for letting herself go to seed. For heaven's sake she was only thirty-three, not sixty-three!

Without further ado, the hair was cut, the tumbling copper locks shaped into a softer shorter style that framed her face and made her look ten years younger. She started exercising with the help of a shape tape and exercise bike; and even after a week of dieting and exercising she began to notice a difference. It was a sparkling vibrant woman who ran up the steps of the ILAC library the next week.

Adam did a gratifying double take at the sight of her and she laughed aloud. "Just got the old mop cut," she said lightly. But her eyes sparkled as she met his clear dark-lashed hazel ones.

Their weekly meetings gave her something to look forward to. Adam was so cool and laid-back, yet full of enthusiasm for her writing ventures, quite unlike her husband who dismissed her "scribbling" as a waste of time. They swopped ideas, gave each other encouragement and enjoyed their hour in the library each week.

When Adam told Maggie of a writer's workshop starting up in his local Arts Centre Maggie jumped at the idea. Terry was not at all impressed when his wife informed him that from now on, every Monday night, she would be going to a writer's workshop and he would have to mind the children. "For Christ's sake, you're wasting your time with that nonsense. Couldn't you take up knitting or rug making or something useful?"

"I'm not wasting my time. And if you don't like it, you can lump it! You're out half the week anyway," Maggie retorted crisply.

"That's business and you know it," her husband growled.

"So is this," his wife informed him calmly.

The classes were a joy! It was wonderful to mix with other people who shared the same interest, especially when you were sitting beside a guy who made you laugh constantly with his witty asides and who made you feel young and lighthearted again and not the mother of three demanding young children. Looking at herself in the mirror one night before she went out, she felt like the Maggie of old—vibrant, alive, ready for anything. How glad she was that she had got herself out of the soul-destroying rut she had been in.

thirty-five

One morning several months later the postman presented her with a large brown envelope and Maggie felt her heart sink to her boots. Without opening it, she knew it was her returned manuscript. She hadn't won the competition! Maybe she had been kidding herself all along. Maybe she had no talent as a writer. To compound her misery, her washing machine chose that particular morning to flood the kitchen and it was a very depressed Maggie who set about cleaning up the mess.

For the first time in months she decided not to go to her writers' class. What was the point? And anyway wasn't it time she got sense? Half the reason she went to the class was because Adam went. She must be crazy! He was almost eight years younger than her, and probably had a luscious twenty-year-old girlfriend that he hadn't mentioned. And besides...she was married.

So was Terry when he had the fling with Ria! The thought came unbidden to her mind. "Oh stop it Maggie," she muttered aloud, grabbing Michelle who, in her enthusiasm to kiss her baby sister, was almost smothering the child.

The evening dragged. Terry fell asleep in front of the fire, the returned manuscript reproached her accusingly from the coffee table and she felt miserable. The following morning, she was feeding the twins their breakfast and listening to Gay Byrne when the phone rang. "Hi! What happened you last night?" inquired a familiar voice and Maggie felt a warm glow envelop her.

"How did you know my number?" she asked.

Adam laughed. "Maggie, my girl, I'm a thriller writer par excellence who just hasn't been published. Putting my detective skills to good use, I looked up the phone directory and found the only Terry Ryan who lives in Castleknock. I then deduced, brilliantly if I may say so," he added modestly "that since you were married to him you must live in the same house and therefore share the same number. Are you impressed?"

Maggie had to laugh. "Absolutely. I'll have to call you Sherlock Dunne from now on."

"Why didn't you come last night?"

Maggie stayed silent for a moment. "My washing machine broke down," she said glumly.

"And?"

Adam was so perceptive. It was one of the qualities she liked in him. Besides it was only fair to tell him the real reason she had stayed away. "I got my manuscript back yesterday," she admitted.

"Ah, Maggie! I'm sorry. It's an awful feeling, isn't it?"

"Yeah," she admitted with a sigh.

"What's wrong with the washing machine?"

"I don't know. Water flooded all over the kitchen. Someone is supposed to be coming to repair it the day after tomorrow."

"Poor Maggs." She could sense that he was smiling at the other end of the phone.

She laughed. "I'm feeling so sorry for myself, I feel like flinging the typewriter and the washing machine out the window."

Adam laughed. "Just make sure there's no one passing by. You don't want to be sued to add to your list of woes."

"OK," she smiled, feeling much better. "See you Friday?" she queried.

"Hmmm," he responded. "Have to go, Maggie. Take care."

Around the middle of the afternoon she answered a knock on her door to find Adam smiling at her. "I fix washing machines in my spare time!"

"Why aren't you at work?" Maggie laughed.

"I was owed some time so I took it. I figured I'd better get you back on the straight and narrow with your typewriter."

"Idiot!" she grinned, feeling strangely happy. He handed her a blue book.

"It's the CLÉ *Directory* and it's got the manes and addresses of all the Irish publishing houses. So get cracking. Get in touch with some of them and put the kettle on and make a cuppa for us while I have a look at your washing machine," he instructed her good-humouredly.

As she moved around her kitchen making tea she was deeply aware of him as he lay, long legs all over the place, trying to fix her recalcitrant washing machine. He sat up boyishly, his hair awry. "I can see what's wrong. I'll have to get a part. Can you wait until tomorrow? You can cancel the other bloke and save a few bob," he suggested.

"Thanks, Adam," she said, smiling at him.

They sat facing each other at the table, Maggie with Fiona on her lap, the twins playing on the floor.

"That's a beautiful baby you've got there," he said as Fiona gripped one of his fingers in her tiny hand and made eyes at him. "Motherhood suits you, Maggie," he said softly.

She blushed. There was a warmth in his eyes that excited her. It was a long time since a man had looked at her like that. Too long. Terry looked at her these days and never even saw her. Couldn't see the loneliness inside her that was causing her to turn to a younger man for companionship. They stared at each other and Adam said, "I'd better go, I'll see you tomorrow."

"Thanks, Adam." Her voice was husky; she felt like a sixteen-year-old.

She watched him drive away. She was confused, scared, elated. He made her feel so attractive again. God, she could stand up in a leotard these days in a class at CITY GIRL with girls ten years younger than her and not be ashamed. That's what Adam Dunne had done to her. He made her feel like a woman again and not a drudge!

He arrived as promised the next day and this time she was ready for him. Her hair was freshly washed, her touch of make up was just right and a faint hint of *Laughter* adorned her wrists and throat. She watched as he deftly fitted the piece in the machine, noticing his long well-shaped fingers. She'd like to feel those fingers caressing her body. A strange fear suffused Maggie. She hadn't felt like this since she was a young girl with Joe Conway. What was she thinking of?

Adam stood up and saw the expression in her eyes. They stared at each other in silence and then very gently he reached out and took her face in his hands. "Maggie, you're beautiful," he said, before lowering his mouth to hers. They kissed slowly, sensually and she felt weak with longing but a yell from the playroom penetrated their passion.

"My children," Maggie murmured apologetically "like to be seen *and* heard."

Adam laughed. "It's just as well maybe because I could very easily get carried away."

Maggie stared into his smiling hazel eyes. "Me too," she said honestly.

"Maggie, I have to go to London for a month. Telecom are sending some of us so I want you to promise me one thing."

"Anything," she said, dismayed that she wouldn't see him for a whole month.

"Get back to your typewriter, go to your classes, and get in touch with some publishers. There's a rake of 'em in that directory and some of them will at least read your novel, and if they've any sense they'll publish it. It's a great read! Now promise!"

Maggie hugged him. "I promise, Adam."

She stood in the sunlight watching him drive away. He waved and she returned the wave. She felt so strong and renewed. Would she have an affair with him? She couldn't swear that she wouldn't. That was something to be decided in the future. For now she felt incredibly happy. Lightheartedly, Maggie walked into her kitchen and started to prepare her husband's evening meal.

Epilogue

The three friends greeted each other warmly when they met in the plush foyer of CITY GIRL.

"You're looking pretty pleased with yourself, Maggs," Devlin noted as she pressed the button for the lift.

"I am," Maggie grinned as they stepped into the elegant lift and it glided swiftly, silently upward.

"What's happened?" Caroline asked, dying to know. Just wait until she told them her news!

"I'll tell you after class at breakfast"

"Tell us what?" chorused Devlin and Caroline.

"At breakfast," Maggie repeated firmly.

The other pair grinned. "You won't be able to wait that long. You're bursting to tell us. Come on! Don't be so mean," expostulated Devlin who was dying with curiosity to find out what had made Maggie looking so radiant. Maybe she had slept with Adam. No! It couldn't be that. Wasn't he in London? He had certainly brought the sparkle back into Maggie's eyes. She just lit up when she spoke about him. "Come on, Maggie."

"Patience is a virtue," Maggie teased as the lift stopped and a beautiful girl in a white uniform stepped in to join them, ending the conversation.

"Morning all."

"Hi Aoibhinn," they responded to the chief beautician of CITY GIRL.

"Any chance of a make-up job for the TV thing?" Devlin grinned.

"I'm sure I could squeeze you in to my schedule. Mind, with your mug it could take a couple of hours."

"See the awe and reverence my staff hold me in," said Devlin in mock disgust as the lift came to a smooth halt and Aoibhinn glided gracefully down the carpeted corridor to her domain.

"You shouldn't have gorgeous-looking girls like that working for you, Dev. They'll give your clients complexes," Maggie said, as she pulled the muscles of her stomach a little tighter.

"The way you look this morning, it's you who'll be giving people complexes. Now stop getting away from the subject and tell us the news."

"Now, come along, ladies," Janet the pint-sized aerobics instructress ordered crisply as she passed them on her way into the gym.

Caroline threw her eyes up to heaven. "We'll have to wait, Dev, to hear Maggie's news. You know Janet—she's a stickler for time."

"It won't hurt you," grinned Maggie as they trooped into the gym and took up their positions.

"Morning, ladies. Let's all prepare to live long and prosper by getting our bodies into shape. If our bodies are well, our minds will be well and we can face anything we have to. Let us begin." Janet's musical voice floated down the floor as she began the warm up exercises. "Shoulders back and down and back and down..." The girls got down to work.

An hour later, glowing and invigorated, they sat at a window table of the restaurant that overlooked Stephen's Green, tucking into muesli, fresh fruit, croissants and coffee.

"Now!" demanded Devlin.

Maggie gave a huge grin. "The novel's being published."

"MAGGIE!" The other two shrieked with pleasure, delighted for their friend.

"Look," she said proudly, showing them a cheque.

"Two thousand five hundred pounds!" Caroline read in awe.

"It's my advance," bubbled Maggie. "It came this morning. Isn't it a hoot?"

"Does Adam know?" Devlin asked excitedly.

Maggie shook her head. "It all happened so fast and he's been in London for the past month. He'd due home next week and I just can't wait to show him this and the contract I signed. I got a copy of it with my cheque this morning."

"You kept this all to yourself. How could you?" Devlin remonstrated smiling.

Maggie laughed. "I know, I know. It was so hard, but I wanted to make sure everything was signed, sealed and delivered before I said anything, just in case..."

"How did you go about getting accepted so quickly?" Caroline asked curiously. "I thought it was a long slow process."

"I was just lucky," Maggie said modestly. "Remember when I didn't win the competition and I was pissed off?" The other two nodded, agog. "Well, Adam gave me this directory with all the names and addresses of the Irish publishers and then I took Terry Prone's advice in *Write And Get Paid For It* and sent one of them a sample chapter. Two days later I got a phone call from an editor who said she'd love to read the manuscript. So I delivered it to her. A week later they contacted me, said they loved it and it was going to be a bestseller and it's being published next spring. I signed the contract last week. I just can't believe it."

"It sure is going to be a bestseller, I hope they realise how lucky they are getting you as an author. You've a half dozen books inside that head of yours! You'll make a fortune. Ria Kirby turn green and puke," Devlin laughed.

Caroline chuckled, "Just wait until everybody recognises themselves—then there'll be wigs on the green!"

They all guffawed. When the excitement had died down their talk turned towards arrangements for the week-end. "I was thinking," murmured Caroline casually. "that I could drive us down."

"WHAT!" Exclaimed her two friends.

"I said," repeated Caroline calmly "How about

coming down in my car?"

"But you haven't got a car. You can't drive," Maggie said, confused.

"Oh yes I have! And I can!" Caroline grinned proudly. "I passed my test last week and Richard bought me the most gorgeous little Fiesta. I collected it from Des D'Arcy's in Donabate yesterday. Oh girls you should see it!" Caroline enthused. "I've called her Bluebell! I didn't tell you because I wanted to give you a surprise."

"Aw Caroline!" said Devlin leaning over and hugging her friend.

"You've certainly surprised us. Congratulations! We'd love to go to the Harbour in your...in Bluebell. Wouldn't we Maggie?"

"I couldn't think of anything nicer," agreed Maggie, delighted by the glow of pride in her friend's eyes. Imagine Richard buying Caroline a car! Things seemed to be much better between them in the last few months. Since Caro had received treatment for her drinking she was a different person and she had much more confidence in herself. It was great that she had started to work again too. It would give her a sense of independence.

"I've nothing exciting to surprise you with.," Devlin remarked ruefully. And then remembered. "Well, I might have something nice to tell you later."

"What's that?" asked Maggie curiously.

"Oh, just something I've been meaning to do for a long time. I'll tell you when we get to the

Harbour." Then she excused herself. "Have to rush. I've just seen Mary and Julie with their camera equipment. They're going to shoot the new brochure."

"*That* will cost you," Caroline replied knowingly. The two girls ran the most exclusive photographic agency in Dublin.

"Nothing but the best," Devlin said cheerfully. "See you later."

"Ya sure will baby," Maggie assured her. "Come on, Caro. Let's move it or we'll never get to Rosslare!"

***

Four hours later they were moving at a sedate forty miles an hour along the wide Dublin-Wexford road in Caroline's brand new baby blue Ford Fiesta. They were just a few miles from Arklow, where they planned to stop for lunch. Caroline, proud as punch but just a trifle apprehensive, sat up straight, hands gripping the wheel, tongue between teeth as she prepared to overtake a tractor ahead of her.

"You're doing fine," Devlin said encouragingly as her friend put her foot down on the accelerator.

"Wowie!" hollered Maggie as they flashed past the ancient farmer.

"Stirling Moss, look to your laurels," put in Devlin and they all guffawed. It was a journey of lighthearted laughter and anticipation and by the time they finished a delicious lunch they were all relaxed completely, the pressures of city life entirely forgotten.

"Do you think we should have a 'Sin Bag?'" Devlin asked with a gleam in her eye as they came out of the restaurant. They grinned at each other and without hesitation marched into the first sweet shop they came to and bought all round them.

"If Janet could see us now," Caroline said happily, helping herself to a bullseye.

"Now, we're not going to put on half a stone like we did on the Shannon!" Maggie said warningly.

"No" said Devlin, cheeks bulging with Turkish delight. "We're going to put on a stone!"

They all giggled uproariously, delighted to be in each other's company on the weekend they had looked forward to for so long.

The sun was still high in the sky when they reached Devlin's farmhouse and at her urgings they changed rapidly into bikinis and ran down the wooden steps leading to the beach at the foot of the cliff. They plunged into the white foamy surf, letting the sea caress and soothe them, stretching limbs that were cramped after the journey. Later, they lay on loungers on Devlin's secluded patio as the sun warmed them and they began to go gently brown. Eventually the only sound to be heard was that of the humming bees as they fed from the honeysuckle and hibiscus and the skylarks trilling their happy song and the soft slow breathing of the three friends as they snoozed in unashamed pleasure in the middle of a Friday afternoon.

That night, Devlin took them to a restaurant in Carne, The Bakehouse, where they dined magnificently. Devlin knew the proprietress, Marie, an attractive young woman, who had taken over the restaurant when it was nothing but a shambles, and turned it into a beautiful eatery. The three girls sat in a lamplit secluded alcove with a view of the small picturesque harbour, watching the sun set, its rays painting the sea until sky and sea were a blaze of pink and gold.

They dined like kings on seafood cocktail that contained chunky portions of a variety of shellfish and was almost a meal in itself. This was followed by a melt-in-the-mouth stuffed wild sea bass in an exquisite sauce, of Marie's own invention. The accompanying vegetables, crisp, crunchy and perfectly cooked, were an added delight. It was touch and go as to whether they would be able to eat any desert, but when the dessert trolley arrived, and they saw the selection of truly mouthwatering confections, they got their second wind, and added another few pounds to their hips. It was a superb meal and they had thoroughly enjoyed themselves.

It was all hours before they got to bed as they sat up talking for ages. It was an evening of shared confidences and renewed closeness between them as they told each other the most intimate secrets of their lives.

Devlin confided that she had taken her pride and thrown it out the window in order to ring Lydia after years of estrangement. They planned to meet the following week. It was a start.

"I'm glad, Dev," Caroline said, hugging her friend. "Your dad will be so pleased."

"I know he will," Devlin said thoughtfully. "I think Mum is too. She was crying on the phone. She hasn't really had much of a life, I suppose, and I think she feels terribly guilty about Lynn and Kate." She smiled at her friends. "Luke will be glad too. He's always on at me about it."

"He's a lovely man," said Maggie softly.

"Yes he is. I love him dearly."

Maggie told them that she planned to have her tubes tied. Three children and two frightful pregnancies were enough for her and besides she was practically certain that her relationship with Adam would develop into an affair.

"I love Terry in my own way, I suppose, but he destroyed my trust with his affair with Ria, and Adam gives me so much more encouragement and support about my writing. He's a man in a million and I'm going to make the most of him."

"You're right!" said Caroline firmly.

To a reaction of shocked silence she told her two friends about Richard's homosexuality.

"Jesus, Caroline!" exclaimed Devlin. "Why didn't you tell us before now?"

"I couldn't, Dev, until now," Caroline replied

simply.

"Are you going to stay with him?" Maggie asked quietly.

Caroline smiled. "For the present. You see, he needs me."

"And what about your needs? You actually told him to go ahead and resume his affair with Charles!" Devlin said incredulously. She didn't condemn Richard for being homosexual, but she despised him for marrying Caroline to cover it up.

"It doesn't bother me, Devlin. They really love each other and Charles is a very kind and supportive person, so why should I stand in the way of their happiness. I was as much to blame as Richard, I should never have married him. I ignored all the signs and deluded myself that everything would be fine when I was married. I married for the sake of getting married and look where it got me? Believe me, Dev, I'm happy enough the way I am for the moment. I've conquered my dependencies. I'm standing on my own two feet at last. My time for happiness with a man will come. Who knows I might take a figarie and fly to Seville and contact Ramon again!" she said wickedly. She had told them about her night of debauchery in London.

Maggie laughed. "I wouldn't mind an introduction to him myself! Maybe when I'm researching my next novel!"

"You've enough for a novel here," Devlin remarked as she got up to make yet another pot of tea.

"Now, that's an idea," Maggie was intrigued.

The next morning they woke to the pitter patter of rain on the window panes. "Oh goody," murmured Devlin from the depths of her bed, "I won't have to feel guilty about not getting up!" They had a lovely lie in, reading, snoozing, and chatting, and then they had a Cruiser Brunch and went for a walk along the rain-washed beach. Later in the afternoon Caroline drove them to the cemetery and they stood close together at Lynn's and Kate's grave. Devlin was crying softly. The sadness passed and the sun came out, and they went back to the farmhouse and sunbathed.

That night, Devlin told them she was bringing them out on the town. There was only one shower and one hairdryer in the farmhouse so their preparations took a little longer than usual. Devlin was having her shower last, and when she came into Caroline's and Maggie's bedroom, she saw with some surprise that they were still in their underwear and both fast asleep. Devlin grinned. It was the sea air. It had that effect on everyone. Just as well she was used to it! She'd leave them until she dried her hair. It didn't take long to dry the soft silky curtain of blonde hair. She looked at her watch, Ten o' clock. Things would only be getting lively! Devlin gave a stifled yawn. She'd wake the girls in a minute...

She woke up at five past one, and didn't know where she was. Hazy memory came back. She walked into the girl's room. The two of them were snoring gently. "Get into bed," she ordered sleepily, pushing Caro beneath the covers of her bed, and unable to get a stir out of Maggie, she covered her with a quilt.

"Oh the shame of it!" Maggie's eyes twinkled as they sat over breakfast the next morning. "Are we getting past it or what? For God's sake don't ever tell anyone about last night, I've a reputation to live up to!"

That night, they did make it out. Dressed up to the nines they went out to dinner. It was the last night of the most relaxing, fulfilling weekend they had spent in their many years together. The bond between then had grown even stronger. They all knew they would never be alone and that they were secure in the knowledge of their friendship. As they watched another beautiful sunset from the elegant dining room of the cliff-top hotel, Devlin raised her glass in toast. "To the most important thing that anyone, rich or poor, can possess. And that we are richly blessed with." She smiled. "To friendship."

Smiling back, Caroline and Maggie raised their glasses.